GOLD FAME CITRUS

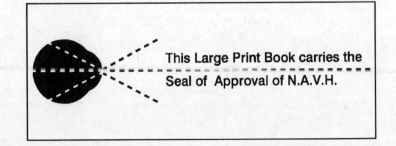
This Large Print Book carries the
Seal of Approval of N.A.V.H.

GOLD FAME CITRUS

CLAIRE VAYE WATKINS

THORNDIKE PRESS
A part of Gale, Cengage Learning

GALE
CENGAGE Learning·

Farmington Hills, Mich • San Francisco • New York • Waterville, Maine
Meriden, Conn • Mason, Ohio • Chicago

Copyright © 2015 by Claire Vaye Watkins.
Thorndike Press, a part of Gale, Cengage Learning.

LIBRARY OF CONGRESS CATALOGING-IN-PUBLICATION DATA
Watkins, Claire Vaye.
Gold fame citrus / Claire Vaye Watkins. — Large print edition.
pages cm. — (Thorndike Press large print core)
ISBN 978-1-4104-8630-1 (hardback) — ISBN 1-4104-8630-3 (hardcover)
1. Large type books. I. Title.
PS3623.A869426G65 2016
813'.6—dc23   2015035711

Published in 2016 by arrangement with Riverhead Books, an imprint of
Penguin Publishing Group, a division of Penguin Random House LLC

Printed in Mexico
1 2 3 4 5 6 7 19 18 17 16

FOR D.A.P.

■ ■ ■ ■

BOOK ONE

■ ■ ■ ■

There it is. Take it.

William Mulholland

Punting the prairie dog into the library was a mistake. Luz Dunn knew that now, but it had been a long time since she'd seen a little live thing, and the beast had startled her. She'd woke near noon having dreamed a grand plan and intending to enact it: she would try on every dress in the house. They hung like plumage in the master closet, in every luscious color, each one unspeakably expensive — imagine the ones the starlet had taken with her! In the dream Luz had worn every dress all at once, her breasts bestudded with rhinestones and drenched in silver dust, her ass embroidered with coppery alleyways of sequins, pleated plumes of satin fanning from her hips, pale confectioners' tulle floating like spun sugar at her feet. Of course, things went one-at-a-time in the lifeless waking world.

It was important to have a project, Ray said, no matter how frivolous. The Santa

Anas winged through the canyon now, bearing their invisible crazy-making particulate, and Ray said she should try to keep her hands busy. She should try not to sleep so much. Some of Ray's projects included digging out the shitting hole and siphoning gasoline from the luxury cars abandoned throughout the canyon.

Yesterday, Luz's project had been to present Ray with a gift of herself swaddled like a chocolate in a fur coat she'd excavated from one of the cavernous hall closets, though she was not so dark as chocolate. She'd roasted under the mink, her upper lip already jeweled over and trembling with sweat when she breached the backyard where Ray was working, into the ever-beaming, ever-heating, ever-evaporating sun. Sun of suns. Drought of droughts. These were their days now, Luz and Ray and the merciless sun up in the canyon, a family of light in this mansion cantilevered into the hillside, a bridge for a driveway. Luz had shucked the preposterous coat to the dirt and instead napped naked on a sun-stiffened chaise under the lines of a leafless grapevine until dinner. The once Ray approached her, sliding his hand between her knees, she'd groaned: too hot for sex. The mink was still heaped out back, sculpture of

10

a failure.

This project was better, she confirmed, twisting before the easel mirror in a peachy silk shift, lovely even against her grimy skin. In the closet was a handwoven poncho of oranges and golds, perfect for the shift, except wool was suicide. Instead, a Hermès scarf — no, a delicate tennis bracelet whose tiny clasp gave her some trouble. Like dewdrops strung around her wafer wrist, something the photographers would have said. But practically everyone was thin now. Luz stepped out of the shift and wriggled into a clinging cobalt mermaid gown dense with beads. It was gorgeous and she was gorgeous in it, even with her filthy hair and bulgy eyes and bushy brows and teeth that jutted out from her mouth as if leading the way, the front two with a gummy gap between them that caused her to seal her thin top lip to her plump bottom lip, even when she was alone, even now as she twirled and the dangly beads went *click click click,* softly. She looked liquid and wanted to show Ray.

Luz tromped down the floating railless stairs in the gown and rubber galoshes and a feather headpiece, baubles winking on every finger and one wrist. At the bottom of the stairs, she froze. Across the foyer, watching her, the tawny, beady-eyed rodent. It stood on its hind legs. It sniffed the air. Its nimble claws worked at something. Kind of cute. Except it dipped its head and maybe came at her. Luz panicked, shrieked, and executed a long-stride slo-mo kick of unexpected grace and force, some long-lost AYSO girlhood reflex risen from the resin of her quads.

They were a tired joke, the galoshes. Ditto umbrellas, slickers, gutters and storm drains, windshield wipers. This place had not seen so much rainfall as to necessitate galoshes in her entire life. But thank God for them, else the rodent might have ribboned her bare foot with its claws instead of flying through the open door of the library, going *scree.* A horrifying sound, that *scree,* and in her horror Luz slammed the blond wood door closed, setting it shuddering on its casters. A cruel instinct she was paying for hours later, for she was now plagued with a hefty boredom and the melancholy of finishing an excellent book — a biography of John Wesley Powell — and had nothing new to read.

The question, now, was whether to interrupt Ray — in the yard constructing a half-pipe from the plywood they'd pried off the windows and doors of the starlet's ultramodern château — or to handle this prairie dog situation herself. *Scree,* it said. She went out onto the balcony and called down to her love.

Ray squinted up at her and whistled. "Looking good, babygirl."

Luz had forgotten about her mermaid ensemble, and a little zing of delight accompanied the compliment. "How's it coming?" she called.

"What an embarrassment," he said, shaking his head. "Ten million empty swimming pools in this city, and we get this one."

The embarrassment was adjacent to his would-be half-pipe: the starlet's long-drained swimming pool, its walls not smooth concrete but a posh cobble of black river stones, its shape not a scooped-out basin but a box. Hard edges and right angles. Patently unshreddable. A shame, was all Ray said when he first knelt down and felt it, though his eyes had gone a pair of those smooth, globular kidney pools in the Valley. Ray had been to the forever war — was a hero, though he'd forbidden the word — and he went places sometimes.

Here, he was shirtless, all but gaunt, torquing his knees against a pane of plywood. His unbound hair was getting long, clumped and curling at his shoulders. On the bottom of the dry pool were smeared a few dreadlocks of dehydrated slime, pea-colored and coppery. Haircuts, Luz thought. Tomorrow's project.

She watched him work a while, leaning on the balcony rail as the starlet might have. It was impossible to be original and inspired living as she was, basically another woman's ghost. Ray could dismantle the starlet, splinter her, hack her up and build with her bones, but Luz languished beneath her. They wore the same size everything.

When Ray said *up in the canyon* Luz had seen porticos and candelabra, artisanal tiles, a working bath with a dolphin-shaped spigot patinaed turquoise and matching starfish handles, birds' nests in chandeliers, bougainvillea creeping down marble columns and dripping from those curlicue shelves on the walls of villas — what were they called? But the place they found was boxy and mostly windows. All slate and birchply, its doors slid rather than swung, the wrong style for columns. Any and all vinery was dead. Plantwise there was the dried pool slime and the gnarled leafless grapevine and spiny somethings coming through the planks of the deck, too savage to kill.

Below her Ray's hammer went *whap whap whap.*

Sconces, they were called, and there were none.

Where were the wild things seeking refuge from the scorched hills? Where was the bird-song she'd promised herself? Instead: scorpions coming up through the drains, a pair of mummified frogs in the waterless fountain, a coyote carcass going wicker in the ravine. And sure, a scorpion had a certain wisdom, but she yearned for fauna more charismatic. "It's thinking like that that got us into this," Ray said, correct.

Nature had refused to offer herself to them. The water, the green, the mammalian, the tropical, the semitropical, the leafy, the verdant, the motherloving citrus, all of it was denied them and had been denied them so long that with each day, each project, it became more and more impossible to conceive of a time when it had not been denied them. The prospect of Mother Nature opening her legs and inviting Los Angeles back into her ripeness was, like the disks of water shimmering in the last foothill reservoirs patrolled by the National Guard, evaporating daily.

Yet Luz yearned for menagerie, left the windows and doors open day and night to invite it, even when Ray complained of the dust, even when he warned that the Santa

15

Anas would drive her insane. Maybe true, for here was this varmint scurrying in her head. Here, finally, was a brave creature come down to commune in the house that wasn't theirs — it didn't belong to anyone! — and what had she done? Booted the little fellow in the gut and locked him away.

Air hazy and amber with smoke. Malibu burning, and Luz's old condo with it. Ticks clinging to the dead grass. Sand in the bedsheets and in her armpits and in the crack of her ass. Jumping bugs nesting in the mattress, all the more pestilent for being probably imagined. Some ruined heaven, this laurelless canyon.

Luz had read that they used to fight fires by dangling giant buckets from helicopters, filling the buckets at a lake and then dumping the water on them. The skies were batshit back then: bureaucrats draping valleys under invisible parachutes of aerosols, engineers erecting funnels to catch the rain before it evaporated, Research I universities dynamiting the sky. Once, an early canyon project, Luz and Ray hiked up the mountain called, horrifically, Lookout, and came upon a derelict cloud seeder, one of those barn-size miracle machines promised to spit crystalline moisture-making chemicals into the atmosphere. Another time they hiked up a back ridge and picnicked above that colorless archipelago of empty and near-empty tanks strung throughout the city. They ate crackers and ration cola and told stories about the mountains, the valley, the canyon and the beach. The whole debris scene. Because they'd vowed to never talk about the gone water, they spoke instead of earth that moved like water. Ray told of boulders clacking together in the ravine, a great slug of rubble sluicing down the canyon. That's what geologists called it, a slug, and Luz was always waiting for the perfect slug, slow and shapeless and dark, filling all spaces, removing all obstacles. Scraping clean their blighted floodplain.

Ray often went up to the ridge with the notebook he kept in his pocket, but Luz had not been back. Some things were beyond her, such as opening the door to a seldom-used library walled with biographies of Francis Newlands and Abraham Lincoln and Lewis and Clark and Sacajawea and William Mulholland and John Muir (whom she had her eye on) and capturing the small gnawing mammal inside.

She went back to the starlet's closet, dumped a pair of never-worn espadrilles from their box and brought the empty box to the yard. "I think there's a prairie dog in the library," she told Ray.

Ray stopped his hammering. "A prairie dog."

Luz nodded.

"How'd it get in there?"

"I don't know."

"Did you put it in there?"

"More or less."

"When?"

"Can you get it out?"

"Leave it," he said, turning back to the half-pipe skeleton. Ray was not a reader. He used to read the newspaper every morning, but now that the newspapers were gone he said he was through with the whole reading and writing thing, though Luz had read the secret poems in his notebook.

"It's not . . . humane," she said, offering him the box. "Plus it's probably crapping everywhere."

He sighed, unbuckled his tool belt — some long-gone handyman's — took the shoe box and loped into the house. She followed. He paused outside the library door. "How big was it?"

"Like, a football? I think it was rabid," she lied. She was beginning to feel ridiculous.

He slid the library door closed behind him. Luz listened. The canyon was hot and still and so was the house. Then came a

18

clamorous ruckus from the library. Ray said, Shitfuck. He said, Jesus.

He emerged like a wildman character making an entrance in a play, vexed and slamming the door behind him.

Luz asked, "Where's the box?" Ray raised a silencing hand and strode from the foyer into the cavernous living room. Luz followed. He paced madly for a minute before seizing upon the sooty black poker by the fireplace and returning to the library.

Luz sat on the second step of the staircase and waited. There was more ruckus, a crash, the screeching of a desk chair shoved along the exposed concrete floor. Swears and swears. Then quiet. She wanted to open the door but would not.

"Did you get it?" she called eventually.

The door slid open a sliver and Ray's red and sweaty head poked out. "You better not look."

Luz put her face in the basin of her hands, then immediately lifted it. She gasped. Ray was before her. Aloft at the end of the poker, the throbbing body of the prairie dog, impaled. Its mouth was open and its fore-paws twitched once, twice. Ray hustled outside.

Luz stood, queasy and overheated. She hovered above herself and saw that she was undergoing one of those moments in which she was reminded that Ray — her Ray — had, as part of his vocation, killed people.

She turned around and lurched up the stairs. She did not want to be around when he returned. Halfway up, she tripped. The floating stairs had always unnerved Luz and now they enraged her. She kicked the leaden galoshes from her feet down to the living room with some effort, staggered barefoot to the darkened bedroom, peeled off the suddenly chafing mermaid gown, climbed into the massive unmade bed and wept in the sandy nest of it.

She wept briefly for the creature, and then at great length for all her selves in reverse. First for Luz Dunn, whose finest lover and best friend was a murderer and perhaps always would be, then for Luz Cortez, mid-tier model spoiled then discarded. Emancipated at fourteen, her father's idea, something he'd prayed on, amputated from him and from child labor laws. Then, finally and with great relish, she wept for Baby Dunn. Poster child for promises vague and anyway broken, born on the eve of some symbolic and controversial groundbreaking ceremony, delivered into the waiting blanks of a speech written for a long-forgotten senator:

Conservation's golden child arrived at UCLA Medical Center at 8:19 this morning, the daughter of Mr. and Mrs. William Dunn of San Bernardino, California. Eight pounds, eight ounces, the child has been adopted by the Bureau of Conservation, which embarks today on an heroic undertaking that will expand the California Aqueduct a hundredfold, so that Baby Dunn and all the children born this day and ever after will inherit a future more secure, more prosperous, and more fertile than our own. We break ground today so that there will be fresh water for drinking, irrigation and recreation waiting for Baby Dunn and her children . . .

Baby Dunn, born with a golden shovel in her hand, adopted and co-opted by Conservation and its enemies, her milestones announced in press releases, her life literal and symbolic the stuff of headlines, her baby book lousy with newspaper clippings:

GOVERNOR SIGNS HSB 4579;
EVERY SWIMMING POOL IN CALIFORNIA TO
BE DRAINED BEFORE BABY DUNN IS OLD
ENOUGH TO TAKE SWIMMING LESSONS.

BABY DUNN STARTS KINDERGARTEN TODAY
WITHOUT GREEN FIELDS TO PLAY IN.

LAST CENTRAL VALLEY FARM SUCCUMBS TO
SALT: BABY DUNN, 18, NEVER AGAIN TO
TASTE CALIFORNIA PRODUCE.

BERKELEY HYDROLOGISTS:
WITHOUT EVACS BABY DUNN WILL DIE OF
THIRST BY 24.

Now Luz was twenty-five and hung up on
the logistics. Had her parents been paid?
Was her envoyery prearranged or hatched
last-minute? Some intern of the senator's
staked out in the maternity ward? Some go-
getter do-gooder from a public Ivy, recorder
in his coat pocket, scouring the waiting
room for a photogenic and verbose new par-
ent? How this young gunner must have
delighted at finding Luz's father, big Ger-
man teeth, a pastor and a salesman, moved
by the spirit to join the Rotary Club, to hit
the gym by six every morning, to display
the apple of his eye in church talent shows,
to spend his wife's financial aid on very
good hair plugs. Billy Dunn would not have
been in the delivery room, certainly not.
Not his business to witness his wife's woman's body undergo its punishment. Not

permitted by his temperament to acknowledge anything uterine, vaginal, menstrual, menopausal, pubescent. Not here, on the day of his only child's birth, nor later when Luz's mother was dead and Luz got leggy and bled purple and shreddy brown, when he could have said what was happening to her and what to do about it, when he could have said, as any man could have, what lay ahead for her. But he did not say, and instead she had stolen a plaid dishrag from the kitchen and cut it into strips with her dead mother's scalloped scrapbooking scissors — such that the rag strips shared the peppy border of her baby book clippings — and tucked these strips up between her labia. Instead, she had learned from the other girls and from the photographers, often.

Luz, said Billy Dunn, is my cross to bear.

It was this she always landed on: her father pious and a chatterbox, maybe nervous, approached by a statesman's underling in the hospital waiting room. Saying her name so it rhymed with *fuzz* before her mother, channeling Guadalajara, had a chance to correct him. Random, how she became the goddesshead of a land whose rape was in full swing before she was even born. Baby Dunn.

The ration hour came and went; Luz heard the hand pump screeching and Ray beneath her, filling his jug and hers. She lay in bed a long time, snotty and damp and staring at the dark drawn curtains and the heaps of clothing she'd mounded all over the room that were the millions of holes that pocked every hillside of the canyon, each with a tiny grainy dune at its mouth. She had thought the holes to be the burrows of chipmunks, but knew them now to be snake holes. Mammals were out. LA gone reptilian, primordial. Her father would have some scripture to quote about that.

After some time, Ray came into the bedroom and set a glass of lukewarm water on her nightstand. He stayed, silent, and Luz said, "Can you bring me John Muir?"

"Sure." He went out, came back, and set the volume on the nightstand, beside her undrunk water. He perched himself on his edge of the bed and leaned over to touch her, gently.

"Say something," she said. "Make me feel better."

"I love you?"

"Not that."

He offered the glass. "Drink this."

She did.

He tried, "I think it was a gopher. Not a

prairie dog."

This did make her feel a little better, somehow. She rolled to face him. "What did you do with him?"

Ray bit his cheek. "Threw it in the ravine. I can go down and get it if you want."

"No," she said. She would have liked to bury the little guy properly — make a project of it — but she was certain that if Ray went down into the ravine he would never come back.

"Come here," Ray said, and hoisted Luz, nude and fetal, onto his lap. He took each of her fingers into his mouth and sucked the starlet's rings off. He extracted the feathered headpiece from her hair and began tangling and untangling it with his fingers, something she loved immeasurably. "It's Saturday," he said.

"I didn't know."

"We could go down to raindance tomorrow. Try to get berries."

She sucked up some snot. "Really?"

"Hell yeah."

They laughed. Ray said, Here, and led Luz from the bed and into the master bathroom. He held Luz's hand as she stepped naked into the dry tub, a designer ceramic bowl in the center of the room, white as a first tooth. Ray went downstairs and returned

25

with his jug. He moistened a towel at the jug's mouth and washed her everywhere. When he was finished he left her in the tub. "Stay there," he said before he closed the door. She stayed in the dark, fiddling with the starlet's bracelet, the diamonds having found some improbable light to twinkle. When Ray finally retrieved her, he carried her over his shoulder and flopped her down on the bed and only when she slipped her bare legs between the sheets did she realize that the cases, the duvet, every linen was smooth. He had snapped the infinite sand from them.

The sun had gone down and the doors to the balcony were open; she imagined the sea breeze making its incredible way to them. Tomorrow they would eat berries. They lay together, happy and still, which was more than anyone here had a right to be. She could tell Ray was asleep when the twitches and whimpers and thrashes began, the blocking of nightmares he never remembered. She held him and watched the bloodglow pulse in the east, the last of the chaparral exploding.

Luz had gotten, even by her own generous estimation, righteously fucked up. This occurred to her as the sun of suns dripped into the Pacific and she found herself barefoot at the center of a drum circle, shaking a tambourine made from a Reebok box with broken Christmas ornaments rattling inside and shimmying what tits she had. Luz was not a dancer; she had never been a dancer. But here the rhythm was elephantine and simple as the slurping valves in the body — an egalitarian tune. She jigged and stomped her bare feet into the dry canal silt. She worried for Ray a flash, then let it go. He was probably well aware of her situation, as was his way. Probably watching her from the periphery of the circle, sipping the home-brewed saltwater mash she'd been swilling all day.

And why shouldn't she swill? They had liberated the starlet's cheery, grass-green

Karmann-Ghia, which Ray called the Melon, and descended from their canyon to the desiccant city, to the raindance, a free-for-all of burners and gutterpunks cater-wauling and cavorting in the dry canals of Venice Beach, sending up music from that concrete worm of silt and graffiti and con-fettied garbage weaving fourfold through the nancy bungalows. They'd set up camp in the shade of a footbridge with its white picket handrails ripped off and Ray had procured a growler of mash and a baggie of almonds and six cloves of garlic the pusher called Gilroy, though nothing had grown in Gilroy for a decade. Happy day, day of revelry and bash, for money still meant in Los Angeles, even in the chaos of the rain-dance, and — hot damn! — Luz *Cortez* had earned plenty of it, modeling under her mother's maiden name until her agency fled to the squalid mists of New York, and she too old to be begged to follow.

So vibe on, sister. Shake shake shake. Don't trip on the fact that even money will go meaningless eventually. Don't go sour simmering on what that money cost you, on UV flashes scorching your eyes to temporary blindness or pay docked for time in the ER or old men pinching your thighs, your fat Chicana ass, the girlish flesh pudged at your armpits, putting their fingers or one time a Sharpie up in you. Yes, you have been to Paris and Milan and London and all the rest and cannot remember a thing about them. But don't feed the negativity, though you were always too flabby, too short, too hairy, too old, too Mexican. Ass too flat, tits too saggy, nipples too big — like saucers, one said. Don't start that old loop of, Take your shirt off, and, Turn around, sweetheart, and, Bend over, and, Put the worm in your mouth, babe, you know what to do. Don't get caustic, even if you were only fourteen and didn't know what to do, had never done it before, had never even kissed a boy. Don't stir up the hunger the hunger the hunger. Don't think it was all for nothing.

Don't think. Dance.

Twirl! Twirl!

Because sweet Jesus money was still *money,* and wasn't that something to celebrate? For now, enough money could get you fresh produce and meat and dairy, even if what they called cheese was Day-Glo and came in a jar, and the fish was mostly poisoned and reeking, the beef gray, the apples blighted even in what used to be apple season, pears grimy even when you paid extra for Bartletts from Amish orchards. Hard sour strawberries and blackberries filled with dust. Flaccid carrots, ashen spinach, cracked olives, bruised hundred-dollar mangos, all-pith oranges, shriveled lemons, boozy tangerines, raspberries with gassed aphids curled in their hearts, an avocado whose crumbling taupe innards once made you weep.

The rhythm went manic and Luz collapsed to the silt crust.

Woozy, she stood and careened stylishly through the party, up to the canal berm, the smooth, sloped concrete patch beneath the footbridge where she'd last seen Ray.

And there he was still, guarding their encampment, the growler of mash in one hand and the starlet's bejeweled sandals in the other. The heel straps had been giving her trouble, Luz remembered now.

"I'm blotto," she said, rubbing her forehead on his warm bicep.

"I know," he said.

"And thirsty."

Ray knelt and set the growler between his feet on the pitched concrete. He took one of Luz's dirty feet in his hand and put a shoe on, then the other. Luz wobbled and steadied herself with his fine broad back. When he finished, Ray dug a ration cola from his backpack, the only drink anyone had plenty of. It was warm and flat and thick with syrup — donated because the formula was off, was the rumor. But it was wet and this alone was reason enough to love him.

She sat and drank and Ray stood — he did not like to sit much — and consulted his list. Ray's tiny notebook, looted from the back of a drugstore, was the old-timey reporter's kind with the wire spiral at the top, such that before writing in it he should have licked the tip of his yellow golf pencil, gouged to sharpness with the Leatherman he carried.

Luz snooped in Ray's notebook whenever possible, skimming his secret poems and skate park schematics and lists. Ray was a listmaker. He did not live a day without a list; Luz had never made a list a day in her life — their shtick. His lists went:

- matches
- crackers
- L
- water

Or:

- shitting hole
- garage door
- L

31

– water

Or:

– candles
– alcohol
– peanuts
– L
– water

Or:

– axe
– gas
– shoes
– L
– water

Or:

– charcoal
– lighter fluid
– marshmallows for L
– water

Or:

– Sterno
– eyedrops
– calamine
– kitty litter

– L

– water

Or, often, only:

– L

– water

"Hey," said Ray, batting her with his notebook. "I heard of a guy who has blueberries from Seattle."

"Seattle," she whispered, the word itself like rain. "Can I come?" She had never been on a procurement mission, as Ray called them.

"You want to?"

Luz squealed in the affirmative and finished her ration cola. Then they set off, hand in hand, Ray's eyes as phosphorescent as the day she witnessed him birthed from the sea.

Ray had the blazing prophet eyes of John Muir, and like John Muir, war had left him nerve-shaken and lean as a crow. The ocean had restored him. The way he told it, a city of a ship bearing the emblem of the motherland deposited him in the riverless West, at San Diego. He was released — honorable discharge, had medals somewhere — but the whole way back he'd been jumpy, sleepless, barely keeping the darkness at the edges. Nothing soothed him until he heard the white noise of the breakers. So instead of going home to the heartland he liberated a surf board from someone's backyard and made his home in the curl. He had a mind to surf through all crises and shortages and conflicts past and present. He would make a vacuum of the coast, nothing could happen there, even the things that had happened before he was born. He was surfing the day they pronounced the Colorado dead and he was surfing the day it was dammed, a hundred years before. When some omnipotent current ferried him northward toward LA, he allowed it. He surfed as that city's aqueducts went dry. He surfed as she built new aqueducts, wider aqueducts, deeper aqueducts, aqueducts stretching to the watersheds of Idaho, Washington, Montana, aqueducts veining the West, half a million miles of palatial half-pipe left of the hundredth meridian, its architects and objectors occasionally invoking the name of Baby Dunn. Ray surfed as concrete waterway crept up to Alaska, surfed as the Mojave and the Sonoran licked the bases of glaciers. He was surfing each time terrorists or visionaries bombed the massive unfilled aqueduct canals at Bend and Boise and

Boulder and Eugene. He surfed as states sued states and as the courts shut down the ducts for good. He surfed as the Central Valley, America's fertile crescent, went salt flat, as its farmcorps regularly drilled three thousand feet into the unyielding earth, praying for aquifer but delivered only hot brine, as Mojavs sucked up the groundwater to Texas, as a major tendril of interstate collapsed into a mile-wide sinkhole, killing everybody on it, as all of the Southwest went moonscape with sinkage, as the winds came and as Phoenix burned and as a white-hot superdune entombed Las Vegas.

Then, one day, Ray emerged from the thrashing oblivion of the Pacific at Point Dume, and there was a chicken-thin, gappy-toothed girl sitting in the sand beside a suitcase and a hatbox, crying off all her eye makeup.

Seawatery, gulping air and clutching his board to him, Ray approached her. What was the first thing he said? Luz could not now remember, but it would have been sparkling. She did recall his hands, gone pink with cold, and his pale aqua prophet's eyes, and herself saying in response, "I haven't seen anyone surfing in years. I forgot about surfing."

His hope naked, Ray asked, "You surf?"

35

She smiled thinly and shook her head. "Can't swim."

"Serious? Where you from?"

"Here."

"And you can't swim?"

"Never learned."

They sat quiet for a time, side by side in the sand, hypnotized by the beckoning waves.

"Where are you from?" she said, wanting to hear this wildman's voice again.

"Indiana."

"Hoosier."

"That's right." He grinned. He had an incredibly good-looking mouth.

"Why'd you come here?"

"I was in the military."

"Were you deployed?"

He nodded.

"What did you do?"

He shrugged and snapped a seaweed polyp between his fingers. "You've heard that dissertation."

He said his name and she said hers and then they sat again in quiet. At their backs, gone coral and shimmering in the sun's slant, was a de-sal plant classified as defunct but that in truth had never been funct. They'd heard that dissertation, too.

Luz asked, "You going to evac there, Indiana?"

"Nah."

"Where, then?"

"Nowhere."

"Nowhere?"

"Nowhere."

He told her about the sea and his needing it and then, when she suggested Washington State, he said California had restored him, that he would not abandon her. And eventually he told her too about the younger sister born without a brain, only a brainstem — so much like brain*stump* — that she was supposed to die after a couple of weeks, but she was twenty-one now and a machine still breathed for her, which made Luz think *iron lung* even though that was not quite right. The wrong mote of dust could kill her, said Ray. One fucking mote. And because of this his mother was always cleaning, cleaning feverishly, cleaning day and night, cleaning with special chemicals the government sent. She didn't want Ray around. "It's too much for her," he said. "Anyway they're screening pretty heavy in Washington now, and the only skills I have I never want to use again."

"You've got charm," she said. "Charisma."

"I think they're maxed out on charisma."

"You can surf."

37

"You know, I put that on my application."

"What happened with it?"

"An orca ate it, actually."

People always claimed they were staying, but Ray was the first person Luz believed. "So what are you going to do?" she asked.

"Some people I know have a place. Even if they didn't, Hoosiers aren't quitters. California people are quitters. No offense. It's just you've got restlessness in your blood."

"I don't," she said, but he went on.

"Your people came here looking for something better. Gold, fame, citrus. Mirage. They were feckless, yeah? Schemers. That's why no one wants them now. Mojavs."

He was kidding, but still the word stung, here and where it hung on the signage of factories in Houston and Des Moines, hand-painted on the gates of apartment complexes in Knoxville and Beaumont, in crooked plastic letters on the marquees of Indianapolis elementary schools: MOJAVS NOT WELCOME. NO WORK FOR MOJAVS. MOJAVS KEEP OUT. A chant ringing out from the moist nation's playgrounds: *The roses are wilted / the orange trees are dead / them Mojavs got lice / all over they head.*

But Ray smiled and his kind mouth once again soothed Luz. "We're stick-it-out people," he said, but what he really meant, she knew, was they could be Mojavs together.

Ray brushed a hank of hair from her eyes and said, "You look like I know you." Had he seen her before? Luz said maybe and sheepishly described the decaying billboard surveying Sunset Boulevard, her in sweatshop bra and panties, eyes made up like bruises, crouched over a male model's ass like she was about to take a bite out of it. Get those freaky teeth, the art director had not even whispered. One papery panel peeling off now, so her bare legs looked shrunken, vestigial. "The zenith of my career," she said. "Minus a commercial for wine coolers."

Ray said, "No, somewhere else," then Luz kissed him.

After, there was more silence between them, but it did not feel like silence. It felt like peace.

Ray asked, "What about you? You going to evac?"

They took you by bus. Camps in Louisiana, Pennsylvania, New Jersey. No telling which you'd end up at and anyway it didn't matter. It was temporary, they said. The best thing you could do for the cause. She knew better, but she was scheduled to go anyway.

The suitcase beside her was filled with novels and wads of designer clothes, the hatbox heavy with her savings. But she hated crowds, hated every human being except this one beside her. She suddenly and fiercely did not want to get on a bus tomorrow. She wanted to fall in love instead. Frightening herself, she said, "I was."

So Ray took her home, to the gutted Santa Monica apartment complex from which his friends staged their small resistance. They had sex on Ray's bedroll in the laundry room. After, he said, "I need you to promise me we won't talk about the war."

She said, "Promise me we won't talk about the water."

He said, "Wouldn't dream of it."

Now, dusk was coming to the dry rills of raindance. Luz followed Ray along the berm and, though it scared her, into a man-high rusty corrugated drainage culvert, where the berry man was supposed to be. Inside, a stench met them, fecal and hot. Something scraped about back in the darkness, something screeched. As the light at their backs wilted, Luz put one hand to her mouth and groped for Ray with the other. This was, she realized, probably not a good place to be a woman.

40

The starlet's sandals began to slice into Luz's heels again and she stumbled. "You okay?" Ray whispered. She nodded though she was dizzy and hot and there was a new pressure on the underside of her eyebones, and though Ray surely could not see her nodding in this semiterranean dark.

Soon, Luz's pupils dilated wide enough to accept Ray's silhouette ahead of her. She clung to him with one hand and traced the other along the metal wall of the pipe, flinching at its rust splinters and steadying herself as she lurched over knee-high sediment dunes and dry knolls of sewage. The culvert forked into a smaller pipe where Ray had to stoop. The sounds went human now; voices of people gathered to haggle and score ricocheted down the tube.

Fresh socks here, all-cotton socks.

Ovaltine, whole can, hep!

Luz and Ray continued, the culvert soon clogged with the crowd's collective fetid lethargy. Wherever the pair walked, bodies blocked their path. Luz would have liked to hear some Spanish, to be reminded of her mother, but even here there was none, influx long ago turned to exodus. Ray lightly lobbed the words *blueberries* and *Seattle* into the darkness and what came back was *Not me, white boy. Deeper, brother,* and then,

41

Um-hm. Careful. He nasty.

Finally Ray called *blueberries* and was tossed *Here, son.* From the darkness materialized a shirtless, ashy-skinned daddy-o, bald head glistening, tiny mouth gnawing on a black plastic stir straw. Beside him stood a Filipino with scarred hands and a backpack.

The daddy-o held a drained cola can aloft in the darkness. "King County blues. One-fifty."

Ray took the can and examined it. He handed it to Luz. A handful of berries padded inside the aluminum. She put the can to her nose and thought she smelled the dulcet tang of them.

"Give you seventy-five," said Ray.

The daddy-o bowed reverently to the can. "All due respect, son, these is some juicy-ass berries. Juicier than juicy pussy." He winked at Luz. "Can't give them up for less than a hundred."

"Eighty then."

"Eighty," the daddy-o said to his partner. He sucked his teeth.

The Filipino said, "Used to be a nigger could make a living in this city."

"That's all I got," said Ray, though it was not.

"All you got, hmm," said the daddy-o. He

reached out to retrieve the can from Luz. She handed it over, but instead of taking the can from her, the daddy-o torqued his long-nailed index finger through the starlet's tennis bracelet, still strung like dewdrops around her wrist. He yanked, but the bracelet held. Luz pinched her breath in her throat.

"I doubt that," said the daddy-o.

"Hey," said Ray, but Luz was saying, "Take it," her fingers panicking against the mean little clasp.

The daddy-o flung Luz's own hand back at her. "The fuck you think I am?" To Ray he said, "Two hundred."

Ray gave the daddy-o two bills he'd brought from the hatbox they stored in the starlet's drained redwood hot tub, took the can of berries and pulled Luz away. Her head was swooning and her sense of direction had left her. She wanted to flee on her own but was not sure she could find her way back through the culverts. It was all she could do to follow Ray, who kept dissolving into the darkness then rematerializing to tug her along. "Christ," he whispered, meaning *Christ, be more careful,* and *Christ you're stupid,* and *Christ, I love you and you're all I have and therefore you have an obligation to take better care of yourself.* Luz gazed ahead, needing a glimpse of the daylight they'd left, but she saw only bodies, bodies. Someone trampled the heel of her sandal and she stumbled. She needed to get away from these fucking people, but they were everywhere. Then, mercifully, Ray led her into a dark, clear space.

Her eyes slowly registered the solid perimeter of people they'd broken through. Their mouths hung open, dumb, staring at her. No, not staring at her. Luz followed their gaze and saw beside her an old woman sitting on a collapsible metal lawn chair. She wore a dress that in its day had been festooned mightily but was now threadbare and freckled with cigarette burns. She wore watersocks, and dug into each of her livery shoulders was a huge macaw, one red and one blue.

Luz stood and watched the birds, fearfully transfixed. The circle of bodies pressed in closer. The red macaw pinched a nut or a stone in its beak, working at it with its horrid, digit-like black tongue. It twitched its head. It blinked its tiny malarial eye.

Suddenly Luz was breathing everyone else's foul, expelled air and Ray was angry and gone and there was only so much air down here and everyone was sucking it up and where was he? Had he not heard of girls carried up out of the canal into one of the vacant houses whose dry private docks jutted overhead, homes once worth three and four and five million and now, every one of them, humid with human fluids? Had he not been with her the night she'd seen a woman stumble out of one of the houses, used and bewildered, and start to make her way back down to the canal and the music, only to be dragged back up again?

Luz stepped back from the birds and collided with a sickle-thin teenager. He wore a white T-shirt with some meanness written on the front in marker, and sagging holes where the sleeves should have been. Through these holes flashed his tattooed cage of a chest. There was a long tear up one leg of his jeans and along it dozens of safety pins arranged like staples in flesh. He held a rope, and at the end of it was a short-haired, straw-colored dog, wheezing. The boy laid his rough hand on the bare skin between Luz's shoulder blades. He rubbed.

"Easy, sweetheart," he said. From his mouth escaped the scent of rot.

Something leaden and malignant seized Luz's heartmuscle. She wrenched away. "I can't breathe," she said, barely.

Ray turned. "What?"

"I can't breathe."

"What do you mean?"

"I'm dying."

He put his hand on the back of her neck.

"I can't breathe," she said. "I fucking can't breathe."

Ray didn't laugh at this, though it was laughable. Luz knew it was even now, except the knowledge was buried somewhere in her beneath bird tongue and daddy-o and sweetheart asphyxiation.

"You're okay," he said. "Listen."

She gripped his shirt in her hands and pulled. "I can't *breathe,* Ray."

"You're all right," he said. "Tell me."

One of the birds went *wrat,* impossibly loud, and Luz flinched. *Wrat* again and she began to claw at Ray's midsection. People were looking at them now, some laughing, and she had designs to open her boyfriend up and hide inside him.

Ray took Luz's two scrambling hands in one of his like a bouquet and looked her in the eye. "You're okay," he said again. "Tell me."

"I'm okay," she said, though she was also dying.

"Tell me again."

She looked at him; she breathed. "I'm okay."

"We're walking," said Ray, taking her by

46

the shoulders.

They walked and breathed and walked and breathed and soon a dim disk of light floated ahead of them. Ray led her to it, miraculously, Luz saying, I'm okay, I'm okay, I'm okay, I'm okay.

Their blanket — a duvet meant for guests of the starlet — was still under the footbridge when they got back, another miracle. Ray sat Luz down. He passed her his ration jug. She refused it and he passed her hers.

He watched her as she drank.

"Thank you," she said after some time.

"Do you want to go home?" he asked. He wanted to see the bonfire, she knew. He said, "It's fine if you do."

What she wanted was a few Ativan and a bottle of red wine, but those days were over. It was cooler in the canal and the air was freshish, or at least it moved. The long shadows of the mansions stretched to shade them and the blanket had not been taken and there was Ray, trying. She told herself to allow these to bring her some comfort.

"No," she said. "Let's stay." She sat on the blanket and breathed. Eventually, Ray asked whether she wanted to go back to the drum circle.

"Can we just sit here awhile?" she said.

"Sure."

"Sorry."

"Don't be," Ray said, which was what he always said. He motioned for her to lie back and rest her head in his lap. She did. She fell asleep and dreamt nothing.

Luz woke needing to pee. It was nearly dark but fires were glowing along the spine of the canal, the bonfire down the row throbbing brightest of all. Ray had taken his shoes off and was lying on his back. Luz sat still, studying him in the smoky light: his willowy hands, his steady chest, the tuft of black hair in the divot of his collarbone, barely visible above the neck of his T-shirt. His flat, slightly splayed feet. Everything about him suggested permanence. She rose and kissed him on the head. "I have to pee."

Ray started to stand.

"It's okay," she said. "I'm okay."

Luz made her way up the wall of the canal. The trench beyond was dark and balmy with stink, but she was feeling much better. She straddled the trench, lifted her dress, urinated, shook her ass some then stood up. Yes, she was feeling better. The sun had gone down and the canals were cooling off, the nap had dissolved the throb in her head, as a good nap will. She was okay. She would have some more water, eat something. There were blueberries in Ray's backpack and mash in the growler. She was all right. They would go back down to the drum circle. They would dance. They would bonfire. She would not ruin everything after all.

Descending the smooth dusty pitch of the canal, she looked down at the bonfire and then beyond it, where someone had set off a bottle rocket. She saw the little puff of smoke and heard the snap. Just then — at exactly the instant the snap reached her, so that the moment was ever-seared into her memory as a tiny explosion — something slammed into her knees. She looked down to see a shivering, towheaded child wrapped around her legs.

Luz could not remember the last time she'd seen a little person. The child was maybe two years old. A girl, Luz somehow knew, though she wore only a shoddy cloth diaper, its seat dark with soil. She looked up at Luz with eyes like gray-blue nickels, sunk into skeletal sockets. Her skin was translucent, larval, and Luz had the sense that if she checked the girl's belly she would be able to discern the shadows of organs inside.

"Hi there," Luz said.

The child stared unblinking with her coin eyes.

"Are you lost?" asked Luz. "Where's your mommy?" The girl's forehead bulged subtly above the brow and she pressed it now into Luz's crotch. Luz, embarrassed, tried to pry the girl from her legs. But the child clutched tighter and let loose a high, sorrowful moan. Luz went weak with pity.

"Shh," she said. "You're okay." Luz patted her back then, unthinkingly, put her fingers in the child's whiteblond hair, tufted like meringue at the nape.

Luz managed to separate from the girl long enough to kneel. The girl squirmed to reestablish herself in Luz's lap, hinged her bony arms around Luz's neck, and sobbed. Luz held her, her dress pulled taut where her knees pressed to silt. She expected someone to come for the girl, but no one did. No one was paying any attention to them.

Soon, the girl stopped crying. She regarded Luz a moment, curious, then reached one hand up and laid it plainly on Luz's face, partially covering her right eye. The small hand was moist with snot or saliva, slick as a wet root.

"Where's your mommy and daddy?" Luz said again.

The girl ignored the question if she understood it. She rotated her hand so it lay diagonally across Luz's brow. The child pinched her mouth in concentration. She pressed, then positioned her other hand at Luz's jaw and pressed again, as though getting some information from the sensation. Luz felt uncannily at ease. The raindance had slipped away and left the two of them alone in the smoky twilight, only the fires pulsing lure-like in the distance. Luz smiled, and the child smiled too, and when she did Luz felt an unbearable welling of affection, both for the girl and from her.

Then, with her hands still at Luz's face, the girl said, "Piz kin tim eekret?"

"Tim eekret?" Luz tried.

The child squenched her face in frustration. "Piz kin tell you secret?" she repeated.

"Oh," said Luz. "Okay."

The girl stretched to Luz's ear. Luz strained to make out what she was saying until she realized that the child was not saying anything, only replicating the feathery sounds of whispers. *Spuh, spuh, spuh, spuhst.*

When she finished, the girl leaned back and said gravely, "Don't tell, okay?"

"Okay."

"Don't tell *anyone.*"

"I won't."

Just then a figure strode through the dusk and toward them. It was Ray, looking purely mystified at Luz where she knelt on the ground, whispering with a child. "What's going on?" he asked.

"She's lost," said Luz.

"Did you ask around?"

"It just happened."

Another figure drew near them. Caved and tattooed torso, the chain of safety pins along his torn jeans. As he came closer Luz recognized the teenager who had touched her in the sewer. Several heavy chains drooped between his back pocket and a belt loop, swaying as he approached. The jagged black marker on his shirt read *I knew I was a nut when the squirrels started staring*. He did not seem to recognize Luz. His eyes were on the girl.

"Get over here," the Nut said to the child. He gestured down the berm, and Luz became aware of a scattering of rangy, dull-eyed young men camped out on the canal bottom, shirtless and unwashed. They cradled mash growlers and other incovert alcohols; one gripped a filthy glass water bong. The straw-colored dog scavenged among them, the rope still tied around its neck but trailing now behind him. (Baby

Dunn had always wanted a dog, but her father had not allowed it.) Among the men were two girls, teenagers. The first straddled a man whose age was undoubtedly a multiple of her own. His one hand pinched a filterless cigarette while the other grazed beneath the girl's tank top. His thick arm pulled her top up and the knuckles of the girl's spine rose as she bent to take the man's tongue into her mouth. The second girl was heavy, with rounded shoulders, large breasts drooping into a bikini top and a doughy midsection spilling from tight jean shorts. She watched Luz through hair cespitose and greenish from ink dye, not with anger or concern, not with anything except perhaps a dullness that left her mouth slightly open. Under this dead gaze Luz realized she was still holding the child.

Luz pointed to the group. "Is that your mommy?"

The child shook her head. *No.*

The Nut said, "Her mommy's not here." The tattoo on his bicep was a smeary green cross, blurred lines and imperfect proportions. The cross came closer now as the Nut bent to take the child by the arm. The baby — as Luz had come to think of her, though she was not a baby — scrambled into Luz's lap and flung her arms around Luz's neck.

Luz looked up at the Nut. She did not want him to take the baby, but he would, of course.

Ray laid his hand on Luz's shoulder, protecting her from the Nut or from herself. Luz rose, forcing the child to slide from her lap. "Time to go," Luz told her.

"No, no, no!" the girl cried.

The Nut took the child's arm roughly and the girl screamed, "Okay!" She wrenched her tiny arm from him. "But please can I tell her a secret?"

The Nut sighed, then nodded, and Luz bent down again, letting the child up to her ear. Ray looked on. Again the girl made whispering sounds but said no actual words. When she was finished she looked at Luz and said, "Tell everyone, okay?"

Luz said, "Okay, I'll tell everyone."

"Then come back to me."

Luz glanced up at Ray. "I can't come back to you," she said to the girl. "I have to go."

"Okay, but please can I tell you a secret?" The Nut exhaled loudly but Luz leaned down to the girl again. The child made no breathy sounds this time, but spoke clearly: "Please may I have a glass of water?"

Luz stood and in the tone adults use to speak through children she said, "I'm sure your friends can get you a glass of water."

The Nut once again took the girl by the arm. Before he left he told Luz plainly, "We don't have any water."

Luz watched him pull the baby back to the group, where he sat her down between the doughy teenage girl and the man with the bong. He said something sharp to the child, but Luz could not tell what.

Ray took Luz's hand. "Let's go," he said, though his face looked as sick as hers must have. They walked away from the group, back toward their blanket. Luz looked back but already the child was out of sight, blocked by a stand of partakers. They walked on.

It was Ray who spoke first. "That didn't seem right."

Luz stopped. "Let's go back," she said.

"And do what?"

"Watch her. Make sure she's okay."

"Why?"

"What if those weren't her people?"

"What do you mean?"

She took a short breath, knowing how the next part would sound. "I have a feeling."

Ray frowned and swept a strand of hair from her eyes. "Babygirl —"

"I'm not drunk anymore," she said, though she was not sure if that was true.

"I didn't say you were."

"Let's go back, just to see if everything looks okay." Ray ran his hand up and down her bare arm, as if she were cold. She wasn't cold but she was trembling. "Please," she said.

Ray looked back toward where they had left the child. "All right."

They walked a wide loop into and out of the canal and circled back on the other side of the footbridge. They stopped where they could spy down on the area where Luz first found the girl. The canal had gone from gleaming gray and bleach-white to fireglow and a misty blue-black. They turned to face each other, pretending to talk the happy talk of young people in love.

Luz stood with her back to the canal so that Ray could look over her shoulder. "Do you see them?" she whispered.

Ray nodded. "There."

"What are they doing?"

"The same thing. Sitting."

"Do you see her?"

"No."

Luz knew instantly that something unspeakable had happened to the baby, and that it was her fault. She resisted the rising urge to turn around.

Ray's eyes raked the chaos of the canal beyond. "Wait," he said. "There she is."

"What's she doing?"

"She's playing. Running around."

Luz could not stop herself from turning now. She spotted the child stepping softly in the hot silt, alone. Beyond her, the Nut and the fleshy girl who was not her mother and all the rest were back in their circle, taking rips from the bong, playing roughly with the dog. The thin girl was kissing a different man.

Luz and Ray watched the child — this strange, coin-eyed, translucent-skinned child. She approached a young woman with a ragged Mohawk who sat cross-legged on the concrete slope. The woman wore a crinkly purple skirt and a canvas backpack. She was topless, her breasts painted as two drooping purple daisies, her nipples the polleny yellow cores. The child hopped forward now and waved her hand emphatically in the young woman's face.

"See," said Ray, "she does that. Goes up to people."

The topless woman said something and the child solemnly rose up to touch the woman's Mohawk. She pancaked the inky flattened wall of hair between her two hands. The woman laughed, perhaps uneasily. Ray put his hand between Luz's shoulder blades, where the Nut had first touched her.

"She's just a weird kid," he said.

The child brought her hands to the woman's face and rubbed it all over, as she had done to Luz, and Luz was betrayed, somehow. "You're right," she said.

Ray stepped toward the bonfire, urging Luz in that direction with his large hand. But after a few yards Luz shook him off. "You saw the way she grabbed me," she said. "She was afraid."

"You don't know that."

"I have a feeling. I don't want to ignore it."

"What do you want to do?" he asked, kindly. He was handling her. He thought she was drunk and sliding toward hysteria, though he knew better than to put it that way. They had been here before, the culvert only the most recent episode. An impromptu party at the complex where she'd sat on the waxed lip of the dry pool, tight, smoking and arguing about the drought with some of Ray's nomad friends. They were shouting really, and Luz was shouting loudest. It was late and someone asked them to keep it down. Someone else asked them to take it somewhere else. Luz refused. Everyone there pretended to be so bohemian and radical but really they were all worried about offending everyone else and

58

she was fucking sick of it. She informed the others that they would not be keeping it down, that they would not be going anywhere, that there were entire towns dying of arsenic poisoning and if they thought they were so hard-core, so of the earth, maybe they should forego their trips to the ration truck parked on Pico. She called her beleaguered audience, among other things, cunts and fascists and bores. One weary comrade went back to where Ray was camped, and by the sonic magic of courtyard echoes, Luz had heard her asking Ray to intervene. "She listens to you," she'd said.

Ray's response: "If you want Luz to do something, you have to make her think it's her idea."

Another time — things with the friends souring, just before they'd left for the canyon — Luz had approached the gate after a ration trip and someone said, "Luz is back. Don't make any sudden movements."

"Can we move our stuff over here?" Luz asked now.

"What?"

"They don't have *water*, Ray? What does that *mean*?"

"I'd just like to know what you hope to gain here. Your goal."

"They're taking her rations."

"You don't know that."

"That's why I want to watch."

Ray yielded. "If it will make you feel better."

They fetched their things and rearranged them on the other side of the footbridge, where they could see the girl and her people. Luz could not take her eyes from the child flitting through raindance, darting around fires and garbage heaps, collecting sticks and stalks of shimmering trash into a bushel in her hand. She approached more strangers, farther and farther from her people, sometimes latching onto them as she had to Luz. She was a weird kid. She just went up to people. Yes, but it was also true that some evil was going down here and Luz knew she was the only one who could see it. For the first time in her life, she was absolutely essential. "I am acutely engorged with purpose," she whispered. Ray told her to have some more water.

The Nut did not come after the child again. Another man with another dog had joined them and the group was now captivated by the two dogs, who often erupted in snarls. Without anyone's noticing, the child ventured farther and farther. Luz eavesdropped on the group shamelessly and caught some of their words — *whore, ream, fuck rag, cum dumpster* — words Luz herself used, and whose explicitness had always delighted her, but which seemed now repugnant and unequivocally *inappropriate,* a word she never used.

"Did you hear that?" Luz asked after one of these affronting words reached them. But Ray was making a show of eating almonds. He was, he said, through spying on people.

Luz was not through. Not hardly. She was spellbound by the group's filth and their relentless youth and their drug-depleted gazes — indeed, the more she watched them the more they embodied stories she'd heard of vile things happening in the Valley. Traffickers charged quadruple for children, and many hosts refused to take them, so toddlers were left to cook in cars, older kids locked in the apartments parents fled. Or the children became the currency. These tales, along with the group's obvious and unforgivable neglect of the child, confirmed for Luz their malevolence.

Then, the child spotted Luz once more. She smiled a crooked smile, but it wasn't until she came toward Luz, at an all-out tottersome run, that Luz recognized how she ached to hold the girl again. The baby bowled into Luz and toppled into her lap.

"Hi," said Luz.

The girl said nothing, only stared up at Luz. With dusk her chameleon eyes had gone a milky heather, her hair dull pewter. She smelled strongly of urine.

"Are you thirsty?" asked Luz.

The child opened and closed her mouth like a carp.

"Want some water?" Luz tried, dangling her jug over the girl.

The child squealed and lunged for the water. Luz unscrewed the cap and the baby drank heartily and with some difficulty, spilling down her bare chest and letting out big wet gasps between gulps. Ray watched, trying and failing to hide his alarm at her intense thirst. Luz fetched the can of blueberries from the backpack.

"You hungry?" she said. Ray gave Luz a look and Luz said, "What?" He looked over to the Nut and the others. Luz looked, too. The Nut saw them. Luz wilted, expecting him to retrieve the girl again. Instead, he waved. It was not a friendly wave, not to give Luz permission to hold the girl or to feed her, but an ambivalent flash of the hand to signal that he didn't give a damn what she did.

So Luz shook some blueberries out of the can and offered one to the girl. She longed for the child to take it between her corpulent thumb and index finger, but instead she jab-bered something and Luz stared at her, baffled.

The girl slapped impatiently at the blanket and jabbered again.

" 'What is it?' " said Ray. "She's saying, 'What is it?' "

"What is it?" the girl said again.

"Blueberry," said Luz.

The baby did not know *blueberry*.

"Here." Luz took the fruit and split it in half with her thumbnail. The child looked on in amazement. Luz offered the vein-colored, butterflied meat of the blueberry to the girl and she took it into her small mouth. Immediately the child grimaced, squenched her face up in revulsion and opened her mouth. Luz cupped her hand beneath the child's chin and the girl let the spitty fruit drop out. Luz tried a berry and found it a tasteless mucus. "Sorry," she said. Ray chuckled a little and the girl told him to shut up. Ray balked. "Shut up!" the baby said once more, gleefully. Luz said, "Be kind," her own mother's line.

"What's your name?" Ray asked.

The baby regarded Ray suspiciously and he asked her again. Then the girl made a sound like *Ig*.

"Ig?" asked Ray.

The girl chugged amusedly, "Ig, Ig, Ig," like some small engine.

"Ig," said Ray, laughing, and the girl laughed too. She dismounted from Luz's lap and began to roll around on the concrete, saying, "Ig, Ig, Ig, Ig," her face still flecked with black bits of blueberry skin. Ray and Luz laughed and the girl, little showboat dynamo, little ham, rolled more furiously, going, "Ig, Ig, Ig, Ig." They were having a good time, the three of them.

Then, sudden as a ghost, the child stopped rolling and popped up and bounded back to her wretched encampment. Luz felt a great reservoir of joy drain from her.

Ray watched her go, too, saying finally, "She's sweet."

"I don't like those . . . people," said Luz.

"What's wrong with them?"

Luz scowled at her Ray. "They're high —"

"Everyone here is high. They're letting loose."

Luz knew he didn't believe this. "Something's wrong with them."

"You're paranoid."

"Don't do that to me. Having a drink doesn't make me an idiot. I know what I feel."

"Stop," he breathed.

"Look at them. Please."

Ray turned, finally. They watched the girl skipping and hopping irregularly between her people. "Keep looking," Luz whispered, urgent with the fear that Ray would not see what she saw, burdened with the weight of his waiting. This was the last chance, she knew, the last he'd humor her this evening.

The girl got on all fours and crawled to the new dog, pressing her plank face dangerously close to the mutt's. Ray was unfazed.

Then the child lost interest in the dog and crawled along the silt crust to the young man who had been serving as steward of the water bong. He sat cross-legged in the dirt. The girl put her head in his lap. Ray shifted and Luz felt his attention fading.

Just then, the Mojav brought his hand down on the back of the child's head, not a blow but a grip. Palming her head, he pumped the baby's face into his groin twice, three times. His friends chuckled and he did it again. This time he hoisted his free hand into the air, a bull rider's pose. The group howled raucously as he mashed the baby's whiteblond head into and out of his crotch, then released her.

Ray recoiled. "Jesus."

The gesture sickened Luz too, because it was sickening, but also because it was so wholly validating that she felt she had somehow asked for it, willed it into being. She said, "See?"

"We should get someone."

"There's no one."

"Red Cross."

"They won't come down here. Even if they did. They'll talk to them and they'll tell them some story and Red Cross will leave and they" — she flung her hand toward the wretched gang — "will leave." Her hand hung in the air, trembling as if the last barrier of resistance against the force threatening to pull this child back into the endless asphalt maze of the Valley. "They'll take her away and we'll never see her again."

Ray began to speak. "Listen," he might have said, but beyond Luz the Nut came toward them. The little girl followed, stumbling to keep up.

The Nut stopped at the edge of their blanket and pushed the girl in front of him. He spoke without looking at them, chewing the raw skin around his thumbnail. "Could you guys watch her a sec?" He gestured back toward his group. "We have to do something."

Ray began again to speak. Luz feared what was coming: *Where are you going? How long will you be gone?* Ray always asked the questions that needed to be asked and suddenly, fleetingly, she found this quality of his unbearable.

"Sure," she answered before he could. "No problem." Luz extended her arms to the girl. The child regarded the pose a moment, then leapfrogged instead onto Ray's outstretched legs. Ray released a sitcom groan, which delighted the girl and sent her up and leaping again.

And so another nonsense game was in full swing as the Nut and his jaundiced entourage receded, bong, dogs and all, along the corridor, disappearing into the swell of the raindance.

Ray chided Luz — " 'Sure! No problem!' You were so creepy." — but he entertained the child with unchecked joy. The three of them played at piling little anthills of sand in one another's hands and then played at blowing them into oblivion. They played at Ray lying still then popping his eyes open and saying *boog* and the girl squealing and hiding behind Luz. They played at arranging all Luz's hair to cover her face like a curtain. The girl was a fiendish collector and loved nothing more than scouting the canal for like things and depositing them with the adults. Thus Ray's pockets filled with pebbles and dead sticks, while Luz's backpack became a repository for dust-

67

chalked plastic bags and small shining sails of garbage. During her depositing the baby would sometimes do her dynamo chant: *Ig, Ig, Ig, Ig, Ig.* And when the child set off, Luz and Ray chugged it to each other, "Ig, Ig, Ig, Ig," laughing in their old easy way.

An hour passed, then another, all the while no sign of the Nut or anyone from his group. Ray went responsible periodically, looking around and asking, "Where *are* these people?"

Beneath the silliness, they noticed an eerie adult quality about the girl. She touched. She moaned to herself. Her speech lurched forward and back, progressions and regressions. Sometimes she spoke like a miniature adult, skeptical and weary. *Don't tell anyone, okay?* Other times it was only alien syllables, sending her into a rage at her own incomprehensibility. But she swung easily from tantrum to slapstick to affection, her bulbed brow leading the way. Her torso was taut as a balloon, some pressure inside, and her pale arms dangled from it like vestiges when she ran. Depositing a specimen she often paused to lay her hands on Luz or Ray. She pinched as often as she pet, though her unwashed hands did seem to favor stroking Luz's throat, a disquieting stroke described by nothing so truly as the word

68

sensual.

"What is that?" Luz said once, after the child had tromped off for another micro-expedition. "The way she *feels* everything."

Ray nodded. "Like she's seeing with her hands."

Night was full-on, though it was a night obliterated by bonfire now thoroughly raging, letting off a chemical pungency where someone had heaved in a sofa. Soon the girl — whom they had started to call Ig, affectionately — tired of her collecting and began to whine and mash her fists into her eyes. Luz made a pillow of Ray's hoodie and coaxed the girl into lying down, then took up a corner of the duvet and burritoed it over Ig's soft body. There, the child fell into a fluttering sleep. In the distance a long, manic drum riff crescendoed, sending up trills from the partiers. Ig had been with them for hours now.

"We should have asked where they were going," Ray said.

Luz swaddled the duvet over the sleeping girl more snugly, wishing for something more substantial to wrap around her, wishing she could free her from the putrid diaper. She laid her hand on the bundle of Ig and rubbed softly.

"Maybe they're not coming back." She

said it nonchalantly — almost a joke — but she knew it was true. She had known it since they left.

Ray didn't laugh. He looked at the sleeping girl, unable or unwilling to hide his pity. "Who leaves their kid with *strangers*?"

"Maybe she's not their kid."

Ray was quiet, though Luz could tell he had plenty to say. He was doing the dutiful stoic bit that so provoked her. Around them, people scrambled to set up camp where they could get a good view of the bonfire. Luz felt herself pulled taut with the urgency that had been distending in her since the girl plowed into her life. She was close to bursting, and frantic to make Ray feel that bursting, too. She was desperate to make him desperate.

"How could someone do that?" she said.

"What?" said Ray.

"Hurt a little one."

He frowned down at Ig, pushed Luz's hair back behind her shoulder. He knew about the photographers, was maybe thinking of them now. "I don't know."

"Ray," she said, startled to find herself near tears. "We're going to have little ones and they're going to be hurt."

"You wouldn't do that."

"Neither would you. But someone will."

"Babygirl, don't get like this."

"There's too much hurt in the world to be avoided. More than enough for everyone."

"You just do your best."

She leaned into him and gripped the inner meat of his thigh. "Then let's do it."

He inhaled and stiffened. "Do what?"

"Our best."

Ray looked at her, miniature bonfires winking in his eyes.

"It's been hours," said Luz. "Maybe they wanted us to have her."

"You didn't even think those were her people."

"They abandoned her, Ray."

"You sound like a crazy person," he whispered.

"Don't say that."

"You do. You sound crazy."

"I'm not," she said. Was that true? She was beyond determining her own fitness and had been for some time. And yet, here she felt solid — righteous. She peered fiercely into Ray's prophet eyes aflame. It had been such a long time since she believed in anything. "I cannot accept that there is nothing we can do. I won't."

An ebullient shriek went up from the crowd. The drums pounded on and the

71

bonfire swelled with mattresses and furniture and driftwood. There was a flare in the distance, and an orb of yellow-white gaslight bloomed overhead. Then another flare, another fireball, another ripple of pandemonium traveling through the canal. Ray said nothing.

Someone detonated a round of mortars, a purely sonic cluster of explosions that left pale smoke blossoms in the starless night and woke Ig. She startled in her bundle, then sprang up, wailing. Luz tried to take hold of her but the girl scrambled away, afraid. She stood on the smooth and cracked concrete infrastructure, shuddering, her soiled diaper drooping between her bowed legs. More explosions came and Luz knew as she had known anything that the child was on the verge of tearing off into the darkness, through the dry canals to the channel that was once the Los Angeles River, streaking all the way to the black and infinite and worthless sea.

Suddenly, in one purposeful and athletic motion, Ray was off the blanket. He strode to the girl and scooped her into his arms. She wailed still but he pressed her to him and held her. Luz went to them. She tucked the hoodie around Ig. Ray paced, jouncing the child lovingly and murmuring into her pale head. Eventually she calmed, slackened, and fell back to sleep.

Luz watched. At the cacophonic arsenal of the bonfire's climax she pressed her hands over the child's small ears. It was useless, she knew, but Ray gave her one of his endlessly warm, instantly soothing smiles and she kept them there.

The bonfire caved in on itself and the drummers followed. Soon, another ineffectual raindance would disperse up and out of the canal. Luz folded their blanket, packed the growler, berries, and water bottles in the backpack and donned it. Ray watched, Ig still in his arms, her glowing head draped over his shoulder. They stood looking at each other. Ray's eyes were reddish and bleary now and seeing them made Luz's hurt, too. She wanted to go home. She had the sense that they were standing on the edge of something and she wanted to step off, together. But Ray did not move.

Then, his eyes widened.

Luz turned, looking for what Ray saw instead of her. Below, across the dark dry canal, a serpentine figure moved easily through the churning crowd. He came toward them, the Nut.

Luz did not breathe.

The berm was dense with people. It was

possible the Nut had not seen them. They could flee. She wanted to say all this and more but before she could manage a word Ray leaned into her. He released two firm syllables, the finest she had ever heard: "Go. Now."

She followed Ray swiftly, wordlessly, away from the Nut, through the throngs, up and over the berm. On the lip of the canal, Luz looked back, the bonfire a dying star behind them, the Nut coming at them, maybe.

"Here," said Ray, leading her through a gouged redwood gate dangling from its post by one hinge. They weaved through the sacked backyards of the abandoned craftsmen, past their shredded Burmese hammocks, drained koi ponds, groves of decorative bamboo gone to husks. Upended kilns, mosaics of pottery shards, slashed screens, slivers of smashed Turkish lamps lynched from what had once been a lemon tree, hummingbird feeders still half-filled with pink nectar, wire skeletons of dissolved paper lanterns, a splintering croquet mallet, terra-cotta pavers, disintegrating block walls, gutted cushions, a burnt-out miniature pagoda, a canoe filled with excrement and ancient newspaper. All the while Luz watched the baby's glowing haloed head where it bounced on Ray's shoulder, nodding *yes*. It led her to the starlet's car, to Ray, and together he and she fled to their canyon, with their Ig.

Luz woke at daylight on the living room floor with her head split in two. Her aching brain like some dim-witted oracle slogged through the night before: the affectionate half sleep, she and Ray with arms gently tangled, rolling back together when they parted, each always reaching out for the other. Ray twitching. Luz holding him, uncoiling his clenched fists. Ray at some hourless hour, pressing gently into her from behind. Her encouraging him drowsily, tilting her pelvis back so he could get at her. Him urging himself inside and riding her silently, her face pressed to the rug. Him coming quickly, rolling her over and stroking her clit for a bit, then her taking over. Ray with one big hand around her throat, his index finger curled up and into her mouth, puckered with moisture and rind-tasting. Her diddling madly, coming, and falling back to sleep.

The raindance only a zany, phantasmagoric dream, except Ray rolled on top of her now, kissed her deeply with mash on his breath, and above them, on the starlet's space-age couch, the child began to cry.

They stared at each other, at what they'd done.

The child went on crying, a tight sound leaking from her. Luz dressed quickly in one of the starlet's robes, and as she did, Ig climbed down from the couch butt-first. Luz had untied the child's sagging dirty diaper and lay her on the couch the night before, she remembered now. They looked at each other for a while, the three of them. Luz said, "We should wash her."

Ray said, "We should feed her." He pulled his pants on and went to the kitchen. Ig stood nude in the sunlight flooding through the wall of glass. She regarded Luz a moment, opened her mouth slightly in concentration, and loosed a stream of gold-brown urine on the starlet's birchply floor.

Luz said, Shit, oh shit.

Ray ran in, holding a box of graham crackers. "What — oh. She needs a diaper."

"I know that." Luz ran upstairs and came back with a maxi pad and a psychedelic Hermès scarf. Ray was mopping up the pee with a monogrammed beach towel and Ig was crawling along the stone ledge in front of the fireplace, wagging her bare bottom.

"Come here," Luz said, but Ig screeched, wanting to finish her journey along the ledge and back. Luz waited, then took Ig squirming and flailing and laid her on the ottoman. "Can you hold her?" she asked, and Ray did. "Hey, hey," he said, trying to distract the baby with weird faces and gestures, none of which Luz had ever seen before. Finally and with considerable trouble, Luz cinched the scarf through Ig's spindly bow legs. "Just for now," she said to Ray, whom she could feel watching her.

Ray released Ig and she ran, stumbled, and nearly put her head through a glass end table. She lay where she fell and howled tremendously. Luz rushed to her and gathered her up into her lap. Ray handed over the box of graham crackers and Luz broke one into quarters and tried to soothe Ig with a piece.

"Can she eat those?" Ray asked.

Luz shrugged. "She has teeth."

Ig went on wailing, her flat face tomatoed and shiny with tears. Luz waved the cracker but the baby went on screaming bloody murder, as Luz's mother would have said. And indeed it seemed if Ig did not stop soon she would kill herself, or them. The sound was sharp-edged as a siren and sliced into the softest, still-sleeping or still-drunk parts of Luz's brain. Ray was doing a freaked-out little dance, hopping fretfully from one foot to the other. Luz wished he would stop. She waved the graham crackers helplessly. Then Ig stopped crying, took a cracker in each hand, and stuffed one into her small, saliva-webbed maw.

She ate another and another. Each time a cracker disappeared into her mouth she would wail for another to replace it, so she was always managing three, two in her fists and one disintegrating in her mouth. Luz waved Ray to the kitchen for more and he came back with an unopened box. He set it on the couch beside Luz. "Something to drink," she said.

Ray came back with a ration cola and Luz looked up at him. "All we have," he said. They'd drunk yesterday's water yesterday. Luz helped the baby with the cola and watched as the syrup mixed with the crackers to make a mealy puck in Ig's open mouth.

Then Ig wanted to go outside and so they took her into the backyard. On the deck Ray kicked away the spiny somethings as Ig transferred both crackers to one hand and took Luz's index finger into her other chubby nautilus fist. Ig led them to the chaise, its canvas cushions already baking, and said, "What is?"

Ray said, "Chair."

He said, "Pool."

He said, "Fountain."

"Frogs."

"Trellis."

"Hot tub."

"Fur coat."

"Half-pipe."

"Rocks."

"Rocks."

"Rocks."

"Rocks."

They were in the rock garden — though there was not now much to distinguish the rock garden from the garden garden, except the rock garden had been arranged according to some flimsy interpretation of the word *Zen* — when Ig started tugging at the scarf. Luz untied a knot to adjust it and a little mustard turd rolled out. She picked up the baby and rushed over to the corner of the yard, to the shitting hole, and held her over it. Ig dropped her crackers and began to cry. Luz said, "I know," and Ig squirmed and flailed in the air as saffrony pellets of poop dropped from her, some of the poops landing on Luz's bare feet. Luz tried to shake them off but one had established itself between her biggest and second biggest toes.

"Jeez. What did she eat?" said Ray.

Luz wiped Ig's rump with the maxi pad, wiped her own toes with it, then let the pad and the Hermès flap down into the shitting hole. "How would I know?"

Ray looked down the hole as if regretting the ignoble burial of the beshitted scarf. "Should we keep those?"

"She has a million of them."

Ray dragged the couches and the mod low-slung armchairs from the library and the foyer and the drawing room and with them built a baby corral in the living room. He cleared out all the ouchies, as he called them, and put duct tape over the outlets though they had no juice. He hoisted the glass end tables onto his shoulders, carried them out front and chucked them down into the ravine. For toys Luz unplugged an antique rotary phone from the library and placed it in the baby corral. She gathered up the starlet's collection of glazy babushka dolls, Guatemalan worry people and cottonwood kachinas from a guest room and, though Ray asked if letting a child play with a kachina wasn't to invite a wicked hex, she put those in the corral, too, along with a taxidermied desert tortoise, the thickly lacquered and glass-eyeballed head of which Ig promptly began to gnaw.

From then on out it was The Ig Show, an onslaught of enslaving cutenesses. Ig seemed to need a dress, so Luz outfitted her in one of the starlet's French silk camisoles cinched up on the side with a scrunchie. Ig was a cracker junkie, so Ray emptied the pantry to find her favorite. Ig took everything into her mouth, so Luz cinched dry ration rice into a pocket of gauze and made what Ig instantly called a *nini,* for her to suck. Ig was savage for walks, so Ray made her shoes out of packing tape and corkboard prized from the walls of the library and Luz let herself be pulled endlessly round the starlet's backyard, shading the baby with a cherry-blossomed paper parasol, big bloom of gauze sprouting from Ig's face.

Together Luz and Ray deciphered her tells: fists mashed into eye sockets, walking bowlegged and tugging on her silk diaper, a carp-like opening and closing of the mouth, the bulging of her coin eyes.

They cataloged her tastes. Likes: crackers, rocks, ration cola, questions, her new shoes, the *ding* the antique phone made when she bashed it with the earpiece, opening and closing the sliding doors, the tool belt, the burbling sounds Ray made for her benefit, mounting and dismounting things, i.e. the stairs, the fireplace ledge, the space-age sofa.

Dislikes: the shitting hole, being changed, the empty pool, glass, the fur coat going crusty in the backyard, certain textures (polyester, chintz, velvet, shag), certain sounds (the hand pump squeaking, heavy footsteps on the floating staircase, Luz humming), the sun, the mountain.

Ig could be impossibly silly, her clucking laugh like a seizure, a little worrisome. A spaz, Ray called her with love. Little pill. She was moody, became pensive or enraged without warning. She went berserk at the sight of a plate of saltwater noodles Ray fixed her for lunch, sending up painful-sounding screeches. If they reached for an empty cola can before she had decided she was through with it, she let loose an autistic, unsettling moan, which they made every effort not to hear. After the first day, only Ray could change her, for Ig bit Luz whenever she tried.

The child let loose her meanest mean streak on her toys. She scolded them in her private, wrathful language. She hit them, despite both Luz and Ray begging her not to. She chucked the worry people to the floor and was especially hard on the kachinas, whose legs she wrenched apart, popping them out of their indigenous sockets. After walloping the jujus mercilessly she would put them to sleep, draping them with a tissue and whispering fluffy comforts to them. She was kind to the tortoise, though, whose name she said was also Ig. She carried tortoise Ig everywhere, eventually caving his head in.

Nights Ig soothed herself to sleep by stroking the frayed edge of gauze back and forth across the tip of her nose and moaning. The baby starfished on the floor of the corral beneath a chenille throw with her brain-damaged tortoise double, Luz and Ray collapsed head-to-toe on the space-age sofa above, where they did not say, "What have we done?"

Nor, "We have to get out of here."

Nor, "I've never been so happy."

Though all were true.

For it was blissed-out chaos up in the canyon, it was joy and love, love for the coin-eyed baby and for each other and for everything, everywhere. But it could not last. (Nothing here could.) Luz spent her afternoons following post-nap Ig around the backyard with the parasol. Days went by and the baby went jumpy, twitching at the crunch of gravel in the rock garden or if Luz snapped open a ration cola.

"What is?" Ig would cry fearfully at the sound.

"Soda," Luz would say. Ray, "Pop."

Sometimes Ig jumped at nothing and stood staring at the mountainside, petrified, the Santa Anas keening through the canyon. Luz froze too, her heart gone manic, palping the way Baby Dunn's had after her father taught her of mountain lions, *You won't see them until they want you to see them.*

"What is?" said Ig, meek as dust.

Luz managed, "Nothing, my love," though she too was trembling. Perhaps Ig knew something they didn't, felt her people coming for them, somehow. Felt all the horrors creeping up the canyon.

Luz was exhausted, was not drinking water, could never remember where she put her jug. Was maybe sleepwalking.

"You're *holding* it," said Ray, and there was the jug cradled in her arms.

He was not sleeping at all. All night he paced along the wall of windows, peering over the bridge driveway and the laurelless canyon beyond. Ray's decency had always been a succor, an anchor, and it was still, though now Luz feared it was an anchor buried in the wrong sand.

At night Luz listened to Ray's patrol and made the first list of her life, unwritten.

What we must do:

- leave
- go to Seattle
- find a little cottage on a sound where the air is indigo and ever-jeweled with mist
- take Ig walking in the rainforest, barefoot
- show her velvet moss and steady evergreens and the modest gibbous of glacier on Mount Rainier
- encourage her to stroke gently the fins on the underside of orange mushrooms
- pry open rotting logs and watch grubs and slugs and earthworms at their enrichment business
- let her take some of the sweet colloidal humus into her mouth
- come upon a moose, his antlers splayed like great hands raised to God, his ancient beard swaying as he saunters silently through the forest
- return home, where Ray must be stirring a big pot of chili and I must assemble a rainbow salad and Ig must set her dolls kindly on the redwood windowsill, all in a row

– eat dinner on a picnic table or on the porch Ray built, sipping from tall beaded glasses of ice water, watching orcas breech across the sound

One night, Luz came to at the lip of the starlet's dry unshreddable pool, the moon a pale blade overhead, her fingers in a jar of capers. She blinked; she did not even like capers. She stood staring at the inky mountainside, its sinister stillness, the slug of it, tasting the vinegar tang inside her mouth. She saw the Nut trailing them in circles around the yard, saw his mongrel dog hung by its rope leash from the barren lemon tree. The daddy-o on the driveway bridge. The starlet going wicker in the ravine. Ig stumbling from the wrecked raindance bungalows.

She returned to the mansion and found Ray sitting in the hallway opposite the unyielding wall of glass. She slid down beside him and took his face. "Let's go to Seattle," she said.

He frowned drowsily. "There's militia at the Oregon border. You know that." Washington State had stopped accepting Mojav relocation applications.

Luz said, "Idaho then. I read there're these mountains near Boise and when the sun sets they turn purple. Every day. Something about the altitude. And in the foothills there are these marshes and in the spring they pulse this electric green. You almost can't look at them."

"Still?"

No, no more wetlands in Idaho, no grass whatsoever west of the hundredth. "Oh yeah," she said. "In Idaho? Hella. Idaho's *golden.* We'll take Ig there, she can run around, spaz out. Go apeshit, like kids are supposed to. No more circling the pen."

Ray smiled at the glass, spacey and fatigued. "That sounds nice."

Luz wished they were not in the hallway, the ravine of the house. She could not convince him of anything in the hallway. She looked into his reflecting eyes. "They're going to come for us."

He shook his head.

"The trucks, Ray."

"They don't come up here."

"They will. Eventually they will."

Luz watched Ray's face where it hovered in the glassy black, hollow, ghostly. He clenched his jaw, his impression of a Marine. "I won't let them," he said.

"There's nothing you can do, bub." She touched him. "We need to get legit."

Just then, a thin little wailing came to

them from Ig's pen. Ray nearly sprang up, but Luz tethered him down — "Wait her out" — and they sat still as wolves, with Ig calling out in her Ig language. Ray made prayer hands and tugged on his lips with them. It hurt him to leave her this way, Luz could tell. It hurt them both, physically, her voice twine tethered to their bellies, looped around the nodes and coils of their hearts, lungs, bowels. Already, that was so. Finally, the child settled into silence.

Luz whispered, "We'll have a chance, on the list."

"Put ourselves on it? *Volunteer?*"

She nodded.

"Our part for the cause."

"I'm serious, Ray."

"What about her?"

Luz said, "We'll get her a birth certificate." Their old group had ways of procuring such documents.

"Luz, I can't —"

"We'll say we're married."

"Luz —"

"That we got married in the church." It surprised Luz, how happy even the prospect of this lie made her. She had not thought of herself as someone who wanted to be married, let alone married in a church, but apparently she was.

"Luz, I have to tell you something. Will you listen?" Ray took in a slow, bottomless breath and looked Luz in the eyes. He giggled.

It was not a sound she would have guessed was in him. He gasped shallowly, embarrassed, and out burbled more giggles. "I — he he heh — I can't go. Ha ha! I can't go on the list."

"What?"

"I mean, heh, look — ha ha!" His eyes were wide and manic. "There's just nothing — ha ha!" He clasped his hands over his mouth. "I'm sorry. I can't stop. I'm afraid. But I'm being serious — hee hee hee!"

Luz said, "I don't . . ."

Ray pressed his face between his hands. "Okay: in the service — heh. Hee hee! Okay: I was in medical school. Did I tell you that?" He had not. "But I quit. Dropped out. Went into the service. I was a medic, sort of. Guys would come to me, all fucked up. *All* fucked up. I didn't know what to do. I gave a few of them pills. Standard. I took them, too. So we could sleep. Hee hee — we couldn't sleep, Luz. More guys came to me. More and more. I gave them what we needed. We took Roxicet, oxy, fentanyl lollipops. Whatever I had." He stopped giggling. "They were just so *fucked up*. Every-

90

body was."

Luz watched his shapes moving across the glass wall. "Lollipops?"

"We were on leave — in San Diego," his voice on the upswing, as if San Diego were a friend they had in common, "and one of the guys, his buddy had been busted on patrol with morphine patches plastered all over his ass cheeks. They were going to get me. I mean, I'm the only one with a case of fucking made-in-the-USA morphine patches. Fort Leavenworth." Then, when she clearly did not know what the words *Fort* or *Leavenworth* had to do with any of this, he said, "Prison. Military prison. I, well, you know . . . *ran.*"

They watched each other in the glass.

"Ass cheeks?" said Luz. She was just saying words.

"We used to do that — the sweat helps. Zaps it into your system."

Time had gotten woozy under them. It was hard to tell how long they went without speaking. Ray was waiting for something from her, she realized, so she said, "You're." It was all she could summon.

"AWOL, I guess you'd say," then one loud, hard laugh burst from him, "*Bah!* Goddamn it."

"Shh," Luz said, meaning, *Don't wake her.*

"I'm sorry. I should have told you, but . . . I'm sorry."

She was putting things together now. She looked up. "We can't evac."

"Not without a clean ID."

"And if we try —"

"They'll arrest me. Take her for sure."

This was true, and unthinkable.

The wildfires pulsed behind them, and beyond those the Oregon militiamen cleaned their fingernails. The gatemen at Lake Tahoe changed shifts, one pausing to pluck a tendril of red thread from the other's uniform. Everything here was ash. Chalkdust and filament. Everything here could be obliterated with a wave of her hand, and she waved her hands *all the time.*

Ray wept, briefly. Luz touched his face. "We're lost," he said eventually, and Luz whispered, "We're not." But Ray said again that they were, and Luz was convinced.

And so, lost, they succumbed to sleep.

If Ray thrashed his nightly thrashing, Luz did not know it. She woke raw, bewildered, sore deep in her hips and in the shoulder she'd slept on. Her love was gone, already awake and away, a tiny betrayal, no matter that it happened daily. She rose, discovered Ig gone too, and searched for them in the half-light. She found Ray pacing in the indi-goed backyard, holding Ig to him, speaking something into her glowy head. He looked up at Luz. His features were defeated, even his gorgeous mouth eroded by the expectation of dawn.

Ray came around to Luz, a new posture of resolve. "I'm sorry about all that, baby-girl. I am."

"I know."

"I'll fix it. I will. We'll get the birth certificate, a clean ID. I'll take care of everything." That was what he'd been telling Ig, that he was going to get his shit together, be on top of every damn thing from here on out. Also how quickly one's beliefs and values and principles and philos-ophies — all the biggies — could be reduced to a matter of paperwork. Ray said, "We'll need to go to see Lonnie."

Luz inhaled. "I don't want to go there."

"I know you don't." He kissed her temple. "I don't either. But we have to."

It was a question whether Lonnie and Rita and the others would still be at the complex, a question answered when Ray approached the building made of snagging stucco, pink like the inner swirls of a conch, so much like the inner folds of a cunt, he thought, and bashed his open hand against the metal gate, bashed as so many others had bashed when he and Luz lived here. Shapes responded in the morning haze, moving along the periphery of the courtyard. The building was constructed like many apartment buildings in Santa Monica: a two-story square with a courtyard and a pool in the center, one heavy metal gate, the architecture of fortification, of circled wagons, as if the city had known what was coming, which, it hardly needs saying, she had.

"Go the fuck away!" said the shape at the gate, hood up and bandanna pulled over its face. A new guy.

Ray said, "Be cool man, I know Lonnie."

"Fuck you do."

"Yes, fuck, I do."

"Get the fuck out of here, you fuck, before I blow your fucking brains out."

Ray sighed. "Okay, fella. Just tell him Ray's here. Ray and Luz. Could you do that?"

The shape hesitated — scrutinizing Ig where she was on her notmother's hip, maybe — then receded. Luz hung back with the baby, wishing Lonnie's face would and would not materialize behind the grating.

It did not. Instead it was Rita, Lonnie's girl, her carroty hair tufted into berms by body soil, the green-black at the tips the last of her grown-out dye. A relief, even though Rita hated Luz now — probably everyone here did. Rita's tiny eyes, fringed by pale lashes, squinted behind the grating, then went for a second up, where a thick swath of tar had been slathered atop the complex wall. From the tar jutted sharpened sticks and spearheads of broken glass. That was new. Rita stowed something in her billowy skirt — a weapon, they didn't have to guess — and opened the door.

She embraced Ray, who nodded overhead and said, "Bit overkill, don't you think?"

Rita rolled her eyes. "I know, right?" Then

95

she saw Ig.

She took a small step back. Rita did not come to Luz — Luz did not expect her to — only stared, vaguely horrified, at where the child clung to Luz, grunting drowsily like some lesser primate.

They hadn't seen Lonnie or Rita in eight months. It might have been eight years. Rita had been stocky, plump as a flounder, big shelf of an ass and gigantic breasts that led her around, made her seem powerful. Luz had always been afraid of her, even when they were supposedly friends. But Rita was thin now, so thin that her tattoos seemed withered. The half-sleeve art nouveau Holy Mother on her right forearm, cherry blossoms and thick gashes of Sanskrit up the inside of her left, Johnny Cash giving the finger from the bicep, a fish skeleton fossilized along her neck, supposedly traced from an ancient urn, all sagged a little, except the asterisks signifying assholes on the spit of bone behind each ear. Even Rita's signature bullring drooped now from her septum as though her cartilage was fatigued. She'd removed the disks from her ears and the lobes now dangled in melting *O*s that, Luz noted vindictively, Ig could have put her fist through.

What was Rita before the water went?

(Before they *took* the water, Rita would've said, and Luz once, too.) She should have been the drummer in a punk band in a scene so far underground, it would never see the light of day. She should have been barefoot, murdering the double bass pedals on a cover of "Too Drunk to Fuck," cracking her cymbals, pulverizing her sticks and chucking the splinters into the crowd. She should have been spitting blood on the boys who deposited plastic cups of liquor at her feet. But it had been a dude unloading on the double bass, her boss spitting the blood, Rita depositing the liquor and doing his grocery shopping at the nice Ralphs in the Palisades, Rita driving him to and from LAX, wiping his chow chow's ass.

"You look like run-over dog shit," Rita said to Ray. "Are you drinking enough water?"

Another tired joke, but Ray laughed generously. That was his way.

"Come in," said Rita. "He thought you'd be down."

Inside the complex, Luz saw that the trees that had once stood in the corners of the courtyard had been ripped up, which did not necessarily surprise her — pretty much all the trees in Santa Monica had been hacked down, even the landward planks of the pier had been scavenged for firewood, the carnival unmoored out on its island of pilings, the Ferris wheel unmoving, unwheeling. Rather, it was the holes where the trees had been that unsettled Luz, dark, expectant as graves. There were never so many hazards in the world as there were today. Love made you see them all.

"What is?" asked Ig.

"Holes," said Luz.

"Oles," said Ig.

At the center of the courtyard was the dry swimming pool, its lip glistening black with grind wax. Ray paused over the enviable glob. Chalky sky blue, a color named such before the sky went bloodred with ash, and that before blood went xanthic for want of iron. Luz waited, squeezed Ig to feel the baby resist. Beneath their shoes were the spots where Lonnie's grandfather, the Persian Jew slumlord of Koreatown, had scattered huge hunks of rock salt along the wet concrete, wanting to mimic the popular pocking of American midcentury driveways. But the salt took forever to dissolve — no moisture — and instead of the subtle stippling of Pasadena, it left behind craters the size of unshelled peanuts. Among those craters, heartening and forgotten imprints where Lonnie's oma had laid leaves from

neighborhood trees atop the wet pour: mela-
leuca and magnolia and camphor and jaca-
randa and sweet gum, all the citizens of the
so-called urban forest long since charred to
carbon.

Luz would have liked to leave Ray beside
the dry pool and show Ig the spot Ray had
shown her, near the laundry room that had
been their room, where the fossil of a spruce
sprig was flanked by two gentle divots:
Oma's fingerprints, from where she'd laid
the spruce. But to go to the sprig would be
to go to the laundry room, would be to go
to the chemical and supposedly orchid smell
of an ancient half-gone box of dryer sheets,
would be to slide down the greased worm-
hole that scent can be, to their first time, to
go to Ray's bedroll, his canvas duffel, his
nine Red Cross candles lined up on a shelf
beside his can opener, which she could not
stop counting the night — their last in this
complex — when she woke Ray and told
him, I kissed Lonnie. I let him kiss me. And
touch me. We —

— I know.

— I'm sorry.

— Did you want to?

— No. It just happened.

— Why?

— I don't know. I was fucked up and flattered. I liked that he wanted me.

— Everyone wants you. It's your job.

— Not anymore. Not like that.

— I want you.

— I know you do.

— Do you want me?

—Yes, Ray. Of course I do. It wasn't about that. I liked that he liked me.

— Did you like it?

— No. I don't know. Liking didn't really come into it.

— Jesus.

And later, because she could not resist:

— How did you know?

—What?

—You said, "I know."

Ray, disgusted: You came to bed smelling like him.

Luz had to pull it together now. They were here for a reason. Ig squirmed to be put down but Luz told her to shh.

Rita retrieved a wreath of gold keys from the folds of her skirt and unlocked the red door to the apartment she shared with Lonnie, back in the far corner of the complex.

Ray said, "You're locking doors now?"

Before, all five doors opening onto the courtyard were always wide open or taken off the hinges completely — all except for the storage room, unit B. No locks at the compound, no structure, only frolicsome joy and jam sessions, pranks and all-night debates, raids of merry looting and after these a Christmas-morning vibe. Anyone and everyone was free to come and go, so long as they were committed to the cause and traveled light. No rules was a rule, no labels, and no hierarchy, stressed Lonnie, who owned the place.

Now, all five doors were re-hinged, shut and outfitted with shiny new deadbolts. Rita jangled her keys. "Ch-ch-ch-changes."

But Lonnie's apartment was as it had always been, owing to Lonnie's pathetic Oedipal preservation of the décor meticulously assembled by his mother, the shikse feng shui guru. Here were her star charts, her compasses, her astrolabes of brass and some of lacquered wood. Here were her gnomon, her trigrams, her incense coils gone scentless. There, her dragon head medallions, her color wheels, her innumerable bouquets of plastic bamboo, jabbed into vases half-filled with iridescent glass droplets. Here was her coffee table Zen fountain, now merely a bowl of rocks. Here, here, here, swallowing everything, dense drapes, drapes upon drapes, drapes atop drapes, drapes intertwined with other heavier, darker, mausoleum-making drapes.

Rita directed Luz and Ray to an L-shaped sofa in the darkened living room. She left to find Lonnie. Luz sat on the floor with Ig. She took tortoise Ig from the starlet's orange crocodile birkin-turned-diaper-bag and presented him to human Ig with some other toys — not the kachinas, she had thrown the kachinas in the ravine. Ig did not bother with the toys. Her coin eyes rolled in their sockets, looking for Rita.

Luz, jealous, leaned down and whispered to the child. "Pay no attention to the man behind the curtain."

"I wouldn't lead with that," said Rita, returning.

Lonnie loped in behind her, wearing some kind of orange-gold robe, itself once a drape, Luz was sure. The robe was cinched around his narrow waist with a chain of sterling silver conchos, each faceted with a gob of turquoise. Lonnie had dressed this way on occasion, the solstice or the Fourth of July, a joke or a near-joke. But there was no joke in it now. He stood in a way that begged to be described as regal. His head was shaved though his black eyebrows were as intense as ever. A long, dense goatee hung from his chin, sculpted square and unmoving, facial hair of the pharaohs. Luz wondered fleetingly where he got the razor.

A stupid question, for Lonnie was the great procurer; why they'd come.

"Brother," he said, pulling Ray into an embrace. He waited for Luz to stand, too. When she did he grinned and hugged her chastely.

"You're kidding," Lonnie said down to Ig. "I thought for sure she was fucking with me." He knelt and Luz fermented inwardly at the thought of him touching the baby. She's not a baby, Ray would have said and indeed had been saying. To which Luz would reply, She's a relative baby, meaning maybe that she was closer to being a baby than a girl, or meaning maybe that they just got her and so she was newborn to them. Ray would have said, too, Please behave yourself — was in fact at this moment saying it with his breath and his posture and his darting eyes and the taut filaments of his facial muscles, all of which served to remind her that Lonnie was the only person who could help them, and that she should be gracious, or do her best impression of someone gracious, despite the fact that in any other context she would have hated him.

Squatting, Lonnie said to Ig, "Hello, pretty girl."

No, she hated him here.

"Say hi, Ig," said Ray. "Ig, say *hi.*" Ig

refused. The car ride had lulled her to sleep, and she had perhaps not forgiven them for yanking her from the buttery backseat. "Can you say *hi*?"

"She doesn't want to," said Luz.

Lonnie adjusted his robes and sat at the vertex of the L sofa, Rita beside him. Ray sat at the end of the L's long leg and Luz returned to the floor. Ig, free to do as she pleased now, crawled beyond the coffee table to Rita — she had reverted to crawling lately — and offered her Ig the tortoise.

"She's giving it to you," said Luz.

"I'm good," said Rita, though Ig insisted and finally Rita let the saliva-softened tortoise corpse rest on her lap.

"This is something of a novelty," said Lonnie. "How old is she?"

"One," Luz said, already wanting to keep her young forever.

Rita scoffed. "Big for one." They sat with that awhile.

"So what's the deal?" Lonnie asked finally, aggressively caressing his shorn head. "Luz making some extra money babysitting?" Luz did not meet his gaze.

Ray said, "What do you mean?"

"I guess what I mean is the last time I saw you two you didn't have a baby. Luz was not pregnant, so far as I could tell,

104

you two were not in the process of cooking up a puppy. And you certainly, so far as I can recall, did not have a newborn. Did they have a newborn, Rita? Or am I demented?"

Luz pulled Ig back from the glass coffee table, almost thankful to Lonnie for forcing the question. Did what they'd done have language in Ray's mind? And what were the words?

Ray's Muir eyes were dry when he told Lonnie, "We found her."

Lonnie leaned back and smiled. "I know how that is. We found a Red Cross flatbed. We found a few dozen guns."

"It wasn't like that," Luz said, by which she meant, *We're not like you.*

"No, I'm into it. Upend everything. Snatch all the Montessori canyon babies from their cribs. I just wish we'd thought of it."

Rita muttered that all the Montessori canyon babies were gone.

"Truth," said Lonnie. "Where then?"

They did not answer.

"Don't say it."

Ray rubbed his mouth.

"Jesus," said Rita.

"Fuck me, Ray," said Lonnie. "Some serious cats down there. Some serious cats even

I wouldn't want for enemies."

"I know," said Ray, which was puzzling because he had never said as much to Luz, so either the genuine dangers of raindance had just occurred to him or — and this was the truth, she knew — he had been thinking it all along, those serious cats had been with him those sleepless nights in the canyon and he'd kept them to himself. *Here comes Luz, don't make any sudden movements.* She was not a serious cat.

Ray said, "We came here for a favor."

Lonnie leaned back on the sofa and stretched both his arms to rest atop it. "Naturally. Only reason anyone comes here anymore."

Ray took a breath. Luz saw how brutally he wished he were not about to say the thing he was about to say. "We're leaving. Going on the list."

Rita scoffed. Ig body-slammed her tortoise self on the glass coffee table, shuddering some stones from the fountain and setting them spinning on the glass. Luz retrieved Ig, fetched her nini from the birkin and used it to coax the child into lying in her lap.

Lonnie was still, then neatly took the dislodged Zen rocks into his hand. He looked stunned — even saddened, Luz saw, which was so unexpected and baffling that she kept watching him until she was sure that was the expression. Then she realized: he must have thought they were coming back. That they had come now to ask his permission to rejoin the complex. Of course. He'd donned his best Krishna curtains in preparation for their groveling. He was a small, needy creature who looked now as though he might utter a disgusting phrase, something along the lines of *I believed in you.* (Almost as unforgivable as the bald admiration he'd whispered before he'd had her, those months ago: *Oh, Luz, in another life!*) Luz rubbed Ig's back and prayed he wouldn't make a scene, though she would not have called it prayer.

Lonnie sniffed once and dropped the stones back into the bowl, eyeing Ig as though she were a strange dog come upon them. Luz saw Ig then as Lonnie must have: stunted and off, lopsided head, eyes lolling of their own accord. She had the hot urge to scream that there was nothing wrong with Ig. *Nothing, nothing, nothing.*

Finally, mercifully, Lonnie said just, "California, the failed experiment."

Ray tiptoed over his old friend's withered pride and said, "We have to, Lonnie."

"Clearly."

"We need a birth certificate," said Luz.

"And an ID for Ray."

Lonnie raised his eyebrows at Ray. "So she knows? Good for you, brother."

Ray nodded. "Can you help us?"

Lonnie flattened a seam of his curtain robe. "Can't do it. No one can. Can't be done anymore."

Ray said, "We can pay you." They'd brought the hatbox.

"Don't insult me. There's nothing I can do."

"Come on," said Luz.

"A clean ID, a *birth certificate* — it's too much. Six months ago, maybe. But now . . . Everything's contracting, everyone's drying up. Even if I could, man, do you know what they do to us in those places? It's not a vacation, Ray. First thing they'll do is give you each a number, next thing is split you up, paperwork or no. Men one way, women another. Whole garrisons just for kids. 'Boarding,' they call it. Labor camps. Your part for the cause. Only way out is to enlist, and I gather that's not available to you."

They were quiet awhile, even Ig.

Ray said, "Another way, then."

Lonnie brightened. He needed to be needed. Indeed, there were endless other ways, he said, each illegal and treacherous. He got a visible charge as he listed them all, a little danger boner. One was Oregon, yes. The militia could not be everywhere. There were the tunnels, of course, dug by former dairymen with subsidized earthmovers, though the dairymen were not fond of dark complexions, and their tunnels had a habit of collapsing. "Better to drive up to Crescent City," he said. "Hitch to the border, swim out around the seawall."

Ray shook his head. "Luz can't swim."

Lonnie said, "I thought she was Mexican."

"Her mom was."

Lonnie inspected Luz. "And she didn't teach you?"

Luz was not going to bite. She focused on grazing her fingerpads along Ig's nape.

"She couldn't either," Ray said. She had drowned, Luz's mother. She had drowned herself.

Lonnie tugged his Osiris goatee. "The gorge, then. Hike the badlands. Take you two weeks, maybe three."

Ray frowned toward Ig, limp under Luz's feather strokes. "We need something safe."

"You want safe, bribe your way into Tahoe."

"Or Napa," Rita said. "The Vintners Society could pay people to stand around and spit."

Lonnie laughed, then went serious.

"Maybe through Texas."

Ray said, "We don't have enough gas."

"No one does," said Lonnie.

"What if we went south?" asked Luz.

Rita snorted. "Mexico's a war zone. A complete and utter war zone. Worse than here. Approximately a thousand times worse."

Lonnie squeezed Rita's knee. "The Amargosa is blocking it anyway. They'd be stranded in Baja."

"It's that big?" Ray said. "The Amargosa?"

Rita said, "Getting bigger every day."

Lonnie tapped one of his conchos absently. "The Amargosa, now that's interesting. If I was going anywhere — which I'm fucking not — I'd go to the Amargosa."

Rita nodded.

"What for?" asked Luz. The Amargosa was sand, a dead swath of it blown off the Central Valley and the Great Plains, accumulated somewhere between here and Vegas.

"There's supposed to be a town out there," said Ray. How did he know this? How did she not know everything he knew?

"There *is* a town out there," said Lonnie, "run by a prophet. Very spiritual place. Very primal."

"A town," said Luz. "Without water."

"This prophet," Lonnie said, "is de-

110

scended from a long line of dowsers. Incredibly gifted. He finds the water."

This again. There was always some savior out in the wilderness, some senator, some patent, some institute, some cell. So familiar, this stagey faith. Luz's father had had it; it was how he kept himself atop everyone around him. He believed harder in stupider things, and there was somehow authority in this. Luz exhaled audibly and rolled her eyes. Ray put his hand on her shoulder.

But Lonnie was getting worked up. "There is water, Luz. Just because you can't find it with concrete and bulldozers and dynamite doesn't mean it's not there."

Rita added, in a cool, inward way that made Luz miss her, suddenly, "Just because they say it's gone doesn't make it gone."

Silence then. A stalemate, a standoff, a standstill, a stillborn. A rain delay. How it was always to end, except Lonnie bounced up and announced, "Let's do a reading."

From a drawer in the kitchen he fetched three golden Sacajawea dollars and his tattered catalog of hexagrams, *The Book of Changes.* He set these on the coffee table, beside that a mechanical pencil and a tiny top-tab spiral notebook, the same kind Ray carried for his lists and poems. Vile, to see

111

Lonnie with it, though of course it had been Ray and Lonnie both who said, "We're going to run some errands," before they lobbed a cinder block through the glass doors of the Wilshire Walgreens, a box boasting POCKET SIZE among their loot.

Lonnie fondled the coins now and told everyone to think on their worry, to project their question into the Sacajawea dollars.

Ray said, "All of us?"

Lonnie nodded. "A hexagram," he said, "is the exponent of the moment it is cast." Their endeavors, he said — meaning, Luz assumed, a looted journalist's pad, a mechanical pencil whose red plastic clip was gnawed and three dollops of copper sheathed in brass and stamped with the image of a Shoshone girl kidnapped at twelve and wed at thirteen, when a Frenchman won her in a card game — would correct for their secretmost selves.

Luz had too many worries to think on just one, and her secretmost self was not secret enough, but while it was all undeniably bullshit, she found herself trying.

Here was one worry. Ig. She was worry pooping into an Hermès scarf, worry with skittering coin eyes, worry moaning in the daytime, worry panting at the heat, worry howling through the night. Worry strung out

112

on ration cola, worry with its bulbed head in Luz's lap. Worry drowsy but fighting it, always fighting it, worry worrying the gauze blooming from her mouth. Worry gathering all other worries to them. But Ig was too delicate to resent, too pearly-skinned to solve, and right now, stroking the tip of her nose with the tip of the nini, vastly too gentle, so much like a godsend.

Lonnie shook the Sacajaweas from his hand and let them land noisily on the glass coffee table — *ting ting ting* — oblivious or indifferent or likely hostile to Ig so near to nap.

The coins skittered to rest. Two Sacajaweas with two baby Jean Baptistes on their backs, and beside them a bushel of wheat — or maybe arrows? — wrapped in a blanket. Lonnie annotated the whims of the coins in his notebook. "A broken line."

He took up the coins again.

Luz looked to Ray. She could see him and Lonnie in the same glance and hated herself. Would she always be so hungry? She had taken much from Ray — his home, his friends, his sleep, his sea. Was there no end to her appetite?

Ting ting ting: Three Sacajaweas, three lady Salmon-Eaters with three Little Pompeys, as Clark had christened him, barely born. A line unbroken.

And through that line rose the worry of worries: in what way was Ray no longer her Ray? Luz did not want to take this from him — California, all that it still meant to him — but was glad to, in a way. The sacrifice was a good sign. But what would it cost them? They were lost, yes, but lost together.

Ting ting ting. On one coin, Janey and Pompey, and on the other, an eagle and the other the arrows. A broken line.

"Wow," Lonnie said. "Oh, wow."

Ray's eyes were closed now and his dark lashes met in small, furred slivers. There he was, her Ray, Ray always on the move, his knees ever bouncing. Ray who took her fingers from her mouth so she would not bite them bloody. Ray with the exquisite mouth and its Indiana lapses, saying "pop" or "frigging" or that something was "funky." Ray who once said he envied her imagination, but also that the places her mind took her frightened him. Ray who said she ought to have a project — Napping is my project, she'd say, but she had not napped since Ig. Ray who said she ought to pay attention to the ration hour, Ought to keep your eyes peeled, he said, as though hers were still coated with a glittery scrim of cosmetics, which they likely were. Ray who tethered her to rock, rock she was now ripping him from.

Lonnie tossed the coins again. *Ting ting ting.* One Sacajawea looking over her shoulder at her boy or at home, beside her an eagle, beside that the blanket-bound arrows. A broken line.

Ray with Muir's eyes and wavesickness and a list in his pocket.

L.

Water.

Ting ting ting. An eagle, his twin, and Sacajawea with her little Pomp. A broken line.

Here was a worry: Luz. Her whole self a worry. How had her father put it? *Luz is my cross to bear.*

Ting ting ting. The eagles, gliding through rings of stars, and beside them, the bouquet of wheat arrows wound with the blanket. An unbroken line.

Lonnie moaned, as if his own wisdom pained him. He set the pad on the coffee table, the miniature sheet lined with addition sets and beside those:

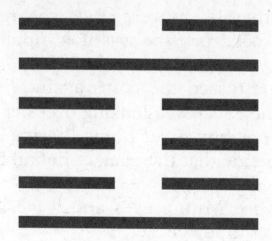

He consulted a chart, then an index, then flipped through the pages. He cleared his throat. *"Chun,"* he read. *"The abysmal, the arousing. This hexagram connotes a blade of grass pushing against an obstacle as it sprouts out of the earth — hence the meaning 'difficulty at the beginning.' "* He looked up at them, in case they had missed this profound foreshadowing. *"The hexagram indicates the way in which heaven and earth bring forth individual beings. It is their first meeting, which is beset with difficulties. The lower trigram, chên"* — he tapped the pad — *"is the Arousing; its motion is upward and its image is thunder. The upper trigram is the Abysmal, the dangerous."* Again, another glance, which said, *Are you getting this? "Its motion is downward and its image is rain. The situa-*

tion points to teeming chaotic profusion; thunder and rain fill the air." Here, he cocked his head apologetically. "This edition's a little outdated."

He went on. "But the chaos clears up. While the Abysmal sinks, the upward movement eventually passes beyond the danger. A thunderstorm brings release from tension, and all things breathe freely again."

Luz leaned over to check if Ig was asleep. She was not. She was lying tranquil, slack, still stroking the tip of her nose with the gauze.

"Times of growth are beset with difficulties," read Lonnie. "They resemble a first birth." Rita snorted wickedly. "Everything is in motion: therefore if one perseveres there is a prospect of great success. Fascinating."

Lonnie turned the page. "Let's see, let's see," consulting the pad. "Nine, six." He popped another page. "Here: Nine at the beginning means: hesitation and hindrance. It furthers one to remain persevering. It furthers one to appoint helpers." This last he said as though the word were a good friend he had not seen in a long time, the way Ray had said San Diego: Helpers! He flipped another page. "Six. Six in the second place means: difficulties pile up. Horse and wagon part."

117

He slowly closed the book. Rita said, "Hmm," and so did Ray.

Lonnie stacked the pad on the book and the pencil beside it and leaned back. "This is what we'll do," he said after some conspicuous reflection. "I have a man in St. George. If you can make it there, to Utah, he'll get you to a train in Lawrence, Kansas. The Carolinas, I think he takes them. Ultimately Savannah."

"You have 'a man'?" Luz said.

Ray said, "Easy," but it was too late.

"Yes, Luz, I have a man. I have all kinds of men —"

"Shh," said Luz. She spread her hand across Ig's bare back, her pinky and her thumb finding the child's floating ribs. "I'm sorry."

"Damn right you are. Come here asking for a favor and criticize the way I do business —"

"Business," she said.

"Ease up," said Ray, though it was not clear to whom.

"— playing the baby makes three up in the canyon while we've had to *survive* —"

Lonnie went on. In fact there was no water crisis, he maintained. Theirs was a human crisis. What they called drought was merely the mechanism of a long overdue

118

social contraction. A little agony was just what this place needed. Reintroduce hardship into the regional narrative. Sift out the posers and moneymen, the tourists, the sunbathers, the whores. Slough off the bourgeoisie! Euthanize the comfort culture! After: a pure city, liberated from its toxic pecking order, rid of its meet-ups and mixers, its principals and agents and managers murdered, a city of freed assistants, a city pure of heart.

Luz had heard it all before. She went lichen, pressing her palm to Ig, her own flat, cool boulder. She and Ig and John Muir were slate blue and sea green. They were a tuft of moss in Yosemite before Yosemite was a dry, ruined chasm ringed by hot granite knobs. They were a spray of fungi leaning out over Crater Lake before it went entirely crater. They were lichen on stone, dormant beneath the snowpack of a hangnail glacier in a crook of the Cascades that no one knew about, that no one even knew the name of. Lonnie was saying, ". . . giving them *exactly* what they want . . . resist . . . endure . . . sickening." Luz hunkered, unfurled her sagey petals, breathed through boreal ruffles, absorbed with her felt fins snowmelt and fog and mist and dew, all things moist, all things cool, and passed them to Ig.

Lonnie said to Ray, "Didn't I tell you? Didn't I *say* it? I told you about her. I *told you.*"

"Told you what?" asked Luz, returned.

"It doesn't matter," said Ray.

"Tell her!" cried Lonnie.

"Things are different now." Ray looked to Ig.

Luz said, "Tell me, Ray."

He might have — Luz hoped he wouldn't but he might have, she could see this — but Rita rose. "Come with me, Luz."

"Good idea," said Lonnie. "I can't fucking talk to her."

Luz did not want to go with Rita. She looked at Ray, motioned to Ig in her lap. She wanted him to come and lift them both and take them away from here.

"She's fine," he said. "Leave her."

Luz insisted with her eyes.

"No," said Ray. "We're not doing this now."

Despite Ig's wan objections, Luz left her lying on the floor.

Outside, the sun had made its way over the walls of the fortification, burnt the dawn from the courtyard and was now doing its evil bake work above. Luz followed Rita to unit B, though the brass *B* was gone, leaving only two nail holes and its shadow in the lacquer. Luz had never been in unit B. She had never seen anyone go into unit B. She had never seen anyone come out. Rita unlocked the door now and jerked her head to say, as Ray had said at raindance, *Go*.

Luz went.

Rita shut the door behind them. It was lightless inside, all smells: desiccate cardboard, dust, hot plastic. It occurred to Luz that Rita might want to hurt her and she was fine with that. She had it coming. There could be some comfort in at last getting what was expected and deserved.

Luz stepped forward and crashed her shin into something sharp and stumbled. Rita moved toward her — Luz felt her approaching in the dark — and then easily past. From the back of the apartment came a shaft of sun, wobbling where Rita pinned a heavy drape behind a tower of cardboard boxes. All around them were boxes, the unit filled with them. A small city of boxes and heavy-duty garbage bags squatting among the boxes like fat black ticks.

Without speaking or looking to Luz, Rita began to pilfer. She wedged herself between towers of boxes, sending some swaying, heaved some boxes and bags from one pile to another. Occasionally she punched in the sides of one and stripped the packing tape from its seam. She glanced inside, extracted something, resealed it and moved on. The boxes read SYSCO and WINCO and FRITO-LAY, many smiled a logo smile, nearly all had arrows pointing skyward. Rita moved fast and methodically; she knew the boxes by heart, Luz realized. This and what came next would follow Luz into the desert.

"Take this," Rita said, from somewhere deep within her box borough.

She gave Luz a garbage bag. It was half-full but heavy and Luz held it open like a child asking for something. "What's this?" Inside was slick plastic in pastels, puffy teal cubes and countless doughy faces, all of them caught in the act of laughter.

Rita put more bounty into the sack. "He's too good for you, you know. Ray."

"I know."

"It's not your fault, though. He's too good for anyone."

Rita rifled still, and into the garbage bag went more diapers, rubber nipples, a thermometer, burp cloths, bottle of powder, bottle of oil, tube of rash cream, tube of ointment, a bushel of used onesies. Two cans of formula.

Luz said, "Why do you have all this?"

"Doesn't matter. Here." Rita presented

Luz a car seat.
She was a good woman, Rita.

The A/C had quit outside Santa Clarita, started blowing hot, syrup-smelling smoke in what was once strawberry country. "What is?" Ig asked from the backseat, and though she knew Ray would scowl at her for it (and he did), Luz had said, "A very bad omen." But Ig was asleep now, and because Luz did not know how to drive stick — even the phrase she found unpleasant — she sat in the passenger seat in the starlet's slip, sweating and watching the crusty wasted fields fold past. She rolled the window down, hoping to smell the sea, but they were well inland and the wind was not cooperating and all that came in was a vicious cyclone of heat and dust that whipped her across the face with tendrils of her own dirty hair. She would never smell the Pacific again.

She rolled up the window. She'd sweated through the starlet's slip in places — eclipses leeching from her armpits, a Rorschach line below her breasts — and the silk clung to her. She wanted to sleep — needed to — but could not. The dress she'd peeled off outside Ridgecrest was wadded somewhere on the floorboards in the backseat. She should have worn shorts, a tank top, boots. Ray had said as much before they left, but Luz ignored him. After one last round of dress-up she took Ray's hand as they stood facing the starlet's indifferent, cantilevered villa.

"Say good-bye with me," she said. "Be a husband."

Ray saluted. "Good-bye, house."

Luz frowned. "I meant silently." She closed her eyes, keeping his hand in hers. Behind them, on the bridge driveway, was the Melon, loaded with diapers, rubber nipples, a thermometer, burp cloths, bottle of powder, bottle of oil, tube of rash cream, tube of ointment, bushel of onesies. Two cans of formula plus eight Sparkletts bottles filled with gasoline, two with water, a flat of ration cola, a cubic foot of graham crackers, another of dry cereal, a plastic grocery bag filled with PowerBars, canned food from Rita and Lonnie's stash — sardines, mostly, and some tuna — scarves, sunglasses, hats, biographies, six tiny notebooks bound together with a rubber band, the hatbox with the rest of Luz's money in it, about one hundred thousand dollars, and in the glove box a manila envelope with the name of an intersection in St. George, Utah, and Lonnie's guy — Samuel, whom Ray was calling Sammy the Bull — and both of their original IDs, though Ray had wanted to burn his. Also in the envelope, with Sammy the Bull and Ray the Hoosier and Luz Cortez of Malibu, CA, was the birth certificate of Baby Dunn: Luz Eleanor Dunn, six pounds, nine ounces, a greasy smear of black hair atop her head, labia and teats inflamed with her mother's hormones, a dark, spinachy meconium collecting in a rectum the diameter of a wedding band, a coat of translucent hair all over her body, setting her ashimmer in the sun of suns. A mascot before her mother would wear the velvety fuzz away, loving her. A logo before the ink on the certificate was dry.

Standing in front of the starlet's, Ray had closed his eyes and sighed peacefully, which had made Luz feel at peace, too.

But that peace had left her now, and an irritable, fidgeting anxiety had taken over. Luz pressed her bare feet against the windshield already smudged with her footprints, then removed them. She consulted the map Lonnie had given them, an old map on

126

which he'd traced a large oval with a question mark inside — "I think that's where it is." They would skirt the Amargosa to the north. Each moment she was farther from home than she'd ever been. She couldn't get comfortable. Whichever way she arranged herself there was something to burn her: the metal tongue of the seat belt, the hot nub on the e-brake, the dash gone waxy, the scorching leather against her thighs, sweating as though still some live thing's hide.

Her thoughts went to helpers: St. George, Lawrence, Savannah. They sounded like people who couldn't be trusted. The Carolinas were two mean girls from grade school.

She looked back at Ig, strapped in Rita's car seat. The seat was not the right size, maybe, and the child slept with her head rolled down and to the side at such an angle that her neck looked broken. Wisps of her yellow-white hair gone lank with perspiration. Dry cereal rings were confettied all over the backseat, one stuck to her blood-flushed cheek. Luz stretched and brushed it off, then touched the back of her hand to the child's warm, bulbed brow.

"She's still hot," Luz said.

Ray glanced in the rearview mirror. "Let her sleep."

"What if she's hurting?"

"Wouldn't she wake up?"

"I don't know," said Luz. She cupped the child's thick, dimpled knee with her hand. "I don't know."

The sun at their back was dipping, finally, setting the bald and hazy mountains in the distance aflame.

"She doesn't have a name," said Luz. She might know how to mother the child if only she had something proper to call her.

"She does," said Ray. "Only we don't know what it is and never will."

"She's an orphan," said Luz. "Like us."

"We're not orphans," he said.

"We are, kind of. We don't have anyone."

"That's true," said Ray. This made her feel good, annihilation. She would have liked to kiss him, rest her head on his shoulder, but her guilt would not allow it. The visit to the compound had put Lonnie's scent on her again. But they'd both made mistakes, hadn't they?

Luz studied the mountains ahead, watched the sunset coloring them as the things gone from them: lilac, plum, lavender, orchid, mulberry, violet. Pomegranate, one of the last to go. John Muir had written how when we try to pick out anything by itself we find it hitched to everything else in the universe.

Above those spoilt purple mountains materialized a glowing wedge of light, whiter than the sun, thin, blurred, and radiant. Snow, Luz thought, unable to stop herself. She'd seen snow only once, from a train skirting the Italian Alps, but she had never touched it and already she was zigging up there, ramming her fingers into the cool blue bank until they stung, crunching the puffs of sparkling crystals in her teeth, falling backward to make angels in the airy drifts.

But there was nothing cool or blue or airy about this calcium-colored crust capping the range. It throbbed with heat, glowed radioactive with light. Luz said, "What is that?" just as the answer came to her.

Ray said it. "The dune sea. The Amargosa."

"It's that close?" They were barely beyond the city.

Ray shook his head. "It's that big."

This knocked Luz off balance: The dune was not atop the empurpled range before them but beyond it, beyond it by miles and miles. The white was not a rind of ice, not a snowcap, but sand piling up inland where the Mojave had been.

They watched this sandsnow mirage, hypnotized by fertilizer dust and saline particulate and the pulverized bones of ancient sea creatures, though they did not know it. Did not know but felt this magnetic incandescence working the way the moon did, tugging at the iron in their blood. Knew only that it left them not breathless but with their breaths exactly synchronized. Ray reached for Luz, took her hand as though he'd never before touched her. They went on, silently transfixed by the immaculate flaxen range looming before them.

Ray whispered, "We could name her Estrella." After her long-gone mother, he didn't have to say.

"We could," said Luz. "Do you want to?"

"Let's," Ray said. "Let's call her that." Though they almost never would.

Night and the moon was high and fat as a fat face — but beautiful! — and Ig was awake with her feet raised and her fingers curled around her big toes, saying, *Bab bab babby bab bab.* Luz had a good feeling. The Melon and its cargo had been born of the city and now sailed along the crests and trundles of the straight-up desert. It was better than surfing, Ray said, driving at night on an empty road between the swervy prehistoric hills. They emerged from a batch of bare hillocks and saw before them a great alluvial valley, yawningly vast, the dune beyond dreadful with moonlight.

Then, an iridescent glimmer, a figure in the road. Ray downshifted, slowing the Melon, though Luz told him not to. There were patrols and worse. Bandits. Highwaymen. So she'd heard. As they approached, the figure went from in the road to alongside it, from a being to a box. A dollhouse. A storage unit. No, a booth with a sliding glass window and maps pinned to a corkboard, bleached blank. Before them a mechanical arm, spangled with reflective strips, busted at the joint and part supine on the asphalt. Ray swerved around it and the mechanism lurched, whining, raising the pinched arm so it dangled, flapped, begging amputation.

Ig laughed.

Admitted, they descended below what was once the snow line. The road took them down into an immense forest of silver yucca. On and on for miles staggered the woody skeletons, the monocrop broken only occasionally by a feathery date palm, drought-weary, bowed in half, its fruitless head laid on the lifeless ground. But the palms were rare and in the main the valley stretched on and out and up in tessellations of pale soap-tree yucca, spiny heads grafted to thick and hearteningly hairy trunks.

"Look, Ig," said Luz, twisted around in the passenger seat. "Trees!"

But Ig was a baby and could be dismissive in the baby way. She did not take note of the trees.

"Her first forest," said Ray.

"Let's stop."

"A milestone!" Ray steered the Melon to the shoulder.

"Look, Ig." Luz wanted the baby to see the forest. She wanted the baby to see every new and magnificent thing in the world. Already there was no limit to her yearning on behalf of the baby.

With the Melon's cuckoo clock engine turned off, the valley was quiet as a shadow. Luz lifted Ig out of the backseat and went off from the road. "Be careful," said Ray. He had been saying this lately.

Luz held Ig to her as she walked among the moon-cast shadows of the yuccas, smelling charcoal, saline. The baby went quiet, as if even she, irreverent devil that she was, recognized they were traipsing through something sacred. The yuccas were white in the moonlight and some had holes bored in their shaggy trunks, holes so perfect the wind would have whistled through them, except there was no wind. Some of their spines were gauzed with glistening webs.

Surely there were creatures tricksy and nocturnal to be spotted within. Ray noted the holes, too. "Look," he whispered at one, and Ig did.

They walked on and on through the forest, the wise firecracker heads of the yuccas motionless above. The Melon became an enamel droplet on the tarry road behind them. "These are ancient," said Luz. "They must be." Ray touched her elbow lightly, then scooped Ig from her. He pinched a knifey yucca frond between his fingers — "Look, Ig. Tree. Can you say *tree*?"

"Eee," tried Ig.

He brought Ig closer, her small mouth agape, agog, and as he did he pulled on the frond. There was a sound then, an incongruous sound, like the tearing of very delicate fabric. Gossamer, or cheesecloth. A crepeish rip, and the massive hairy yucca swayed, somehow. Luz and Ray staggered back and the tree fell between them, sending up a dry veil of dust. Ig said, "Uh-oh."

"What the fuck?" said Ray. He pressed his foot to the felled thing and where he pressed the trunk collapsed, papery. Ig laughed like a hiccup. They investigated the broken stump and found it completely hollow, save for some dry, twiny marrow inside.

Luz pushed carefully on the trunk of

another towering yucca and it too crumpled to the ground, setting Ig agiggle.

"They're dead," Luz said. "All of them." Dead, without moisture enough to rot.

"The groundwater's gone," said Ray, though he'd promised he wouldn't.

Luz plucked a yucca tine from its socket, then another and another, revealing an arid cavity inside the tree. She looked out over the miles and miles of pale lifeless specimen. This was no forest but a cemetery. Ray felled another plant husk and crushed it beneath his boots, its desiccate death rattle vastly satisfying. Ig reprised her hiccup laugh and clapped. She had never clapped for them and so Luz clapped, then toppled and crushed another tree. Ig clapped again, triumphantly.

"Watch this," said Ray, and then held Ig aloft as he kicked the spindled torso of an adolescent yucca to dust. The baby went hic, hic, clap, clap.

"Watch *this,*" said Luz, hoisting a sandstone to her shoulder and shot-putting it clear through the stout trunk of a grandfatherly yucca.

"Bah!" said Ig, clapping like mad.

"Here," said Ray. He handed Ig over to Luz. He set himself, took a breath, leapt into the air, yipped and torqued a kung fu—

type roundhouse kick through the body of a massive hollow plant, splintering it profoundly and sending the spidery head to the ground. Ig laughed and clapped and laughed and clapped.

They continued like this, crushing large swaths through the papier-mâché forest, trampling the flimsy giants, pulverizing the ghostly gray cellulose carcasses and sending up great clouds of dust and cinder. Desiccation vibrated in their sinews, destruction tingled in their molars. Finally, they stood breathing in a clearing of their own gleeful debris, no night breeze chilling them in their sweat. A supernatural stillness overtook them, the fear they had tried to laugh away.

Ray picked up a silvery shred of yucca skin and gave it to the baby.

Ig said, "What is?"

"I told you," said Luz, starting back toward the road. "A very bad omen."

In the womb of a dream Luz is hiking along a rocky ridge with William Mulholland and Sacajawea through no country she's ever seen, and though Mulholland has on inappropriate footwear and spiny somethings are everywhere, they are making good time. There is a tang of frost in the air and in the ravine below tremble the heads of plum-

135

colored cottonwoods. Mulholland, his Irish
*R*s bubbly, is talking up home birth, a position Luz supports, though she also has a
little devil in her, a little devil who lives in
her throat, who makes a hammock of her
hyoid bone, the only bone in the body that
connects to no other bones, said her home-
schooling anatomy coloring book. This
devil, suspended in his web of ligaments
anchored distally to the tongue, says, "It
doesn't add up, Willy," and Mulholland
says, "I invite you to look at the facts. We
rank fortieth in the world in infant and
mother mortality. Behind Cuba!" Luz has
no hat on suddenly, and the tree-size lilacs
in the ravine are swooning, swooning. Sacajawea is a bronze statue on her back and on
Sacajawea's back is Jean Baptiste, stillborn,
marbled with blue. Willy Mulholland is saying, "Hospitals are designed for death."
Willy Mulholland is saying, "Septic! Septic!"
Sacajawea's bronze body scorches — what's
become of that frost tang? In the ravine
there is a creek running with shreddy brown
blood and Willy Mulholland is saying, "Isn't
it amazing what a little light can do?"

She woke near dawn, the car stopped and
Ray gone. Ig's seat was empty, too. Luz
found Ray filling the gas tank with Ig on his

hip. Luz offered to take her.

"She needs to be changed," said Ray, handing her over.

"Are you stinky, Ig?"

Ig said nothing.

"Be careful," said Ray again. Luz turned to walk around the front of the car and stopped. Up ahead, maybe twenty yards from the nose of the Melon, the road disappeared. Luz squinted in the dim — *Crow's-feet!* screeched a makeup girl who prescribed ground pansies with garlic juice for Luz's eyebags. *Powdered horsetail, fresh yeast dissolved in boiling spring water for these nasty blackheads. Ten young, fresh nettles to drink up all this oil. Pick them away from the highway! If you would only practice the merest self-care you wouldn't be in this chair for so long.*

Luz approached the nothingness where the road ought to have been, turning to put herself between Ig and this void. A massive pit, perfectly round, walls sheer and plumb, like a cork had been popped from the earth, except on the lip where huge slabs of asphalt had cracked and threatened to slide off like melted icing. She could not convince herself to seek out the bottom.

"What are we going to do?" she said.

"Lon said this would happen," said Ray,

who smelled of gasoline. "He said there'd be trails." He pointed to the side of the road, at the improvised detour of other Mojavs, then took Ig and changed her. Luz fetched a clean shirt from the front trunk, one Rita had contributed, with a choo-choo grinning from the chest.

The tire-wide ruts led them worming around the sinkhole and back to the road. They rejoined the asphalt and soon left it again where another cavity had engulfed the highway. Reunion, separation. Hello, good-bye. The pits were growing, it seemed, for they were off on the trails for miles at a time and even the trails encountered other chasms, detouring the detour. Lonnie's map lay useless on the dash. They needed only to go east, to get to I–15, Lonnie had said. I–15 would take them into St. George. No longer than a day, Ray said he'd said. But also that it would depend on the trails. Keep heading east. East was all. But without the sea, Luz had lost what little bearings she had. She would have liked to check with Ray — wanted him to say *This is east* in his surest voice, the voice that made things sound truer than they ever were in her mind. But they barely spoke as they drove, waiting for a trail to swerve back to where the road might be, a trail trampled by people who, for all they knew, died in its blazing.

Instead of talking, Luz opened a plastic barrel of chalky peppermint puffs that Ray had stolen on one of his projects, her favorite kind: innards airy and white, red-striped husks with sugarsnow inside. Ig saw the candy and dropped her tortoise into the canyon between the car seat and the door, grunting. Ray frowned but Luz passed her a candy anyway. "At least take the wrapper off," he said. "She'll choke."

"I was going to."

"I don't see how."

Luz's technique was to pop the candies from their wrappers straight into her mouth, then imprint her front teeth into the mint before shearing off segments in good-feeling planes. Ig's technique was to hold the mint globe in her mouth for an alarming while then spit it out, softened, and roll it around between her hands and along her bare chest and in her hair until she was wet and pink and her fingers webbed with sticky, sugary spittle. For every mint she passed back to Ig, Luz ate ten or twelve. She could not stop. Each shearing brought with it a cold-hot release, like glaciers shedding into the sea, and the sensation lured her back for more. She stuffed the wrappers in the ashtray but the ashtray got full and then wrappers would leap from the tray on the wind and whirl around the cab like locusts before zipping out the window, which annoyed Ray, so Luz let the clear, crinkled wrappers fall to the floor at her feet, where the wind was unable to lift them.

The trail, unfurling for miles now, agitated Ray. "We have to get off this," he would say. "This is not going to get us there." There was a small sea of cellophane at Luz's feet now, moving like the heat lake ever wiggling on the horizon. Luz went on shearing, grinding, building up little deposits of mint in her teeth.

Finally, they found asphalt again — Ray exhaled with relief as the tires started their even, mellow whirring. The candies were gone and Luz was left with sores on her gums and wrappers crinkling beneath her feet and the realization that she had not offered Ray a single one.

Ig grunted for another.

"No more," said Luz. "All gone."

Ig demanded with a whine.

"No more, Ig. They're all gone."

Ig considered this, looked Luz straight in the eye, and began to wail.

"Here." Luz leaned back and retrieved the tortoise from the floorboard. "Ig, here.

Look, Ig. Look."

Ig bashed the tortoise in the head, sending him back where he came from. She bellowed, shrieked.

"Where's her nini?" Ray asked the rearview. Ig's face was red now, slick and horridly disfigured by her screams. He reached behind his seat, feeling around for the nini, and the Melon surged hungrily toward the soft, bankless shoulder.

"Jesus," shouted Luz, reaching for the wheel.

"I got it. Find her nini."

Luz groped along the baseboards and under Ray's seat. She forced her fingers into all the spaces in the car seat and beneath it, Ig screeching and slapping at her all the while. Luz snatched one of the child's hands out of the air and leaned in toward her small, lumpy, snot-smeared face. "No, Ig. No hitting." Ray watched in the mirror. Ig's eyes dilated with shock — shock and fear, surely — then squinted in resolve. With her free hand she smacked Luz in the face.

You cunt, thought Luz. She captured Ig's other hand and held them both in a sticky nest. She squeezed, hard, hard enough that it felt good. *"No,"* she said. "That is *not* okay."

Ig's face fell to sorrow then, genuine

wound and heartbreak, with real tears springing to blur her gray eyes. She pulled her hands away and covered her face with them. She sunk her head, ashamed, and wept.

Luz went to stroke her head but the baby recoiled. Her cage of a body was trembling, seizing where Luz touched her. "I'm sorry," said Luz, her own tears springing now. She unbuckled the car seat and, with much effort, lifted Ig from it. Ray started to speak but stopped. Luz took Ig onto her lap, limp and burbling softly. She held the child to her, all shame and need. Then, in a gesture of pure grace, Ig put her spindly arms around Luz's neck. Luz cupped her hand to the back of Ig's large white head and whispered love and apology and contrition and affection into her neck.

The Melon slowed.

Luz looked up. Before them the road went on, did not slide like melting icing into an interminable pit. It went on, on and on east to St. George, to Lawrence and Savannah, where Ig would grow up, maybe saying, *I was born in California,* maybe one of the last, onward into the fine future, leaving behind the starlet and Lonnie and Rita and John Muir and Sacajawea and the photographers and the nettles and the Nut, except this road — which was to lead them to . . . to what? Kudzu, maybe, and Spanish moss; hurricane season and whatever the Outer Banks were — this road went onward and buried itself beneath a thick tentacle of sand stretched out from the dune sea.

"Fuck me." Ray whapped the steering wheel. "Sorry, Ig."

Ray turned the Melon around. "We don't have the gas for this," he said to no one. They doubled back, then Ray pulled off onto the trail from where they'd come. This forked off along a barbed-wire fence to a washboard cattle trail, which veered south and threatened to shake the Melon apart. All the while the dune lorded over them, in front of them and behind them, to the east and to the west, somehow. A passively menacing sight and Luz could not take her eyes from it. No more than a day, Lonnie had promised, but it had been two and they were farther than they'd ever been from anything.

They took a bald dirt track eastish. Promising for miles, until it was bisected by an ancient gully, its bed loaded with head-size boulders. Ray skidded the Melon to a stop. "We won't make it," he said.

He looked as if he might cry, or shatter the too-close windshield with his hand.

143

Ray's deflating faith was terrifying. Disbelief was Luz's way. Or rather Luz believed only the most absurd Disney fantasies — the canyon menagerie, the Hollywood escape — so that their failure to materialize was proof that all things would always fail to materialize. She could certify sinkholes, arsenic poisoning, a world of hot undrinkable brine. But where her mind was miserly, Ray's heart had room for all things, all modes of being, for water and for the promises of coins. He was, she realized, the essential opposite of her father, whose meanness and fear she'd inherited, though none of his industry. How sustaining it might have been to have that room, to not be ever at capacity. The ultimate project: to believe. That way, when the day came — through some fermentation of will and time and miracle — when the three of them emerged from this desert and Ig plumped and spoke and lined her dolls along a windowsill and asked, "Where did I come from?" faith would surely, if Luz could begin to cultivate it now — no, *cultivate* was not the right word. One didn't cultivate faith and one did not cultivate anything here, save thirst and thirst and insanity. But if she might have somehow by then made room in herself, might have evicted the photographers perhaps, erased the year she probably should have followed her agent to New York, the year she was twenty-two but writing seventeen on all her forms, faith or belief might have let her respond, without saccharine or strychnine, "God gave you to us."

"We can make it," Luz said. She cajoled Ig's limbs through their straps and buckled the apparatus over her despite the child's whining. "Go," she said, "before she has another meltdown."

Ray nodded. The Melon plunged into the wash, the three of them lurching within. Rocks pinged violently up into the undercarriage. The Melon's European engine whirred as her wheels spun frantically in the detritus, then caught, miraculously, ejecting the car up and out of the wash. Ray and Luz cheered. Ig cried until Luz freed her and reinstalled her on her lap. Luz held Ig, smelling the slight scabby smell of her head as the trail dipped dramatically and the desert scrub shrunk away and the trail went bankless, stretching now through a vast blinding rockscape. Luz had never seen anything like the craggy bleached white rocks rippling along the side of the trail, like water froth made inanimate, capped here and there with daubs of brown.

The sun was at its perfect apex, which it seemed never to leave. Beyond them, the blurry summits of the dunes in the distance blazed as if they made their own light. Down and down they sank, and the blanched, calcium-crusted oven of the valley broiled. Luz remembered something from her father's idea of school, stacks of outdated trivia cards skewered on rings by subject: the lowest point in the US? Badwater. She was drinking more than her share.

She helped Ig drink, too, though still she spilled. "I'm good," Ray said too pleasantly when she offered. Soon, Luz had to pee.

"Low on gas anyway," said Ray, chewing at the skin beneath his nails. They were facing south now — she was almost positive — though they did not acknowledge this between them.

Luz set Ig down so she might waddle around, burn off some energy. "You have her?" she confirmed, fearing the little one impaled by the jagged rock pinnacles jutting skyward in crags like parched coral. And like something once alive, the rocks crunched under her feet, more delicate than rock ought to be. She squatted, hanging her head to look between her splayed feet. She grasped a spire for balance, prepared for it to burn her. But instead, the spire snapped off in her hand. She caught herself and looked to the crushed filtrate glittering uncannily. Teeny honeycomb crystals in her palm. She peed and watched between her legs in awe as her near-brown urine melted a tunnel in the rock. She finished, shook her rump in the air diligently and on her walk back found a pure white fist-size crystal. She licked it.

"It's salt," she said, marching clumsily back to the car. "It's all salt. Ray, taste."

Ray had opened the hood of the Melon and was leaning inside with his shirt off, as if the little coupe was politely eating him. Ig was stooped in one of the ruts of the trail, collecting little somethings in her hand. Luz approached Ray with the rock outstretched but he did not look to her. In the dark shadow of the hood his back was angry — cords in his neck and throat pulled taut, the flanks spread across his shoulders drawing his scapula up around his ears. Obviously not the time, and she congratulated herself for realizing this. She would go show Ig instead. But before she could turn and leave Ray to his trouble, whatever it was, a scent dizzying and unmistakable confronted her: gasoline.

She covered her mouth with her free hand, tasting somewhere beneath her dread and horror the salt residue there. "What happened?"

"Gas tipped over. When we went through that gully."

She put the salt crystal to her side, not sure whether to drop it — too melodramatic — or hold it until it dissolved in her fist. "Jesus."

"The lid was off."

Their last stop. She'd pried the plastic cap from the Sparkletts bottle and whiffed from it so as not to accidentally fill their drinking jugs with gas. She'd congratulated herself, scooting the gasoline aside and reaching for water instead, silently commended her own prudence while neglecting to replace the cap. Now, a clear, greasy crescent of the fluid swayed in the once-full bottle where it lay on its side, scarves and baby clothes and adult clothes soaked, the carpets glistening with fuel.

"I'm sorry," she said.

"Me too. That was our last one."

"What do we do? Turn around?"

"We'll never make it through that gully from this side. Even if we did."

"So, what? Keep going?"

"Maybe there'll be a road."

"How far can we get?"

"Not far."

Then what? no one said.

They went on, the journey a stillborn they had to birth. The Melon's steering wheel was a simple chrome circle — surely blisteringly hot, though Ray said nothing — with another half circle of chrome upturned inside it like a smile. The speedometer, notched with kilometers, was one eye and the other, a little smaller, was a clock stuck near three thirty. Onward they rolled, no need for speed now, through the salt fields, quiet except for the crunch of the trail and Ig whispering her Ig language. The steering wheel face grinned at them idiotically, maniacally, while Luz and Ray silently watched its third eye, the gas gauge, tick nearer and nearer the orange hash marked *R.*

"What do you think that stands for?" asked Ray after some time.

"Does it matter?"

"I'd like us to explore it."

"Are you doing the thing where you ask questions just to be talking?"

"Yes."

She sighed. "Refill."

"Reserves," he said.

"Replenish."

"Rejuvenate."

"Regenerate."

"Regurgitate."

"Reinstate."

"Reject."

"Restore."

"Rejoice."

"Reconnoiter."

"Rescue."

"Residue."

"Roam."

"Rome."

"Romans."

"Romance."

"Remnants."

"Run."

"Rest."

The salt rock was still in her hand somehow, but the salt fields were behind them, and Luz did not notice when they left them and so she did not get to say good-bye, and wasn't that her shallow, selfish way? Before them was the dune: magnetic, candescent, on three sides of them, as consuming as sky. The needle leaned on *R,* now engorged with denotation. The trail narrowed. Shallow, boiling pools came up on either side, their waters fluorescent yellow, stinging to the eye. The smell of rotten eggs seeped into the car.

"That color," said Luz. "Look at the color, Ig."

"Ig, Ig, Ig," said Ig.

"Mine tailings," said Ray. "Sulfur."

In the sulfur pools squatted slick, bulbous mineral hives, steam surging from their slit openings like eyeless worms surfacing, belching mustard gas into the air. The thick

151

rankness carried Luz to her father's living room, where she was drinking a smoothie made from fruit powder — some powder was caked at the bottom and if she put her straw too deep she'd sip up a mealy mouthful. Her father with a bolo tie and too much skin for his face held a glowy yellow specimen in his palm and said to a room of grown-ups, This is Satan's little stocking stuffer. This is how he tells you he's a-coming.

"Brimstone," Luz said to Ray. Together they knew the names of everything.

The Melon lurched once, twice; something knocked around inside, then stopped. And then, casually, as if it weren't pinpointing the specific patch in a field of poison where they would die of thirst, the car began its final, quiet, excruciating coast.

Ray got out. Luz did too, as if there were something to be done. Ig whined after them and Luz climbed into the backseat to free her. From there she heard it, a sharp, wet bark, then another. She started and looked through the filthy windshield to Ray, pacing up and down the trail, his long legs stabbing berserkly away from the car and back again, his body atop them a live wire, convulsing, seizing, his hands clawing at his red face, wet somehow. (Spit, tears.) He

152

screamed again, a pinched shriek like a mutt beneath a car and with it more spittle flinging from his lips, and then again, this sound slower, seeming to come from deep within him, a tremor traveling up his racked torso and bursting from his mouth. His feet skidded from beneath him and he collapsed on his back in the dirt. He lay there, trembling. The man with the specimen would have called it a possession, and Luz would have, too. A possession by rage and fear and profound, unyielding despair at this most inarguable failure.

Ig was still in her seat, silently shaken. Then she began to cry. Luz lifted her, jouncing and cooing, and walked with her away from where Ray lay in the dirt, his chest heaving, making scary murmuring sounds. Ig wanted down, then wanted to face-plant into the lovely toxic shore beyond the trail, so Luz squatted down and wrapped her arms around her. The child leaned into the hug, and what a tremendous satiating feeling that was, better than clean water.

When they returned Ray had collected himself, risen from the ground and was now leaning against the open trunk, folding the gasoline-soaked clothes. "Did she pee?" he asked.

Luz lifted Ig and sniffed her rump. "She's

good," she said. "She wants you." But Ray went on, folding the gas-smelling clothes. Making piles. When the clothes were folded and sorted he lifted Lewis and Clark and Sacajawea and Francis Newlands and William Mulholland and John Wesley Powell from the starlet's leather satchel and stacked them beside the clothes. He would not look at them. Luz was beginning to think she'd never known this man and never would.

"Is this clean?" he asked, holding a super-saturated cobalt scarf with golden links of illustrated chain strung across it.

"What are you doing?"

He had a project, a plan. He tied the scarf loosely around his neck. He put his half-full jug in the satchel, and a dirty T-shirt and three cans of tuna.

"What are you doing?" Luz said again, though she knew now. "Stop it."

"Come here," he said to Ig, and she did. He held her and squeezed her and she let him. He kissed Ig on her head. Again and again he kissed her. Luz wished he would stop, and that he would never stop. He tried to pass the child to Luz, but she refused.

"I don't want you to go," she said.

"It's gonna be fine. I'm just going to get help."

"Where?"

He kissed Ig again. It was horrid, his lips hesitating on her feather-soft hair the worst of omens. "It's gonna be fine," he said again, though it would not. "I'm just going to go ahead to a road and find someone, get some gas and get us out of here."

"There's nothing out there, Ray."

To Ig, with his high, soft Ig voice, he said, "I'm going for a walk now. Just a little walk down the road here."

Ig said, "Road here."

"That's right," he said, passing the child to Luz. "Go to Mama."

Luz took the girl on her hip.

Ray fastened the satchel. He was doing penance for the AWOL thing. He was going to leave her alone to watch their child die, to prove what a good man he was.

"We'll go with you," she said.

Ray stroked Ig's head. "It's not safe. She needs shade. Water. We can't carry enough." He let Ig make a fist around his index finger. "She's too delicate. She'd slow us down." It was unclear whom he was talking to.

Ray kissed Luz then, kissed her as if he were embarking on his morning commute, as if he were the manager at one of the burnt-out banks along Wilshire. "Please," said Luz. "No."

"Listen," he said, trying words on the wordless. "I don't . . . You won't . . . I'm sorry. It's just . . ." He squeezed Ig's calf and shouldered the satchel. "Get her out of the sun, okay?"

"Please no. Please! I can't do this by myself." She wanted him to say, *Sure you can.* He used to be so good about saying what she needed to hear.

"You don't have to," he said.

"No," she said.

"I'll be right back."

"Take more water at least," she said through a thick sob. "Fill your jug." She reached for the Sparkletts barrel, nearly full of water, and tugged it to the edge of the trunk. Then, epiphany.

She could not lift the barrel with Ig in her arms, and everywhere there was to put her was scalding or venomous or glistening with gasoline. She pried the plastic cap off with her free hand, saw herself tipping the whole heavy, sloshing aqua of it, spilling the only water they had onto the dry crust of the trail. Water came in three lethargic *glug*s, instant mud spattering against her ankles.

"Don't," cried Ray, righting the bottle. He grasped her wrist and pried the plastic cap from her hand. He shoved the cap back on the barrel. Between them the water disappeared into the ground. Whispering now, he said, "Don't you fucking dream of it."

She might have tried again — wanted badly to, wanted badly to be capable of that. She wanted worst of all to press a cold pint glass against his neck and ask him if he remembered his longboard, the two of them leaning back and riding it down Canyon Drive. Ask him to help her once more onto the handlebars of his liberated mountain bike and ride them both down the center of PCH, helixing through rivulets of melty tar, him swerving, putting little phantoms in her heart, so that he could whisper *I got you.*

Ray tugged the scarf up over his mouth and nose. Against the infinite cobalt of the silk his eyes were colorless, clear, already gone. "Don't cry," he said. "I'll be right back," he said, though he would not.

The light went on forever out here, and so it was a long, long time before he disappeared. "Where him go?" Ig asked a few times, dry-eyed. Luz was the only one weeping.

"To get help."

"Elp?"

"Help."

Horse and wagon part.

Luz knew enough to stay in one place. That was the thing lost people never did but she would do and they would be rescued because of it. "It has nothing to do with inertia or helplessness," she told Ig. "Or fear." And to prove it she took the girl on slow walks in one of two directions: back, in the wake of the Melon, the way Ray'd gone, or forward. They paced the trail so ceaselessly and so slowly — Ig was ever distracted by a clod or a rock — that Luz might have forgotten which way was which if not for the Melon gazing blankly ahead. As they walked Luz watched the horizon, too, watched it until it went meaningless, until she could no longer distinguish the valley floor from the dune field marching across it, nor the smeary peaks of the dunes from the white sky. At home base — this she called it for Ig's sake, somehow — she thought to pinch the starlet's clothes in the rolled-up windows, but even in the shade the car became an oven, so she rolled them down again.

She opened the trunk to check the Sparkletts barrel, then conferred with the stopped clock on the dash. She promised Ray and Colonel John Wesley Powell that she would adhere to a strict regimen: a swig for Ig every hour, one for herself every three.

Dawn and dusk they could move finally. Diurnal as Muir's mammals, they ventured out walking or embarking on a project. She stacked her biographies in the driver's seat. She swept the peppermint wrappers from the floorboards. She removed Rita's car seat and set it in the road carefully, as though she might return it one day. Ig had tortoise Ig and her Russian nesters and free rein of the backseat. Luz read to her and Ig parroted some words: *Axe. Beaver. Shoshone. Rapids. Fur. River.*

Luz vowed that they'd get a good nap routine going. That's what the creatures here did, yes? She'd read something about lizards sleeping in the shadows of barbed-wire coils. Owls burying themselves in the sand. She took the corner of a scarf in her mouth and sucked until it was wet, then ran it along Ig's hot neck. She fanned the girl with books. Still, the child was the color of the mountains from the starlet's balcony, the color of flames and waiting cinders. She had heat rash in the crook of her legs and rosy polyps speckled across her crotch. Luz taped the soiled diapers into dumplings and tossed them way out into the sulfur pools. When some unseen tide brought them back, she practiced not acknowledging her severe and persistent preference to be the first of the two of them to die.

Ig did wilt into a nap sometimes, but Luz could not get her eyes closed all the way. When she did manage, Ig burst into her dreamlessness, lurching Luz into consciousness only to find Ig asleep, a cracker in each fist. The child detested protein, was surviving on starch and salt. Luz slurped sardines, spines and all. She drank the oil. The water she saved for the baby. She let her own saliva puddle in her mouth and swallowed it, trying to coax her brain back from the sunstroke on which it was so hell-bent.

The water, she knew, was trying to drive her mad. It was important to maintain the upper hand. She resisted checking the trunk when she could, which she often couldn't. When she did open the trunk — because she thought she'd heard the jug fall, because it had likely been an hour — she braced herself, and still the level was always lower even than she'd feared. Many times, Luz felt compelled to dump the last of it so the goddamned waiting would be through.

When the Melon's doors got incredibly heavy she left them open, even though Ig might tumble out and swan-dive into the stinking chemical lake. There was no breeze. The mustard gas from the vents expanded as released. What was it her father said about sulfur? When you smell sulfur, you know Satan has been coming round. Billy Dunn worked on oil platforms in the Gulf of Mexico and sometimes, he said, they drilled too far and very suddenly the platform might fill with that rotten egg smell and that was, he said, brimstone coming straight up the pipeline from hell.

When she poured the last rivulet of water into Ig's sippy cup the quickness of it shocked her, though the shock registered somewhere behind the stabbing sensation in her eyes and the hot, constant pulse inviting her to ram two sticks deep into the soft spots behind her own earlobes.

The nights were terrifyingly beautiful, stars gaudy and tremendous, a dense and blazing laceration of them bisecting the black dome crosswise. Sacajawea would have known the name of them. The white sands of the dune fields caught the moonlight and held it. It was impossible to think these had always been here. Stars fell frequently and Luz watched for them, replaying Ray's return in her mind, for she'd been told as a girl that the thought thought the moment you spy a shooting star always comes to be. It was a risky strategy, for her mind would move without her permission from Ray bouncing down the path in a Red Cross truck to Ray facedown and bloated in the sulfur pools. There he was one night when a falling star kept falling in a long line across the valley floor, fell and became a car on the road.

Luz sprung from the Melon and screamed at the car — "We're here! Here! Here!" But the light continued on its path and kept on even when Luz remembered the horn. *Meep! Meep! Meep!* cried the Melon in the desert. *Meeeeeeep!* it said, and Ig woke and started to cry and Luz screamed all her voice away and all three of them were doing their part though the light was gone, and had been gone for some time.

After, she held Ig in the passenger seat, soothing her and staring at the stopped clock, waiting to see if she could feel the moment it was right.

It was the next morning or the next — time was getting shifty, smeary as the summit of the dune sea in the distance, but the two events abutted each other psychically, to be sure — when Luz spotted a dark shape floating in the sulfur pool: a bighorn sheep, bloated, its horns sawed off, though bighorns were extinct. It floated, swaying slightly in the brine. Its hoofs had been sawed, too, and there were bloody stumps where they should have been. Luz watched it a long time, Ig indifferent until Luz started tossing clods of dirt at it. Ig joined in then, selecting a clod, and then flopping her arm near her head, sending the clod into the dirt at her feet or sometimes straight up above her. She was ambidextrous, and smiled smugly when one clod finally plopped into the pool. When Luz landed sweeping underhanded arcs on the creature's neck and taut, distended belly, Ig said, "Again," and Luz obliged. "Again," Ig said, "again." Luz let herself hear, "Omen."

"That's right," Luz said.

The bighorn was gone in the morning, and so was the island of diapers, and Luz had to tamp down her own tardy sense of abandonment. Ig did not cry anymore, which was not good.

You can hear them screaming, her father said, the demon pleas for mercy coming up the pipe. Maybe so, because Luz did hear things at night, or felt them. Rumblings. The ground rolling beneath her. Once, she felt something pressing on her chest and when she opened her eyes a cloudy green light quivered in the sky in front of the Melon. When she shifted in her seat, it zipped away faster than anything of this world could move.

Friends, her father was saying, and he had so many friends, *have you ever sat yourself down on the porcelain throne to answer nature's call and been engulfed by the smell of rotten eggs? Sulfur! Gastrointestinal brimstone! A portent from the demons living in your rectum!*

Day, night, another day. Day. Day. Day. Why was there so much more day? Why were the nights not cool anymore? Luz asked, What season is it, Ig? Ig answered or didn't. The child lay silent on the floorboard with the tiniest nesting doll on her bare chest, her scalp blistered and bleeding, and when had that happened? Light, she thought she heard the nameless baby who was not a baby say. As in, Let there be. And there was. More than enough light. Enough light. Enough with the light. Luz was light, she was light-headed, light within light, her head hollow as any yucca carcass, shriveled as a blueberry, filled only with hot, stupefying light she could feel ricocheting mercilessly inside. It was the last thing she felt.

■ ■ ■ ■

BOOK TWO

■ ■ ■ ■

A land of lost rivers, with little in it to love;
yet a land that once visited must be come
back to inevitably. If it were not so there
would be little told of it.

Mary Austin

From space it seems a canyon. Unhealed yet scar-tissue white, a wound yawning latitudinal between the sluice grafts of Los Angeles and the flaking, friable, half-buried hull of Las Vegas. A sutureless gash where the Mojave Desert used to be. In the pixel promises of satellites it could be the Grand Canyon, its awesome chasms and spires, its photogenic strata, our great empty, where so many of us once stood feeling so compressed against all that vastness, so dense, wondering if there wasn't a way to breathe some room between the bits of us, where we once stood feeling the expected smallness a little, but also a headache where our eyeballs scraped against the limits of our vision, or rather of our imagination, because it was a painting we were seeing though we stood at the sanctioned rim of the real deal. Instead we saw a photograph, blue mist hanging in the foreground, snow collars

169

around the thick rusty trestles. Motel art, and it made us wonder finally how we could have been so cavalier with photography, how we managed a scoff when warned that the cloaked box would swallow a part of the soul. Although in this instance the trouble was not, strictly speaking, the filching of the subject's soul, for while our souls are meager, nature has surplus. Yet something of the mechanism's subject was indeed dissolved in that silver chloride, flattened then minted as those promiscuous postcards we saw now, which we could not now unsee, for we had accepted unawares a bit of the Canyon each time we saw a photograph of it, and those pieces, filtered and diluted, had accumulated in us, so that we never saw anything for the first time. Perhaps the ugliest of our impulses, to shove the sublime through a pinhole.

But scale is a fearsome thing. Scale is analogy. When understood correctly, scale expresses itself mostly in the bowels. See to the east there? See that red thread flagellum? That hair on the lens, that mote in the vision, that teensy capillary is the suicidal region's dry vein, opened. That is the Grand Canyon, where the silty jade Colorado once ran.

Returning our gaze westward, the mind

lurches vertiginous. The vast bleached gash we once took for chasm protrudes; the formation pops from canyon to mountain. Another optical lurch as strata go shadows, as mountain goes mountains.

Closer and the eyebrain swoons again: these mountains move as if alive, pulsing, ebbing, throbbing, their summits squirming, their valleys filling and emptying of themselves. Mountains not mountains. Not rock, or no longer. Once rock. Dead rock. The sloughed-off skin of the Sierra, the Rockies, so on. Sand dunes. Dunes upon dunes. A vast tooth-colored superdune in the forgotten crook of the wasted West.

Buried beneath:

The world's tallest thermometer.

An iconic cohort of roadside fiberglass dinos.

Goldstone Deep Space National Laboratory.

The Calico Early Man Site, first, last and only dig of the National Geographic Society's New World archaeology project, its excavation led by the world-class archaeo-paleontologist Dr. Buzz Leonard, Ph.D., who dated Calico's bountiful stone tool cache of obsidian flakes, chert blades, flint scrapers, hammerstones, handstones, and knobbed querns earlier than Lucy by fifty thousand years, the new oldest evidence of *Homo sapiens sapiens*'s habitation in the world and thus shifting the origin of man from Africa to the Americas, relocating the cradle of humanity to Southern California, thereby upending the scientific consensus while confirming the hypothesis long-held by all southern Californians.

Buried beneath:

The Rio Tinto borax mine, birthplace of the twenty-mule team.

The Rainbow Ridge Opal Mine, from which was pulled "Black Beauty," the largest, purest, most expensive opal in the world, whose 3,562 carats overburdened every gemological scale at the Golden State Gemological Society and Rockhounding Club in Sacramento and had to be weighed on a butcher's scale down the street, the opal that Leland Stanford purchased, had carved into the shape of a sea lion, and presented to his wife, Jane, as a push gift upon the birth of their only son, Leland Junior, namesake of Leland Stanford Junior University.

The Potosi mine, which made the lead that made the bullets that made such quantities of blood bloom in the Mountain Meadows massacre that Brigham Young was forced to revise his grand plan for Deseret.

Buried beneath: Quartz country. Talc country. Arrowhead country. Petroglyph country. Rain shadow country. Underground river country. Ephemeral lake country. Creosote forest country. Joshua tree country. Alfalfa field country. Solar array country. Air Force base country. UFO country.

I–15, I–40, I–10 and all the unincorporated pit stops astride them: Zzyzx, Ludlow, Essex, Needles, Victorville, Barstow and Baker.

The date groves and pastel tract houses of Indio.

Snow Creek Village, a lifestyle community designed for miniature-size adults.

The movie-set city of Pioneertown, including Pappy & Harriet's Pioneertown Palace and the Pioneer Bowl, the oldest continually used bowling alley in America, where retired movie chimps worked as pinsetters until the evacuations, when, forgotten in the chaos, they were left behind, perhaps bowled a few frames of their own before flight or entombment.

The low, gravel-roofed, rectilinear Neutra imitations of Twenty-nine Palms, their cracked clay tennis courts, their empty stables.

The eerie auroral throb of Palm Springs swimming pools, dry, but with solar lights charged to bursting and ablaze. Each of that city's 2,250 holes of golf a tinderbox begging for flame.

Naturally, there were efforts. The Essex town board planted the wild grasses they were told would deter the steady intrusion of sand. With seeds donated by the Sierra Club, FEMA funding, and meltwater from glaciers tugged down from Alaska, the town surrounded itself with thousands of acres of hearty, supposedly indigenous grassland. Still came the dune, rolling over the grasses like so many swaths of peach-fuzz, the world's most invasive species no species at all.

Baker and Ludlow erected fifty-foot retaining walls, Baker's made of high-tech perforated flexfoam developed at the Jet Propulsion Laboratory in Pasadena, Ludlow's old-fashioned concrete and rebar. The dune buckled both.

Windbreaks were constructed, tree lines were sowed, thousands of truckloads of gravel were dumped. Scrappy Needles — a town of three hundred truck drivers and rock hounds and recovering alcoholics — offered the mightiest fight, or at least the best-documented, stationing Caltrans trucks and the tanker from the county volunteer fire department at the edge of town and continually spraying the advancing sand wall with oil. Still came the dune.

Still came sand in sheets, sand erasing the sun for hours then days, sand softening the corners of stucco strip malls, sand whistling through the holes bored in the ancient adobe of mission churches. Still came the wind. Still came ceaseless badland bluster funneled by the Sierra Nevada. Still came all the wanderlusting topsoil of Brigham Young's aerated Southwest free at last, the billowing left behind of tilled scrub, the aloft fertilizer crust of manifest destiny. Ashes in the plow's wake, Mulholland's America.

Still came the scientists: climatologists, geologists, volcanologists, soil experts, agriculturists, horticulturists, conservationists. In fluxed new-booted, khaki-capped men and women from the Northeast, stalking tenure in L.L.Bean. Still came journalists, deadline-hungry, sense of subtlety atrophied. Still came BLM and EPA and NWS and USGS, all assigned to determine why a process that ought to have taken five hundred thousand years had happened in fifty. All tasked with determining how to stop the mountain's unrelenting march. All

175

of them failed.

Or half failed. How it happened they could explain, a microchronicle even the layest Mojav might recite: drought of droughts, wind of winds.

Unceasing drought indifferent to prayer, and thanks to it rivers, lakes, reservoirs and aquifers drained, crops and ranches succumbed, vegetation withered, leaving behind deep, dry beds of loose alkali evaporate.

Scraping wind, five-hundred-year wind, the desert's primal inhale raking the expired floodplain, making a wind tunnel of California's Central Valley. In came particulate, swelling simultaneously Dumont Dunes and their southerly cousins, Kelso Dunes. In barely a blink of desertification's encrusted eye, the two conjoined across the eighty miles that had long separated them, creating a vast dune field over one hundred miles wide, instantly the longest dune in North America.

But knowing how it came would not stop it from coming. Still came the wind, hoarding sand and superlatives: widest dune in North America, tallest dune in North America, largest dune in the Western Hemisphere. The dune field overtook I–15 in a weekend, reaching a corpulent four hundred square miles, insisting upon its reclassification from dune field to dune sea.

Still rose the dune sea, and like a sea now making its own weather. Sparkling white slopes superheated the skies above, setting the air achurn with funnels, drawing hurricanes of dust from as far away as Saskatchewan. Self-perpetuating then, the sand a magnet for its own mixture of clay, sulfates and carbonate particles from the pulverized bodies of ancient marine creatures, so high in saline that a sample taken from anywhere on the dune will be salty on the tongue.

So came the name, *amargo* being the Spanish word for bitter; Amargosa being the name of the first mountain range the dune sea interred.

In the blurred background of the Pulitzer Prize–winning photograph, the remaining citizens of Needles, nine men and three women — the Needles Dozen, as they will be briefly known — are frosty with sand mortared to their oil-slickened bodies, white specters with dark holes demarking gas masks or goggles, handkerchiefs pulled over mouths, a dish sponge tied to a face with a shoelace. They look to the dune, perhaps rather than acknowledge each other stepping backward across the besieged playground they've vowed to protect. In the foreground a toddler — the caption called him "the forgotten child of the Mojave" — squats naked in a sandbox. A plastic bulldozer lies on its side at his feet, rumored the photographer's salt. The child's crusted face is tilted skyward, to the ration jug he holds inverted over his head. His tongue is a violent belt of glistening red, the last drop of water dangling from the lip of the jug. A wink of light in the droplet, too pure to be digital.

Still those once of Needles lingered, stationing themselves at the foot of the dune for three weeks after the town was buried, accepting only rations from Red Cross, wanting perhaps to stay as close as they could to their interred lives. They looked to the hot white whale glittering in the sun and saw their homes, shops, their football field entombed in sand. Preserved. Like those quaint towns they'd read about, long ago drowned by dams but reemerged, mudlogged and algaed and alien-looking, as the reservoirs drained.

But the base of the dune was not sand, reporters reminded the Needles Dozen at a press conference held in a tent with generators shuddering behind it, and had not been sand for some time. Question: Did they realize that the dune now behaved more like a glacier, albeit a vastly accelerated glacier? Question: Were they aware that geologists had ascertained that the base of the dune — the foot, they called it — was rock? That it carved the land more than covered it? Question: Did they wish to comment on the fact that the buildings they envisioned, in which they had spent the entirety of their short lives — their homes, say, or their twelve-step club — had already been crushed, were now but fossil flecks in banded sandstone?

And so retreated even the hard-nosed dreamers of Needles, California. So dispersed the last of the true Mojavs, though the term had already outgrown them. They were reabsorbed by New England, the Midwest, the South, all those moist and rich-soiled places their wild-eyed forefathers once fled. Some were granted temporary asylum in the petite verdant kidney of the Pacific Northwest. In retreat, the stalwarts of Needles comforted themselves by categorizing the dune as a natural disaster, though by then it had become increasingly difficult to distinguish the acts of God from the endeavors of men. The wind was God; of this they were confident. As were the mountains funneling the wind.

But the sand, all that monstrous, infinite

sand. Who had latticed the Southwest with a network of aqueducts? Who had drained first Owens Lake then Mono Lake, Mammoth Lake, Lake Havasu and so on, leaving behind wide white smears of dust? Who had diverted the coast's rainwater and sapped the Great Basin of its groundwater? Who had tunneled beneath Lake Mead, installed a gaping outlet at its bottommost point, and drained it like a sink? Who had sucked up the Ogallala Aquifer, the Rio Grande aquifer, the snowpack of the Sierras and the Cascades? If this was God he went by new names: Los Angeles City Council, Los Angeles Department of Water and Power, City of San Diego, City of Phoenix, Arizona Water and Power, New Mexico Water Commission, Las Vegas Housing and Water Authority, Bureau of Land Management, United States Department of the Interior.

Metaphors were unavoidable. The Amargosa was a disease: a cancer, a malignancy, a tumor. A steamroller, a plow. A hungry beast, a self-spawning corpulence, a bloated blob gobbling land, various images of appetite, projections of our ugly, innermost selves.

The Amargosa was angry, cruel, or uncaring — personification inevitable and forgivable too, for at times the mass did seem to move with discernment. Witnesses describe occasions when it seemed to pause its march, or reach its steady foot around a town rather than atop it, as though in embrace, allowing the citizens time to hitch their trailers to their trucks and haul them from harm. Its storms once lifted a child playing jacks in his yard and deposited him unscathed atop the dumpster behind the Terrible's gas station where his mother worked. But just as effortlessly, a sandalanche humming ten miles away veered to take an entire town in minutes. It has been called the devil incarnate, but also the wide, open eye of God.

With the Needles Dozen, the last of the newspapermen, the lingering specialists from this institute and that withdrew. Civilization retreated; the frontier reasserted itself. Their staff and charges evacuated, local sheriffs' offices disbanded de facto. Sinkholes gulped the interstate, rendering highway patrol moot. State troopers ceded jurisdiction to the Department of the Interior, whose last vestige of authority is a fee booth at the northwest entrance to Death Valley National Park, a shack with a busted mechanical arm flopping out front, a bulletin board tacked with maps bleached blank and disintegrating.

USGS concluded its modest survey efforts when an SUV with government plates was ransacked, stripped, and set on fire, the assessors found four days later, wandering the edge of the dune naked and nearly insane. As the *New York Times* put it, AMARGOSA DUNE SEA INTERNATIONAL WATERS.

No complete map of the Amargosa Dune Sea exists. Partial maps of one face or another are etched almost immediately to obsolescence by the ever-shifting sands. The most informed estimate of the terrain describes "nearly exponential exaggeration of features," wherein each chain of dunes gives way to another taller, wider, hotter, until these crescendo at the Six Sisters, a chain of crestcentric dunes whose sandstone feet are estimated to be as wide as they are tall. Any one of the Sisters would easily be the tallest sand dune in the world. Atop these, the hypothesis goes, reclines the summit: a nameless five-crested star dune, entirely unmapped and ever shawled in rainless clouds. Though never scaled, the summit is suspected to be the second tallest mountain in North America. At last count, geologists estimate seven thousand individual peaks and crestlines accumulated to form the dune sea, though sandalanches and extremely hostile environs make an ac-curate count impossible. And anyway, funding's dried up.

No one has circumnavigated the Amargosa, no one has ventured into its interior, and no one has crossed it. Unmanned IMQ-18A Hummingbird drones sent on scouting patterns inevitably encountered a "severe electromagnetic anomaly," transmitting back only an eerie white throb. Satellite-imaging attempts were similarly frustrated, yielding only ghostly blurs.

BLM's *Survey of the Area Surrounding and Encompassing the Amargosa Dune Sea* reports a population of zero. The one-page document — the Bureau's shortest survey to date — is itself salted with words like *inhospitable, barren, bleak,* and *empty.*

A desert deserted, the official line.

Yet stories circulated the stuffed cities, rumors whipped around the social networks, urban legends rippled through the besieged green East: amassed at the foot of the dune was perhaps a colony.

Some versions people the colony with stubborn Mojavs, the calculation being that for every thousand fleeing the Amargosa, one stayed. A welder from Needles with fifteen years of sobriety refused to board the National Guard lorry with his wife and twin daughters. A high school geography teacher, supposedly a descendant of Meriwether Lewis, insisted on staying to finish the new maps. The ranger who once manned the fee booth at Death Valley National Park built himself a yurt and lived there with three teenage girls he called his wives-in-Christ.

The versions circling amongst the professional set populate the colony with refugees of the bourgeoisie. A spinster assistant professor failed to submit her tenure box in the fall. The environment desk lost contact with its Ivy League greenhorn. The anal-retentive manager of the illustrious lab failed to renew his grant application. A brilliant but antisocial postdoc did not return to his carrel at the Institute.

Underclass iterations have the colony an assemblage of shrewd swindlers, charlatans, and snake oil salesmen, hearts inherited from the forty-niners, awaiting the oil bonanza when the tremendous sand mass squeezes out its inevitable pods of petro, or the adventure bonanza when the summit outgrows Denali and helicopter rides to base camp go to the highest bidder, when brightly clothed cadres of the stubbled wealthy stand atop their piles of money to be the first to summit.

184

On the left it is a survivalist outpost, vindicated doomsayers with homes of abandoned freight cars of rusty oranges and reds and clear crisp blues and stockpiled with guns and canned goods and bottled water and military rations. Home to Libertarian drifters and vagabonds, tramps, wanderers preferring not to have an address, a garrison for the familiar cast of trigger-happy vigilantes scowling and squirting tobacco juice across the New Old West.

On the right it is ground zero of the eco-revolution, vital utopia where the beatniks of the Enchanted Circle have relocated from Big Sur — or the aging acidheads of Atlas City from Tucson, or the free rangers of No Where Ranch from Santa Fe, or the wispy vegans of Gaia Village from Taos, or the kinky paramours of Agape from Sebastopol, or the anarchist pinkos of Ant Hill Collective from Oakland, or the burnouts of Alpha Farm from Grass Valley, or the lesbo Amazons of Girlhouse from Portland, or the junkies of the Compound from Santa Monica, or the burners of New Black Rock City from Minden, or the shorn monks of the Shamanic Living Center from Ojai, or the jam band Technicolor Tree Tribe from Santa Cruz — all with their wheeled zero-footprint

185

Earthships made of tires and bottles and clay.

Rumors of a colony are nourished by the many who saw the dune sea firsthand and thereafter ascribed to it a curious energy. While it's a fact that certain places woo, the Amargosa's pull was said to be far beyond topographic charm. It was chemical, pheromonal, elemental, a tingle in the ions of the brain, a tug in the iron of the blood. The dune beckoned the chosen, they said. "I was overcome with this very powerful feeling," one Mojav refugee told CNN of the first time she saw the dune sea. "A feeling of, well, belonging."

Another refugee said, "I miss it. Sounds strange, I realize. But I do. I truly do."

Another described the Amargosa as "a feeling, like that swelling inside you when you hear a song perfectly sung."

"I saw it from the air, from very far off, back when there were flights out West," wrote a mirage-chasing New York stockbroker on his blog.

The PWI [Palisades Water Index] had been banging against the ceiling for weeks, so of course I'm flying to pitch water derivatives in Silicon Valley, or what was left of it. A lot of my guys had gone

186

back to Boston when Stanford closed, but there were still some whales floating around. I was polishing my presentation when the captain came on the intercom and said if we looked out our windows we could see the Amargosa. I thought, Bullshit. We were hundreds of miles north. But I looked out my window real quick and there it was, glowing. It was so bright, like a light I'd never seen before. I felt very full then, and couldn't take my eyes off it. When we passed out of sight I felt just bereft, like someone I loved was dead. I've come to realize I need that full feeling. Very full but also incredibly calm, like heaven, or the rush of warmth before you freeze to death.

This last simile, those parting words of the stockbroker's final post before he disappeared, was perhaps especially apt, for among the called the Amargosa is both siren and jagged reef, its good vibes a blessing, its curse just as likely. Fickle, it is said to be, false and traitorous. Others, wounds less fresh, describe it simply as an arbiter, allude only vaguely to its methods of exiting the unwelcome. You might have heard it on the eastbound evac lorry: *The dune is rejecting me.* Or later, among the jilted devotees in the Mojav camps: *The mountain has turned its back on me.*

See now from our imagined sky-perch. See through blurs of sand and waterless cloud and obfuscating energy. See the stoss-side base of the dune sea, glittering. It is colloidal, this light, the sun wiggling as if across a braided river from above. A mirage, for the water's run out. This is the sun reflected by aluminum, glass, the roofs of vans sandblasted smooth, mobile geodesic domes, shanties of salvaged metal. Nomads and neo-Bedouins belonging to no district, aligned with no representation, knowing no laws save their own.

The colony.

And beyond that, in terrain not yet subsumed by the dune, an anorexic wannabe orphan languishes in a vintage car on the shore of a sulfur lake, abandoned with the nameless child she took. Through playing house, dying of thirst.

When Luz came back it was her body that came first, tugging her behind it. Her skin was screaming. Her lips split, clefts puttied with scabs. The flesh around her nose was raw to cracking, like the plates along the bottom of a dry ancient sea, no moisture left to yield. The insides too, surely, for the simple, vital intake of air stung. Her fingers were swollen beyond bending, waxy and violet-tinged. Crimps of black vein ventured near the surface. Her windpipe was evidently collapsed, for she could not breathe, not exactly. Her tongue surged unavailingly against her palate, her airway clamped shut by her own forgetting how to talk to the different parts of herself.

She breathed, finally, though what passed through the flattened airway was altitude-thin and hot; it dissipated before making it all the way to the bottom of her lungs. Eventually, she did breathe deeply, and then the woozy smell of diesel came to her.

She was lying in a nest of dust-crusted pillows in a long dim narrow room. Its gently domed ceiling was low, and colored the last pale shade available to green before green becomes taupe, a shade insisting so obstinately on tranquility that it was surely blended for asylums, an interior decorator's attempt to divorce the mad from their madness. Below the domed ceiling, the walls of the long room — it was more a hallway — were lined with blankets, swelling and slackening like sails. Behind the blankets was surely a row of high windows encircling the room, for these backlit the blankets, which were two-tone and faded, depicting scenes of vanished nature: wolves howling, a mustang and foal rearing, a mountain range foregrounded by evergreens.

Luz shivered. The shadow of the starlet's slip was writ onto her by sunburn, but the dress itself was gone and she was naked save for a quilt laid over her, its batting leaking from the eroded cloth. She was chilly, though it took her a long time to recognize the sensation and to understand what to do about it. She pulled the quilt around her. The pillows beneath and about her were in fact couch cushions, filmed with a silky white dust that rose from them when she shifted.

She thought: Ig.

She rolled to prop herself up and cracked her elbow instead on some hard surface that gave a hollow clang at the blow. She burrowed one fat, blood-glutted hand into the cushion nest and felt a floor of rubber and a neat row of rivets.

Luz concentrated on breathing. Behind the blankets the open windows rattled gently. At the far end of the room, above a patchwork of more hanging blankets, was painted a silhouette of a dove — no, not a dove, a bluebird, for there were the words astride it, BLUE and BIRD. And beside that a placard with two hands reaching for each other and scripted beneath them, BE SAFE. On the ceiling was a skylight hatch made from ancient yellowed plastic and on the floor a black rubber strip ran from beneath the bluebird and back to her, and as it ran the room was not a room but a bus, a school bus with the seats ripped out: the accordion door, closed, the long metal arm attached to it with its lever mechanism, the first aid kit mounted on the wall, the elevated driver's seat upholstered in olive green and flanked by many mirrors. In one mirror Luz caught a glimpse of her own face. It made her a little unsteady, her reflection, because the angle was all wrong and so were the eyes: small and lashless, bolstered by plump cheeks where Luz's cheeks were pointy and hollow. The plump cheeks lifted a little now, and Luz touched her own face. She was not smiling.

The driver's seat creaked, and down on the long, slanting gas pedal, the toes of a bare foot curled then relaxed. The eyes in the mirror watched, still.

When Luz opened her mouth, her lips crackled. "Hello?"

A rusty scrape came from inside the apparatus of the driver's seat.

"Where's my girl?" Luz's voice was not her own. "I had a girl with me."

"Shh," went the eyes in the mirror.

"A toddler. Where is she?"

The figure — a woman — turned in the seat now. She slowly extended both her bare feet — fat, pink bottoms black, grazed by the soiled hem of a flowing, wrinkled white skirt — into the aisle. She was topless, with wide hips crowned by rolls and a soft paunch resting on her waistband.

She clutched a bundle of cloth to her chest. "Easy," the woman said.

Luz caught her tone. "Oh, God."

The woman stood. She was massive, her

head threatening the ceiling of the bus. Her hair hung lank and greasy and gold-flecked from beneath a filthy bandanna. Another was cinched around her neck. The woman came toward Luz. Her gait was tender, but not tentative. From the bundle hung a pale spindle leg. Long toes. Hard bulb of knee.

"No," Luz said. "No."

The giantess came at her still.

"Get away," said Luz, loud.

"Shh," said the woman again, kneeling with some difficulty beside Luz. "She's eating." She leaned close — Luz smelled a sourness rising from her — and there, in the wad of cloth was Ig, suckling the giantess's left breast.

Luz felt her breath come back to her, and other things with it: relief, joy, the weight of responsibility, a seasick sensation born of both having and having not failed the baby. Ig caught her with one gray eye but continued suckling, her mouth twitching rabbity and the breast plumb against it. Luz touched her head but pulled back when she saw the scabs along Ig's hairline. "Is she okay?"

"Hungry. Goes to town whenever she gets the chance."

They watched the child in silence awhile. "I'm Dallas," whispered the big woman.

"Luz," said Luz. "That's Ig."

"Ig," said Dallas, fondly.

"There was a man with us," said Luz. "Did you find him?"

Dallas shook her head no. "Drink this." She passed Luz a green glass bottle filled with cloudy liquid.

Luz smelled it.

"It's water," said Dallas, "mostly. You need vitamins, too. Drink it."

Luz did, wiping her mouth after. "How long have we been here?"

"More there."

Luz hesitated at the plastic blue barrel, its water low.

"Go on. They found you yesterday."

"Who?"

"Levi. Out walking." She gestured to Ig, who watched them still with her one eye like a squid's, catching light. "You want her?"

"I don't . . ." Luz looked at her own austere breasts, her dark nipples veering slightly away from each other. "We gave her formula." Though she hadn't. The can Rita gave her was somewhere in the Melon, still sealed.

Dallas said, "I see."

"We had to."

"That's your decision."

"Now she's too old."

Dallas shook her head and adjusted the blankets around Ig. "I hate to see young people eating that poisonous crud. My oldest was on the breast until she was four. Kid was the healthiest little nub in Mendocino. Happy, too."

Luz nodded.

"She's back East now," said Dallas, by way of full disclosure, perhaps, a gesture to her own motherly imperfections. Luz appreciated it, but she fixed her gaze on the fresh magenta stretch marks radiating along the woman's brown belly. The oldest was not the child about whose whereabouts Luz was curious.

Dallas winced. She detached Ig, turned her around, and put her other nipple in the child's waiting mouth. "Learning with teeth does make a difference."

Dallas reminded Luz of the water. Luz drank, grateful that the water was warm because she was still freezing. She hugged the quilt around herself, all the while cupping Ig's foot in her hand. She could not stop touching the baby.

"That's the heatstroke," said Dallas, nodding to the quilt. "Mindfuck, isn't it? Bet you haven't been cold since you were a baby."

195

Baby Dunn said, "Not even then."

"Chemicals. You know you're in a bad way — you know you're *close* — when your brain starts thinking in terms of quality of life."

"Where are we?"

A raised brow. "You don't know?" Dallas reached up over her head, grasped a fistful of the mustang blanket and pulled. "You've heard of the dune sea? This is shoreline property!"

White sun screamed into the bus, stinging Luz's eyes. She shielded them and saw Dallas do the same for Ig. Luz decided then that this woman could never leave them.

"Take a look," said Dallas.

Luz gathered the quilt around her like a clergyman's robes and stood, dizzy, the blood in her head suddenly at low tide. When her brain accepted color again it was blue: arresting matte pops of blue spattered along an encampment of dun, blue in slabs, one-dimensional — water, she thought, though it was water as Baby Dunn had drawn it, one flat plane. Oases going snap in the wind. Between the tarps, like boulders to their lagoons, clustered camping tents, cars and bench seats from vans, structures of two-by-fours, plywood and chicken wire, a geodesic dome of PVC pipe. Large aluminum globules with windows also covered in aluminum winked beside corrugated white cuboids splashed with maroon or teal lettering: *Wanderlodge, Born Free, Chieftain, Four Winds.* The one called Holiday Rambler had a TV antenna swaying high overhead, a red brassiere wagging from it. Everything was covered in dust: plywood, canvas, tires, barrels and boxes and bicycles. The tip of a teepee in the middle distance. Beyond this, a wall of glittering white. Luz shivered again and pulled the quilt tighter. She looked for the top of the dune but could not find it.

"I'm going to need one of those bikes," she said.

Dallas sighed. "Sit down, will you?"

"I have to find him."

"We need to cool you off first," said Dallas. "You're sick. You're weak." She passed Luz a plastic spray bottle. "Keep moist," she said. "Get your blood back where it belongs."

"He's out there."

"Have a seat."

"I won't wait. It's not possible."

Dallas stood. "Sit on down now, would you please?"

"I have to find him."

Dallas clutched Luz's arm with her free hand. She held Luz steady with her gaze.

"Listen," she began. Then, after some fortification, "They already found him."

"What? What are you —"

Dallas said, "I'm sorry."

"You said . . . No."

"I'm sorry," she said again and meant.

Luz might have left anyway — might have charged off into the desert like a conqueror, like John Wesley Powell on his velvet armchair strapped atop his raft, directing, with the one arm the Minie balls at Shiloh allowed him, his expedition's deadly slide down a mile-deep canyon. Might have, like Sacajawea, given Ig a wad of leaves to gum, slung the child into her papoose and set off for home, except when she tried to lift the baby from Dallas's arms her own quivered and the thew straps along her midback seized and Ig, perhaps sensing Luz's unfitness, let loose one of her agonized shrieks.

Dallas eased Ig down and urged Luz to sit beside her.

"Your muscles are essentially suffocating," she told Luz, meticulously reattaching the mustang blanket across the exposed streak of windows. "You might walk now. You might run. You can get out there on adrenaline. But they'll quit on you all at once. You won't even have a little sports car to protect you. Dying in that bucket will start to look

198

like heaven when the birds come for you. Vultures, grackles. Never mind the movies, they won't wait for you to die. They'll take that child piece by piece, baby."

"Watch her for me then."

"Afraid not. Plenty of hurt in this place without signing this girlie up for more." Dallas let the blanket fall silently over the washed-out vista beyond. She fetched another bottle of hazy water and sat beside the cushion nest. "Come. Lie down."

"Where is he?" asked Luz. "His body."

Dallas patted the nest. "Come on."

"Tell me."

"Levi found it — him. You'll have to ask Levi."

"Where? When?"

"You'll have to see Levi." Dallas passed her the spray bottle. "Got to cool your blood. Got to give your heart a rest."

Luz would not accept the spray bottle. To accept it would be to give time permission to go on. The gesture would be an after-gesture, as every gesture would now be, every gesture and glance, every meal, every milestone, every empty sob. "Did he suffer?"

"Levi can tell you that."

Through tears Luz watched the light beat through the mustang blanket. It was after-light, and though it was almost twin to fore-light it was of a different quality entirely. "You keep saying that word."

Luz went prone and stayed that way, trying to get a feel for the afterworld, the world without Ray in it. A long time passed like this. She would not remember the plates of food Dallas brought — clean leafy greens, supple strawberries and a golden smile of cantaloupe — nor would she think to ask where these came from. She would not remember the carnival of resurrection the fruits danced across her tongue, nor the paroxysmal shits they visited upon her later. She would not remember Dallas chattering to Ig, Dallas nursing Ig until she fell asleep, Dallas pointing to the child's blisters and saying that though she was badly burned Ig was in better shape than Luz inside. She would not remember Dallas telling her to spray herself down and she would not remember Dallas misting up her left leg and down her right when Luz refused, Dallas misting from her left fingertips across her chest and neck, to her right fingertips and — because by then her left leg was dry, the skin having swallowed it, or the thirsty air — starting again. She would not remember Dallas spritzing the blankets or soaking torn segments of cloth in water and instructing Luz to lay these where the blood was closest: her neck, armpits, lower back and groin. She would not remember Dallas telling her to picture the tubes clustered near the surface, the blood coming in rusty and over-hot, surging right up against the cool rags and turning beryl, turquoise, robin's-egg. Do you feel it? Dallas hummed, those chilly vessels evangelizing out and back, the icy platelets taking that nip inward, refrigerating her baked organs, hydrating her withered inners. Do you feel it? Luz would not remember saying, Yes, yes.

Luz did rise, eventually, and together the two women bathed Ig in a blue plastic barrel filleted lengthwise into a trough. A new halo of freckles at her brow, Ig at first grunted her displeasure, then wailed it, and Luz had to lean over and let the baby scratch at her, let Ig clutch her about the throat while she held her close and cooed into her white head. But soon the child grew bold and wiggly, beaching herself on her taut belly, sitting and slapping the water while releasing high honks of joy. Strange, Luz thought, that such a sound was still possible.

"Easy," said Luz. "We don't want to spill."

"Let her spill," said Dallas, baldly charmed.

The grace of this was staggering, and Luz could barely manage. "She's never had a bath before."

Days passed, many of them. Barrels of water appeared and appeared again, full and clean. More fruit came, and vegetables too, and sometimes charred rounds of rustic yellow bread tasting of fire. They saw no one but Dallas, who went out sometimes, Ig whining after her. Luz never slid the blankets back after that first time, had no intention of leaving the Blue Bird bus whatsoever. Dallas said that was perfectly okay and returned with cloth, gifts, rations, once a sweet ruby grapefruit, which Ig returned to again and again despite the way it made her face collapse in pucker. The baby's glottal moans went unremarked, her bulbed head and low heavy brow undescribed. Dallas fed them both salt crystals surely harvested from the badlands they had visited with Ray a lifetime ago.

Ig would have lived in the trough tub, but her lips went blue and quiversome after only a few minutes in even tepid water. "She's so thin," Luz said to no one, for Dallas would not feed Luz's worries. Together they bathed Ig twice a day and as she built her tolerance, Ig's rash receded and her blisters shrank. Once, Dallas was out fetching supplies and Luz left Ig quietly enthralled in her favorite bath-time game of watching a pair of stones Dallas had brought her sway to the blue bottom of the trough, then retrieving them. Suddenly, the baby shrieked behind her. Luz turned and dashed down the bus to Ig, who was squealing with delight and running circles around the trough, a puffy turd giving chase in her wake.

The first time Ig stayed tending to her sinking rocks long enough for her fingertips to wither, she stared at them, horrified, whispering, "What is?" until Luz kissed all ten of them and said, "It's okay."

"It's okay, it's okay," Ig repeated, petting her raisins against her own lips with the same sensuous intensity she'd had at the raindance.

"She's always been like that," Luz said, wanting Dallas to say either that something was wrong or that nothing was.

"She's a feeling being, is all. Probably got that from mom and dad."

"Dad, probably."

"He was a feeler?"

"He used to have these nightmares. He'd thrash all night. Scream, sometimes."

"What about?"

"He never remembered. That's what he said."

"You didn't believe him."

"I don't now. He was always wanting to protect me."

"Hm," said Dallas.

"What?"

"Why did he leave you out there then?"

Luz took an affronted breath. "He didn't *leave* us."

"Then where was he going?" Dallas was obstinately frank, and this confirmed Luz's assumption that she'd had a difficult life. People with hard lives don't waste time on euphemisms or manners.

"To get help," Luz said. How ridiculous that suddenly sounded.

Dallas again said, "Hm."

"He was being a hero. I let him. Made him."

"You didn't make nothing."

"I was always needing saving. That was our deal — damsel, woodsman."

Dallas wiped Luz's face. "Some people got to fix everything around them before they can get right with themselves."

Ig splashed. Luz said, "It's just. You spend your life thinking you're an original. Then one day you realize you've been acting just like your parents."

Dallas told her story then: her father one of the last holdouts against Big Pot, his the last family farm growing organic Mendo Purps, beautiful six-footers with plum-colored leaves thick as velour and buds frosty with resin. This was the heyday of the NorCal ganja boom and Dallas — named for the site of her conception — grew up bussing tables in her mother's vegan restaurant, getting tipped with dime bags. "I was high for all my girlhood," she said, combing her fingers through Ig's fine hair. "Both my daughters', too. I try to see my oldest as a baby and I can't. I was numb and it took them killing my pop to get me sober. Pot wars was in full swing. He was missing for ten days . . . Found him at the bottom of a dry dam. Some *Chinatown* shit."

"There was water."

"What?"

"In *Chinatown*," said Luz. "In the reservoir, remember? It's a freshwater reservoir but later they find salt water in Mulwray's lungs?"

"Well, no water in my pop, salt or fresh, but they did knock all his teeth out with a baseball bat. Closed casket. Wanted to send a message and I got it. Packed up my mom and my girls and went to San Francisco.

Got there three days before the bridges went outbound only. Still, there was no place to live. We were broke. We slept in Dolores Park. My daughter wrote an essay about it and got into Carlisle University on one of those Mojav scholarships."

"How did you end up here?"

"Same as everyone. I was summoned."

"I need to see him," Luz sometimes said.

"Who?" Dallas asked, though she knew.

One bright, milky morning, Luz lay naked on her nest, Ig asleep beside her. Dallas was out — where, Luz did not know and did not want to know. She had this Blue Bird world pinned down: trough, cushions, rocks, blankets. It was all she could manage. She sprayed the prickle of mist on her slowly mending skin, listening to Ig's even breathing.

Then the back door of the bus — which Luz had not known about — swung open, swamping the place in unwelcome light. Dust billowed in, its glittering particles adhering immediately to Luz's damp skin. She reached for the quilt to cover herself, setting Ig moaning. A figure stood in the light.

"Dallas said you wanted to speak to me."

Like every hoodwinked dreamer assembling at the stoss-side colony, like every huckster and pioneer before him, Levi Zabriskie came to California chasing a mirage. He came via Albuquerque, where he'd been recruited to conduct research for an initiative to reanimate the Southwest's sluggish tectonics, a project he never finished and perhaps never began.

For this project Levi was granted the highest clearance level available to civilians, Clearance Zed. To attain and maintain his clearance, Levi's friends and family were asked to file personal reference questionnaires quarterly. The questionnaires went:

ZABRISKIE, LEVI H.
HCR BOX 89
SALEM, UT 84653
CLASS: ZED
89980-682-34409J

1. TO YOUR KNOWLEDGE DOES THE APPLICANT LISTED ABOVE EXIST?

    ☐ YES
    ☐ NO
    ☐ I AM UNABLE TO SAY.

2. TO YOUR KNOWLEDGE IS THE PERSONAL INFORMATION OF THE APPLICANT ABOVE AC-CURATE?

    ☐ YES
    ☐ NO
    ☐ I AM UNABLE TO SAY.

3. HOW LONG HAVE YOU KNOWN THE APPLICANT?

    ☐ 0–1 YEARS
    ☐ 1–2 YEARS
    ☐ 2–5 YEARS
    ☐ 5–10 YEARS

☐ MORE THAN 10 YEARS
☐ I AM UNABLE TO SAY.

4. IN WHAT CAPACITY DO YOU KNOW THE APPLICANT?

☐ FRIEND
☐ FAMILY
☐ COLLEAGUE
☐ INTIMATE
☐ OTHER
IF OTHER PLEASE SPECIFY:

_____

5. ON AVERAGE, HOW OFTEN DO YOU INTERACT WITH THE APPLICANT?

☐ DAILY
☐ WEEKLY
☐ MONTHLY
☐ SEMIANNUALLY
☐ ANNUALLY
☐ BIANNUALLY
☐ LESS THAN BIANNUALLY

6. DOES THE APPLICANT LACK IN ANY OF THE FOLLOWING WELLNESS ARENAS? MARK ALL THAT APPLY:

- [ ] INTELLECT
- [ ] DISCIPLINE
- [ ] PERSONAL FINANCE
- [ ] HYGIENE
- [ ] MORAL COMPASS
- [ ] PHYSICAL FITNESS
- [ ] TIME MANAGEMENT
- [ ] PRAGMATISM
- [ ] NONE OF THE ABOVE

7. TO YOUR KNOWLEDGE DOES THE APPLICANT HAVE ANY ADDICTIONS? MARK ALL THAT APPLY:

- [ ] ILLEGAL DRUGS
- [ ] PRESCRIPTION DRUGS
- [ ] OVER-THE-COUNTER DRUGS
- [ ] ALCOHOL
- [ ] GAMBLING
- [ ] INTERNET
- [ ] PORNOGRAPHY
- [ ] FANTASY SPORTS LEAGUES
- [ ] MASSIVE MULTIPLAYER ON-LINE ROLE-PLAYING GAMES
- [ ] SHOPPING
- [ ] SEX
- [ ] OTHER

IF OTHER PLEASE SPECIFY:

_____

8. HAVE YOU EVER HEARD THE
APPLICANT CRITICIZE THE
FEDERAL GOVERNMENT FOR
ANY OF THE FOLLOWING?
MARK ALL THAT APPLY:

☐ FISCAL RECKLESSNESS
☐ DISTRIBUTION OF WEALTH
☐ HUMAN RIGHTS — DOMES-
TIC [RACE]
☐ HUMAN RIGHTS — DOMES-
TIC [CLASS]
☐ HUMAN RIGHTS — DOMES-
TIC [GENDER]
☐ HUMAN RIGHTS — DOMES-
TIC [DISABILITY]
☐ HUMAN RIGHTS — DOMES-
TIC [SEXUALITY]
☐ HUMAN RIGHTS — DOMES-
TIC [REGIONALISM]
☐ HUMAN RIGHTS — DOMES-
TIC [OTHER]
☐ HUMAN RIGHTS — FOR-
EIGN [AFRICA]
☐ HUMAN RIGHTS — FOR-
EIGN [ASIA]
☐ HUMAN RIGHTS — FOR-

EIGN [EASTERN EUROPE]
- ☐ HUMAN RIGHTS — FOREIGN [SOUTH AMERICA]
- ☐ HUMAN RIGHTS — FOREIGN [CENTRAL AMERICA]
- ☐ HUMAN RIGHTS — FOREIGN [UNACKNOWLEDGED NON-NATIONS]
- ☐ HUMAN RIGHTS — FOREIGN [OTHER]
- ☐ GENERAL "HEGEMONY"
- ☐ FOOD SAFETY
- ☐ FOOD SCARCITY
- ☐ INDIAN AFFAIRS/"GENOCIDE"
- ☐ "RAMPANT CONSUMERISM"
- ☐ "POT WARS"
- ☐ INFRINGEMENT OF STATES' RIGHTS
- ☐ CLANDESTINE GOVERNMENT OPERATIONS, INCLUDING BUT NOT LIMITED TO: ASSASSINATIONS, DOMESTIC USE OF CHEMICAL WEAPONS, COUPS D'ÉTAT, EXTRATERRESTRIALS, SUPPRESSION OF TECHNOLOGIES, BLACK OPS, GHOST DETAINEES, "THE PLAN"

☐ ENVIRONMENT — EPA [IMPOTENCE OF]

☐ ENVIRONMENT — EPA [OVERREACH OF]

☐ ENVIRONMENT — WATER CRISIS [ALASKA PROJECT]

☐ ENVIRONMENT — WATER CRISIS [GREAT BASIN ENHANCEMENT ACT]

☐ ENVIRONMENT — WATER CRISIS [VERDANCY INITIATIVE]

☐ ENVIRONMENT — WATER CRISIS [COLORADO RIVER RESCUE CORPS]

☐ ENVIRONMENT — WATER CRISIS [RATIONING JUSTICE]

☐ ENVIRONMENT — WATER CRISIS [SIERRA SNOWPACK CULTIVATION INITIATIVE]

☐ ENVIRONMENT — WATER CRISIS [RELOCATION AND EVACUATION]

☐ ENVIRONMENT — WATER CRISIS [OTHER, INCLUDING: DESERTIFICATION, CLOUD SEEDING, ARSENIC POISONING, DISMANTLING OF NATIONAL PARKS SYS-

TEM, MASS EXTINCTIONS 6
& 7]
☐ FOREIGN POLICY — "FOR-
EVER WAR"
☐ FOREIGN POLICY — OTHER
☐ GOLD STANDARD
☐ INFLATION
☐ ELECTORAL COLLEGE

9. DO YOU HARBOR ANY GEN-
ERAL MISGIVINGS ABOUT
THE APPLICANT'S TRUST-
WORTHINESS AND STABIL-
ITY?

☐ NO
☐ YES
☐ I AM UNABLE TO SAY.
☐ I WISH TO DISCUSS THE AP-
PLICANT IN PERSON.

These surveys had, like all things, unin-
tended effects reverberating outward from
them. One such effect was to evoke in their
authors a vestigial intimacy with the applicant: By sitting at their desks every three
months to consider Levi Zabriskie's superlative character, his family and friends developed the impression that they still knew the
young man quite well, though they did not.

For example, each of his recommenders indicated that they spoke with Levi "Weekly" or "Monthly," though by the time he was discharged from the project he had not visited, phoned, written or otherwise interacted with anyone from home in many years.

And where was home, exactly? His first — an FLDS compound founded by his paternal great-great-grandfather, Clester Snow, a polygamist apostate — went to vapor the day his father deposited him in front of a shopping mall in Salt Lake City for getting an erection. Despite Levi's being only twelve, he would, his father recognized, soon know what to do with it. Levi's brutal second home, Pioneer Park, mercifully evaporated when he found his third, a ward, and in that ward his fourth and penultimate home: the sheep ranch above the Dream Mine, run by his adopted family, the Zabriskies. It was mainly the Zabriskies who filled out the questionnaires.

The Zabriskies were an old Mormon family. A young, mute Zabriskie had survived the Haun's Mill massacre in Missouri and carried the news to Far West, scratching the slaughter on a sheaf of birch bark. Zabriskies had been among the founders of Nauvoo, that short-lived asylum on a spongy crescent of the Mississippi River. Erasmus Zabriskie served as scribe for the Zion-bound Vanguard Company of 1847, where he grew tired of counting the revolutions of a wagon wheel and, with the aid of mathematician and apostle Orson Pratt, fashioned the ancestor to the odometer. Two Zabriskies — ten-year-old Orrin and baby Cecil — died during the Westward Exodus, both of tick sickness, both along that pitiless stretch between Winter Quarters and Fort Laramie. Orrin was buried in Wyoming but Baby Cecil stayed pressed to his mother's bosom beyond Fort Laramie, grief-stricken mother and lifeless son pulled into the Salt Lake Valley on a handcart, the baby buried in what would become Pioneer Park, where Levi Zabriskie would live the winter he became a teenager. Hyram Zabriskie founded the Elk Mountain Mission in 1855, but abandoned it soon thereafter under Paiute attacks. Hyram's eldest, Leroy, led the charge to resettle Elk Mountain, later called Moab, later called the Uranium Capital of the World. It was state congressman Xan Zabriskie who banned this nickname, insisting instead on "Canyonlands Cathedral." Xan's nephew Travis consulted for Gaucho Energy, TEVX, and the Astrid Group, arranging for Moab to supply the

Manhattan Project with its ore biscuits. Travis's second cousin, Neal Zabriskie, became a dean at BYU, and afterward sat on the Utah Supreme Court where he cast the deciding vote in *Utah v. Alaska,* moving Utah to the tip of the Western phalanx marching toward tundra mining. The Zabriskies had a book with all of this written down.

Mrs. Zabriskie, whom Levi called Candice or later Mom, was the kind of woman who could not sit still while her family enjoyed the meals she'd made. With all her boys save Levi away on missions or at school, and Levi not disposed to facilitate her doting, she turned her feverish industry toward remodeling their big ranch house. Candy Zabriskie's energy was so boundless that she often had two teams of contractors in the house at once, one upstairs and one down. She never hovered over the decisions that gave most housewives pause, though she was a slave to trend and her swift assuredness would sometimes conjoin with her need for chic so that by the time she worked one crew from the guest bath to the den to the sunroom to the gym to the library, the guest bath was no longer to her taste. She fawned over Levi when he let her, but her attention made an ornament of her adopted son, so more often Levi fled out-doors, folding himself into the rhythms and mechanisms of Zabriskie Farms.

Levi found salve in the operations of his adopted family's ranch, its chores and puzzles and solitudes. He slaked himself with the enterprise, taking on essential projects like revamping the entire irrigation system, and also those unglamorous duties reserved for the migrants, shit-shoveling and posthole-digging. None of the Zabriskies' other boys had displayed much interest in manual labor, and Mrs. Zabriskie feared their ward would think they'd adopted Levi to work him to death. Thus began her campaign to get him to join the youth group's Wednesday night volleyball league. Levi became a devilish outside hitter, and by the fall of his senior year he was offered volleyball scholarships to Ohio State and USC. USC was, by then, the last university with athletics in California and, having absorbed those ropey beach boys who ten years prior might have donned the jerseys of now-shuttered UC Irvine, Pepperdine, Stanford, and Long Beach State, the Trojans were national champions nine times over and chomping for a tenth. But Levi was afraid to go too far from home, and his adopted mother even more afraid he would, and thus his early decision for Southern Utah University and the euthanasia of his Olympic aspirations.

Owing to a brief leave of absence for his mission in Toronto — its Soviet deprivations, often noted by his companions, were lost on Levi — he was among the final class at SUU. Levi wearied of that institution's nostalgic handwringing, so much so that he disappointed his adoptive parents by not attending commencement. He disappointed too his housemates — two of them future fillers of government questionnaires — who had, in the spirit of celebration, driven across the Nevada border to fetch real beer. Disappointment or no, Levi would not submit to a group photo to be juxtaposed with SUU's first class, thirteen blond boys in white hoods standing rigid in front of the Ward House on loan from the Church, a photo marked *Cedar City, Iron County, Utah Territory*. This was his first act of blatant rebellion, though the milestone would not make it into any questionnaires.

Instead of attending his graduation, Levi returned to the ranch, becoming the operations manager under the man who was by then his father. While farms across Utah collapsed, Zabriskie Farms hung aloft, thrived even, thanks to Levi's impossibly innovative irrigation system, which brought him some notoriety in the field, though no one else truly understood it. He made a name for himself in Fish and Game, then Conservation, and at thirty-one, was recruited by the National Laboratory for the project they said would save the Southwest.

The project took him to Albuquerque, where he grew lonely and morose. Unused to scholarly solitude — a dreary, deadening brand of aloneness compared to the bracing and alive quiet of nature — Levi occupied himself with the team's lead physicist, his first older woman (twelve years) and his first gentile. She was distant and literal and secretly doubted Levi's inclusion on the project team. They did not live together — they each had their own pods on the National Lab campus — so pulling away from her ought to have been easy. But Levi doubted his own inclusion on the project team too, and each evening, as he thought of returning to his pod, to the bound technical manuals stacked on his only shelf, the generator shuddering in the corner, he veered toward hers instead. By day they sat side by side at lectures and roundtable discussions, where Levi was routinely presented with the choice between attending to her erotic disdain of him and the agony of paying attention to the sessions themselves — sessions that seemed to bore even those who had organized them, even those who were, at that very moment, participating. Again and again, he chose to occupy his mind with the proximity of his shoe to hers, the press of his thigh on hers, the brush of the back of his hand against her bare knee. In this way Levi was quite successful in diverting his attention from the topic at hand, be it evaluating the fricative qualities of two tunneling prototypes, modeling fault slippage, or the projected patterns of ash dispersal. Soon, he was almost entirely oblivious to the theory underlying the initiative's endeavors: new faults would tap new aquifer.

Another diversion was offered by his mountain bike, which he'd brought to New Mexico, and which — when he could resist his grim, transfixing lover — he rode not in the mountains, but into the city, by then almost completely abandoned. Aside from Toronto, he'd not spent any time in a city since the year he spent on the streets of Salt Lake, panhandling at the Gateway mall, sleeping in dry drainage culverts where the coldest day of winter took two of his toes. In Albuquerque he rode through Old Town, the rounded brown backs of adobes huddled into squares, in their center always a bronze Catholic with excellent posture, always looking West, many of the placards blacked out with Sharpie where they'd once read SAVAGES or PRIMITIVES or GREAT CIVILIZER.

He rode until dark, and then past dark. As Christmas neared he rode along the fences of the wealthy subdivisions, looking for houses with luminarias lining their rooftops, real candles flickering in their bags. When he found one, as he occasionally did, he stopped pedaling and stood straddling his bike beside the tall iron fence protecting the rich, smelling their fire.

That winter wanted to snow but was unable, lacked the moisture, and gusted its frustrations. Levi often rode into the train trenches for shelter, and to admire the graffiti and, with luck, to see some movement, for a few trains did come through still. One day he descended into the trench and discovered a train stopped, which he had never before encountered. He walked his mountain bike along the narrow canal between the train and the trench wall, grazing his hand along the grated cars. Something asked him to stop and peer into one grated container. He put his face to what he realized too late was an airhole.

The container shuddered and a shape came at him: graceful, lethal, very much alive. It roared, charging the grate. Levi staggered back, pushing himself against his bicycle and the concrete wall of the trench. His eyes groped the darkness beyond the grating, where materialized the massive medicine-ball head of a tiger. It roared again from its container, a cavernous bellow more felt than heard.

Despite the animal's closeness, Levi found himself queerly unafraid. The tiger went on roaring, his bellow traveling up and down the train trench. The naturalist within Levi noted the tiger's long canines like stalactites streaked with rust, the very small, very worn teeth between them. He noted the beast's gums, pink, splotched with continents of black. He looked deep into the creature's mouth, its white-haired tongue, the brown pits where its molars once were. He looked, finally, into its yellow eyes, fearful gems. A warm stink hovered in the trench, drawing Levi's gaze up and down the train to its many like containers. Levi heard something like a loon cry, then from another grated car a slow scraping of a creature massive and, somehow he knew, elderly. The train's brakes hissed their release and the cars lurched forward, impounding the citizens of

223

the Albuquerque Zoo east on the Santa Fe Railroad, the old line that brought all the trouble west.

As the train began to move, the tiger stumbled sideways, and as he vanished Levi knew his trembling fatigue. Cars flashed past and Levi somehow knew too the hippo's thirst, the crocodile's nausea, the mania of a pair of wombats trying to burrow into steel, the communal madness of a pack of Mexican gray wolves pacing ceaselessly, the aches of a mother giraffe with legs folded beneath her, long neck crimped to the confines of her container.

He recognized the sensation. Their voices were the voices of Zabriskie Farms, of the sheep and of the sandstone above the Dream Mine, and of the deep netting of aquifer he'd found there, which fed the ranch. They were the voices as he'd first heard them in the dry clay streaks along the Salt Lake culvert, which first woke him on the coldest day of the year. They were the voices of the matted lawn of Pioneer Park, which urged him to walk, stagger on feet gone clubs from what he did not yet know was frostbite, to the Temple lawn, which beckoned him inside, to the vestibule where the basin of holy water whispered, faintly and finally, *Rest,* whose voice he was heeding, nearly eternally, when Brother Zabriskie arrived very early and nervous, for he'd been invited to give, that morning, the Fourth Sunday Address.

In the Albuquerque train trench, Levi felt immense grief at the zoo creatures' leaving. They called to him the same way the rock and dirt of Utah had, though their voices were not literal, the way some in his ward described the voice of God. The call was a sensation rather, a sudden seeping of their experience into his heart. Had anyone asked, he might have described it as a rapport with Creation, though in his mind he named it simply *the call*.

In the train trench and beyond, Levi yearned for the call. He ached for it. He'd not felt it in too long, and could no longer do without it. He ignored his lover, the minor flutters she sent up from his loins now insulting in comparison to this higher tug. Alone in his pod he remembered long-forgotten sermons by his grandfather, sermons that had always frightened him, telling of the Snows as a touched people. Stone seers, he called them. The records had been destroyed by the Quorum of Twelve, family lore insisted, but among other lesser miracles a Snow had looked to an egg-shaped agate in a white stovepipe

225

hat and predicted Brigham Young's impossible ascendancy.

His yearning urged him out again, his fearsome legacy transmuted now into desire. He shirked his duties, stalked the city on his bicycle, wrecked, intolerably aware of the vacancy opened up in him. One day, it took him to a bridge spanning the dry wash where the Rio Grande had been. He listened at its rail, futilely, then left his bike and climbed down to the waterless plain. He sat on a flat rock once submerged and listened. He stroked the hot stone. He dug his hands into the dry loam. He turned over and pressed his torso against the rock, feeling its warmth all through him. He felt, finally, a welling of harmony, a communion with the rock and the silt. He was a vessel, clutched fistfuls of gravel, moved as their covenant told him to move. His feet, touched by divine nature, tingled, and he shuddered against the stone.

The dry wash of the Rio Grande awakened something in him, and from that moment onward his ears were reattuned to the gift delivered him in Salt Lake City the day he nearly froze to death. He could hear the ancient murmurs of the sand in the basin, which ferried outward, to the Sandias and the mesas, the raspy voice of the escarpment, the gentle caress of the gully, the open arms of a canyon, the groans of the boulders along the foothills. He summited Sandia Peak along a trail weaving between the towers of the useless ski lift, in conversation along the way with the mountains themselves, nodding his gratitude to every secret burrow and tomb. He had purpose, then. He had meaning and a reason for being. Did she know what he meant?

Luz did.

Levi told her this while they rode in a pedicab chariot, its tugging tricycle rigged with huge tires off an ATV. He told her this while another man pedaled, while she watched the desert and the sweat spot at the man's neck bleed down to his rump, until he — Cody, her host called him — finally removed the shirt. He told her as they heaved across the desert, making dust of scrub beneath them. He told her as they rode away from the colony, away from the dune sea, and then somehow, without turning, toward it again. All this after she'd said, "I need to see for myself."

"I understand," he'd said. "But I'm responsible for these people. It's too dangerous to go alone."

The chariot stopped, wedged in the sand,

and Luz followed Levi into the dune.

"I have to see him," Luz had said back in the Blue Bird world, wrapped in her dust-crusted quilt. Now she wished she hadn't. Levi had gone silent. The knolls before them were bone white and sparkling. Dallas had Ig. Luz wanted to get back to her, suddenly, to make sure she was real. But she went onward, the dune sucking at her steps.

Levi walked slowly, his hands clasped together at his navel, the tips of his index fingers pressed together in a steeple. Luz watched as his hands began to tremble. Suddenly, his index fingers dipped toward the ground, and he halted.

"Here," he said, but there was nothing.

"I don't understand."

He hesitated. "The dune, it's always moving."

"I know that."

"He's here." Levi reached into his pocket and withdrew a cobalt scarf, balled up. He handed it to her. Inside, Ray's ID and his Leatherman.

Luz said, "I don't . . ."

"The dune has him."

It came to her after some time. "You didn't bury him?"

"He is buried."

She unraveled the starlet's scarf. A greasy

228

stain dead-center. "Yes, but."

"I apologize," said Levi. "We should have. It's just. We find a lot of bodies out here."

There are three ways to learn about a character:

1. What he says.
2. What he does.
3. What other characters say about him.

This from an acting coach, a big woman who wore half a dozen bright resin bracelets on each wrist and whose hair might have been called ringlets except over the years the ringlets had lost most of their coil and now scattered across her back in long, static-plagued scribbles. Three ways and three ways only, and oughtn't Luz have thought a little more about these?

1. What He Says

Hoosiers aren't quitters.
California people are quitters. No offense.
You've got restlessness in your blood.
Your people came here looking for some-
  thing better.
Gold, fame, citrus.
They were feckless, yeah? Schemers.
That's why no one wants them now.
I want you.
Do you want me?
You look like I know you.
You came to bed smelling like him.
You're all right, tell me.
I think it's time we headed up into the
  canyon.
It's important to have a project, no matter
  how frivolous.
The Santa Anas are coming, try to keep
  your hands busy.
Try not to sleep so much.
Keep your eyes peeled.
Looking good, babygirl.
You surf?
Shitfuck. Jesus. You better not look.
Ten million empty swimming pools in this
  city.
Drink this.
Be careful.

You're drunk.
You're paranoid.
You're crazy.
You're all right, tell me.
Babygirl, don't get like this.
You just do your best.
Who leaves their kid with strangers?
Go, now.
We're stick-it-out people.
Be careful.
Rocks. Rocks. Rocks. Rocks.
Roxicet, oxy, fentanyl lollipops.
Brainstem, brainstump.
Don't make any sudden movements.
We couldn't sleep, Luz.
We're lost.
I love you?
You've heard that dissertation.
We could name her Estrella.
Be careful.
I'm going for a walk now.
Be careful.
Just a little walk down the road here.
Be careful.
If you want to make Luz do something
   you have to make her think it's her idea.

2. What He Does

Dig out the shitting hole. Siphon gasoline. Impale gophers and throw them into the ravine. Keep a notebook in his pocket with lists and secret poems.

– matches
– crackers
– L
– water

Or:

– shitting hole
– garage door
– L
– water

Or:

– candles
– alcohol
– peanuts
– L
– water

Or:

– axe
– gas

- shoes
- L
- water

Or:

- charcoal
- lighter fluid
- marshmallows for L
- water

Or:

- Sterno
- eyedrops
- calamine
- kitty litter
- L
- water

Or, often, only:

- L
- water

How did his poems go? She'd read them
a few times, looking for herself, but quit
when she was nowhere to be found. So
Ray'd gone to figment now, his papyrus
shredded. She remembered some words —
resignation, pocket, kill switch, kitchen, spine,

dispatch. She remembered hard *C*s: *cost* and *cunt, costume jewelry, custard,* maybe. She remembered ampersands & mothers, or at least dowdy women making demands like *press your doubt / under your tongue,* or *wait & wonder / at the window.* She remembered desert words, *arroyo & ocotillo, Rancho Cucamonga.* But the poems looked east, she thought, or maybe backward. Either way, away from her. Then there was this couplet, chimey and risen in her now like a singular bubble from a tar pit: *Let's bless the first to go / it will be the other's fault.*

3. What Others Said About Him

He's too good for you, you know.

So. The woodsman was a deserter, as obvious as a grammar lesson: one who deserts, and what a desert he'd made of Luz. She held Ig tight to her, kept the Leatherman and the ID on the window ledge. The scarf billowed in slo-mo. No sudden movements indeed.

Dallas had another theory. "The dune curates," she said. "It knows who it wants to be here, brings us to it. Pushes others away. He wasn't right for this place, though I know it hurts you to hear it. Trust me, I know. We're all where we're supposed to be, believe me."

And Luz did! The space where Ray used to be was full of surprises like that. For example, there was the relief: with Ray gone he would never tell Ig her rotten origin story, as Luz had feared and known he one day would. Ray was dead and thus the secret dead inside Luz. Though she could not be said to have honored anything in her life to this point, she would, she knew, honor Ig's first request: *Don't tell anyone, okay?*

Another surprise came those times Dallas told Ig, "Leave Mama be. She's not well." Because Luz *was* well. She was waiting for the crack-up that never came. Though she did weep, of course, and her sobs puzzled Ig, drawing the baby to Luz where she'd crumpled, asking, "What is?"

"Sadness," said Luz through a webbing of snot. "Grief."

"Geef?" tried Ig, a new word for her. Other new ones, too: *Ouchie. Daddy. Peas* and *Tank you. Uh-oh* and *Why*.

Ig knew "more," but Dallas taught her the sign for it anyway, taught her to kiss all ten fingertips together, and soon the sign ousted the word. Dallas taught her "milk," a nautilus fist squelching a phantom teat, a sign Dallas always saw. But Ig's pantomimed refrain was *more, more, more. More,* Ig said without saying, pinching her fingertips into each other. *More,* sighing as though it gave her some release just to say, with her hands, *Mama, I've got so much want in me.*

Mama — Dallas's word in Ig's mouth, though all three of them needed it. Dallas talked through Ig, offered counsel this way. She taught Luz how to tell when Ig needed to poop or pee, watch for her squirmy tells. Dallas trained Luz to train Ig to squat in the dirt and work it out. They made a game of burying their waste, of watching their water guzzled by the dry ground. We don't need diapers, do we, Ig? We were never meant to shit our pants, right, Ig?

Through Ig, runty conduit, Dallas taught Luz the siesta schedule with which they slept away the brutal hours. Soon Ig and Luz had gone circadian, up before dawn into early morning, then rising again for sunset and the first, sane half of night. A bronzy girl Luz's age came with outfits: muumuu for Luz, shroud and sling for Ig, all the same gauzy white Dallas wore.

Dallas taught them how the colony existed as a perpetual motion machine, how on their rippling day those whose encampments lay closest to the encroaching mountain pulled their stakes and resettled at the farthest edge of the camp, so the shantytown rippled just ahead of the dune's march, like the endless children's game of stacking hands wherein the bottommost hand is removed and laid atop the topmost hand, and then the bottommost hand is removed and laid atop the topmost hand, and then the bottommost hand is laid atop the topmost hand, and then the bottommost hand is laid atop the topmost hand . . .

When it came their day to ripple, other colonists appeared. They greeted Luz, grinned at Ig. Luz surveyed them as they worked and wondered whom she was seeing. Women mostly, all in white, white robes, white muumuus like Luz's, billowy white skirts like Dallas's. The men seemed young — boys, really — though one was very old, with a mangled face and an earned industry about him.

Luz assumed they were to push the Blue Bird. But Dallas said, "Solar," and the bus rumbled to the outskirts. In this way, Luz discovered order in the colony, alleyways radiating from the dune like the spokes of a wheel, sunbeams between metal and PVC and tarp, which explained why when they moved the Blue Bird it had to be parked just so.

Dallas taught Luz which questions to ask:

Couldn't the self exist in a single word? Meaning, *water.* Meaning, *war.* And what if that word was not allowed?

Could a person promise another his dreams? If he nightmared instead, who was at fault?

What ego must have throbbed within her to believe that she could pin Ray down?

Yes, the gall. But whose?

All that time he let her think she was the flimsy one.

At night, the dunes sang.

When its roll had accumulated enough flammable debris to host a bonfire, the colony came alive after sunset. One such night, Ig was stir-crazy and Luz coaxed her into her sling, then helped Dallas roll their empty keg toward the smell of something clean burning. They entered the circle of the bonfire and the pulse of hoots and chatter slowed. There was, for just an instant, stillness. For her, Luz realized, for the squirming baby and its young mother.

The commotion picked up again, mild and soothing — no raindance racket. Someone strummed a guitar, someone urged reedy notes from an elementary school recorder. Dallas excused herself to tend to the keg, leaving Luz to jounce Ig and watch.

Soon Ig was asleep in Luz's arms. She had not spoken to anyone, and this seemed as it should be. Firelight ghosted brilliance on the colonists where they swayed, talking.

They touched each other a lot, with an easy intimacy Luz envied. Tending the fire with affection, wrangling empty kegs, braiding each other's dirty hair. Mojavs, undoubtedly, and Luz attempted to attach to each a Mojav story. But the word conjured hunched people scrabbling in the dirt, where these people were grimy but buoyant. Happy. They laughed. Hard to imagine them digging for brine or spraying the dune sea with tar. Hard to imagine them mourning anything.

Then, Luz saw him across the flames: Levi, his square head bare, his light hair shorn, his nearly translucent beard ablaze in the firelight. She had not seen him since he'd given her what was left of Ray. She considered going to him but felt very content where she was, watching.

He was a large man. She had somehow not noticed this in the dune or before. His skin glowed coppery behind his pale tangle of beard, as though the sun had evacuated all the pigment from his facial hair and relocated it to his face. Firelight gathered at his cheeks and his small teeth winked as he chewed something. He held a ration cola, though he was not drinking from it but gleeking into it discreetly as he received the other colonists.

Levi was their north. Their compass needles quivered in his direction. His stance was wide, as though he were readying himself to shoulder a great burden, a burden he would lug willingly and with grace, his little teeth winking all the while. Even Dallas, sturdy as a mountain, appeared at Levi's side and leaned into him. As they embraced, another gust bolstered the fire, melting their two forms together.

Luz watched the fire, which was somehow blue at its core, flames licking green and black. Later she would ask Cody what they were burning, what made the strange color, and he would show her boxes and boxes of evac pamphlets. LEAVE OR DIE, the pamphlets said in bright bubble letters.

She rubbed Ig's back, round as a beetle's against her. What it might have been to carry her.

Levi noticed Luz then. His gaze would have been intense if it did not so soothe her. She did not look away. Natural, an instinct, and when was the last time she'd honored the tug of instinct? As if to answer, Ig shifted, then settled. A sense of calm was rising in Luz, and some heat descending, too. What was attraction if not a form of telepathy? The wild luck of two people feeling the exact same thing at the exact same time. That word again: *purpose.*

Ig woke. Luz turned so the little one could see the fire. Ig watched the flames and Luz did too, the two transfixed as moths until Dallas came around, rolling the blue plastic keg, now full.

In the end, the damsel had no talent for acting, regardless of how often her coach waved her cottage-cheese arms above her head, setting her bracelets aclack and proclaiming, *Dear, you're positively* made *for the pictures*!

But maybe it was only that she'd never found the right part. After the bonfire outing, Luz and Ig took to walking the spokes of the colony at dawn, before nap time, before the sun of suns took over, shrouded in the white that turned out to be cut from parachutes that had delivered pallets of evac pamphlets.

And as they walked, people watched, and Luz caught something novel in their gaze. It was a wondrous change from those she had, without knowing it, become accustomed to. At work: the exasperated looks of photographers mumbling from behind their massive cameras, the defeated gazes of editorial directors, for there was another girl — a Colombian — who looked just like Luz (spindle limbs, scapula like malformed wings, a fat and drooping bottom lip, even a gap between her teeth) except this girl's ass was smaller and sat higher and her legs dangled from it like a puppet's. The other girl was more expensive and had to be reserved very far in advance, so if Luz booked a shoot it was often because they were compromising, because the campaign had been scaled back or the editorial sliced in half and so they would have to settle for the poor man's Colombian. "One good thing about Luz," said her agent, "you never have to tell her not to smile."

On the street, at parties and restaurants: those looks of preoccupied recognition, the brain nag that they had seen her somewhere, but where? ("You look like I know you," the woodsman had said.) Not altogether terrible, except for the guesses, other lives that might have been, always painfully better than her own — the indie that swept the festivals, the cellist from the new band, this It girl or that. But she was professional wallpaper, her job to replicate a human being without the mess of one, and so they would scowl at her, a problem never to be solved. The woodsman had sometimes looked at her as though she were a tick clinging to a stalk of grass.

(He had another look, too, but she would not quite allow herself to remember it. Something that made his smile go lopsided, a cord bulge in his jaw, a look that meant all the ways and reasons he loved her were at that instant rising in him.)

But at the dune she was regarded in a way she had never been regarded. The girls thought her and Ig cute, and said so, but also seemed a little repelled. The men were harder to decipher. Since girlhood, the gazes of men and boys had been a kind of consumption, gulping her in not because she was beautiful — because with her bad skin and bad teeth she was not beautiful, not without the tricks, "certainly not street pretty," her agent often barked into her earpiece — but because she was thin and her bones showed in places like a partridge on a plate. But at the dune, instead a glance to her face, then her feet, then to Ig slung around her. Pity? There was some. The story got around, she knew: a wife lost her husband, a widow with a baby. But something beneath the pity. A smile that, she realized in time, meant the child was triggering the saddest memories of their happiest moments. That old man called Jimmer, the heart side of his face purpled wurst, whose left hand moved without him, mumbled either "Mine's grown" or "Mine's gone."

Usually, the men said nothing, giving her a wide psychic berth for reasons she did not understand and would not understand for some time.

No matter. Here, the damsel delivered her greatest role. She played long-suffering, she played pure. A mother.

Only — and her coach had said this would happen, the miraculous transmutation into character, a notion that Luz had always found a little frightening — she wasn't playing. Another surprise. Here, she was a good woman.

Like a mother, Luz worried.

Dallas

There's nothing wrong with the child, nothing wrong on this Earth and surely not here. I believe that. Take her to Jimmer in the teepee if you don't believe me. He's our healer.

Jimmer

Was the little one baptized, and if so did she drink of the baptismal water? Did she cry when she was born? She's not anything-handed — which arm did you first put through the sleeve when you put on her baptismal dress? Don't worry, doll, no one ever remembers. Did she have much hair when she was born? Children born with too much hair cannot think straight, for the hair tugs on their brain and drains it. On the other hand, children born without any hair are dim, because the hair is still inside the head and it clogs the brain. Did you tickle her much? You mustn't tickle a child before she speaks, it can cause a stammer or even muteness. Freckles come from drops of rain drying in the sun, though I assume that's not the case here. Did you and the father speak much the day she was born? What day of the week was that? A Saturday baby will be stupid, but only for a bit, because Saturdays are lazy days. If we scrape the dirt from her nails and put it in her water she may be cured of that petting, but I advise against it. For the insomnia you need to get your jing flowing again. Yes, there's a blockage above your kidneys. That Holiday Rambler there, with the brassiere flag. The girls live there. At the very least they're up all night. Sew a salt crystal into your hem, for the heartache.

The Girls

We come from all over. We're here because we want to be, our contribution. We don't use money, not in a five-senses form. We've never been this good at anything, never particularly good at sex, even. Speak for yourself! The Rambler is not a brothel. Think of it as a bathhouse. Think of it as a sanctuary. Think of it however you like, or not at all. We relax you, we do what comes to us and what comes to you. A haven from inhibitions and negativity. You don't know how negative thoughts weigh you until you float free of them, then there's no putting them on again. The Rambler is a medical tent. We knead the worry out of you! There's no shame here. We embrace after each orgasm. Orgasm is God in the body. Before we got here, we were sensual atheists. Orgasm is a leap of faith. They call it a leap because you have to leave your body. We're not shackling anyone with our expectations. But we are willing to receive seed when it seeks us. We have to be. There are no divisions here, no lines between the erotic, the sublime and the divine. No space for the worldly. There are clusters of nerves all over the body and each of these can be stimulated to heaven. We can coax an orgasm from the earlobe, the Achilles' tendon, the tip of your nose. We can come by watching others come. Just sitting is fine. Sit as long as you like. It's nice to have some company. Relax. Give us your burdens.

Jimmer

For arthritis wear the eyetooth of a pig. Chew newspaper to stop a nosebleed. A salt mackerel tied to the feet cures bunions. Cut off a head cold by tying a long stocking around your neck. Rub warts with pebbles, rub warts with chicken blood, rub warts with a slice of raw potato and stow it in the eaves, rub warts with thistle leaves and throw them into a grave, scratch a wart with a nail from a coffin until it bleeds. In the Army I carried the Ninety-First Psalm in my pocket and the bullets never touched me. Do not wear a man's hat unless you intend to keep him. Did you whistle when you carried her? Pardon my French, but this will retard surefire. In what direction did you sleep while expecting? Feet to the north could tie the child's tongue. Have you taken the short end of a wishbone lately? Bad things come in threes, miracles in pairs. Never point at lightning. If you kiss a man with the raw heart of a turtledove in your mouth he will fall in love with you and never out. The first to go to sleep after consummation will be the first to die. If a body of a drowned person cannot be found, toss a loaf of bread in after it. The loaf will hover above it. Some of this is not so useful these days.

The Girls

It's arsenic poisoning, Jimmer's face. Have you never seen a case? You'd think he'd be more grateful, ugly as he is. Though that twitchy hand can do some tricks between your legs. Can it? Ig is not what you would call cute, is she? Cute is the worst way to be. Cute is an act of erasure. Cute is gynophobia writ large. We all have a snake or two in our hair. Even you. Especially you.

Dallas

The girls were lost before they came here. Wanderers, like all of us. They have a very specific definition of ministry, let's say. But who am I to tell another woman what counts as divination? For that matter, who are you?

Jimmer

Dallas has an ardent soul. Very awake. One of the few who truly grasp the mystery of the dune sea.

Dallas

At the dune sea two cartographers can walk the same trail and draw different maps.

Jimmer

Two artists can sit side by side, sketching the same peaks, sharing the same tin of charcoal, and their drawings will emerge as though they were sketching two different ranges on two different continents.

Dallas

That sound you hear at night, the singing, it's a vibration. You're hearing the dune move through you.

The Girls

The food comes from the greenhouses. You've seen the Volkswagens? Rolled over a VW mechanic and gutted them for grow pods. Tomatoes, kale, strawberries. You've met Cody? Our grower savant?

Cody

Here you've got your snow peas, your watermelon, over there your cantaloupe, your leafy greens. Everything organic, everything heirloom. No tubers, no winter squash, no rice or wheat or trees, of course. Before this I was an urchin, you could say. I'd never belonged to anything. When the Amargosa rolled over my school it was the first time I was capable of considering the existence of a benevolent God. The Wide Rock School for Errant Boys. Basically a labor camp. One of those places where they use wilderness as a cage and see no irony in it. Blueberries? Sure. I think I can manage blueberries.

Jimmer

The dune sea does not exist, insomuch as we define existence. How is that little one? Put a nub of brute root under her pillow.

Cody

The root is Levi's creation, I can't take credit for it. Basically he spliced cannabis with cocoa. There's some peyote in there too, or a cousin of it. No paranoia though, no freakery. A truly flawless hybrid. Inspired. Genius. Chew the root to clear your mind. Levi takes them on vision quests.

The Girls

They go at night, while we sleep. Levi needs peace to dowse. He and Nico take the empty kegs and fill them at the ephemeral rivers. They distribute the full kegs at bonfire. He dowses with his hands, rather than a rod. The phallus would defile the process. Men have wagged their rods at the Earth plenty.

Jimmer

The kids call them vision quests. I call it listening. He uses his hands because he can't find branches. When was the last time you saw a tree?

Dallas

For Levi, using a tree branch to find a river would be like using a severed arm to find a shallow grave.

Jimmer

A gifted dowser can divine with anything for anything, so long as his desire is honest. He can dowse for oil or ore. He can tell whether something is safe to eat or drink. He can find lost objects or missing people. He can solve crimes. He can find anything buried: unmarked graves, mineral deposits, long-healed injuries, subconscious fantasies. He can feel sickness, he can feel lies. Intuition enters the mind in a way Western science has yet to explain. Moses was a dowser, probably Jesus too. Though they did not have the benefit of dune buggies.

Cody

Oh, no. We'd be fucked if we were still on gas. Nico rigged the buggies with solar and wind. Like sailing on land. He's a genius with machinery. Don't I know you from somewhere?

The Girls

Nico was Tesla in another life. He was Tesla and he was Vlad the Impaler. You've got one of those déjà vu faces.

Dallas

Nico is a savage. That's his Chieftain there.
Leave him be.

Jimmer

If you open your eyes to the sun at dawn
and dusk, when its energy is purest, you will
absorb all the day's nutrients via the ocular
ducts. It's a mainline to the brain, nutrients
converted directly to brainpower. Einstein
did this. Bach, too. Picasso's Paris studio
faced east and he would stare out the
window for an hour each morning to invig-
orate himself. He painted *Guernica* in three
weeks.

So Luz began her sungazing, began pacing up and down the Blue Bird with Ig and letting the child pull a dusty blanket aside and ask, "What is?"

"Sunrise," Luz said, staring. She wanted a better brain, wanted to make beguiling, impressive things, or at least to need less. She drank up the morning rays until her eyes stung, keeping Ig in shadow. So far she had not felt much resembling rejuvenation or genius. The only tangible effects of her sungazing shone when she closed her eyes and the sun remained there, both darkness and light. Then one day, pointed somethings beneath it too.

She opened her eyes and looked not at the sun, rising, but at the structures on the horizon below. A mirage, surely, but a queer one: dollhouse silhouettes, gingerbread houses all in a tidy row. She squinted harder against the sun, thinking she was maybe

256

cracked up after all. NORTH POLE OUTLETS, a sign reassured her.

"Dal," she said. "I think I found something."

The colony swarmed, darted across the asphalt lanes, between the planters and decorative lampposts, beneath eaves dolloped with plaster snow, to shops with brown paper taped over their windows, chains across their glass doors. Luz went too, with a wet shroud over Ig to keep the heat away. Luz had spent a lot of time in malls, as a preteen and after. It was where the suave young handlers from the agency always took them when they traveled, if they had any downtime. She strolled the outlets as she might have were it not abandoned, Ig swaying in her sling.

Meanwhile, the others lifted forest-green trash cans and chucked them through the store windows, sending glass down like rain, making Ig clap. Through one such waterfall came Nico with left-behind batteries, phones, cameras, laptops, wires and plugs — contraptions Luz had not seen for a long time and had not missed. In another shop Dallas filled a duffel with puffy plastic packages of linens. From another shattered window Cody emerged cackling, with shoes

257

on his hands.

"What size are you?" he called to Luz.

She could not remember, had to check the bottom of the starlet's sandals.

Cody came back with boxes stacked big to little, a cardboard wedding cake. He gave Luz a pair of sensible mom tennies with yellowed gum soles, pink Velcro light-ups in every baby size for Ig. Though it was too bright out to see whether the light-up cells were dead, Ig liked Cody, perhaps saw that he needed her enthusiasm, and faked some.

Newly shod, Luz and Ig went exploring. The baby walked and walked. In one courtyard cul-de-sac they found Santa's Village, maze of plastic presents, one nutcracker sentinel toppled. Ig was uninterested. They went on.

"What is?"

Luz followed Ig's gaze to a carousel, its bulbs surely dead but its mirrors and gold trimmings gleaming. Luz lifted Ig over the wrought-iron fence and climbed after. They walked among a pearly menagerie: no horses but pairs of unicorns and zebras, two-humped camels, dignified giraffes. Luz said all their names, though Ig could not or would not repeat any:

"White tigers, Ig!"

"Look, jackrabbits!"

"Cheetahs!"

"Ostriches!" long-legged and confident.

"Eagles!" with wings splayed.

"Dragons!" tongues and tails forked.

"Dolphins!" sleek, lunging muscular through the air.

"Mermaids!" with iridescent tails.

All ahover on candy cane poles, waiting. A wide swan bench for lovers.

Ig stroked and inspected, and gradually the others joined them to marvel at the carousel. When Levi came he told everyone to hop on. Luz perched Ig in the saddle of a fat panda, cinched the dirt-crusted straps around the child's tiny torso, and climbed on behind her. When everyone was on, Levi, Nico and a boy named Lyle from Cody's school pushed. Jimmer helped with his good hand. It seemed impossible the wheel would ever turn, but it soon yielded, its insides groaning, the opalescent animals lurching up on their poles then gliding down, coaxing synchronized squeals from their passengers. Above those squeals came music, a warbled underwater tune from somewhere deep within the contraption. As they whirled, a breeze came to the riders, cool and awakening, bringing them lost sensations and forgotten memories.

A girl named Fern remembered her brothers' launching her from a trampoline.

A girl named Cass remembered clinging to an indifferent beau on the back of his dirt bike.

Luz remembered luging down Canyon Drive on Ray's longboard, his impossible laugh in her ear.

Cody remembered flinging himself down a ridge beyond Wide Rock, the once he tried to escape.

Dallas remembered floating on her back in the last warm dregs of the Yuba River.

Jimmer remembered his boy.

They laughed anyway.

In the gilt-framed mirror overhead, Luz watched Ig: startled but brave, then cautiously merry, clenching her mama and Mama clenching back. Luz wanted to feel this way forever.

Up ahead, Jimmer swung himself around the pole he'd been pushing and hopped on. Cody and Lyle soon did the same. Levi pushed and pushed, sweating, laughing, hollering for everyone to hold on. He finally jumped on too, shouting *whee,* and Ig said *whee* too. Luz wondered if he'd heard her, wanted to catch his eye and mouth *thank you,* but soon the carousel was succumbing to its old inertia, the tune above stretched slow and sorrowful.

After, Cody kept congratulating Luz.

"For what?" she said finally.

"You found this," he said.

"The carousel?"

"The whole damn place!" said Cody, admiring his new loafers.

"Amazing eyes," said Dallas, still aglow from the ride.

"Beautiful work, Luz," confirmed Levi, watching Nico inventory his devices.

"You would have found it without me," she said. "Anyone would have."

"Not true," said Dallas. "Things aren't so reliable out here. The dune could take this place by sundown."

"And we were out scouting last night," said Levi. "Didn't see it, didn't hear it. This is a gift for the very attuned. Unequivocally so."

In this way word of Luz's offering spread through the giddy colony assembled in the shade of the carousel, assessing their haul. Many posited that Luz possessed such qualities as knack and grit and presence of mind. Luz watched Ig do bobbleheaded, bow-legged laps around the carousel in her light-ups and considered the possibility that she did. It was the first time she had ever been a good omen.

The colony reconvened that evening, when someone swung a girthy branch of mesquite into a bomb casing pilfered from Travis Air Force Base, sending a gong throughout the settlement, a solemn series of *om*s that summoned all to bonfire.

Cody was scurrying about, feeding mall debris into the fire. He passed near them and squeezed Ig's knee.

"Watch," said Luz, and set Ig on the ground. Free, Ig tottered, her light-ups' pink carnival beacons flashing underfoot.

"Wild!" said Cody. "You're tricked out, Ig."

Ig seemed not to notice, concentrated instead on running.

Luz spent some time hunched, chasing after Ig and redirecting her away from the fire. Ig had by now become a kind of mascot at the colony, and people Luz had never spoken to tutted *Ig, Ig, Ig* as the baby

262

chugged by, lighting their faces with red siren lights. Jimmer smiled at the child from where he sat on a bench seat from a gutted van, whittling a stick. "Psychedelic," was his assessment.

Ig wanted up, so Luz lifted her. Ig wanted down, so Luz put her down. Ig pulsed her two curled fists skyward, asking for milk, so Luz found Dallas.

"Relax," said Dallas, encouraging Ig to latch. "We're not going anywhere."

A pretty girl made room for Luz on a log near the fire, where smoke whipped into her face. Smoke follows beauty, said Billy Dunn, wherever he was. She blinked the ash from her eyes and saw Levi, or a mirage of him, watching her. Thick arms, sturdy trunk, still. Planted, or rooted. But those metaphors were expired here and the word that came instead was *embedded.* Suddenly, Luz arrived at a simple and perplexing fact: in the few siesta hours since the carousel, she had missed him.

A gust swelled the fire and brought Luz Mojav stories. They seemed ridiculous to her now. That the well-shaped girl beside her was a park ranger's bride-in-Christ. That Nico, sitting cross-legged on a papasan in the bed of a truck, fiddling with some electronic he'd rigged to life, had a desk at an institute somewhere, unreturned term papers in a drawer, two yellowed strips of glue on the wall where someone had pried his nameplate free. That Jimmer was one of the Needles Twelve, his lost boy the forgotten child of the Mojave. That she might smell the oil on him still. That she might find black smirks still under his fingernails. That Levi had refused to board the National Guard lorry with his wife and twin daughters.

Beside Luz, the pretty girl spoke. "I want to admit that I've been doubting," she said, and the others went quiet. "In the past. And recently, even. I've been unsure of why we're here." Her voice wobbled. "I'm ashamed to say it but it's true."

Someone said, "It's okay, Cass."

Cass said, "In a way it was easier when I first felt pulled. There was clarity there. It was stark, undeniable. Plus I had nowhere else to go."

Many laughed.

"But being here is different, not so clear. I get a now-what feeling sometimes. I don't know, maybe it's easier to be lost than found. At least there's energy in lostness. Something to be done. I know we're supposed to trust the place, to embrace its mystery, to keep our eyes open, and I try to do that. I do. I try to be a vessel. It's hard though, hard not to wonder what we're supposed to be looking *for*. But today I knew. Today I was a vessel filled. It's true — if we're open and honest we will be consoled. I was."

Nods all around.

"I want to offer my gratitude for that, and to tell anyone who's feeling that now-what feeling to hang in there. To stay open, honest, willing. Like Levi says, we can't force wonders. Can't insist on signs. But they do come." Here, she looked at Luz. "And when they do you can't miss it."

How lovely Cass looked, pliant and bare. Luz envied her. The Amargosa curates, Dallas had said. *Spiritual* was Lonnie's word — the memory brought Luz old shame from new sources: how she'd scoffed at the very idea, the well-trod path her mind inevitably strolled, a straight line downhill to cynicism and disdain. She wished Ray were here, to buoy her with his capacity for belief. The world had been wider with him in it. She looked again to Levi, who could hear the earth. He seemed to want something from her.

"I've never really been a part of anything," Luz said, without knowing why except it felt right. "Or, anything I could believe in. I guess what I've been thinking about a lot lately is that idea, belief." Some nodded. "I haven't ever had a believer's disposition. But lately I've been getting comfortable with the idea of something bigger than myself — I don't want to say 'God.' When I was growing up people around me used that word in all the wrong ways. It was a weapon, that word. 'God's love' was this scrap everyone was fighting for, something you could win by dressing with modesty and having a clean face, by sitting quietly. But why should those people and their fucked-up nonsense have anything to do with my experience, is what I've been thinking lately. Can't I decide who I am? I've never been a very good listener, but today I felt I could be."

Many nods.

"I know what you mean," Luz said to Cass. "About it being harder to be found. It's like there's been this momentum carrying me forward, this energy, and I wasn't sure where it was taking me. Scary, that feeling." Several moaned their assent, urging Luz on. "But freeing, too. In a way. And now . . . I don't know. A lot of it hasn't made any sense. Or maybe it makes too much sense? I don't have a lot of experience with clarity or . . . significance, I guess you'd say. I've never been good at it . . ."

Her voice went wet with emotion and Cass patted her shoulder.

She went on. "You can't see that from the outside, how frightening it can be to believe. Believers always seem so serene. I've never felt serene a day in my life." Some laughs. "But I think maybe it's been taking me here, that energy. I don't know if that makes sense. Does anyone else feel this way? Maybe it's just me . . ."

"No," said Levi. "We all feel all of that every day. You are supposed to be here, Luz." He went on. His words had a way of making the complicated comforting, making the listeners' abundant fears instead evidence of sensitivity and keenness. He somehow unearthed confidence and serenity from deep wells of fatigue, revealed the sublime subtext in the long list of civilization's failures. He brought, as he spoke, a verdant world to them — transformed the colony from a place of isolation and hardship to a place of beauty and abundant blessings. He invited the yuccas to lift their tired heads, regrew the wild grasses, reran the rivers, cleansed them of their saline and fertilizer and choking algae, replenished aquifers and refilled swimming pools, plucked the woodworms and emerald ash borers from the trees, rid the forests of their malignant fungi, swelled the snowpack, resurrected the glaciers, refroze the tundra, returned the seas to their perfect levels. It seemed possible, as he spoke, that his words might summon thunderheads, that his voice might bring rain.

Levi was human again beneath the sun of suns, his head draped in cloth, though Luz saw that his eyes had the same electricity as she offered her hand to help him up through the open back door of the Blue Bird.

Inside, he nodded to Dallas. "Give us a minute, would you?"

Dallas plucked her nipple from Ig's mouth and went without a word.

"I brought you these," he said to Luz, and offered a plastic shopping tote gone matte with dust. Inside the bag, Sacajawea, John Muir, Lewis and Clark, Mulholland and John Wesley Powell.

Luz accepted the bag. "You had these?"

"I saved them. Only things of value, so far as I could tell. Car was completely useless. Stylish, but suicidal."

Luz lowered her head. Strange to see her books here, as though people from her past were visiting her, assessing her new life. She did not want to open them; to open them would be to open herself to their scrutiny.

She put them down on her cushion nest.

"This too." Levi offered her the hatbox filled with money.

"I don't want that," she said.

He set it in the corner. "Dallas is taking good care of you?"

"Yes."

"And you're comfortable here."

"Yes." They were saying these things but meaning others, it seemed.

He said, "I wanted to thank you for sharing last night. And for finding the outlet mall, of course."

Luz said, "Thank you. For the carousel."

"I wasn't sure if you —"

Ig interrupted. "What is?"

"Levi," said Luz, lifting Ig and pointing.

"Eev-ai."

"*Lee*-vi," Luz corrected. But Ig was through with the elocution lesson and instead thrust herself into Levi's arms. He caught her. He had held a baby before, apparently. "Ig, Ig, Ig," she chugged, milling her pelvis on his forearm. They laughed. Ig moaned then as though hurt by their laughter — perhaps she was — and rubbed her bloated head against Levi's chest. It was a new gesture for her.

"She's never done that before," said Luz. "That's the first time. It's wild how quickly she changes. The minute I know what to do with her she morphs."

"A changeling."

"It's maddening. Sometimes I think it's making me crazy." Ig continued waxing Levi's pectoral with her forehead. "She's a feeler," Luz added.

Levi rubbed her back. "I can relate."

They watched her a little more — she gifted Levi one of her sinking stones and then cried for its return. "How old is she?" asked Levi.

"Two."

"Small for two."

"Almost two."

They looked at the books where they lay on her bed, beneath the window, so Sacajawea and Little Pomp stared up at Ray's Leatherman. Beneath them John Muir, who had comforted her the day Ray impaled the prairie dog, on the last day of what had passed for normal then. These artifacts from the mansion seemed to confirm Luz's bonfire inkling: inevitable that a little creature would dart into the starlet's foyer as Luz was playing dress-up. Impossible that Ray might do anything other than skewer it with the fireplace poker. They had to get to Ig, to the colony, through whatever maze of carnage and threat necessary, through gopher and raindance and daddy-o. Through the Nut; somehow she had not thought of him in a long time.

Luz took Ig from Levi and set her down. "Can I ask you something?"

Levi nodded. "Of course."

Ig wanted up again, but Luz ignored her. "You said you find a lot of bodies out there."

"Yes."

Ig pinched her ten fingertips together, meaning *more.* But Luz went on. "How often do you find people alive?"

Without hesitation he said, "You're the first. You two."

"How? How did you find us?"

"You may not believe me if I tell you."

"Try. Please."

More, signed Ig.

Levi hesitated.

"How did you find us? Did you hear something? That . . . voice?"

His head tweaked up.

"You did." *More.*

"Yes."

"Yes what?"

Levi said, "There was a bighorn. They're supposedly extinct. I tracked it."

"I saw. In the sulfur lake. It was dead."

"Yes. I followed its death rattle, you might say."

Luz lifted Ig finally and stroked her great head. "Last night you said you think we're supposed to be here. Ig and me."

Levi looked to her as though he'd just been resuscitated. "I do. You are."

"Why?"

"I heard that voice. It wasn't just the bighorn dying. An alarm of sorts. It said we needed you."

"Me?"

"It was a sense that someone important was fading from this place."

"Important how?"

He reached down for Sacajawea and moved her aside. He lifted John Muir and opened him. Luz wanted to reach out and stop him, to protect the Blue Bird from the starlet's library, to keep this chimeric colony as far as possible from the laurelless canyon. But from John Muir Levi withdrew a manila envelope, and from the envelope, a piece of paper, creased and bluish. "I knew I knew you," he said, handing her her own birth certificate.

She said nothing. Ig batted at the paper.

"I remember that photo of you, on the soccer field," Levi said.

" 'Field' is generous."

"I remember the caption. 'Baby Dunn at a California Soccer Clinic.' The picture was

272

all over the news when I was in college. We did a unit on you in my English class. 'Visual Rhetoric in Politics.' " He laughed. "Can you believe it? That's what we were doing then. Making posters. I wrote a paper about you. 'Angelic Symbols in the Secular Media' or something. I said the picture was persuasive because you looked like you were about to cry."

"I wasn't about to cry."

"The way you were clutching the ball, confronting the camera."

"My mom was yelling at the paparazzi. I was trying to stop her."

"I got an A."

"She was yelling in Spanish and I was embarrassed."

Then, Dallas reentered the Blue Bird.

Levi took a barely perceptible step away from Luz. "Come see me sometime, okay?"

"Okay."

"I'm in the dome."

"I know."

"Come soon."

If she went, she would have to leave Ig, which she had not done since Levi had taken her to the place where Ray's body was interred and which she did not want to do ever again. If she went she would have to ignore that instinct and ask Dallas to watch Ig. She would have to tell Dallas where she was going, which she did not want to do though she did not know why, exactly. If she went she would have to go after bonfire, when Ig was sleeping, but before Levi went out dowsing. If she went she would have to lie to Dallas, to say, I think I'll take a walk, and she would have to endure Dallas's mysterious disappointment anyway. If she went she could take Sacajawea and John Muir, to remind her who she was. If she went without them she might find out. If she went she would go as Baby Dunn, little changeling. If she went she would know what he knew, and would thereafter be a better listener, would perhaps look inward with his same sureness and serenity. If she went she would run her hands along the patchwork cloth of his geodesic dome, a place she had walked by many times before she realized the others did not walk by it, it was a place circumvented out of deference, a place whose entrance and exit were not immediately evident. If she went she would pause to look up at the night sky and see it blighted by stars, their glow radiating from the dune, their moon. If she went she would have to call out to him in the dunelight, but if she went it could not be a call but a whisper, which would be stolen by the wind. If she went she would whisper again, pressing her hands into the canvas coverings, run them along the spines of triangles upon which the whole structure rested. If she went she would feel something pressing back, like a child stretching in the womb, and she would recoil and feel for Ig where the baby did not hang from her. If she went she would marshal her courage and reach for that which was reaching for her. If she went she would feel a hand through the canvas, and pause there knowing it was his. If she went a geometry of darkness would open in the blankets and his voice, bodiless, soft as sand, would beckon her inside. If she went she would smell sleep must and dried sage. If she went they would stand together beneath the patchwork canopy of blankets. If she went there would be a small fire pit dug at the center, with faint coals like flotsam swaying in the bottom and all the colors of the blankets would be above them and feathers would be hanging from the rafters, feathers and little bones and bound clusters of herbs and pecks of a mottled golden root. If she went he would ask her to sit. If she went he would offer her some root to chew, and if she went she would take it and they would sit side by side on his bed, a Red Cross cot, and he would teach her how to knead the root in her molars, releasing its fusty juice, to swish the juice around in her mouth before sending it into a ration cola spittoon. If she went she would get used to the root's fustiness and it would give way to an earthy oolong flavor and the softest sensation of floating. If she went he would say, I don't use that word, *dowser.* It's a gift I have. You've probably heard that the summit is permafrost year-round? It's not. There's a cycle of thaw and freeze, but it's incredibly rapid. The rivers appear for a half an hour, often less. A pattern more felt than known is the best I can describe it. There are trends conventional methodology cannot reveal. Processes we have yet to catalog within our cosmology. Undocumented happenings beget themselves, if you follow me. Imagine a super-speed evolutionary time warp. It's not unprecedented. You've heard of Calico? The Early Man site? Do you know what they found there? If she went he would list them — camel, horse, mammoth, saber-tooth cat, dire wolf, short-faced bear, coyote, flamingo, pelican, eagle, swan, goose, mallard duck, ruddy duck, canvasback duck, double-crested cormorant, grebe, crane, seagull, stork — and she would see each hovering above the coals. If she went he would say, Those are just the fossils. The Amargosa has been categorized as a wasteland. Inhospitable, they say, as though nature should offer you a cup of tea and a snack. Barren. Bleak. Empty — my favorite. Nearly every species that once inhabited the Mojave Desert has purportedly been erased from this area. It has been described as the deadest place on the planet. But these so-called surveys have been conducted over a mere fraction of the dune sea. The University of Michigan surveyed two percent, BLM only one. The Fish and Game study, the most widely cited paper on the Amargosa — the one that named it the Amargosa — looked at point-oh-oh-one percent of the total area. Studies have been conducted over shockingly short periods of time — a week, ten days. They don't like to get dust in their eyes. The Harvard study spent more time describing the team's dry skin than biodiversity. No serious rigorous survey of the flora and fauna of the Amargosa Dune Sea exists.

"But there is life here. That's what I'm trying to tell you. There is so much life."

If she went she would leave with another book.

■ ■ ■ ■

NEO-FAUNA OF THE AMARGOSA DUNE SEA: A PRIMER

BY LEVI ZABRISKIE

■ ■ ■ ■

BLUE CHUPACABRA

This hairless relative of the coyote is characterized by its bluish-gray skin. Pups are born covered in vibrant turquoise fuzz, which they quickly shed at weaning. Adults gather in a troubling to hunt.
Family: *Canidae.*

BURROWING DWARF OWL

The only known species of social owl, Burrowing Dwarf Owls live in parliaments of four to six. Diurnal rather than nocturnal, they spend twenty-two hours per day in micro-hibernation below ground. Classified as a micro-owl, the largest Burrowing Dwarf specimen to date measured 9 cm, about the size of an adult's palm.
Family: *Strigidae.*

CARNIVOROUS PLANTS
(Appendix A)
The lack of conventional nutrients in the soil at the dune sea has forced several plant species to become carnivorous. Methods of capture include pitcher structure with highly acidic pools, jaw structures, strangling tentacles and poison webbery. Prey include gnats, moths, Scorpion Bees, micro-owls, and Albino Hummingbirds.
See also: Wandering Joshua.

COLOSSUS VINEGAROON
Very similar to the Heirloom Vinegaroon (*Thelyphonus doriae hosei*), relative of the scorpion, whose venom will cause its victim to taste only vinegar. Principle difference is the Colossus Vinegaroon can grow as large as a dachshund.
Family: *Thelyphonidae.*

DUMBO JACKRABBIT
Easily identifiable by its enormous ears, which grow four to five times larger than the rabbit's body and serve as a cooling system in the extreme heat of the dune sea. Unlike its herbivore relatives, the Dumbo Jackrabbit is an insectivore.
Family: *Leporidae.*

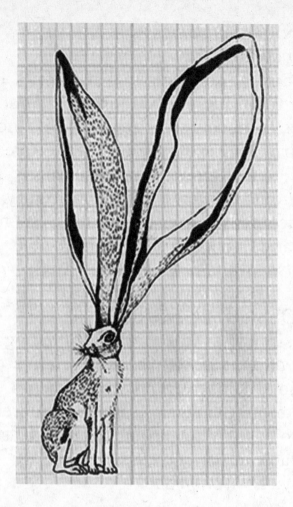

GRAVEDIGGER ANT

The predation strategy of this ant species is its burrow, a steep-sided funnel constructed in the troughs of dunes. The burrow is dug at an angle that causes prey — Land Eels, Colossus Vinegaroons, Jelly Scorpions and Woolly Chuckwallas — to perceive it as a safe trough until they are inside. The ant uses its front pincers to "fluff" the sand on

the sides of its burrow, so that efforts to dig out result in collapse, entombing the prey and preserving it for the ant's return.
Family: *Myrmeleontidae*.

GREATEST ROADRUNNER
Descended from the greater roadrunner, the Greatest Roadrunner can reach speeds of up to 70 miles per hour for sustained distances, making it the fastest creature on land. Its tremendous speed is likely a result not of predation — as in the ostrich — but of the enormous distances it travels between its feeding grounds at sand reefs.
Family: *Cuculidae*.

HUMMINGBIRD, ALBINO
A symbiote of the Blue Chupacabra, the Albino Hummingbird harvests the gnats that gather in the chupacabra's mucus glands — eyes, ears, nostrils and sphincter. As was the case in the Arctic, albinism is an evolutionary advantage on the Amargosa Dune Sea, for purposes of camouflage.
Family: *Trochilidae*.

INCANDESCENT BAT
This keystone species nests in decomposing yuccas. Their bioluminescent abdomen is thought to be a communication system, perhaps to aid in finding mates at long

distances.
Family: *Lampyridae*.

JELLY SCORPION
Hermaphroditic and translucent, this arthropod likely dissolved its exoskeleton over time, the gummy body being better able to survive sandalanches.
Family: *Thelyphonidae*.

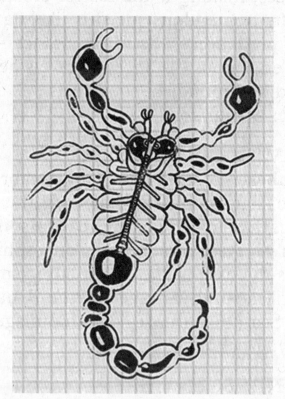

LAND EEL
This augmented asp is completely covered in spines, which both protect it and serve as

camouflage from predators — Stiltwalker Tortoise, Blue Chupacabra — which often mistake the asp for ocotillo. Chief territory is the leeward face (formerly northern Arizona) where ocotillo once flourished.
Family: *Atractaspididae,* possibly *Loxocemidae.*

LILLIPUTIAN RATTLER
Long mistaken for a common earthworm, this is the rattlesnake cousin of the blind threadsnake. Growing to a maximum length of only two inches, its rattle is the size of a shelled sunflower seed.
Family: Unknown.

MOJAVE GHOST CRAB
Like the Jelly Scorpion, the Mojave Ghost Crab has rebuffed its hard carapace — which does not regrow after first molt — with the exception of its superclaws (chelipeds, propodus, semisoft carpus), which less resemble typical crab claws with pinching chelipeds than a trough like that of a backhoe, which it uses to dig down to ephemeral aquifers (the subterranean counterpart to ephemeral rivers) and to the egg caches of Stiltwalker Tortoises and Land Eels, on which they feed.
Family: *Blepharipodidae.*

OLYMPIAN KANGAROO RAT
Another superlative creature of the Amargosa, the Olympian Kangaroo Rat can jump up to fifty feet. A subterranean burrow snatcher, Olympians squat in vacant or abandoned warrens of Burrowing Dwarf Owls and Gravedigger Ants.
Family: *Heteromyidae.*

OUROBOROS RATTLER
Nearly indistinguishable from the Mojave sidewinder, except by its form of locomotion. Rather than sidewinding with its characteristic "J" track, the Ouroboros Rattler inserts its own tail into its mouth and locomotes via axial revolution.
Family: *Elapidae.*

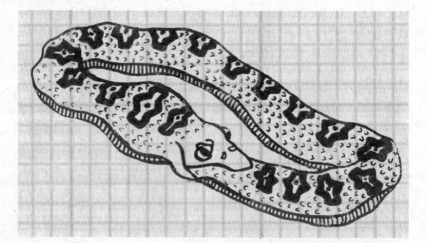

PARASITES *(Appendix B)*

The parasitic population of the Amargosa Dune Sea is among the most resilient in nature. One example is the Common Bowel Worm, which, rather than attaching to intestine or stomach at a single fasten point, replaces the entire digestive tract, beginning at the esophagus and including rumen, omasum, abomasum, cecum, small intestine, large intestine, colon, rectum and anus. The Common Bowel Worm is just one of at least three dozen intestinal parasites of the dune sea that are capable of thriving within mammal, bird, reptile, rodent, insect or human.

RAINBOW CHUCKWALLA

A vegetarian relative of the Komodo dragon, this ectothermic basker is chromatophoric. Colors observed include black, pink, olive, yellow, turquoise, red and white. Notably, the Rainbow Chuckwalla's color camouflage depends not on the environment but on its predators. For example, when encountering a troubling of Blue Chupacabras, the Rainbow Chuckwalla will turn golden yellow, a color the chupacabras cannot distinguish from the white of the dune sea.

Family: *Iguanidae.*

SAND CORAL

Composed primarily of zoanthids, polyps and feathery pinnules, Sand Coral feeds on microorganisms that consume saline and silica, though some larger formations do emit palytoxins, which they use to paralyze and decompose Sand Krill and Jelly Scorpions. Like sea coral, Sand Coral reproduce primarily through asexual gonads and secrete saline silicate underskeletons, which form reefs at particularly salty deposits, such as the Amargosa's north-facing stoss slope, which is exposed to a megaconcentration of saline and fertilizer from California's Central Valley. Vastly delicate, these sand reefs constitute the most diverse ecosystem in a dune and, after ephemeral rivers, sustain the most life.
Class: *Anthozoa.*

SAND KRILL

These shrimp-like creatures are actually members of the worm family. Found in large numbers on Sand Coral reefs, this keystone species not only feeds birds, lizards and rodents at the dune sea, but, most crucially, consumes sand that, upon excretion, provides sustenance for microorganisms.
Family: *Lumbricidae.*

SCORPION BEE

A stinging apiforme, likely crossed from Africanized honeybees and tarantula wasps; its most notable adaptation is its ability to regenerate its stinger after an attack. Extremely aggressive, and known to be fatal.
Family: *Pompilidae.*

STILTWALKER TORTOISE

The Stiltwalker Tortoise (also called the Dalí Tortoise) is named for its extremely long legs and neck, which grow six to ten times longer than those of a desert tortoise. These allow it to walk long distances without the dune baking its torso. The Stiltwalker's adaptive behaviors are astounding. Due to the lack of conventional vegetation at the dune sea, it has become the only known species of tortoise that is a facultative carnivore. Because the Stiltwalker has yet to develop teeth conducive to the shredding of meat, it tucks carrion in its shell until decomposition renders it soft enough to eat. Stiltwalkers have been known to transport carrion for up to thirty days and hundreds of miles, depositing the bones and claws of their prey well beyond those species' known range, a behavior that long baffled this researcher.
Family: *Testudinidae.*

TINE SHREW
A cousin of the pocket mouse, the Tine Shrew makes its home in the tines of cacti, where it suckles its large litters on tine glue. Family: *Soricidae*.

VAMPIRE GRACKLE
It was initially believed that the Vampire Grackle's sharp, proboscis-like beak was adapted to extricate the fruit of cacti. However, the bird — glossy red-black with a white bow tie — has been observed to use its beak, which can measure up to twice the length of its body, to extract the blood of mammals, chiefly the Dumbo Jackrabbit

and the common coyote.
Family: *Icteridae.*

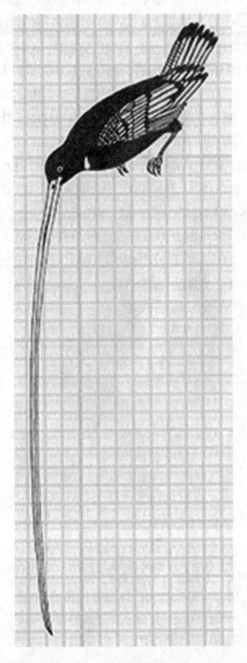

WANDERING JOSHUA

The myth of the wandering tree dates back to the Chemehuevi Indians and likely before. Botanists have widely dismissed the wandering tree as cultural legend. The "wandering" is made possible by the Joshua's unique root system — a horizontal blazing star structure equipped with a double-thick taproot and a meristematic zone capable of sensing moisture. The taproot grows in the direction of water, while allowing roots growing in the opposite direction to atrophy, essentially dragging the plant toward water. Some wanderers can travel up to one hundred yards a day.

Family: *Asparagaceae.*

Luz carried this bestiary everywhere she went, showing no one but Ig. It felt secret, sacred, and she needed to be close to it. Ig was mad for the book, asked for *more* and *more* and *more* — drawn to and focused on Levi's drawings as Luz had never seen her. Together they read and reread the primer in different places — alone in the Blue Bird, in Levi's geodesic dome, in the Holiday Rambler while the girls were working, in secret at bonfire. Luz needed to meet the beasts in different lights, and with different people swirling about, to be sure that they were real.

Though she'd been warned by pretty much everyone against straying from the colony alone, she left Ig with Dallas and walked as far into the Amargosa as she ever had, clutching the primer to her. She walked until all she could see of the colony was the red bustier flapping from the antenna of the

Holiday Rambler and then she stood, listening. On the wind she heard the dune she'd once thought barren flourish and thrive and teem, heard creatures great and small blazing new paths to abundance. The primer turned a world once shriveled into a locus of succor. One day, as she was leaving the colony, Luz watched a crackled blue tarp escape on a gust and soar off into the Amargosa. She watched idly until it disappeared, annoying Camille and Dot, the sisters whose shade was wriggling out of sight. By then the dune sea was inarguably alive. The tarp could be going anywhere. It could settle upon a tomb dug by a devious ant. It could be a queer surface rolled over by a forever snake. It could shade a parliament of miniature owls. The world was that expansive. Now there were tortoises out of Dalí and Technicolor lizards and wandering trees for Ig. Suddenly this was a land of *could*. Flamboyant, vibrant, polychrome and iridescent, there was turquoise, pink, olive, yellow and red. Glossy red-black with a white bow tie. The taste of blood and vinegar. Acid pools and poison webbery, egg-suckers and salt munchers, mucus slurpers and vampires, so many inspired ways to eat and be eaten. And what was vibrancy but being very, very alive? She and

Ig were an example in her mind. It was soon very obvious that the world was made of unseen wonders, which we might call miracles.

And if she did not yet believe in miracles, one morning Levi returned from dowsing early and sent Nico to bed. Instead of going to bed himself he took Luz and Ig out for an expedition. As Luz climbed atop the buzzing solar dune buggy, Levi paused to wrap Ig's bare head with the cloth from his. *Do not wear a man's hat unless you intend to keep him,* Luz recalled.

They did not ascend into the dune but rode away from it, through the land of *could* to a patch of sky pasted on a sandblasted billboard. As they neared, the billboard went from sky to water, water with a wiggly veinery of white light.

Here, they turned onto a gravel road. Eventually a bubble rose from the earth, clay gray, snub-ended. Ig said, "What is?"

It took Luz a moment to find the word. "A . . . building."

Its doors were waffled fiberglass, green, chained closed but curled up from the bottom by some vandal's effort — Levi's, Luz soon realized. He crawled through this space, then reached for Ig. She clung to Luz at first, but went with some urging. Luz crawled in after.

Inside, she had some trouble breathing. The air was viscous, resistant to inhale. Gas, was her morbid thought, an oven. She looked for Ig. But the cement beneath her was relatively cool. Moisture, she remembered. Humidity.

"What do you think?"

The ceiling glowed yellow, and there was movement on it. She looked for its source and saw a shimmering square of jade: fluid, liquid light ribboning. So much color it stung, soft turquoise streaked with evergreen algae and, above, gold. Grassy water plants grew at the cracks of the pool, and a pump burbled somewhere. Impossible.

"Solar," said Levi, pointing to coils of black tubing. A towel hung petrified on the back of a plastic chair. Mounted opposite them was a long rod with a hook at the end. A sign beside a Styrofoam life preserver said, NO LIFEGUARD ON DUTY. A municipal oasis, mineral water once drawn from a spring and now just circulating, was Levi's theory. Indeed, a rime of salt had dried on the tiles ringing the edge: 3″, 5″, 9″, 12″, NO DIVING. A ring of buoys strung across the pool's midpoint, the rope rotted black. Luz could not adjust to the languid green of it all. The parts of her eyes for processing green had perhaps atrophied. Another fragment from Ray's notebook, something about chintzy rods & cones.

Luz closed her eyes. Being in the bubble was like being in an angel's inner ear, echoes of their voices and also its own hum. A seashell sound.

"How did you find this?" she asked eventually.

"Something like this is an earbug for me."

"Like a song?"

"A song the way the deaf hear it. Like music you feel."

"How does it work? Your . . . dowsing."

He laughed. "Have you ever felt the tension between a couple arguing in front of you? Or walked into a building and gotten a bad feeling? Met someone and known, instantly, that they could not be trusted?"

"Of course."

"Voices are loudest when they're negative, but there are others too. Think about the feeling of someone watching you. A lover admiring you from across a party. Or thinking of someone and at that moment they call. Or déjà vu. These energies are all around us, all the time. I happen to have an ear for the organic. But anyone can do it."

"Jimmer says it's a kind of listening."

"Yeah, sure."

"I've never been a very good listener."

Levi shook his head. "That sounds like someone else's idea of you."

Ig squirmed and whinnied. "She loves the water," Luz said.

"I know she does." Levi pulled his shroud over his head, folded it once and laid it on a chair. "Let's take her in."

He waded in, naked, his trunk refracted at the water line. "So nice," he said, then went under. Ig squealed. "It's okay," Luz said. "He's swimming. You want to try?" She undressed Ig and passed her to Levi. At first she was still, then she began to cry, her face going red and warped. She grasped Levi savagely, her feet wanting bottom. She shrieked for Luz — *Mama!* she was all but saying. So Luz immediately pulled her own shroud off and slid in. The gentle mineral water held her — what it must have been like in the womb. Luz wondered, involuntarily, whether the same thought had occurred to her mother as she allowed herself pulled under. Death by drowning was warm, supposedly, but the Pacific had been cold every time Luz plunged in, cold and rough and loud. Luz took Ig from Levi and soothed her. Filth washed from them and floated away in shimmering floes. Ig settled and loosened her grip on Luz's hair, which was disintegrating from clumps to strands again. In the water, they weighed less. Luz was not at all afraid, though she had always feared water.

"Come on," said Levi, treading toward the rope.

"I can't," she said. "I can't swim."

He pulled her deeper.

"Don't," she laughed.

Ig let Luz lay her prone, but ignored her and Levi when they said together, "Kick, kick, kick!" Her pale rump bobbed placid above the surface. The bottom of the pool was slime-slick, and when Luz tripped she took Ig under too. Luz came up with Levi's arms around her waist, with Ig in her arms, laughing. Luz was startled for a moment but laughed too, at Ig's clucking.

When Ig wore herself out laughing, Luz wrapped her in Levi's robe and laid her on one of the plastic loungers with the fossilized straps. Luz retrieved Ig's nini and Levi materialized a thin pad of brute root — "For you," he clarified when she looked confused. Luz took the root and Ig took the nini and soon the child lay content and drowsy, the grown-ups moving soundlessly around the shallow end.

Levi's erection was frank and elegant.

With the child subtracted from the three-some Luz watched him unabashedly, and he her. "Is she asleep?" he whispered after some time.

She was, and as answer Luz backed onto the pool steps, reclined against them and opened her legs, slightly, the water like cool cotton against her. Levi approached, unhurried, and when he finally reached her he hooked one thick arm around her waist and lifted her from the water.

She liked the compression of his weight above her and the cool, ungiving concrete deck below. They moved together in silence, eyes closed, feeling everything. Across the bubble, Ig slept.

After, they washed each other. She felt all the parts of his body she'd been curious about: his broad and hairy shoulders, his plump butt and the scoop of sacrum above it. They clung together, weightless, and whispered to each other.

"I can't stop reading the primer," Luz said. "It's . . . magic."

"It's science."

"I can't believe they've ignored all this."

"Believe it."

"Are they just incompetent?"

"I wish they were."

"What do you mean?"

300

"We're told this is a wasteland because they need it to be a wasteland."

"I don't understand."

On the lounger, Ig sighed, then settled.

"I'm going to be honest with you," said Levi. "I feel I can and should be. Are you prepared for that?"

She was.

"What I'm about to tell you is big. Not the kind of thing you can unknow. I want you to be aware of that before you decide. I don't want to force you into anything."

"You're not."

He nodded. "We're told we don't exist because they need us not to exist. They need to take control of the Amargosa. 'Stop it,' everyone says. 'The unrelenting march.' That slogan. Of course, this is a natural process we're talking about. This is the inevitable result of our own savagery. And we want to stop it because it reminds us of our tremendous neglect and of the violence we've done to this place. Your friend Powell knew that. The Amargosa reaches outward on all sides, toward Phoenix and Vegas, San Diego and Sacramento. To Mexico and Canada and New York and Washington, DC. Not good for national morale. Hard to sleep in the green East with a mountain of sand bearing down on you. Step one: establish that it's barren. Step two: destroy it."

"But they've tried that. They've tried everything."

"Not everything."

He took her back to Albuquerque, where he had taken to sleeping in the lab to avoid the woman whose spurning had slashed the thin membrane restraining her outright hatred of him. There, one night, he heard a new call, behind the voices from the sample cabinet, which were always gossiping, behind the murmurs of the biomass slivers pressed between slides. There was something urgent in the call, something that pulled him deep down into the subterranean bowels of the National Labs, swiping his Zed clearance badge along the way. Something was trapped in that bunker, he knew, something freest of free now caged in a coffin, a tomb, he could feel the confines against him even as he slid silently down the concrete stairs. The call engorged as he approached the bottommost level. The corridor was dark but the call urged him onward. Two MPs sat on stools. One nodded at his badge, the other leaned away from him, unnerved by the wildness in his eyes. The voice, Levi realized, was a Utah voice, a call from home, and he had not heard such a thing since he left. Things were aligning inside him, and yet there was chaos in him too. He had to act. He swiped again, pressed his thumb to an electronic pad for another guard without even realizing it.

In a room lit yellow the call became a chorus, a tabernacle choir stretching out a mournful note. A dozen warheads nested in pens, like livestock. From within the physics packages his ex-lover had designed came that Utah calling, his mineral brothers, his isotopic kinfolk, twenty-eight thousand pounds of Moab uranium-235 teetering on the cusp of fission, descendants of Trinity, Operation Crossroads, Operation Greenhouse, Ivy Mike, Castle Bravo, Operation Argus, Operation Dominic, Operation Storax, Operation Plowshare, all humming to be free.

"A nuclear bomb?" Luz asked.

"Bombs," he said. "And not just any. What they call nonconforming design. I'd seen the plans. I'd listened. That woman, the one I was with, she thought I didn't understand her work. She would leave schematics out to belittle me. 'Careful,' she'd say. 'You'll go cross-eyed.' I let her think she was teaching me something; I asked her stupider and stupider questions until she couldn't help but correct me. That package wasn't designed to detonate underground. Not a burrower, like they said. The design was retro, clunky, humongous. Nothing that would fit in a suitcase. The kind they drop from the sky. The OGs: Fat Man, Little Boy. Operation Glassjaw, they call it."

Strands of rot swayed from the black rope, the serene water suddenly choking with them, but Luz blinked these away. "I don't . . ."

"I didn't believe it either. Despite everything I'd seen. And then they sent me here, to survey. That's what they said. An exhaustive survey to address lingering concerns from local environmental interests. But I knew what they meant: find nothing. They need this to be a dead place so they can kill it."

"But why? Just to make people back East feel better? It doesn't make sense."

He tucked a wet strand of hair behind her ear. "What do you know about nuclear waste?"

"It's poisonous. Lasts forever."

"Pretty much. Unequivocally lethal for longer than we've been upright. Two hundred fifty thousand years, then tapering. To compare, the pyramids aren't even five thousand years old."

"And there's a lot of it."

"Making more every day with the last of

304

our water."

"And they have nowhere to put it," she said.

"Barnwell, Clive, Deaf Smith. All failed." He nodded. "Even Yucca Mountain. About a hundred miles from here. Have you ever been? It's finished now — the tunnels, trains, even the warning monument. Landscape of Thorns, they call it. All on hiatus until the timing's right."

" 'Not in my backyard,' " said Luz.

"Exactly."

"But it has to go somewhere."

Levi nodded again, perhaps a little disappointed. "Industry would be delighted to hear you say that. 'It has to go somewhere' is one of the most expensive, most effective covert jingles of our time. See, it only 'has to go somewhere' if it remains as deadly as it is. To establish a national repository is to promise we will use nuclear power forever and never hold the industry responsible for making its waste safe. It becomes the state's problem. They make a product that is poisonous and they've managed to change the conversation so that we accept that as a given: it will always be poisonous, so 'it has to go somewhere.' The question is where? That's *not* the question — it shouldn't be. It's a motherfucking shell game."

He lowered his voice. "We should be spending money on technology to neutralize the waste — industry should have to fund that research. They should have been doing that from the beginning instead of ditching the shit in storage pools and saying it's everyone's problem. But the research is expensive, slow. Last bit of funding was diverted from neutrality to storage after Fukushima. Believe it or not, nuking the Amargosa is cheaper than holding the industry responsible for its waste. Not to mention infinitely more politically viable."

"So they'll put it here."

"No one's backyard anymore. It's a wasteland, remember. All these years have been an elaborate performance, a theater of due diligence so they can conclude that there are no living things here."

"But then what? How do they stop it?"

"Blast it to glass. That's what the National Lab was really working on. They weren't looking for aquifer. They were building a nuclear fireball."

"Then pick up where they left off at Yucca Mountain?"

"Exactly. The Southwest is a dying limb. This is how they'll amputate."

"When will they do this?"

"The minute we leave."

It was true, Luz knew. She should have been afraid, should have been disturbed, but the water was making its own mournful music and really it was just such a relief to finally *see*, such an effortless swoon. How long had she felt doom coming? Ruin, cataclysm, destiny, etc. It was nice to know how.

But she knew something else too, there in the silky green slickness of life. The white light of the dune sea shone into her heart, and she reached for him again. The air thick with impossible moisture and her chest heaving. Like this she could believe all things, the ghastly and impossible truth, plus the lie she needed badly, needed in order to put one foot in front of the other: the baby would never die.

Though it was the colony that moved across the desert, the reverse felt true. It wasn't long before the swimming pool oasis left them — save for the water they drained from it, and the chairs, ropes, sheets of fiberglass, peels of tin and other salvage-ables they pried from it, and the algae, which Jimmer scraped from the bottom and dried for his concoctions. This was life at the colony: the solid, grounded, unyielding world getting up and walking away. Ravines, canyons, ranges, alluvial fans and gardens of boulders, all folded beneath them. They pilfered from abandoned Indian casinos and deserted truck stops. The sturdy was no longer something to hold on to.

Luz needed Levi more in the face of an-nihilation, though she would not have characterized it that way. She was drawn to him with such simple urgent magnetism that it was impossible to attribute her feelings to trauma, circumstance, or the context of emotional catatonia into which he entered. One seemed to have nothing to do with the other.

She began spending her nights in Levi's herb-garlanded dome, where they shared a long finger of brute root and where he undid lies long knotted within her. She saw for the first time the way we fill our homes with macabre altars to the live things we've murdered — the floral print of the twin mattress in her childhood bedroom, stripped of its sheets when she soiled them; ferns on throw pillows coated in formaldehyde; poppies on petrochemical dinner plates; boxes and bags of bulk pulpstuffs emblazoned with plant imagery the way milk cartons are emblazoned with children. A rock on a window ledge, cut flowers stabbed in a vase, wreath of sprigs nailed to the front door — every house a mausoleum, every house a wax museum.

She saw water fetishes everywhere — fountains and saunas and ski lodges. She saw the National Parks for the tokens they were. Everything she once knew of the natural world was revealed to be propaganda or at best publicity. There were interests everywhere. Meanwhile, all that seemed fantasy she hadn't even the imagination to conjure throbbed in the primer, which she memorized.

The others knew some, Levi said, but not as much as she. Even she could not know everything, not yet. He had a plan, but could not yet tell her what it was. Yet everything was coming together and she would know as soon as he could possibly tell her, and *then* they would act instantly and grandly and finally. Meanwhile, at bonfire his talks sculpted the colony's existence into a conical shape, rising in a taper and pointed, climax somewhere in the very near future. He spoke feverishly of culmination, of plans and meaning and our obligation to answer when called.

Privately Luz needed — she knew this without his saying it — to be beside him every possible minute. What mad ecstasy were these nights up late and early, talking, then touching each other to surrender, then talking some more. Levi had an unhurried way about him, sturdy and mellow, even when the enormity of his words brought him tears. His easy openness drew tears from Luz too, and also words, all words except her three secretmost — *we took her* — which would die within her, one day, and which she hardly recalled now, so lost was she in unloading the injuries of her lonely girlhood in the wasted West. When Levi spoke, all was weightlessness, even when he spoke of the horrors to come. When he left to dowse Luz did nothing much but succumb to her longing, an enjoyable ache.

At the Blue Bird, Dallas watched over Ig without being asked. Luz took the scarf and the Leatherman off the shelf. She should have thrown them away — should have let the wind take the scarf, should have let the dune bury the Leatherman as it had its owner. But instead she forced both into a cushion through a small tear in its seam.

One night after bonfire Dallas said, "To Levi again."

" 'Again'?" Luz said.

"Baby, do what you want. But own it."

"Is that how you really feel?"

"How should I feel, Luz?"

"Maybe you think I shouldn't be moving on. Maybe you think I'm disloyal. Maybe you think I'm a whore."

Dallas laughed. "I don't believe in whores, Luz. My worldview does not accommodate the concept. Your process is your own."

"Maybe you think I'm not good enough for Ig."

"You're her mother. Good enough doesn't enter into it." Dallas lifted Ig. "I'll take her. I'll always take her. But don't make the

311

mistake of thinking I'm doing anything for your sake. There's a whole great goddamn world out there that has nothing to do with you."

Luz should have gone then, should have kissed Ig and whirled away and onward, but some imp inside her whispered *push*. "Levi, then," she said. "You're doing it for Levi."

Dallas said nothing, and the peculiar quality of her silence helped Luz put things together. "Oh Christ. That's why your milk was in."

Dallas pressed Ig to her and turned away. Luz, quieter, asked, "What happened to it?"

Dallas said, "He came out dead."

"I'm sorry."

Dallas waved one hand in the air. "Not meant to be." She was doing her best to believe it. "That's what Levi said. The Amargosa had other plans for us. It curates, he said. Then you showed up."

"I didn't know."

"Seems you're the plan, now. Apparently the Amargosa requests I be your wet nurse."

Luz wanted to go to her, but something about Dallas's posture, the private way she held Ig to her, would not allow it. "I didn't know, Dal."

"Don't call me that. I'm not your pet."

She began to nurse Ig, rubbing one finger along the bridge of the child's nose. The motion always soothed them both.

Then, "He may be a bastard, Luz, but he's all we have. He grasps things we can't. He has an incredible gift. I believe that." She paused in her stroking to gaze upon Luz. "After everything, I do believe that."

Levi continued to make his excursions — he rose while Luz still lay in his cot, dressed, kissed her good-bye and tugged on her earlobe, his reminder to listen. She rose after, to watch Levi and Nico disappear into the dune on the rumbling, shuddering lorry.

At his leaving, Luz returned to the Blue Bird, where Ig and Dallas slept curled side by side as if in a womb. These early mornings, as Luz watched Dallas sleep, she did listen, as Levi implored her, listened for rustling soft chomping life beyond. But she heard nothing, saw instead: Levi with his arms around Dallas, Levi taking Dallas's heavy breasts in his hands or mouth. Nights after bonfire, Levi needed Luz. In the ember light they made love, rowdy and vital, and after he plummeted into sleep she extracted herself and pressed her palm to the dirty arch of his bare right foot, lopsided with its two smallest toes missing. A zone of vulnerability, according to Jimmer, with potential

313

for thought transference. What she wanted to know was whom he dreamt of, and how.

Most times, she dreamed of the day she'd just had. Not dreaming so much as remembering. She wondered if a person could go insane this way.

One morning, as Levi was about to exit the tent, the lorry grumbling outside, a desperate question escaped from Luz where she sat on his cot.

"What happened between you and Dallas?"

Levi turned and let the tent flap fall closed behind him. "Dallas is a dear friend," he said.

"You had a child together."

"We did." He took a root from where it hung on the ceiling. He sat beside her on the cot and cut himself a sliver.

"Tell me, please."

He offered her some root.

She shook it away. "Don't make me beg you."

"What would you like to know?"

She watched the coals, expiring now to ash. "Were you in love with her?"

"We loved each other, yes. But that love existed only between us. It had no greater dimension. It was . . . of a measly scale. The baby's death was a symptom of that. It was

314

an intervention of sorts, a resetting of my path, though I didn't see it at first. Not all doubt is spiritual doubt."

The grumble of the lorry rose, then idled. Nico was waiting.

"Dallas and I buried the child together. We set him on an altar at the mountain. It had been completely still that day, but the moment we placed the body, the Amargosa took him. It lifted that trauma from us. I heard nothing then. I knew the mountain was comforting us, Dallas and me, by its actions, but I couldn't hear anything. I was utterly alone. I could barely make my way back to camp. The mountain was shunning me. I wandered, hoping to hear, trying to reconnect. I went three days without it. Our water supply dwindled. Still, the mountain would not guide me. Such utter, encompassing loneliness. It was the darkest my life has ever been. I considered leaving. Can you imagine? Abandoning everything we have here. Rejecting the mountain and everyone who relies on me. But I was prepared to go. And then I heard the bighorn."

Luz curled into herself, crossed her arms over her ugly knees. "You could have told me. You should have."

"Listen to yourself. Come here."

He pulled at her but she jerked away, saying, "I feel like a fucking idiot."

"Luz," he sighed. "These are the smallest concerns on this Earth. They're too small for you. That's what my relationship with Dallas was like, in the end . . . *earthly*" — as though the word had a foul aftertaste — "I wouldn't even call it a bond. You and I have something larger. More expansive. Or I thought we did."

She loosened her grip on herself, whispered, "We do."

"I believe that. I think of the circumstances that brought you here, all the forces at work to bring you and me together, *here.*" His voice began to wobble. "I was lost without you. I had a gift and no one to give it to. I heard a voice but could not speak back. You and I, we have a voice together. Don't you hear it? Don't you?"

Luz listened. She heard the idle of the lorry and the faint fizz of the coals. She heard Levi, who had begun to cry beside her. She loved it when he cried.

"Don't you?" he asked.

She drifted toward him, the old magnet. She stroked his back. "Yes," she said.

"You do?" His eyes bright. "You do?"

"Yes," she laughed. "I do."

He reached for her. "Can I hold you? Please? I need you."

He took her and they lay down and he held her from behind, both of them trembling. "You belong here," he said. "Right here. Do you know that?"

"Yes," she whispered.

He pressed his mouth to her neck. "Wherever you are I'll be. Do you know that?"

Luz did.

It was around this time that Luz began having proper dreams again. In them, the places beneath the dune sea told their stories.

The binder does not say "mole men." The mole men are a rumor, a legend. So the old, pinkened blind man with the puckered skin and long, translucent, prehensile whiskers we found in the desert near the repository is not a mole man.

The binder, given to us ages ago by a gentleman representing the US Department of Energy, says the nuclear waste repository at Yucca Mountain, just up the road from our tiny gamblers' settlement in the desert, is unmanned. The binder — which we stored until now as directed: on the wall of the county commissioner's office in a glass-faced case with a tiny hammer dangling from it — says the repository is unmanned, that the silent white bullet trains disappearing into the mountain and reappearing out the other side, empty, carry only casks (we read "caskets") of spent fuel rods and pellets and are unloaded by a gleaming robotic arm. The binder has pictures.

The binder, whose protective glass face we have shattered with the tiny hammer, says the stainless steel caskets are unloaded by the robotic arm and transported by a fully automated conveyer system (FACS) deep into the hollow earth, down the trellis of tunnels that took one hundred years to dig, to their storage pods, where they will stay interred for one hundred thousand years. There are no people working inside Yucca Mountain, says the binder. The tunnels were dug by a state-of-the-art tunnel-boring machine (TBM).

We are soothed by the authoritative acronym-loaded binder delivered to us ages ago by the gentleman embodiment of the US Department of Energy and stored in its secure glass-faced case beside the MSDS and the old Terror Alert Color Wheel, for since there are no people who dug the dark tunnels of Yucca Mountain, nor people working as stewards of the nation's nuclear waste deep inside, then it is only a rumor that there is a subterranean population at the Yucca Mountain Nuclear Waste Repository, only local lore that below us, in a town perhaps identical to ours, move once-human creatures whose genes the department tweaked over generations until their skin went translucent, until a scrim of skin grew over their useless eyes, until two thick, cord-like and translucent whiskers sprouted from their faces, sensitive as a catfish's barbels, and their mouths gone a little catfish too, a side effect.

The not–mole man was discovered, sun-singed and unconscious, by a gang of teenagers at the Landscape of Thorns. Regarding the Landscape of Thorns, the binder quotes *Expert Design of an Architecture of Peril to Deter Inadvertent Human Intrusion into the Nuclear Waste Repository at Yucca Mountain* by Magnus S. Geister (Cornell University), Manuel Brink (Sandia National Laboratories), H. S. Traverse (University of Pennsylvania), Linda Gillis (Eastern Research Group, Inc.), Yuki Takashi (University of Washington), and R. C. Tung (Purdue University): "The marker is pan-cultural, pre-linguistic, post-linguistic, ominous and repellent [. . .] It evinces the repository site as a non-place."

The Landscape of Thorns was erected atop Yucca Mountain to frighten our distant and curious descendants on a primal level. It is an assembly of multilingual stone message kiosks and concrete spikes jutting from the mountain, skewering the sky. Our teenagers like to go up there to skateboard, rollerblade, bounce their tiny bicycles off its menacing concrete javelins. We've scolded them against this but we live in a dinky desert town with one paved road; our young people are fiends for concrete.

When they were in elementary school, our young people took field trips to the monument and made rubbings from the message kiosks there. Our children once had the patience for a project like that. Now, they dye their hair inky black without consulting us; they push safety pins through their eyebrows. Our refrigerators are still layered with curled etchings of star charts and the periodic table, of symbols that look like snow angels — triangles within circles — and rubbings of warnings in Old English, ancient Arabic, and something the placards at the kiosks call French. The rubbings say, *This place is a message . . . and part of a system of messages . . . pay attention to it!*

They say, *This place is not a place of honor. No highly esteemed deed is commemorated here. Nothing of value is here. What is here is dangerous and repulsive to us.*

They say, *Sending this message was important to us. We considered ourselves to be a powerful culture.*

Since he is not a mole man, we assume the blind man our teenagers found is a desert wanderer. We come from a long line of desert wanderers, so we intend to treat him well. We set out finding a cool, dark place for him. A gamblers' outpost in the sun-blanched, sand-scraped Mojave — we have many such places. The brothel offered him his own swamp-cooled bungalow, but when he came to he seemed bashful somehow, with his humped posture and pinched nose and the way he stood so politely clacking his pale, brittle claws together. Instead, we looked to the casino, a stucco cube with a gravel parking lot. We put him up in a suite, comped. We enrolled him in the Players Club, with bonus play, express play and multi-play, all comped. We granted him unlimited access to the buffet, where with a bedraggled claw he points to shrimp cocktail, steak and eggs. He tests the doneness of his eggs by probing the yolks with one slow, slick, opalescent barbel.

Despite being a member of the Players Club at the platinum level, the not–mole man finds no joy in playing keno, for though we can see his eyes rolling lax behind the pale vellum of skin, he is blind as an oracle and can take no pleasure from the numbers bouncing around the television. He disdains video poker; his barbels recoil from the slots. When we gave him a bingo dauber he tried to eat it, smeared his lipless catfish gape with a shimmer of teal lipstick. He will throw the bones at the craps table, if you ask him, but only after standing for a long time with the dice cupped solemnly in one hand, running his index claw over their tiny dimples.

Though we suspected as much, the fact that he knows nothing of bingo proves the desert wanderer is no ordinary old man. And though it says nothing of mole men, the binder given to us by the freckled personification of the long arm of the US Department of Energy, which we have retrieved from its shattered glass case, says there may be "contaminants." If a contaminant should enter the community, says the binder, you must quarantine it. Call this number, says the binder. If you cannot quarantine the contaminant, says the binder, kill it.

The danger is in a particular location, say the rubbings.

It increases toward a center . . . the center of danger is here . . . of a particular size and shape, and below us.

Apparently, and according to the binder, we are the first line of defense against a threat that does not exist.

■ ■ ■ ■

Quarantine can be tricky here. Ours is a town where tourists stop on their way somewhere else. Ours is a way station where visitors dock in the dark and then, in the hammering sun of morning, look around them at the burnt husks of muscle cars, at the dented trailers welded together, and say, Who *lives* here?

They move on to the national park, the sin city. We become a story they will tell, the freaks in the desert, the mutants at the mountain, the wasteland. Three times a day the bullet trains spirit into the earth and out again without a sound. Our teenagers ache to go with them, we know. *This place is not a place of honor,* say the rubbings. *No highly esteemed deed is commemorated here. Nothing of value is here. What is here is dangerous and repulsive to us.*

But it is autumn, peak season is sliding away from us, and the red brome is exploding across the alluvial fans. Yucca Mountain is magenta with them, the stalks bowing all around the Landscape of Thorns. And the mole man seems to like it here. The oracle stirs powdered creamer into his coffee with one dignified, prehensile barbel.

Someone wonders, What if he's poisoning us? A good one, because we've long felt hard, lentil-sized nodes beneath our eyes, unshelled walnuts growing in our throats. Our water has tannins of uranium and we have sores that will not heal, dark motes floating in our fields of vision, yellowing sclera, blood in our stool. Our babies are born with webbed fingers and toes, or none.

This message is a warning about danger, says the negative space within our malformed children's manic charcoal scribblings. *The danger is to the body, and it can kill.*

You are in no danger, says the binder.

Also: You are the only thing standing between the rest of the country and radiation poisoning.

The oracle haunts the casino floor, lightly clacking the milky keratin of his claws together. He lurks near the roulette table, listening to the dolly pop along the wheel. Peak season is over and the cocktail waitresses slip outside and cut spears from the aloe plants growing alongside the swimming pool. In the sportsbook, they sit him in a plush maroon chair and glide the slime over his burnt skin.

In the buffet, the mole man gums his flaccid steak with his downturned catfish maw.

The teenagers sit with him, build creamer pyramids, jelly huts, stab gashes into the vinyl seats with butter knives. Sometimes they bring maps. Tenderly they trace the mole man's barbels along the interstate. *Blow this popsicle stand,* they say.

Kill it, says the binder, but there is something of us in the mole man. Bonus play, express play and multi-play are lost on him, and truth be told they are lost on us, too.

The white bullet trains come in and out thrice daily, soundless, only a slight pressing and unpressing of the air. One day the repository will be filled and it will be sealed and it will stay that way for one hundred thousand years, says the binder. One day all the toxic pellets we fear will be stuffed safely inside the mountain. The mountain will be sealed and will remain sealed through flash floods and ceaseless corrosion and the itchy trigger finger of tectonics. The binder says this and we believe it, even though the trains that move through town so silently you cannot hear but only feel them — those beautiful, soundless white bullets — run on the throbbing rods they ferry.

We considered ourselves to be a powerful culture.

■ ■ ■ ■

We have questions the binder cannot answer:

Is a mole man not a man?

How many times did the US Department of Energy say "wasteland" before this became one?

How many times will they chant "unpopulated" before we disappear?

What utterance will emerge from history's longest game of telephone?

Why, of all the rubbings curling on all the refrigerators, all the etchings in all the message kiosks in all the desert repositories of this nation, do none say, *We're sorry?*

The oracle does not speak, and we are glad. We could not bear to hear what he might say.

Instead, we put our ears to the dirt at dawn. We can, maybe, hear a steady rock scrape a mile below. There are someones, somethings, moving through the trellis of tunnels under us, tending the pods of stainless steel caskets, inside the caskets rods, inside the rods pellets throbbing like glow-worm larvae, though we've never seen the glow and never will, promises the binder. We take our iodine tablets. At night, if we lie still, we can feel the silent white bullet trains moving through us.

We have the number to call, but we have long been unable to discern the poisoned from the yet-to-be-poisoned. Peak season is over. Winter is coming to the desert and there are things we want to see: the ground crunchy with frost. The dog's water bowl froze over. The Joshua trees along the highway decorated for Christmas. The red and green garlands winking in the sun, tinsel swaying in the breeze of the bullet train. Soon, the burros will eat the tinsel and for weeks the good-natured BLM boys will spot strands of it glinting in their dung, and we want to be here for that. We want to be here for the one day of snow, when our teenagers run outside in their pajamas to scrape the fine white dusting from the surfaces before it melts. Their flaxen roots grown out now, their eyebrows throbbing and infected, with their webbed fingers they press an entire car's worth into one hard, divine, infinite snowball.

Luz felt the scar before she saw it, a ridge wall she mapped with her tongue. Below, Levi's balls dark and tight as plums, and these too she took into her mouth, individually, adding his must to the taste of brute root in her mouth, wanting to impress him, wanting to please him, wanting him to go limp beneath her, an offering and apology. Hers were the efforts and industries of love, the same that once built glistening golden forts of honeycomb, the same mud and saliva and horsehair and caterpillar silk that once kept nests of swifts and swallows aloft. When Levi said, Stop, she smiled and said, No, wanting to build her monument, to summon their own private flood. But he abruptly jerked her up and atop him, saying without saying, Get to work. She did, hinging at the hips, her joints soon sore, her calves seizing, but pistoning with renewed energy each time he let loose an approving sigh. She was careful to accommodate the curve of him with her motion and her body. He asked her not to stop, and she promised she wouldn't. He encouraged her by circling a finger around her anus, then inserting it inside, a surprise. She became suddenly very attentive. When he slid it out, there was a smell, and also a quiver.

After, she asked about the scar. He told her of an at-home circumcision, his first impossible memory, at the compound where his grandfather was Lord, where his sisters were siphoned off to other trailers when they were ready, which they never were.

Silent, Levi visited that compound for some time. Luz did not know how to bring him back; she wished she'd had a worse childhood so that she would know what to say. When Levi returned, he cut them each a new peel of root and said, "Do you believe in evil?"

"I — I'm not sure."

"I do. Absolutely I do. We need to protect this place, Luz. They are trying to obliterate us. They send trucks in the night. Have you heard them?"

She hadn't, but she was not so powerful a listener as he. "What do we do?"

Levi chewed his root thoughtfully.

She inhaled, excited by the sudden opportunity to be useful. "I have some money," she offered.

He winced.

"I don't even *want* it," she said. "I haven't even *looked* at it." It was true. The hatbox sat in the corner of the Blue Bird, where Levi had first delivered it, an artifact. Inside, what was left of her modeling money, the bulk of it intended for Lonnie's helper in St. George. "I don't have any use for it," she said. "You can have it all. Wouldn't that move things along?"

Levi shook his head, gently.

"Take it," she insisted. That money belonged to another person, a child doll weakling. Baby Dunn, a Mojav quitter. She would be glad to be rid of it.

Levi thanked her, kissed her and thanked her. "But that's just not the paradigm we're working with," he said. "Money . . ." He batted the very notion away. "You'd get more from that money burning it for light." He went on, about her bracing belief, how it nourished him. She chewed her root and watched his beautiful voice comet across the heaven of their dome. She lifted her hand before her face and made patient, shimmering contrails with her fingers. A little disappointed, for she wanted to give him all things there, in their tiny kaleidoscopic universe fixed in the center of the great big benevolent cartwheeling galaxy all around them. There was nothing she wouldn't let go — the freedom of that — this was her thought when he asked for something else.

"Of course if they decide to evac us, really decide, there's no stopping them, nothing even I can do. We will only win, ultimately, if we first conquer the rhetorical sphere. We must tell our story in the language spoken by the rest of the country. We can no longer let them decide whether we are human. You saw it with the Mojavs. They made people into non-people. We must do the reverse. Tell them what kind of a people we are. Prove that we are more human than any of them! It's been done before. We make evac a cleanse, a genocide. Establish ourselves as a chosen people. The Amargosa our Zion. You follow?"

Luz did, though she was too rapt to say so.

"We position our removal not as an injustice — we've failed on that appeal, again and again. The Sierra Club, Save the Mojave, Mojav Rights Org — all peddling injustice porn. Injustice is mundane. No one gives a good goddamn about injustice.

"We need to offer atonement. Deliver

them unambiguous righteousness. We change the scenario, get them off the guilt circuit. We can't drink their guilt. We can't bathe in it. We say, 'It's okay that you fucked half the country, killed rivers, depleted millennia of aquifer, fed arsenic to children and lied about it, forced citizens once again into internment camps, let people die in holding pens. It's okay. It's actually *good* — because look! You created this magical ecosystem. The way the Ukrainians call Chernobyl a national park. You meant to do that, right, America? Well done! Bravo!' "

"Yes," she said. "How?"

He paused. "Baby Dunn's *baby.* Imagine the attention when she surfaces, here in the wasteland, with you, happy — that's the key —"

"What do you mean surfaces?"

"Nico has his devices. Thanks to *you*! You see how it all fits together?"

Luz, slow with root, did not.

"The Christmas Village you found. Your discovery. Some important equipment there, believe it or not. Nico's been tinkering with his electronic stockpile ever since. The cloud and so on — not my area of expertise, but he's confident he can get us access. Hack in at certain crucial junctions. He can get the word out."

"What . . . word?"

"People remember Baby Dunn. They'll see those old headlines — that photo of you playing soccer in the dirt. Do you have that? Never mind, it'll turn up. We take them right back. And then: Ig. The fresh start."

"I —"

"We need you both, and we need it to be big and wholesome and beautiful. Transcendent. Madonna and child."

He saw her hesitancy, perhaps. "Think about it. You of all people were brought here. No one survives out there, but *you* did. *Ig* did. This is Zion, Deseret, the New World's Holy Land. You see? Ig is our baby Moses."

It was brilliant, it would work, and Luz could not agree to it. And yet she already had, in a way, was already swept into the current of his plan. He was the Colorado, raging sculptor. She was not John Wesley Powell but one of his supply barrels, lashed alongside the boat, bobbing.

"Can you see it?" Levi wanted to know.

"Yes," she said, her voice shadows and shapes.

"Yes?" he said.

"Yes, yes, you're right, yes!" She flung the words and watched them burst on the wall. *Yes* went to pieces against the dome, wet

334

and shattersome and dazzling. *Yes* came from her like a column, a beam of *yes* prismed in the room, each *yes* a starburst, a sunbeam fractal tessellation into eternity. Each *yes* a glowing thunderstorm, cool jewels in the deep pit of the earth radiating with positive energy, and though Luz knew each was empty she stuffed their hollow hulls with straw and positivity and stacked these, and with *yes* she kept the bombs at bay.

Beyond this mortar of impossible promises rose a massive, alien mountain range. Though it was the dune that approached the sheer sawtooth mountains, and though the colonists were accustomed to their nomads' vertigo, all at the colony felt the sinister peaks bearing down on them. At first no one spoke this unease, doubt being an unconscionable transgression. Though they knew these mountains were destined ultimately to be dwarfed by the dune sea, they knew too that the craggy range was gargantuan compared to the other mountains the colony had rippled over and through. And those had been clay and soft ash, long-dead volcanoes, while these mountains were of a malevolent shining rock, unyielding razors thrust up from the earth recently, it seemed. Some said they were the Sierras, identified this peak or that as Mount Whitney. Others said no, these were a new, unknown range, without names. Jimmer summarized their collective anxiety. "The dune will have no problem taking those," he said. "But it may take us in the process."

A symptom of some poison at the colony, was Dallas's theory, some infiltrating toxin within. Jimmer conceded this could be the case. He wandered the colony with his smudge stick, deposited agates and crystals in strategic locales. Luz craved a whole cache of them beneath the Blue Bird, for she knew her lies had invited the range.

Luz was and was not Baby Dunn. She had been emancipated from that life, no longer used that name, though it was still hers — Levi had seen the state-issued proof of that, embossed with California's great seal — extinct grizzly beside extinct river, *Eureka!* overhead. Even if Ig could play the role of Baby Dunn's baby without exposing her foul providence, without drawing the Nut or the cops or her horrid people to them, Luz — urgently, desperately, painfully — did not want Ig to be Baby Dunn's baby.

She did not allow herself to ask what Ray would think of her promise and instead her

336

thoughts tramped unfamiliar paths. She found herself longing for Lonnie's coins, his little pilfered notebook, his abstract and outdated prophesying, even sometimes for the man himself, who though repulsive and a poser would at least have a plan. How happy he would be here among the real holdouts, how giddy he'd go to find Luz in such trouble.

Levi refused even to acknowledge the nearing mountains, but that portentous range was always in the corner of Luz's peeled eye nights she sat up nodding, nights Levi spent unfurling the fine points of his plan — the old contacts he would tap, the hordes of media that would descend. He lurched from catalyst to catalyst, groping obsessively in the firelight for the perfect way to set it all in motion. If started exactly right, the movement would create its own energy and feed itself perpetually. Like the dune, Luz did not say. It couldn't come from them, of that Levi was certain. The nation needed to think of the colony as their discovery, its rescue their collective simultaneous atonement and absolution. He kept coming back to a video of the two of them, one they would make. A real mother-daughter moment. Nico apparently had the means for both video and upload, thanks to the Christmas Village haul. A gardening scene, maybe. Or giving Ig a bath.

"You give her lots of baths? She's used to them?"

"Yeah," said Luz, though Dallas had been doing it these days.

"That's perfect, just perfect — you have the water right there, but it's human, domestic, maternal, intimate. There's skin and sound. Heaven lighting. Squalor, but resolve. Some Dorothea Lange shit. And Ig likes the water."

"She loves it."

"Of course she does! Brilliant."

Luz bit her thumbnail. "I don't know, Levi."

"What don't you know? It's perfect."

"What if I can't?"

Levi eyed her, suspicious. "You can — you have to. If you don't, we have nothing," he said. "No recourse. No strategy. All these people here, all the animals, the entire ecosystem. They will blast it all to glass!"

"What about the primer?" she offered. "What if we sent it out places? If people knew about all those creatures, they'd do something. Designate the dune a protected wilderness area."

" 'A protected wilderness area'!" He laughed in her face. "Luz, I've recited the primer to every agency and advocacy group you can imagine. Every journalist and academic. They call it a fantasy, if they say anything at all. No one in the scientific community hears me anymore."

Levi grasped her hands in his and squeezed. "You're all we have. This is why you're here. You must have realized that."

Somehow, Luz did.

Levi became distant after she voiced her doubts, though he assured her he was only under tremendous pressure. The string of insurmountable peaks loomed, and scouts returned from fruitless efforts to find a kind pass-through. Worse, they reported its shape to be not a rigid spine but a bowl, so that on one side swooped the dune sea, their talisman and companion, and on the other loomed the crescent upthrust range, the livable scrub between them ever diminishing.

The colony buzzed with distress, yet Levi declined to soothe them. He was quiet at bonfire, except to invite them to look up at the stars, to remind themselves of their infinite insignificance and the undeniable omnipotence therein. He seemed not to notice the ripple bringing them nearer the stony grip of that impossible range. One night, instead of speaking, he pulled Luz aside and asked her to meet him later at the

Holiday Rambler.

When Luz stepped into the Rambler, the girls offered their cordial, laconic greeting. Levi came in behind her, sending them abuzz. Luz had never seen Levi visit the Rambler, had never seen the girls in this sudden choreography. Someone brought out a platter of brute roots, the largest Luz had ever seen. Levi fed them all, saving Luz for last. He selected a pretty girl called Aza and another, Cass. When they escorted him back, Levi said, "You too, Luz." And Luz went back with them.

She was nervous, a little afraid. She had never seen the back room of the Rambler. It was cleaner than any place she'd seen in a long time. Levi dropped his shroud to the floor and told Luz to do the same. They stood naked, facing each other, and the girls began.

They started at their heads, wiping the dune from Luz's and Levi's brows with wet cloths. The girls circled their eyes, then ears, and scrubbed gently their limp mouths. Luz knew somehow that she was not to take her eyes from Levi and that she was not to speak. The girls went nymphs, quick and diaphanous in her periphery, wiping collarbones and shoulders, backs and chests. They held Luz's breasts from behind and stroked them in circles. Luz reached for Levi then, but one of the girls pushed her hand away. Levi smirked.

Aza wiped Luz's feet, lifting one gently and wiping it, rubbing roughly between her toes and buffing her calluses, then lifting the other. A moist rag went up her thigh, and a little warped cry escaped her. "Relax," whispered Cass, wedging another skewer of root between Luz's clenched teeth. "You'll love it."

When Luz was clean, they laid her on the bed. She looked to Levi but instead of joining her, he watched, amused, as the girls undressed. Aza was a languid creature, a gift. Cass had the hips and tits Luz had always wanted for herself.

Soon, wet clefts found Luz's hands and worked against them. Then Levi took Cass by the hand. She smiled. They were sharing something, perhaps. Levi turned Cass, bent her at the waist, and Luz watched the twin hills of Cass's haunches rise between them. Her chin was propped on Luz's knee now and Luz might have liked to reach down and stroke her hair, but Aza had bent over and urged one soft breast into Luz's mouth.

Levi took two handfuls of Cass. He whispered something and Cass heeded, kissing and licking Luz's clit. It was something Levi never did, and Luz understood this as a gesture of reconciliation, perhaps forgiveness for her misgivings. Aza moved aside and combed her fingers through Luz's knotty hair. Cass lapped at Luz as if she were a sweet. Luz lay her head back and closed her eyes.

"No," Levi said. "Watch."

Luz opened her eyes.

He spread Cass and pressed himself inside her. She moaned into Luz.

He seemed to be saying, *Watch her, Luz. See what loyalty is.*

Levi rocked into Cass, pressing Cass's face hard into Luz. Luz felt the sharp jam of Cass's broad jaw against herself and winced.

"Shh," Aza said. But Levi thrust Cass into Luz again and Luz cried out.

He shared a look with Aza and the girl climbed atop Luz's chest. Aza's black bush was rough against Luz's stomach, then breasts, and though Aza was petite, Luz had to pull hard for air. She looked up at Aza overhead and wanted to be up there, with the air. The girl walked her knees up to Luz's shoulders and pinned them to the bed. She lowered herself. A tangy scent, the taste milder. Luz kept her eyes open, saw only the slope of the girl's belly above her. Luz attempted to lick upward — she was not sure what she was doing — but the girl ground down on her, pressing herself to Luz's jaw and torquing there. Someone laughed. Luz felt Levi through the force of Cass pressed against her own pubis, and in the heaving of the bed. He was everywhere; it was becoming difficult to breathe. She tried to open her mouth for air but Aza ground down hard. Luz wanted to breathe; even more, she wanted to see Levi, to see him pleased with her yielding and acquiescence. But she saw herself as he saw her now — a torso squirming beneath Cass's loyal industry, tiny breasts atop ribs asking for air, two bony legs thrashing now on either side of a better girl. She was embarrassed. She was embarrassed and she was suffocating. I can't breathe, she called out, though no sound was made. She wondered how many such calls for help were up inside each of the girls.

Levi had each in different ways. He showed Luz what they did right, showed her how unguarded they were, showed her what it meant to be truly selfless. This went on for a long time. The girls were very young, Luz thought, and very pretty.

After, the girls rose, wordless and synchronized. Professional. Luz hated them, but did not want them to go. Levi lay across the foot of the bed, glistening. He did not touch her — had not touched her once the entire time.

"I'm sorry —" she began, but he quieted her, gestured for her to lie at the other end of the bed. When he did reach for her, she flinched. He took her ankle and laid her leg across his wet chest. He rubbed his palm against the tender arch of her bare foot. "You're a good girl, Luz," he said finally. "But you're not being honest with me."

"What do you mean?"

"You're blocked. You don't listen."

"I do listen," she said.

"You couldn't hear anything we were saying today. Even the girls couldn't open you up. You are completely closed off."

She tried to laugh. "What are you talking about?"

"I used to be able to open you with my eyes. But you're gone now. Something major is blocking you."

She smiled and tried to pull her foot away, but he held it.

"I won't be lied to," he said.

She wished she weren't naked. Wished for her shroud, her sling, her Ig, but each seemed equally and impossibly far. She wished for Ray, briefly, the easy lank of him sauntering into her mind, then she pushed him out.

Levi dug his palm into her arch. "Tell me about the baby," he said.

She tried to expel Ig from her mind but in came her mustard beads of poop, and rocks, rocks, rocks and, *Please can I have some water?*

"What?" she managed. "I don't know what you're talking about."

"Tell me," he said, tightening his grip on her ankle.

"You're hurting me," she said.

"I'm not *hurting you,*" he spat. "You're hurting me. Do you know what it's like to know the person you love is keeping something from you?" He squeezed her ankle and began to cry.

"There's nothing," said Luz, "I swear." But the Nut was pacing in her brain.

Levi began to scream. "Tell me, Luz! Tell me! Tell me! Tell me! I need you. I need your voice." He yanked her ankle to make her kick him in the face. "Goddamn it, Luz! I love you and you're fucking killing me!"

"Stop!" she yelled. "Please!"

But he struck himself with her again and again. She tried to pull her leg back but he wrenched it and pain burst in her knee. She stopped resisting and he hit himself with her foot in the cheek, the jaw, the ears. She helped. She bashed her calloused heel into his raw ear, his nose and eye socket. He seemed delighted by this, manic and aroused.

"I'll tell you," she said finally, out of breath. "I'll tell you everything."

Luz calmed Levi, smoothed his hair, held his wet, blood-glutted face to her. They shared a nub of root and held each other. "Get out," he called down the hall, and the girls did. "Take your time," he told Luz.

She began: "We took her."

Everything unfurled from there: gopher, raindance and daddy-o. Nut, Lonnie and Rita. Yuccas and Ray. When she was done, Levi thanked her with his body, finally. "I heard you," she said afterward, and he said, "I know you did."

By the time Luz and Levi emerged, the Rambler stood alone at the dune's edge. The colony had rippled away without them and the group had gathered near the Rambler, waiting.

Now, with the colony gathered around, Levi stepped down from the Rambler and turned to take Luz's hand. He had never reached for her in front of the others before. She could have floated down the two iron steps, so unburdened was she by what they'd shared, so airy with affection, but instead she took his hand.

When Luz reached the bottommost step, Levi lifted her by the waist and she wrapped her legs around him. They kissed like newly-weds, long and with their eyes closed. Slowly, the others turned to something at their backs.

Luz was euphoric, repaired, blissfully oblivious to their movement and to the movement high on the white slope of the Amargosa. She and Levi went on kissing. Whispers rippled through the colony: See there, a clot of blue, growing, descending, marching. It approached, and the crowd was silent. Luz opened her eyes, still grasping Levi with her entire body, and there, in the space of the opened crowd, wearing a brittle blue tarp around his shoulders, the starlet's birkin, and a giant Stetson, stood Ray, her Ray.

■ ■ ■ ■

BOOK THREE

■ ■ ■ ■

Heaven knows we need never be ashamed of our tears, for they are rain upon the blinding dust of earth, overlaying our hard hearts.

Charles Dickens

Rage fueled Ray through his first day of flight, tuna cans tinking in the starlet's buttery satchel. Luz had all these rooms inside her — library, well-stocked pantry, smoky bordello, circus ring. All these wondrous rooms and yet she sat in the one that was blank, with nails poking from the plaster where portraits once hung. It had been his task to take her hand and walk her, each day, to a different room. Today the rumpus room, today the greenhouse, today the heated indoor swimming pool! Sometimes the journey took the entire day; sometimes they never got there. Sometimes he deposited her on the velvet ottoman in the solarium, certain beyond all doubt that this time she would stay. But she was never where he left her. Without him she would return to the bare plaster walls, or, worse, wander off to the root cellar, the spidery shed, the asylum. The inevitable symmetry: all those

351

rooms had once thrilled him, especially those, but now he was done exploring.

He marched onward, keeping the dune at his back, but feeling the need to keep turning to look at it, lest it creep up on him like the ghosts in a retro video game he'd binged on as a boy. The starlet's scarf did its best to keep him breathing. The satchel's lining was soft — satin, or silk even — and he stroked a hole in one pocket just to feel something besides sand dragging across his skin. Occasionally the sun stopped in the sky. That was worrisome.

He transferred the leather satchel from one shoulder to the other, his embarrassment at sporting it the first sign his rage was waning.

I'll be right back, tinked the tuna. *I'll be right back,* whistled the wind across the lip of his open jug.

"I always wanted to come back," Ray said aloud, to see if it was true. "I walked so far I thought I'd make a circle and come back to you."

Later, stabbing at the can of tuna with the bottle opener tool on his Leatherman, working a lip open with its wire cutters, "There was a largeness on top of me, there always was. You lifted it, Luz, but also brought it right back down. Then Ig. Lifted, then right back down. I never wanted to leave her, or you. But it felt good to do it."

I'll be right back. He knew it was a lie — he had never, in all his life, been right back. But what he could not discern was how far the lie extended. Did he intend to come back at all? Yes, surely. But the more he walked, the better he felt, every step if not a good decision then at least his own, so that by the time the sulfur pools disappeared behind him the scarf had lifted closer to his eyes, which must have meant he was smiling.

It would not be so bad to die, went a story he'd told before. No, he would not be returning to that overseas desert in his mind. Instead, he stayed stateside, recalled the hollow solitary yuccas, papier-mâché and dry filament, and the time he and Lonnie broke into a sound stage in Culver City and sledgehammered the foamcore streets of New York, a city neither of them had visited nor ever cared to. He missed Lonnie. He missed the courtyard compound and the first bed he and Luz had shared. How brave she'd been then, leaving her evac ship in the sand, looking right at him as they fucked. He missed Luz then, horribly, and almost turned around. But there was the gully they'd forded, the bone-dry threshold whispering, *Onward.*

Everything was a little better in retreat. From the other side of the gully it seemed possible to walk to the highway, to walk back to Santa Monica, to walk up to Point Dume and drop his satchel in the sand and tap a skinny girl on her shoulder. Approached from the rear everything was mirror image, the bad omens good ones, the impossible possible, the situation improving rather than going straight to shit. The nasty-smelling peppermints went back into their wrappers. Fingers of water stretched back into aqueducts. Lies were truths. Luz got back into his bed and never got out.

Sometimes optimism joined him on his walk. He would find someone, or someone him. Red Cross had to come through here. Evac lorries. Ration shipments. Water trucks. Even better, they would find Luz and Ig without him and send them somewhere moist, the mossy inlet Luz talked about, the marshes and the pines. He would find them there, on a blanket in a meadow slurping smiles of watermelon.

Sometimes gloom stepped in stride beside him. At his back the dune sea was Fort Leavenworth, growing, gaining on him. At some point he noticed he was marching. He'd always been good at that. But then the drills had made it seem so easy. Forward march. About-face. Forward march. As if going back was a kind of going forward, as open and free and boundless, all clear skies and plains. But going back was complicated. Maybe impossible. For one, there was the question of go back where? He might march back to Point Dume or San Diego, could continue to the starlet's, to Lonnie's, to the breakers or the brig. A sea sound took up in his ears and became cicadas dripping from the trees, the carapaces he was forbidden to touch but did.

To look back was to join hands with ghosts, to build himself a house of past frailties and failures and all the unending ways in which he was a disappointment. Ray's house of the past had a matching mailbox out front, and its white lettering read HOLLIS, GREENCASTLE, INDIANA. Here was the corn and here was the creek, here were tornados of gnats funneling over a baseball field. In the neighborhood where he grew up there were barbecues with half-used tins of lighter fluid beside them, folding plastic lawn furniture in every backyard except his. Here was citronella and cut grass and thunderstorms like plush black curtains falling closed overhead. Here were the train tracks and here were the blackberries he was to rinse before eating but didn't. Here were tire forts and bottle rockets and the child-proofing strip busted off a lighter. Here was the Leatherman, found in the otherwise empty drawer of a workbench, surely his father's. Here were peeled, sharpened sticks and the back of a bus seat slashed and an adult who kept saying *vandal* though he was not a vandal — he was a good boy, class monitor.

But here was the Leatherman and here was the seat and hadn't he slashed it? If he was not a vandal then what of that? There were the girls in his class, sharpening Crayola crayons and, later, examining the tips of their hair. Here was the old quarry filled for swimming, the surface of the water rainbowed with suntan oil, here was the floating platform from which he dove deep enough to scare himself, deep enough for the green, sun-warmed water to turn black and arctic. Here was the metal siding and the cloth awnings and the sprinklers and the wide scratchy sidewalk and here was the family room with the piano he'd never seen anyone play. Here, the way other houses had boxes of tissues or Bibles in every room, were boxes of rubber gloves, blue for cleaning, purple for Lucy.

Poor Lucy, his mother never let him say.

In Lucy's room his sister lolled on rubber sheets, a puddle of a person, a body without a brain, and beside her a pylon of monitors where a nightstand might have been. Here were the cleaners who came in on Mondays and Thursdays, a young husband and wife, and here were the pennies his mother had hidden in the corners — behind the dresser, balanced atop the baseboards — to test them, now in a shiny stack on the kitchen island. And here in the window was the prism, a teardrop of glass hanging from fishing line, spraying rainbows across the linoleum floor in the late afternoon. Once, when his aunt was visiting, she and his mother played old music and drank chardonnay in the sitting room and his mother said, What I'm most afraid of is that she can't tell the difference between dreams and reality and she'll have a nightmare and think it was me doing it to her. His sister Lucy stopped breathing every Wednesday night, when Ray went to Scouts and his mother taught him all the ways to say *Come home.*

Fear fueled him through the second day, fear doubled by strange sounds he'd heard in the night and by drinking down close to the last of his water. He spent the second night where he stopped, and he stopped when a massive sinkhole came into view and he hadn't the will to circumnavigate it. He used the satchel as a pillow, untied the scarf from his neck and wrapped it around his eyes to block the audacious moonlight emanating from the dune sea. With his eyes closed he still rocked from side to side, phantom footsteps, and little lightnings of lactic acid fired in his spent legs. He tried to sleep, one hand in his pocket, curled around the Leatherman.

For some time, Ray did not know who was older, him or Lucy. He did not remember a time without Lucy, and so he assumed she'd been there when he arrived, assumed himself the baby and the repair. Lucy's birthdays had no cake and so no wax number atop to correct him, no balloons or streamers, as these were contaminants. It was only when Aunt Breanna was visiting for his father's wake — Ray would have been seven then — that his mother had caught a glimpse of him peeking in on them, summoned him to her, hugged him, her breath boozy, and said, "At least you had us to yourself for a while, sweet boy."

According to Lonnie, this explained a lot: because of his sister's disability and then his father's death, the household instilled no sense of hierarchy via birth order, meaning that Ray's environment had failed to indoctrinate him in the ways of subjugation, making him essentially impervious to hegemony. He had no impulse to dominate, nor had he developed a tolerance for domination. Lonnie had gone to an all-boys boarding school in New Hampshire, where he became an expert in hegemony and domination. Plus, he'd read his stepmother's books about birth order and sun signs. According to Lonnie, the lack of a sense of birth order and his father's early death had made Ray's childhood a distinctly mortal one — the bubble of immortality that insulates most toddlers popped before it could incubate Ray's ego for very long. All this in Taurus ascending made Ray one of a very few capable of genuine altruism.

(*Wow*, Luz had said. *That sounds so much better than* martyr complex.)

Anyway, Ray was special, was Lonnie's idea, which was nice because as a kid Ray had felt mostly ignored. Underfoot, his mother always said, urging him out the sliding glass door with her elbows, so as not to contaminate her purple-gloved hands. Ray did not remember his father, not even his dying, though he did have a cluster of inexplicably rich friends in his memories — they had docks on the river and TVs in their rooms and one had a go-cart with a track wriggling through the woods — friends he never saw again, so maybe he'd been stowed with their parents while his father deteriorated.

It wasn't as if Ray's mother refused to talk about his father. She answered anything Ray asked, but he hardly asked because it seemed there were important questions, right questions, some revelation that might be set free within him if only he could find the words. He couldn't, and that was frustrating, and so he stopped trying. His mother told stories about his father, and so did her two sisters when they came to visit from the East Coast, but they were always the same stories: His father had once fished a grape out of Ray's mouth that had been choking him. His father had built the deck out back but didn't seal it right, so it was warpy. As a boy, his father broke his arm climbing onto a horse named Gidget. It was as if each of them, Ray's mother and his two aunts, had been allotted a story or two about the man, six stories max. They asked whether Ray remembered the trip to Hocking Hills, or Turkey Run, or Nine Lakes. Sometimes he said he did; sometimes he told the truth.

He did remember that after his father

died, his mother had given away all his father's things. Someone came and took them, even the mattress where he'd died, and as a boy Ray could see why that had seemed like a good idea. But he wondered often now what he might have had of his father's, if he had something besides the Leatherman.

A waterfall of too-wide ties cascading from a wire hanger.

A wooden cigar box with earplugs inside.

Dog tags.

Maybe the piano had been his father's. Maybe his sheet music was still in the bench, a favorite tune tattered.

He wondered what kind of a man he might have become with those possessions.

It occurred to him, trying for sleep near this hole in the earth, that if he died out here Ig would have none of his things to hold on to. Ray wondered: would Ig wonder about him? And if she did, would she wonder about her father or the man who took her?

In his dreams he was still walking.

The wind woke him. He sat up and the night was dense with darkness, somehow. Maybe the moon had gone down? He flailed in the dark a moment, the wind wail getting

361

louder, before shoving the scarf up from his eyes. The wail was behind him, somehow, and he turned to see dune light, all ablaze and bearing down on him. He sprang to his feet too fast, and his head went instantly aswirl. He blinked, and the light honed itself, a light within the dune light, then two. Headlights, then, and the wail not the wind but some bizarre engine he had never heard before.

"Here!" he called, making Xs with his arms overhead.

The headlights came right at him, and he shouted with joy. The vehicle bore down on him, not slowing. "Here!" he called again, afraid they would mow him down in the dark. More lights throbbed to life then, doubling the spotlight on him. Surely they saw him. Still, the truck came at him full speed, shrieking its banshee shriek. Ray waited, near-blind. He heard whoops, and the vehicle roared past him, so close he could smell its oil burning. It must have been a lorry or a jeep, because when it passed he could make out the silhouettes of roll bars, KC lights and massive tires.

In the distance, the vehicle slowed to an idle. Ray waited. Deep murmurs came to him across the desert, as though the ground was opening up beneath him. Then laughter.

This was no rescue vehicle.

Ray groped for the Leatherman in his pocket and pulled it out, struggling to extract one of the small blades. He held the dinky tool in front of him, saw it quaking in the moonlight. He steadied himself and stooped to grab the satchel. Ray begged his eyes to adjust, trying to make out whether there was dry pan in front of him or the sinkhole's chasm.

When the vehicle turned, so did Ray. He dropped the ridiculous pocketknife and ran. The whoops and cackles from the jeep suggested this decision was an entertaining one. He fled, or did the best approximation his ravaged legs could manage. The jeep roared at his heels, but did not overtake him. Ray pressed the ground away as best he could, lurching over the pan in front of him. The jeep hung back, then lunged up at him, then receded again. They were playing with him. Then, whoever they were roared up alongside him, the huge tires popping rocks up all around. Another whoop, the engine's unreal screech, and something came down hard on his head.

Ray woke at dawn in the shadows of two men. His head was three times its normal size, or felt like it. He looked immediately

to their truck, a Japanese hybrid deal somehow lower than when it had chased him,
big regal decal on its door: BLM. No roll
bars, no KC lights, lower and seemingly
miniaturized. And why had they waited until
sunup to collect him? Unless this was not
the truck that had chased him.

The rangers gave him water, though he
still had a little bit in his jug. One of them
said, to no one in particular, "Most individuals who succumb to dehydration still have
water on their person."

"My girl and my child are two days' walk
back that way," Ray said.

They only nodded. One ranger removed
the blood-stained scarf from Ray's head and
handed it to him. "Got a gnarly gash here,"
he said, unzipping a fanny pack and fishing
out ointment and a bandage. The other
searched the satchel. "Do you have a
weapon in here or on your person?"

"No sir," said Ray, and the ranger returned
the satchel. He instructed Ray to get in the
truck bed. Ray did. The truck had no roll
bars or KC lights, but it did have a dozen
heavy metal rings installed in its bed, six
down one side, six down the other, for
shackles, Ray realized. Also two huge barrels of fuel. The truck lurched to life; its
engine sound was any other engine sound.

These were not the people who had chased him.

The truck turned and sped away from the dune sea.

Ray pounded on the window. "Wrong way," he shouted, pointing. "You're going the wrong way!" He pounded harder on the window, gestured maniacally. "Go back!" he screamed. "Go back, go back, go back!" He tried to pry the window open, but it was sealed and reinforced with wire mesh. He shouted and shouted. The truck vaulted over the desert, unresponsive except to throw Ray to his ass.

He watched the plume of dust erupt behind the truck, an earthen miasma between him and Luz and Ig. His head felt humongous. Certainly it was filling with some nasty fluids. He reached up to touch his wound but found instead the bandage, plasticky and puffy. The sun was roasting his dome, but when he tried to wrap the scarf around his head, the wind took it and sent the silk snaking off into the sky.

A grim thought came to him then.

He glanced at the cabin and, seeing only the unmoving backsides of two crew cuts, reached into the satchel. He'd stowed his driver's license in the pocket meant for the starlet's cell phone, which he found empty now. The rangers must have taken it. So they knew who he was. If they did, it would be only so long before that game of institutional connect-the-dots drew a picture of a court-martial. The rings rattled in the bed. But why hadn't they shackled him? Nothing made sense.

He searched the satchel again, groped in the cell phone pocket, discovering a rip in the deepest corner of its silky lining. With two fingers he mined the hole, probing desperately until he came up with what he wanted. Checking again whether the rangers watched him, he did what he should have done a long time ago. He rested his arm on the hot rim of the truck bed and with one effortless and almost imperceptible twitch flicked *Raymond Xavier Hollis, 6ft. 2in. 150 lbs, hair: brn, eyes: blue, organ donor, 623 Windy Lawn Lane, Greencastle, Indiana* into the truck's billowing wake.

The truck hauled ass for a very long time. Ray guessed they were going northeast, though the dune sea seemed at times both behind and ahead of them so he could not be sure. The ground went from white to blush to rust and back again. The hills were sapped tan, then chalky green with veins of aqua, then they were lavender mountains with streaks of saffron and marigold, brown,

brown and brown. Ray curled in the stingy shade of the barrels and nodded off, waking when the truck moaned into low gear. They were going up now, crawling high on the haunch of an alluvial fan. Canyon walls rose on either side of them, banded and dry, and the truck lurched steadily up the gully. Soon, it turned and climbed up and into a scooped-out space where the rocks were iron-colored and ore-stripped. The truck summited, then swayed down a sandy road. A padded quiet overtook them, accompanied by a low, smooth whirring. The plume of dust dissipated. It took Ray some minutes to realize that asphalt was beneath them.

He managed to stand again, and turn. Ahead was a bleak, nude mound crowned by crosses. At its foot, settled into the rock, was a colonial mirage: gleaming red Spanish tile roof, smooth pink adobe walls wrapped with wrought-iron balconies and studded with the nubs of roof beams, a bell tower capped by a quivering weathervane, its mustang bounding windward, everywhere archways. In the foreground was a gate of black metal and wood flanked by a medieval turret of pink stone. The truck paused at the turret's narrow window, the driver said, "Medical," and from behind a screen of chicken wire a hairy arm waved them through.

The truck circled around the castle. In its courtyard squatted a compound of blue-gray trailers. They passed these and descended along a wide, recessed causeway walled with Moorish tilework. What was once a moat, Ray realized. The truck stopped again at another gate, red rusted swords stabbed into the ground, cranked out now by some invisible mechanism to allow them into the castle fort.

Ray received medical attention in the cathedral ballroom where his was the only bed occupied. He spent his first several hours pleading for a search party, screaming after Luz and Ig, depicting in frantic detail the road, the path, the gully, the sulfur pools and the Melon. "Not our jurisdiction," one of the guards said, though another said, "We're on it, partner," before he shackled Ray to his bed — a precaution, he said.

Ray spent most of the time thereafter on his back, counting the ballroom's ornately scalloped rib beams overhead. From the twentieth hung a punched tin chandelier, retrofitted with sockets and flame-shaped bulbs. He continued to ask after his family, as he'd begun to call them, and the staff assured him it was being taken care of. The next day, they asked him if he could walk and when he said yes he was led down two spiral staircases — the first lustrous blond wood, the second stone. Gates of latticed iron clanked behind them, summoning high school Poe — crypts and catacombs. The stone walls slouched, tunnels narrowed then turned white, and it got, somehow, very very cool.

Before it became another venue of the evac clusterfuck, the place called Limbo Mine had offered talc for pulping the world's paper, for fire-retarding her plastics, stiffening her ceramics, matting her house paint, drying the palms of her nervy athletes, powdering the clammy bottoms of her babies. The place called Limbo Mine was in fact not one mine but a daisy chain of smaller mines — Colfax Mine, Jericho, Buena Vista, Hazen Pit, Coyote Springs, Lone Pine Pit, Dot's Ledge, Hole in the Ground, though no one knew these names anymore. The individual mines had been bored out, linked together in a three-hundred-mile maze and hastily retrofitted for security by the Army Corps of Engineers, who then ingeniously joined them to the labyrinth of tunnels beneath Clay Castle, William Randolph Hearst's uncompleted winter villa hidden high on the clay preamble to the eastern Sierras, and transformed into Impermanent Retention Facility Nine, the place called Limbo Mine.

Their courses having been expertly schemed by prospectors long dead, the tunnels in Limbo Mine ached to give up their talc, so that the ground beneath the detainees' feet was green-white and silky soft enough to gouge with a fingernail, puffs rising underfoot to bleach their bottom halves, giving each the appearance of an apparition disappearing. Overhead, ventilation shafts had been garlanded from crimped iron buttresses, and from the buttresses hung lanterns illuminated by industrial glow sticks, letting off a pale jade radiance. Despite the paper masks provided them, detainees and guards alike hacked up warm chartreuse phlegm balls.

It was here that Ray was deposited when he was well enough to walk, when he gave them a fake name and said he was trying to get to family in Wisconsin. They took him underground, via Poe stairs and bored-out tunnels and freight elevators and a tiny train, hundreds of green-glowing eyes above paper masks peering at him along the way. They deposited him finally in a cool-walled cell. Processing, they called it, a holding facility until they could locate his sponsors, which they never would because the aunt and uncle whose names he'd given did not exist in Milwaukee nor anywhere else.

Down in Limbo Mine, mostly Spanish softly echoed through the chalky caverns. Ray recalled one of Lonnie's conspiracy theories: busloads of Mojavs arriving in the evac camps whiter than when they'd set out — immigrants and anyone who looked like an immigrant siphoned off before crossing certain state lines, the illegals deported and the legals held until their papers expired, or until nativist legislation could make them illegal. When Amnesty International confirmed the evac camps contained "thirty-one percent fewer people of Mexican and Central American descent than the population of pre-evacuation California," the governor's office issued a statement. A simple explanation, the press secretary said, migrant farm workers went home when drought hit, a victimless ebb in a lagging job market, simple depression arithmetic. Ray saw now how many had in fact been deposited here, in Limbo Mine, and in its innumerable sibling facilities. *Los detenidos fantasmas* — the ghost detainees.

Ray learned there was a women's ward, and though he could never make his way to it, he spent meals and workouts describing Luz and Ig to anyone who would listen. "She's skinny and brown, but doesn't speak Spanish," he said, as a means of distinction, "and the baby is very blond." This often got a laugh.

In the mess cavern, detainees were served the ration colas and crackers Ray was accustomed to, but also a cold porridge he was not. The porridge was concocted to supply all the water and nutrients one needed, apparently with minimal waste. "Astronauts eat it," said Ray's cellmate, Sal, though this perfect food of astronauts looked a lot like creamed corn from a can and produced, in Ray's case at least, considerable waste.

Sal was young and undeniably stupid, though his stupidity was of the rare variety that provoked envy in the more intelligent, rather than contempt, for it would surely leave the boy content for all his days. Sal, a baby-faced homebody who wore a rolled felt cowboy hat and seemed to mean it, had had the cell to himself for some time. Their bunks were anchored into the soft wall, and above each Sal had carved little crannies into the soapstone. He'd also sculpted a pedestal for his chamber pot, of which he generously offered Ray the use, with a magnanimity at first lost on Ray but soon found, thanks to the elucidation provided by the space-age corn porridge. On the wall opposite their bunks Sal had carved an entertainment center where he kept a crank-powered television he'd been given for good behavior, and a collection of curios also carved from talc. Talc was a bitch medium, Sal said, as delicate as it was beautiful. Like a gorgeous woman. Sal's specialty was chess sets, and one of the first questions he asked was whether Ray knew how to play. Ray didn't. "Me neither," Sal admitted, and indeed closer examination of the shelves would reveal that what he called chess sets were simply talc statues of the entire casts of popular television shows like *The Blobs* and *Star Cruiser* and *The Tabernacle Choir Sing-Along.* "I intend to sell these as souvenirs," Sal said, without stipulating when or where or to whom.

It had been a long time since Ray had watched TV — since the shaky satellite feed of the Super Bowl beamed into the barracks. TV was audacious now, he discovered, and it was hard to tell what was a joke and what was not. Pretty much nothing was, assured Sal, mentoring Ray through his TV routine. Together they binged with the volume down low, so as not to disturb their neighbors: first was *Wake Up USA,* then *The Dish,* and *Your Body with Dr. Jax.* Next came Sal's soaps, *The Ties That Bind* and *Thicker Than Water,* during which Sal sneered and hissed and gasped, debriefing Ray with essential back-story only during commercials: "Ignacio is *not* a real priest"; "Hugo and Chrissy were engaged but then Francesca revealed that they were brother and sister. Of course, they'll always love each other"; "Angela cannot be trusted." Next came the game show *Name That Brand,* followed by *America's Funniest Car Crashes.* After a lunchtime check-in with CrimeTV — currently offering nonstop coverage of the retrial of the Eugene Aqueduct Bombers — came *Custody Battle!, Extreme Land Development: Mojav Edition, Spy in the Subdivision* and after all that exhausting deceit and reinvention came the cool pool of *Sasha,* who was wide and wise and segued lovingly into the cold hard truth with her signature catch phrases, "Get set for real talk" and "Sasha gotcha!" Next was either *Embalming with the Stars* or its spinoff, *Real Undertakers of Savannah,* and then on to a few episodes of a widely syndicated sitcom called *Friends of Bill W.,* about a group of regulars at an A.A. meeting. Then came

Sixteen with HIV, Murder Bride, Midgets in Middle Management, and *Shaker Heights,* which profiled a team of spry elderly Shaker mountaineers. Next they watched the same six-minute episode of *SportScrap* three times in a row, killing time before the gritty meta-documentary series *Where Are They Now?* their favorite episodes of which were, in order, *Birthed into a Toilet: Real Stories of Babies Whose Mothers Didn't Know They Were Pregnant, Purrfect Fit: Real Stories of Jaguar-People on the Job Market* and *Shotgun Wedding: I Married an Inanimate Object.*

There was the triumphant medical-inspirational dating show *Leper Love Boat,* whose life-affirmation was rivaled only by the brave men and one woman who risked their lives every day on *Grain Bin Divers.* Then came the news, which they skipped for dinner, and after dinner more reruns of *Friends of Bill W.,* though this time on a different channel running a later season, which was like stepping out of the flow of time and hopping back in downstream, where sweet Katie H. was hiding her pregnancy from Kyle R., where Al-Anon made Hilda G. smug and Timmy S. and Nadine T. had to bring her back down to earth, where sassy Hannah L. married her sponsor and started popping pills, where fat Johnny V.

worked his Overeaters Anonymous program and got skinny, where skinny Gene F. worked his Narcotics Anonymous program and got fat. Cigarettes were smoked, instant coffee was drunk, store-bought cake was cut, chips were collected, newcomers appeared, disappeared, then reappeared, people fell off the wagon then clawed their way back on. Oh, so many ups and downs on *Friends of Bill W.,* where someone was always hitting rock bottom and pretty much everyone had been molested. A lot of triumph and a lot of tears — even during those bright early years on the morning block on the other channel, for Sal and Ray knew what dark days lay ahead. And yet, somehow, it all worked out, and at the end Ray believed the chant he and Sal whispered along with the gang: "It works if you work it, so work it, you're worth it!"

Ray's least favorite was the trivia show *Cerebral Weasel,* for he never knew any of the answers. His self-esteem recuperated during *Money Dash,* and his loins flared throughout prime time, which brought perhaps *The Undead Sheriff, The Reluctant Clairvoyant* or *Torture Trio,* a police procedural in which the CIA's top three interrogators, all single, traveled to exotic rendition locales around the world. Another good one was *Mind/Body,* the erotic drama set in a mental ward, featuring an endless court-ship between a Don Juan albino serial killer and his sultry young psychiatrist. Ray and Sal howled during *Laughing Gas,* a raunch-com about dentists innovating a myriad of ways to violate their unconscious patients, but only occasionally chuckled through two late-night shows whose topical opening monologues they never quite followed, and whose guests' patter made them feel like disappointments, for the stars beseeched them to go see movies they never would. Sal grew defensive during these segments, and classified all the stars into three catego-ries: gaylords, major sluts, and Scientolo-gists. Ray often fell asleep during these interview portions, or during the sketch comedy show that followed, soothed to sleep by canned laughter.

Weekend mornings meant cartoons, which were made by computers now and cheap-ened for it, they agreed. But before those, on Sunday, while many other inmates went to Mass, was Ray's absolute favorite: *Sunday Java,* where elderly commentators asked tough questions, like, *Whatever happened to vacuum repair shops?* And, *What exactly are women carrying around in their giant purses?* "Planners!" hooted Sal, incredulous. "Water bottles!" But *Sunday Java* ran solemn segments, too, genuine weepies featuring cancer babies whose lemonade stands outlived them and retarded boys who made Ig sounds shooting the game-winning baskets and mothers who nearly aborted the children who grew up to supply them with precious life-saving marrow or organ or blood. One *Sunday Java* segment, "On the Lam . . . with Gerald Hopson," always made Ray hold his breath.

Gerald Hopson told the stories of fugitives — murderers and kidnappers, cult leaders and enemies of the state. He conjectured their whereabouts and encouraged viewers, whom he called citizens, to report any sightings to the proper authorities. In this regard, "On the Lam . . . with Gerald Hopson" was far from unique. But unlike his trench coat–clad counterparts, Gerald Hopson was genuinely fascinated by the moral ambiguity of the alleged crimes. He stressed that his subjects were innocent until proven guilty, and he speculated not only about their motives but also the conditions that might have driven them to thievery, fraud, or murder. Gerald Hopson pondered, with gravelly voice and swaying neck wattle, whether each of us had versions of these criminals inside us. The greatest injustice,

Gerald Hopson proffered, was not the crime unsolved but the mind unknown, and it was this stain he begged his fellow citizens to scrub. "Answers to the questions *are* out there," his closing monologue insisted, "and *will* be delivered us *when* the accused *stands* before the mantle of *justice*. Until then, they remain . . . *on the lam.*" That was a nice idea.

Limbo Mine was full of surprisingly nice ideas. Ray did not know how far down they were but found he did not miss the surface. Here it was always cool and dim, always a gentle lime twilight. The abandoned catacombs of desert sourdoughs had delivered him from the unrelenting sun, finally, left him with his notebook, the starlet's buttery satchel, and his jug, though he hardly looked at these. Talc statuettes smiled down on him and the forgiving powder walls absorbed most unpleasant sounds. The TV went on and on, quietly, and simple Sal scraped his figurines and everything always worked out in the end.

It was somewhere in this cul-de-sac of routine that Sal ran out of characters to carve, and Ray suggested he make a politics set. "I like it," said Sal. "More serious. Issues and shit."

And like his work, Sal seemed to turn serious, too. The thing Ray needed to know about Sal was that Sal had a super active mind. He was, he admitted, something of a stimulus junkie. Add that to his ingenuity and he could be hard to keep up with.

"I'm UTW," Sal would announce in what he called his language, which was not a language but a system of inscrutable acronyms. UTW meant Under the Weather, which meant depressed, which Sal had honestly become lately, but could not or would not say why.

At mealtimes there came "DYWYP?" pronounced *dee-weep:* Do You Want Your Corn Porridge? Ray always said he did but never seemed to.

"DYHAGBH?" pronounced *dye-hag-buh* meant, Do You Have a Girl Back Home?

There was "WYHAH?" pronounced *why-ha:* Where You Headed After Here?

Ray declined all of these conversational invitations.

Finally, from beneath the considerable shade of his cowboy hat, Sal admitted that he had come to find Ray a lacking roomie. In all the time Sal had been mateless, he had assembled a perfect bunkmate in his mind, built him mostly of TV clichés, and it turned out that Ray fell short of this ideal in nearly every single way.

"For one, you never ask me, 'What's your story?' " said Sal, which was true. Ray had drawn that line in his mind, because while he could describe Luz and Ig around Limbo Mine for purposes of finding them, to sit in the cell trading stories with Sal about where they came from and for whom their hearts ached would be to admit something that, despite the comforts of Limbo Mine, Ray was not ready to admit.

Sal said, "And we never talk philosophy, for example."

Ray the disappointment said, "I've never really known what that means, philosophy."

Sal sighed. "It's one of those things that's so all around you that you can't see it." He scraped at the talc president's lapels. "It would help if you had something to tend."

"To tend?"

"A mouse, say. Or a falcon. Maybe a snake you raised from an egg."

"I don't have anything to tend."

"That's POP," said Sal. Part of the Problem. Another POP was that Ray never imparted to Sal any chestnuts of wisdom, nor, more troublingly, did he ever in turn ask Sal to expound upon his outlook on life, despite the fact that Sal was keeper of a vast bureaucracy of insight, much of which came to him on the chamber pot, his thinking throne, and which he punctuated by the tipping up then tipping down of his ten-gallon, like the hero on *The Undead Sheriff.*

"Are farts pure methane gas or are there poop particles mixed in?"

"Why do I feel ready to burst the second I take my pants down? Could the butthole have an auto-somatic reaction to fresh air?"

"Doesn't it seem odorless? I think the porridge is engineered that way. Thus, our shit does not stink!"

Detainees awaiting relocation were required to write letters, weekly, to their sponsors. Ray's were addressed to Aunt Hennie and Uncle Randy in Milwaukee, and while early epistles were generic and stillborn, Ray soon took to writing for the entire mandatory hour rather than risk more of Sal's wisdom, for Sal seemed for some reason exempt from the weekly letter-writing session. Soon, Aunt Hennie and Uncle Randy metamorphosed in Ray's mind, the lie of them shuddering silvery gunk from its wings. It was a familiar feeling, and he welcomed the reunion.

Aunt Hennie was of Hungarian stock, devout and stoic, but could turn blubbersome without warning. So emotionally repressed that she cried at commercials for cell phones and fast food but not at the deaths of either of her parents. When Ray came to visit she forced him to scoop big handfuls from a dish filled with M&M's color-coordinated with the season. Every Christmas Aunt Hennie made a different gingerbread house, each year's design more ambitious than the last — a Tudor with icing icicles and working lights, a Cape Cod with white chocolate shingles, a ski lodge made from pretzel logs, a Buddhist monastery, the White House, the Taj Mahal, the Sagrada Família. She worried about Uncle Randy, who was hard and like most men of his generation you had to lube with a few brewskis — local only, for he worked at one of the big brick breweries chugging on the waterfront. Only then would he talk at length about the boy he lost, Ray's cousin Paco (Ray was not good with names), who fell through pond ice playing hockey. Paco had not even liked hockey, that Ray could recall, and even Aunt Hennie had wondered when Paco pulled his musty gear from the basement that bright snap of a morning. No one said *suicide,* but Uncle Randy said that Paco had always been both here and gone. He wished Aunt Hennie could put him from her mind, though he himself could not. Aunt Hennie and Uncle Randy were not perfect, but Ray envied how contained their problems were, not as diffuse and inoperable as black ink dripped into a glass of water. Ray came to enjoy writing them with all the normal advice he was never asked to give: *Talk to her, Uncle Randy, I know you're better than you think you are.* What a salve to heal his beloved aunt and uncle this way, what a relief finally, after years of manning various bellows, to waft away a black cloud! But eventually Aunt Hennie and Uncle Randy's failure to respond hurt his feelings.

One night, during the later late show, Sal said, "I don't suppose you want to do any of the other cellmate stuff either?"

"Like what?"

"You know . . . HJ, BJ, RJ?"

Ray remembered guys in the barracks who announced their success by shouting "Here comes the cream sauce!" In high school some boys had a race in the back of the school bus. Supposedly they each let it off into a Dixie cup and the last one to finish had to drink it. Ray had not been invited to the back, had sat in the front of the bus with the girls and the born-again boys, a brushoff somehow repaired years later with Lonnie, when this new friend who thought he was so special asked Ray to please touch him, to please taste him, and Ray did, marveling how willing we become when simply asked nicely.

Ray was actually considering telling Sal this, was imagining how thrilled the kid would be to finally engage in what he called "genuine bondage," when Luz appeared on the TV. Fragile and folded in another man's arms, she looked shyly at the camera, as if by accident, then away. She laughed. They were on a beach, Luz and this man and their chums, all laughing and drinking wine coolers around a fire.

"That's her," said Ray. "My girl." But when Sal looked, Luz was gone and Ray was once again a foolish young deserter whose pride was still wounded from not being invited to a circle jerk in the back of the school bus.

She'd been laughing a laugh he'd never seen before and could not hear. Perhaps she laughed that way before they met. Perhaps he had extinguished it, if not with his presence then with his leaving. He knew it was a trick of the light, the camera, the music and the jumpy cuts, but she'd been having so much fun there. He'd never seen her have that kind of fun. She was throwing her head back with abandon, and even as Ray could hear the director saying, *Throw your head back with abandon,* he wondered why he'd never glimpsed that gesture or its cousins in all their time together.

That night and for many after he dreamed of Luz in all the ways he'd never seen her. In a robe, pouring coffee and wiping the sleep crud from her eyes. In a party dress wrapping a gift, asking him to put his finger on the knot so she could make a bow. Re-potting a plant, a smudge of soil on her forehead. Curled in sleep beside Ig on a blue, velvet-looking duvet, Ig reminding him of all the ways to say *Come home.*

One night, Sal came down to Ray's bunk and held Ray as he wept. "Is it your girl?" he whispered.

"My family," Ray managed. He was not sure whom he meant — it was becoming increasingly difficult to tell who was make-believe, who was waiting for him and where. He wished he'd told his mother it was a dream catcher, not a prism, that would keep Lucy's nightmares away.

"That's tough," said Sal, a decent clamp on his delight.

"It is," said Ray.

Sal grew hard against him. Ray allowed this. He had not been touched in a long, long time. Sal kindly stroked Ray's mangy

386

hair. "You miss your people?"

"Yeah," Ray choked. "I have a little daughter. Little tow-headed girl who needs me."

Sal rubbed himself against Ray as he spoke. "You poor thing. I can only imagine what it's like to have family aboveground. Being separated. Being alone. I hated being alone. That's why I was so glad when you came." He ground his dick into the small of Ray's back.

"You didn't have anyone," Ray said.

Sal grunted. "No one. But at least I got over to see Mom here and there."

Ray pulled away slightly. "Your mom's down here?"

"Of course," said Sal, reaching.

"You were arrested together?"

Sal held Ray tighter and resumed his grind. "What are you talking about, arrested?"

"Taken in or whatever," Ray said. "Detained."

"You don't know?" Ray could feel Sal trembling with the giddiness of finally telling his story.

Ray was trembling, too. "I don't. I'm sorry. Tell me."

Sal shuddered against him. "I was born in here."

Sal never finished his politics chess set. "No one knows any of the politicians," he said. "Or maybe they know the name but not what the dude looks like and not, like, his job. Plus those guys all look the same."

The project aborted, Ray asked if he could have one of the few pieces Sal had finished: Baby Dunn. Sal had carved her bundled in a blanket, little soapstone chrysalis with big watery eyes. Sal said yes, keep her forever, but Ray would not. Ray would realize he'd forgotten the talisman, left talc Baby Dunn behind in his cell, only as he was inching himself stealthily up an air duct, his satchel slung around him, licking his hands and rubbing the spit on his bare feet where the talc made them slippery.

When Ray finally reached a ceiling in the duct he found it blistering. This he could tell when he scooted his face up near and confirmed by touching the back of his hand to it, as a fireman visiting his elementary school had long ago instructed. It was either the surface of the mine or some fire was burning on the other side. But what choice had he? The air shaft yawned below, six or seven stories of it by now, his limbs were quivering, and even if he survived the fall only Limbo Mine awaited him. He heaved himself against the hatch, hulked his puny mass against it, jamming his legs against the duct best he could without falling, urged his body against this barrier, which he somehow knew was his last, heaved himself again up and out into flames.

They went only to his eyes, his eyelids gone translucent for all the protection they brought. His eyeballs boiled on in their sockets even with Ray's palms pressing the magma from them. Beneath him was not ash but dust, scorching all the same, the sun of suns branding his larval, cave-paled skin. He felt for the satchel where it hung from him, retrieved Sal's liberated ten-gallon and donned it, though its shade did not register. He crawled to make his escape. He scrambled one way and then another, not certain if he was inching back toward Limbo Mine or if a guard was standing over him, smirking. All the parts of his eyes he didn't have names for were crisp, rattling hulls. He felt the duct and the hatch he'd pushed off. He curled up beneath the hatch as though it could hide him and lay there for some time, baking and blind, listening for trucks.

None came, and eventually his brain registered the lifting of his eyelids as faint reddening, which gave way to an oscillating green-black, as though he were looking at an overcast night sky through night vision goggles. He came out from under the hatch. The first shapes he saw with his new sight were crosses, which came to him as gashes of red light. They were for the Indian massacre, some people said. For William Randolph Hearst's stillborn babies, or for the wives he bluebearded. For the innocent victims of drunk driving, or the drunks themselves, catapulted off the shoulderless highway now buried. Below the crosses, he knew, the Spanish tile of Clay Castle gleamed in the sun like an oasis, and beyond that the dune sea, a laceration of light in the distance, utterly reconfigured in the months since he'd last seen it, yet as fearful, as transfixing.

Ray knew he had to move. Insisting to himself that if necessary the red-green forms materializing and dissolving before him would coalesce into a sinkhole or a truck coming, he slid down the opposite side of the hill on his ass, his limbs still noodly and light, not behaving in a predictable way whatsoever. He could not determine whether it was night or day. The sky was a pit above but also somehow aglow, the new horizon a shimmering smear and very far away.

The dune tugged him. His world was a photo negative of itself, a kind of heat vision except the world was all heat. As he walked, purples and oranges came onto the scene, first faint at the borders, then lurid. Colors he'd not seen in a long time somersaulted across his field of vision — Technicolor cells on parade, lackadaisical psychedelia, rainbows prismed then collapsing, the drought of droughts through a kaleidoscope. He knew these colors to be unreal — symptoms of a shorted-out ocular nerve, a spent rod or cone, a fried disc somewhere — but still, they were company. He would find Luz and describe all this to her, she who had always been so hungry for color.

He walked and watched the show, occasionally slurping handfuls of corn porridge from the satchel he'd filled with it. At some point, the colors from his burned eyes seemed to repose onto the real. Auras, Lonnie said, pleased with himself somewhere.

The alluvial fan beneath him was an essential beige flecked with urgent orange. One rocky wash was welcoming lavender, and so he spent the night. Behind him, the mountains concealing Limbo Mine throbbed a cautionary rust. The sun was indifferent black, or some days a deep, infinite navy. And in the distance, always, the dune sea shimmered in sublime, hypnotic, opalescent blue, the color of water at the shallow end of a swimming pool, with a pretty girl's suntan oil sliding on its surface. His damaged sight, though he had stopped thinking of it this way, led him there.

Upon entering the dune sea, he set the modest goal of walking in only one direction. South, maybe. But even this got difficult when his footprints disappeared behind him and the ridges around him shifted from north-south to east-west. But the heartcolors stayed with him, and he continued to let them guide him. He heeded effervescent streaks of emerald, an earnest path of peach. If a valley was spiteful olive gray he went around, then watched from a distant ridge as a sandalanche slid silently to fill it. If a slope of sandy ripples shone a chirpy robin's-egg, he climbed them as though they were the front steps of his own house.

At some point he crested a day-long dune and saw nothing but more dune. Sand stretched out on all sides and above, for he was nowhere near summiting even the foothills of the Six Sisters. But instead of terror he grasped what made these dunes a sea, and for the first time felt the serenity of that. He was as at home here as he had been bobbing on his board, seeing nothing but sky and the Pacific. A real good, deep-oblivion kind of feeling.

In this state, he carried all hurts past and present and future. He thanked his blisters, befriended his burns, watched his migraine move around his head the way he might have watched Ig pull Luz around a play-ground. Pain had its favorite spots — his headaches preferred the nook beneath his eyebrows, heat rash his armpits, and sting nested in the crook of his groin, probably for the shade. Ray made room for these. People and things came to him, and he pretended not to notice.

Some were hard to ignore. Lucy walking boneless was a beautiful thing. He did not turn to see Luz and Ig beside him, for fear of evaporating them, but he did slow down so Ig could keep up. He spoke to some, say-ing, "I appreciate the offer, Uncle Randy, but this is something I have to do myself."

His sturdier companions were his talc hack, his satchel and his jug. Though he felt a little bad about taking it, Sal's ten-gallon was like God's awning overhead. He touched it when he needed to pin down what was real.

Some nights he thought he heard that worrisome banshee shriek way off, though perhaps it was imagined. Either way, he dropped immediately to the ground, made himself flat as a river stone.

He was, after everything, a Hoosier and a guest and so when he dipped his hand into the satchel and found his porridge finished he said, "If I may, sand dune, you are not going to kill me." When his jug went dry he said, "I beg your pardon, dune sea, but I am just here to get my girls. If you would kindly. This is not my first desert, you see. I am not done with my life — I'd say I'm about halfway through. I don't think that's an exaggeration. I am a young white man in America and we typically do quite well here. So if you will excuse me."

He found he was no longer afraid of losing Luz, or of loving Ig — he was content to have those two throbbing slabs of his heart outside his body, walking around. If only he could find them. All he asked was to watch them make their rounds, and occasionally to press them up to their puny kindred plugging away inside him. His vision went a-swamp. He did not know whether they were alive, and if alive where — perhaps even back at Limbo Mine, in some hidden grotto. But he pressed onward along routes of affectionate coral and welcoming teal. He did not know where he was walking but he knew why. He would, he realized, find them or spend the rest of his life looking, and this might not take so long. So be it. All he had ever needed, in that desert or this, was some say in how it went, some reassurance that he would go doing something worthwhile. A sappy idea, but not therefore false. And while his life, it seemed, had been an archipelago of ambiguity and abstraction and impossibility, here was something he could grasp: a designer bag greasy from gruel, a ten-gallon hat. *My girl and my baby two days back.* This was what faith looked like: a phosphorescent world showing the way, a beautiful rose-colored vulture with a cherry-juice beak weaving through the white-hot sky, circling him, then landing at his feet. When the vulture became a great blue heron and the heron a tarp, Ray shrouded himself in it — precious shade, the canvas of discarded wagons —

and walked in the direction from which it
came.

The Girls
We knew something was going down when
he kicked us out of the Rambler. Get out,
he said, just like that. Like it wasn't our
monastery, our vestibule, and hadn't we just
delivered him?

Jimmer
An unnatural portrait, I admit, the girls
huddled outside the Rambler that way, and
the Rambler off by itself. Not right. But he
couldn't let the girl go. Baby Dunn, though
she was not a baby anymore.

Cody
I thought we were to leave the Rambler with
them in it. I did. The ripple was on and then
done and still no one went near it. No one
said not to. We just knew.

Dallas

Ig was with me — she always was then. Luz root-gone and derelict. Shameful. I nearly knocked on the Rambler and told her so, but then they came out.

The Girls

Somehow they were more than two, the two of them. Levi, who taught us that monogamy was a prison built by gynophobic capitalism, that public affection was a bludgeon unless it was extended to all. And here was the proof, her in his arms in front of all of us, ignoring the ripple.

Cody

Until then he had loved each of us with the same heart, if that makes sense.

Jimmer

Certainly the landscape had some significance. The Rambler by itself as we others rippled to that new place on the high plain, tufts of dead sagebrush all around us. Levi out in the open with this Baby Dunn wrapped around him. The sage would have cured us all, in other circumstances.

Dallas
He'd never anointed any woman this way, though he'd had all of us.

Cody
And with all of us there, like we knew, like he wanted us to see.

Dallas
Of course he wanted us to see. He knows exactly what he's doing at all times.

The Girls
And there was nothing to do but watch.

Cody
I keep seeing it in my mind, even now. I don't know why, except that it was one of those few moments when you are in it and above it at the same time. One of those rare moments when you know you're swinging on a hinge in your life.

Dallas
Things were changing, or were just about to, and everyone could feel that.

Jimmer
And down comes this cowboy harbinger.

Cody

Some wild man out of the dune. How he survived I don't know. Stumbling down the slope and grinning. Fucking *grinning*.

The Girls

We saw him and we saw her see him and we saw him see him.

Jimmer

A triangle of very high-pitched energy, and all of us caught inside it.

Cody

That step she took was it, looking back.

Dallas

Levi put Luz down and she took one step away from him, a big step, bigger than seemed possible.

The Girls

We saw it, yes. A divot in the sand where she had been, and another where she stood now.

Jimmer

And the sand between these absolutely pristine. That was crucial, from my perspective.

Dallas

Levi's arms still raised in the shape of her.

Jimmer

It was finished in that step, though its finishing took some time.

The Girls

It hurt to witness, honestly.

Cody

And we all stayed there, even after she took Ig and the three of them walked to the Blue Bird. We stood waiting to see where to go, I guess.

Jimmer

Until the sand whispered around our ankles.

Dallas

After we moved the Rambler we were drawn back to the Blue Bird, waiting.

Cody

We stayed there until bonfire, like the day Luz came, except Dallas was with us, pacing.

The Girls

Locked out of her own place, which wasn't right.

Jimmer

Pacing foretells ill fortune. Doubly when the pacer is a mother.

The Girls

When Luz came out it was dark and she was a different woman. The baby held her hand.

Cody

She did seem changed, I guess you'd say.

Jimmer

Like she'd found a sachet of bird beaks in the eaves and had emerged to fling them out.

The Girls

We needed so much from her.

Dallas

But all she said was, *He's asleep.*

Luz told the rubberneckers outside the Blue Bird that Ray was asleep and took Ig on one of their old walks around the transmuted colony, surveying the new high plain.

Luz chawed some brute root as she walked, feeling the fungal juices leech into her gums before she spat, taking in the new territory. Here and there among the structures were haystack clumps of dead roots, half-entombed in sand. "What is?" asked Ig, and Luz said she did not know. The harvest moon was fat and orange overhead. Ig said, "What is?" and thereafter never tired of whispering its name.

What did it mean to have Ray back? All the anger she'd succored to starve her grief had boiled off upon seeing him, and she was not sure what would fill that space. She was waiting for it perhaps, weaving through the domes and shanties in their new constellations, looking for what would grow in her

403

now that he'd made room.

The bonfire was somber that night, music-less and sparsely attended. The fire itself was paltry, though Ig still grunted her wanting it, staggering toward the blaze in her light-ups and whining tragically when Luz picked her up. Luz was sad not to see Levi there, and her sadness revealed that she'd come looking for him. She could continue looking — she had seen the silhouette of his dome out on the edge of the colony — but knew she would not.

Instead, she lingered on the periphery with Ig in her arms, gazing into the fire. Comparisons insisted. Ray's crescent hip bones and Levi's heaving, hair-damp chest. Ray's flat feet and the cracked yellow callus where the two smallest toes on Levi's right foot once were. Where Ray was riding waves, Levi was half-buried; where Ray was whisking along whitecaps, Levi was hunkered. Where Ray was leaning into the curves, Levi was arms outstretched. Where Ray was brittle grapevine, Levi was boulder. Where Ray was a liquid slug sluicing down the canyon, Levi was the Amargosa's solid sandstone foot. She was drawn to Levi the way Ig was drawn to fire — she should fear him but did not. Meanwhile, going back to Ray was like rolling down a hill.

■ ■ ■ ■

Once she'd touched Ray she'd not been able
to stop. They sat on the floor of the Blue
Bird, her silently stroking his bizarrely soft
and white fingertips and speaking only to
remind him to drink.

"I thought you were dead," she said
finally. "I have to keep touching you until
you're alive again."

"I feel very much alive," he said.

"You look different," she said, "but the
same." He was thinner, burnt, with new
shading in his face, impossible to map.
Bloody crescents where some fingernails
had been. But he was hers: fine mouth and
prophet eyes. Delivered her by some great
benevolent hand. She could not deny that.

"You look just like I remember," he said.
Though he was burnt all over he let Ig into
his lap. He kissed the baby and burbled her
stomach. She squealed and pinched her
fingers together and Luz taught Ray how
that meant *more.*

All his months in Limbo Mine, months
that had not passed in that out-of-time
place, that had instead hovered, waiting, at
the surface, that had shuddered behind him
as he walked, came upon him then. Lost

time flooded through him. His tears came — "I guess I've missed a lot" — and then hers. Luz asked where he had been, and through Ig's demands and diversions he told her, told her everything, even all that was madness.

When he described the attack the night before the rangers found him, she showed him the scarf she had stuffed into the cushion. "Here," she said, stretching the wrinkled silk taut. "Levi brought me this."

"Yes," he said, touching the rusty stain. "That must've been where they hit me."

"Who?" Luz asked, and Ig said, "Ooo, ooo, ooo."

Ray said, "I'm not sure."

Luz also gave him the Leatherman. He looked at it for a very long time. "This was my dad's," he said.

"I didn't know," she said.

He took her face in his hands and they both checked to see if she would allow this. She did, but his hands felt like a skeleton version of Levi's and soon she pulled away. They were silent awhile before Luz said, "What do I look like to you?"

Ray was confused. She added, "With your eye thing. What are you seeing now?"

"It's sort of pink in here, pink and yellow-orange. Sunset colors, a lovely sunset, and you're like a happy purple cloud on the horizon."

"A happy cloud. And Ig?"

Ig was luminous, with dark, hard feet. She was the same size as when he left her, but her head was larger, with spots larger than freckles sprayed along her hairline. "Sun spots. From the Melon." He wept again as she told the story of their afterworld.

Luz was quiet for some time. Her shimmer evaporated. She went dark as coal. "You left us," she said finally.

"I know. I'm —"

"I mean, you left us *to die.*"

"No, I . . . Yes. I was afraid. I convinced myself I was doing it for you, but it was for me."

"I fucking know that," she said. "You're not telling me any news." She took a gash of root from her pocket and nibbled it ferociously. "Everything was like that."

"Everything?"

"You were always convincing me I was a burden. That I needed taking care of. I felt like an infant at the end, and then you left me with one."

"I know, babygirl."

Luz croaked.

"I'm sorry," said Ray. "Habit. Goddamn it, I'm sorry." He sobbed some, binding his hands with the stained scarf. Luz had been so small on Sal's TV, smaller still as he'd come down from the dune sea. He'd known it was her immediately, folded into another man's arms, as she always was. He wanted to be those arms, but knew he never had been and did not deserve to be now. And yet here he was, trying, and in this way he was as selfish as ever, more. Luz was maybe happy without him — no, he would not allow for that. When he touched her, she'd softened. She was his home, and he hers — he still believed that. Finally he said, "I needed you to need me, I see that now. I thought you were my project. I was so afraid, Luz, and I didn't know how to love someone who didn't need me. And you didn't need me, and you don't now. I know that . . . But, have me? Please have me. If you'll have me I'll deserve you."

Ig wedged herself between them and let loose a high, jealous hum. "She's been doing this," Luz said, though this was in fact the first time she'd seen it; until now she'd only heard about it from Dallas. "Remember that moan she used to do? It's more like a hum now." They waited for Ig to do it again, but Ig was nobody's wag.

Luz looked at Ray, found him repentant and tender and tired. She unwound the scarf from his hands and returned it to the cushion. "You need to sleep."

Now, with Ig gone slack in her arms and the few people tending the dying bonfire giving her a wide berth, Luz wanted to take her own advice, wanted to sleep — but where? She remembered what the others said, about the dune curating, about being open to signs and omens. Why had she not accepted its grace sooner — why had she slid into her old stingy self?

Levi's dome summoned from the desert. Instead, she walked beyond the encampment, away from the dune sea. Among the sandy clumps of roots she came upon a downed tree, long dead, its branches burnt to nubs and its silvery trunk twisted like a hank of wet hair. Tomorrow someone from the colony would find it and hack it up for firewood. Everything she saw would go that way, someday.

Ray woke late that night, terrified. Luz and Ig were asleep beside him in the school bus, but from somewhere nearby came an atrocious and familiar yowl. He made his way outside and through the shanties and tents and RVs toward the strange banshee sound he'd learned to fear in the desert. At the edge of the colony, he found the source of that sickening shriek: a gangrenous-colored lorry, with roll bars and K.C. lights, Luz's man and another tending to it.

Rage rose in Ray like water in a basin. Luz's man was big, his bigness the first and second and third thing you noticed about him. He had wide meaty hands and a beefy face that shone violently in the dawn. His buddy — weasely and quick, the kind of guy who noticed everything — said something to him and the bastard turned, saw Ray, and waved.

You look just like I remember, Ray had told Luz, his only lie. Something was different about her, not just her darkened skin or wind-thinned hair or the sand all over her. Beneath all that, she was caved in, fervent. Manic but vacant. A little mad, maybe, or just saddled with a mighty hurt, Ray would have said if Sal or Uncle Randy asked after her. Suddenly it was clear that the big man was to blame not only for Ray's injuries but Luz's too.

Ray waved back.

Luz's big man and his helper mounted the lorry and tore off into the dune sea.

Out beyond the colony, a formation of red, wind-rounded stones rose from the husks of chaparral. A few days later, when he was well enough, Ray invited Luz and Ig to accompany him to the formation.

There, Luz found herself answering the questions she'd so often asked when she first arrived, found herself often saying the name so often said to her.

Ray helped Ig summit a boulder. "Levi. He's the dowser? The one Lonnie told us about? He runs this place?"

"It's so much more than that."

Her adoration cranked a vise on Ray's chest. But he and Luz had spent that first night together, and the three nights since, and though she'd refused his advances, the nights themselves were something. He and Luz had doled out some pain to Levi in those hours.

"He finds water," she said.

Ig hurled herself into Ray's arms. He said, "Tell me about him."

Luz did, her voice shimmering with reverence, bristling with golden zeal. Ray heard it and also another, a gravelly voice from near memory. He saw in his mind a Sunday morning figure, intrepid and windblown on location, marching out the facts with steady indigo objectivity.

He's a scientist, a naturalist. But those

words are so deficient. You know that sense we always had that we were missing something? That there was something fundamentally wrong in the way we approached the natural world? You said that, once. The Amargosa looks barren but it's teeming with life. He's the reason all these people are here. Why they came and why they stay. He keeps all of us alive. He finds water . . . ephemeral rivers, nearly instant . . . the equivalent of coral reefs. He's . . . touched. You know I scoff at this as much as you do, but it's true . . . He's walked through some dark spaces to get where he is . . . learned to listen to the rocks and sand and earth . . . the uranium spoke to him. In a hundred years we'll have a completely different understanding of the natural world, thanks to him. He's like Darwin, or Lewis and Clark . . . a seismic shift in the way we understand the environment . . . blending of the spiritual and the natural. Everything's connected and he can feel the strings. I feel drawn to him, I guess, since you've been gone . . . made me grow in ways I didn't know I could. Tenderhearted . . . demanding . . . Yucca Mountain . . . Opera-

tion Glassjaw . . . A prophet, I guess you would say. It's like the world is bigger because of him — he can see in a different way — like you! And he's a giver like you — he gives himself to everyone here. You would like him, Ray.

Citizens, I come to you today from the Mojave Desert. Behind me lies the Amargosa Dune Sea, the only known landmass of its kind, what geologists call a pseudospontaneous phenomenon, a superdune, a symbol of the drought that has wrecked the American West. It has collapsed agribusiness as we know it, sending millions of refugees, known colloquially as Mojavs, fleeing the Southwest, desperately seeking shelter — and resources. It's a landscape we all recognize, emblematic of a drama each of us is familiar with. But could this superdune be hiding a secret? . . . Some call him a dowser, some call him a visionary, others say he is a fugitive who may *even* have access to *nuclear weapons* . . . He is believed to have fled *here,* to the Amargosa Dune Sea, though how he might *survive* here remains a mystery . . . a whistle-blower to some, to others a disgruntled employee . . . accused of *stealing* state secrets . . . accused of

413

polygamy . . . linked to the disappearance of a female coworker . . . train bombing in Albuquerque . . . extremist radical views . . . *ransacking* aid convoys . . . *Sunday Java* unearthed this exclusive photo in which we see the burnt frames of two lorries belonging to the Red Cross . . . Or is he, as some say, a prophet, possessed of a rare gift much needed in this barren, blighted wilderness? We cannot know until he is brought to justice. For now he remains . . . *on the lam.*

Ray listened to them both. Luz was trying not to hurt him, he could tell, and he was trying to determine whether she was in love with this supposed dowser. When Luz told him she had something she wanted him to see, Ray followed her back to the bus, hoping whatever it was would prove she was not. A consolation he would be denied.

She went to the glove compartment and handed him a notebook. Ray sat down and skimmed it. Luz hovered manic as a hummingbird as he paged through sketches and scrawl — a madman's manifesto.

As he read, Ray fingered the scar at his hairline. Everything's connected, Luz had said, and it felt so then. It seemed he could wiggle the divot of waxy tissue on his forehead and a little bell would ring at the dowser's bedside.

Luz sat before him, her knees folded under her, expectant. "Isn't it amazing?"

Ray did not know how to begin. "What does that mean, babygirl? To 'liberate' a bunch of uranium?"

"It's a way of listening."

Ray scratched his chin.

Luz said, "He found Ig and me that way. We're supposed to be here."

"For what? Why?"

"The Amargosa is a wasteland because they need it to be a wasteland, see? If Baby Dunn and her baby are here, thriving —"

"Baby Dunn? What are you talking about?"

"We disrupt that narrative. It's about showing us as humans. A chosen people."

"You said you hated all that Baby Dunn shit."

"Me and Ig. Videos of us gardening, taking a bath. Make them think they discovered us."

"You and Ig? That's insane. Don't you realize what would happen if they saw you, her?"

Luz stood up. "You're not getting it. We're the rallying cry."

Ray pressed his hands against his face

415

then looked up at her. "Has he been taking Ig?"

"What?"

"I don't want him alone with her."

"What are you talking about? I'm trying to tell you how special this place is. It's in danger. They could come any day. If we don't do something."

Ray stood, holding up the primer. "Says Levi."

"We're under assault here, Ray. I think I can help."

"Help *how*? Turning us in?"

"You're asking the wrong questions."

"What's the most likely scenario here, Luz?"

Luz shook her head, disappointed. "Why is it so difficult for you to believe that I could be useful here?"

"I'm saying it doesn't make sense."

"You'd think that with all that you've seen — are *still* seeing — you could open yourself to the unknown."

In fact, Ray's visions were fading. Even now, as he watched Ig bobble around the bus, she was only faintly opal. Luz was a mute slate, and the light pressing on the blankets told him nothing. His heart-colors would be gone by sunset. Ray said, "I heard

416

a story about him on the news, in Limbo Mine."

Luz scoffed. "The news." She tossed the news out the bus window.

"He's a criminal."

"So are we."

"He's a liar. A fraud."

"You don't want to talk to me about liars and frauds," she said.

Ray was silent.

"He finds water, Ray. You've been drinking it."

"He steals it, Luz."

"You don't get it. It doesn't matter what anyone says about him."

"He hijacks aid convoys. I saw photos of the aid convoys on fire. That's where he gets the water."

"He wouldn't hurt anyone."

"Him and his guys cracked my fucking skull."

"No —"

"He might have killed people, Luz! There's a missing woman —"

Luz said, "Why are you trying so hard to belittle what we have here?" She put something into her mouth.

"What is that you keep chewing?"

"It helps me breathe."

"You didn't answer my question."

"Goddamn it, Ray! You're treating me like a fucking toy. After all this, I'm still a doll to you. It's easier for you to imagine some criminal conspiracy than to think I could be useful."

"It's not about you, Luz — it's about him."

"I know it is! I thought you were *dead*, Ray."

"You've said that. And I've said I'm sorry."

"I will keep saying it until you understand exactly what it means. *I thought you were dead.* I thought you were dead because that's what you wanted me to think."

"I didn't —"

"I thought you were dead. Dead, Ray!"

Ray hurled the primer to the far end of the bus. "And who told you I was? *He* did. He was the one on that lorry — the one who attacked me —"

"Don't."

"I'm fucking sure of it."

Ig was not crying — she was watching — but Luz went to her as though she were. She lifted Ig and held her. She had never been more a mother than when she opened the back door of the Blue Bird and in a voice fossilized with resolve told Ray, "You need to find another place to sleep."

Ray drifted through the colony. Where exactly did Luz expect him to go? He passed RVs with foil over all their windows, tents, the black hand of ash where a fire had been. He passed a man in a teepee, napping, his features obscured by sun and sand and fuchsia mottling like some new map across one side of his face. Ray walked in circles, and each time he passed the man Ray glanced at him. The sun relentless, he eventually lay in the teepee's shrinking shadow and tried to sleep.

When he woke the old man stood above him. "You were thrashing around," he told Ray. "Shouting things."

"Was I?" Ray tried to blink the stains from the old man's face, angered by the last remnants of the visions that had led him here, their whimsical obstruction.

"Arsenic poisoning," the man said. He retreated to the shade inside the teepee and gestured with his jumpy hand for Ray to join him. "You're Luz's man."

Ray shrugged. "I was."

"I'm Jimmer." He extended his hand.

"Ray."

"Back from the dead. Where are they keeping the dead these days?"

"Limbo Mine. You know it?"

"Not from experience."

"Glad to hear that." Ray tried to avoid staring at Jimmer's face.

"Domestic dispute?"

Ray nodded.

Jimmer nested a cloth inside a fisherman's cap and donned it. "Luz said you were a surfer. Do I recall that correctly?"

"Used to be."

"Well, let's not sit here staring at each other."

Jimmer instructed Ray to shoulder two flattened oblong petals of tin, each with four holes punched in it, two loops of rope tied through these. Together, they walked into the dune sea.

"See those?" Jimmer pointed back across the shrinking valley, toward the troubling range where clouds made a calico of the sky. "Gonna have a helluva sunset tonight. One upside to those mountains."

They walked on, the colorless sand sucking at their feet. After some time Jimmer pointed at a steep crescent peak two ridges over. "That'll do," he said. They pressed on, drizzling sweat. Struggling up the final slope, Ray's calves began to spasm. "I wouldn't mind a lift," he said. "A towline, even."

"They'll install all those soon as this thing stops."

"You think it'll stop?"

"Never."

They reached the top of the big ridge, lungs screaming.

"Air is stingy up here," said Jimmer.

Ray said, "I feel it."

The sheets of tin were baking as Ray laid them on the sand. Jimmer showed him how to bind his feet to his board with the rope loops, across the toes, around the ankle and back across the heel. They sat this way, on the lip of the dune, tin obelisks strapped to their feet, the colony below miniature in the shadow of those wicked granite teeth beyond, until Jimmer said, "After you, young man."

Ray stood and leaned down the dune. The sand shifted beneath him, ceded to gravity, and he slid. He glided, faster and faster, beating his arms for balance until the dune bit the edge of his board and threw him down. He came up cackling. Jimmer followed after, bit it, came up shouting, "Goddamn it, that's important!"

Onward they slid. They trembled. They tumbled. They moved first like tentative leaves falling softly from the summit, then in wide dreamy arcs, and finally swift and daring as diving swallows. Sensation throbbed in their groins, their abdomens, their inner ears and trembling glutes. It was a kind of flying, gliding across the sand, swishing down and the air suddenly nipping, cooling where they sweated, which was everywhere. They crowed *Wheeee* at the summit and *Again* at the base. When they fell they somersaulted, coating themselves with albino dusting. When they gathered speed they thrust their giddy fists into the air, for it was a surprise every time. They carved the dune and climbed it again, climb and carve and fly and sing, letting loose all the joyous cries that might have otherwise died inside them.

In time, Jimmer and Ray sat at the summit, panting. Ray surveyed the colony below, looking, he realized, for a way out.

"I can't tell you how long I've been waiting to do this," Jimmer said. "I went snowboarding once, as a kid. Once. Course I mighta dreamt it. Always wanted to move somewhere with snow." He made an hour-glass of his hand, let sand slip through. "But I had a nice little homestead. I had a canyon all to myself. I put a statue down there when my boy went, then another, built a bridge, a walkway, carved a scene into the cliffside, I couldn't stop. Wife left; I hardly noticed. Though she would say I'm the one who left."

"What happened to it?" asked Ray. "Your canyon?"

"The dune came and took it. What I remember most was how quiet it was. I'd always wanted to go out there with a shotgun. Blow it all to smithereens. But the dune just slipped over it, like a clean bedsheet. Merciful, I guess I thought."

For the first time, the word seemed right to Ray, especially here, in sight of those toothy peaks, so forbidding opposite the soft swooping embrace of the dune sea. The heartcolors had left him now, but the sun had set, and as Jimmer predicted, the clouds snagged on the new range, aflame. Ray did not miss his visions — he missed Luz, wanted to ask Jimmer the secret to keeping her, though he thought he knew. When he'd been able to pry her away from Levi, the old Luz surfaced. In the weeks since he returned, Luz and Ig had spent every night with Ray in the bus. He didn't want to know all that had happened between Luz and the dowser — didn't blame her, no, but didn't want to know the details, either. She'd tried to tell him sometimes, in the dark, but he'd stop her. It doesn't matter, he'd say. It all happened for a reason, she'd say. But really Ray did not want to invite the man between them that way. And though he would never say so, it was, he supposed, a story he knew from before, the same that sent them up into the canyon. But this new devotee Luz was bristling, unpredictable, and he didn't want to spook her. Nights together or no, something pulled her back to Levi, Ray knew, and he had been intent on giving her no reason to follow that pull — no guilt and no conditions. Everything clean between them. But that was ruined now.

Below, someone had started a fire. Black smoke helixed skyward and disappeared. Nearby, on a big, palm-flat rock, was the dome Ray knew belonged to Levi. Alone, apart, the first time it'd been so, Jimmer said. The dome glowed from within as darkness came, lovely, Ray had to admit.

Luz tried to nap but the Blue Bird was poisoned, the bad air from the fight pressing heavy on her. She tidied up the bus, returned the abused primer to the glove box and took Ig for a walk.

Levi's dome had been relocated to a flat, rust-red rock from which radiated tremendous heat. In the center of the dome was a pile of stones baked in a nearby fire. Luz entered and was immediately surprised by the intensity inside; she had not known it could get hotter.

Levi lay nearly naked on his stone floor, shining. "Sweat lodge," he said. "The heat in this rock was absorbed before you or I were born. Slow the heart rate. Essentialize the thought processes. Reduce to its basicmost pathways. Go through fight or flight and out the other side. To clarity and truth."

He invited her to disrobe and feel it. She felt a primal urge to do just that. The happiest slivers of her girlhood had been spent on a beach towel on a rhombus of dead lawn in Pasadena, thinking of nothing except absorbing the sun, of the air moving around her setting a chill to the sweat shimmering on her upper lip, of evading the sundial trajectory of the finger of shade cast by the single palm in their neighbor's yard, of an insect screaming near her ear or a snowball of sweat rolling from the scoop of her sacrum into her butt crack. But mostly, there on the towel, she had wondered what she would look like one day, when she was tan or when she was thin, and would there be lines here or creases here? Would there be unwelcome hairs, cellulite pocking? In all her hours lying in the sun and thinking, she had never concentrated on important things, never asked herself difficult questions. She wished now that she had.

Her impulse to join Levi was tempered not only by Ig on her hip, cranky from her truncated nap, but by the pair she'd passed as she'd entered the dome, a girl called Rachel, sex-flushed, and Cody, who failed to meet Luz's gaze, squeezing Ig's bare foot instead. Though Luz knew she had no right to be hurt, she was.

Levi tipped water over the rocks, and they watched it hiss instantly to steam. "You'll want to sit," he said. "Heat rises."

She sat across from him and tried to coax Ig into her lap, but the girl was interested only in climbing on and off Levi's cot. "Let her," Levi said.

Luz began. "I'm sorry I haven't been by. Since . . . Ray . . ."

"We don't own each other, Luz."

"I know. It's just . . . complicated."

"Complications are human inventions."

"I know," she said, "but I'm feeling —"

"Come over here."

"I just wanted to tell you —"

"I can't talk to you when you're way over there."

Luz moved close enough to feel a swell of heat coming off him. "You're burning up," she said.

"That's the idea," he said. "Important decisions to be made. I'm going deep within for answers." He meant the wall of rock coming at them, she knew, and other decisions too.

Luz said, "He's Ig's father."

Levi put his hand on the back of her neck and shook his head. "So you're lying to me? Closing off again?"

"No, I —"

"That's not you talking — it's him. He's toxic. I've seen the two of you together. He's poisoning you."

"He's not," said Luz.

"Listen to yourself. Look at you." He pointed to her crossed arms and her folded legs, her yielding shoulders and drooping head. "You're all walls, all barricades. Your body's a prison."

She uncrossed her arms but had nowhere to put them. "Can I ask you something?"

"Anything." He retrieved a pouch drooping with dried, dark roots. "Here." She added a nub to the one gone pulpy in her mouth.

"I've never been with you," she said, "on a dowsing. I'd like to see that."

"I'm going to touch you," he said.

"Wait, Levi. Please. Will you take me with you one day?"

He kept touching her. "Don't you want to get back to where we were?"

Luz wanted to get back there, she did, even if she didn't know where it was. But wherever it was, Ray would not be there. She looked to Ig.

"Let her be," said Levi.

As if to counter, Ig yanked Levi's blanket from his roll and nearly toppled the cot. "No, Ig," said Luz. "Stop."

Ig began to cry.

"She's too hot in here," said Luz, pushing Levi's hands away. "She didn't get a nap."

Luz tried to comfort Ig. The child's face was flame-red and slick as the flesh of some lost fruit. The tantrum continued, frenzy and agitation rippling like waves through the baby's whole body. She flailed, would have flung herself atop the scorched stones had Luz not restrained her. "Shhh," Luz tried. She didn't know what the fuck she was doing and never had.

Levi peeled a tendril of root from the

pouch. "Give her this."

Ig screamed on. Luz hesitated to take Levi's offering and hated that she did. She could not seem to escape herself — Ray's return was proof of that.

She took the root and presented it to Ig. Miraculously, Ig paused in her rage, accepted the root and, as with everything, inserted it into her mouth. "Good girl," said Levi, his hands on Luz again, making promises.

Soon Ig was suckling quiet and wide-eyed on the cot — "That's her mind's knot untying," Levi said. "Perfectly natural."

Luz let Levi undress her, then slid atop him.

After, heat-sick and dizzy, she said, "You'll take me with you? I want to see you work."

Levi sighed. "Not now, Luz."

"Please," she said. "I need to see for myself."

Levi handed her the pouch of root. "Do you hear yourself?" he said. "You have doubt pouring off you. I can't bring you. I can't have you contaminating the process."

Luz lifted Ig, spaced-out and silent, from the cot.

"I need peace now," Levi said, and Luz showed herself out.

■ ■ ■

Jimmer rebuilt his cathedral canyon for Ray,
there on the high white slopes of the dune
sea, recasting each statue and sculpture,
repainting each mural, rearranging each
altar, reigniting each candle. Ray listened
and watched the luminous dome below.
Shapes moved inside, inky against the light.
Ray did not allow himself to speculate on
who the shapes might be. But then Luz
emerged from the dome, Ig limp on her hip.

Jimmer stopped talking. He'd seen Luz
too and with his silence sanctified Ray's
dejection. Jimmer did not need to say what
he said next. It was a fact both men knew
and both would have preferred not to have
aloud and airborne between them, for they
also knew that for all the glee and speed
and colossal fun of the day, this would be
what they remembered, what it all led to,
the utterance undoing all else, the tug of
the first thread. The knowledge would make
Ray lie when Jimmer descended back down
to the colony, make him say he only wanted
to enjoy the quiet a little longer. It would
keep Ray up in the dune that night. But like
Ray, Jimmer had his little one on his mind,
his cathedral and his son. He was brimming

with everything still unsaid, of and to the child who was no longer. He wanted to say his name, which was the name of the grandfather who'd taken no interest in the boy. Jimmer felt the boy's arm too yielding where Jimmer yanked it, his freckled shoulder abandoning its socket. Jimmer touched his own tongue to the boy's gummy red pit, a tooth yanked free too soon. He felt all things going, and though it was obvious and unnecessary and too late, he told Ray, "Son, you're not safe here."

Luz had chewed the whole sack of brute root and the flames were diamonds and triangles, arrows of light with pretty blue lozenges inside them. People spoke to her and she watched their faces go cubist, the features tectonic and akimbo. She walked. Bikes were sculpture in the new high country, thanks to impeding boulders and sandy sagebrush haystacks, and for a long time she stared at a pile of them, dancing. Jimmer's teepee sprouted skyward like a beanstalk, and had she a little more energy she would have climbed it to heaven. She made a note to do that, if need be. Cody's vans had little constellations of condensation in the corners of their windows, which were eyes wide open to all the alchemy in the world, which even Ray could not smash. She believed in something, would leap over the maybe-Sierras, smiling up at and down on her with their jack-o'-lantern teeth. She could feel ideas as they were conceived in her mind, shooting-star neuron kites with strings grazing her gray matter — a tingle breezing from one side of her skull to the other. She felt this epiphany — that ideas were physical and an attuned person could feel them — the way others felt a sneeze coming on. Which was to say there were all different ways of listening. She heard her brain whispering to her eyes, convincing them anew of such concepts as color and light. She was very still for a very long time. She was inside her own heart, kneeling in a soupy chamber, going at the wall with a ball-peen hammer. She'd cracked a hole there, in the wall between the intellectual and the sensual, and so her thoughts were sensations. She tracked a tremor of relief as it surfed a deep layer of her dermis. She could hear different parts of her going through their involuntary, invisible procedures. They were worker bees or drones, and baked, she remembered, like Dallas had said, the inside of you is baked. Her organs had been tanning, they were leathery or peeling or charred and miserly, and still valves were opening and closing, rings of muscles cinched and uncinched, flaps of skin fluttered to a silent close, and an impossible number of little fingers were waving in some acid bath, saying, *Onward! Onward! Onward! Go! Go! Go!* She said, *Ig, Ig, Ig,* but no one answered. Somewhere someone laughed and the laughter turned to smoke, which lifted skyward and made a message there, an unreadable message whose gist she was almost able to grasp. The very dust on her skin was alive, its mites crawling all over her, and if she could only be still enough she herself would be the ecosystem. It might have been one night, or three. Someone brought her a red ovary to eat and she held it in her two hands until she forgot about it but then it hatched and birthed warm liquid and in it swam smiling larvae and these belonged on her in the ecosystem of her body and so she smeared them upon herself and walked into the dune and dug a burrow where she would wait and see all those wondrous creatures for herself, see them hatch across her.

This is where they found her. This is where they said her name.

But their words were not words until the words were, "Ig is hurt."

"What?"

"They think she was bitten by something."

"Oh Jesus."

"She's with Jimmer."

■ ■ ■ ■

Ig's body told the story: one whole side of her swollen to bursting and black, her left arm bloated and prosthetic-looking, unable to bend, her neck swallowed, her eye sockets screaming red seams between two bulbs of waxy flesh. Ray was with her, and Jimmer too. Ray held a peeled stick in her mouth. "It holds her tongue down." He showed Luz where it was worst: the red-ringed punctures in the baby's blood-glutted head and in both hands, yeasty like over-risen dough, the digits all but indistinguishable.

"Jimmer says tarantula wasps. Or vinegaroons. She can't eat yet, so we can't tell whether it's affected her sense of taste. She probably walked into a nest. You can see that some got caught in her hair. They would sting her head and she'd reach up to stop them and then they'd sting the tips of her fingers. She couldn't understand what it was and no one was there. They would sting her and she'd reach up again. This happened over and over until she passed out. One of the girls found her this morning. Took us two hours just to get the stingers out. No one could find you."

"Keep pressing," Jimmer told Ray. "Her

tongue's as big as a fist." The baby's throt-
tled breathing was unbearable, only worse
those moments it stopped.

"Keep her awake," Jimmer told Ray.

Luz said, "What can I do? Tell me what to
do."

No one answered. Ray began to cry,
quietly, the only other sound Jimmer grinding a stone between two others until it was
green dust. This he mixed with water in a
gourd to make a mud. He began coating
Ig's distended body in this. "Bentonite
clay," he told Ray. "Draws the poison out.
Wish I had aloe but this will have to do."

"Thank you," Luz said. "I don't deserve
your help."

"I am not helping you," Jimmer said. He
handed the gourd to Ray and instructed
him to continue smearing Ig. To Luz he
said, "Come with me."

Outside, clouds were snagged on the teeth
of the maybe-Sierras, dropping rain that
evaporated before it hit the ground. Jimmer
said, "Luz, we all have an obligation to the
people who love us. They've given us this
gift whether we want it or not and it is our
duty to stand up and be worthy. We are not
loved in proportion to our deserving, and
thank God for that, for unworthies like you
and me would find that life a bitch. We're

loved to the level we ought to rise, and even in returning it we are obligated to be gentle. Do you understand me? You chose her; she didn't choose you. She came into this world unawares and not knowing better than to love full-blast. You seem to be doing your best to teach her what a mistake that is. Is that what you're after? To make sure this little one knows what a dreadful business love can be? You're learning that yourself, and so you think you might give her lessons while you're at it, is that right?"

"No."

"No. Because you aren't even thinking about her. That would involve too much foresight and consideration on your part. That would imply a plan and some sitting and thinking about what would be best for someone other than Luz, and you haven't ever done that, have you? Now, I've made mistakes. I've lost people. But you've thrown them away. There is an important difference. You're waiting for someone to come scoop you up. Well, you want to know who comes along and does the scooping? Scavengers. You're busted up, anyone can see that. But tell me why you've got to bust up this little one, too. Are you lonely? You want a companion down there, in the sinkhole you've become? Shame on you."

437

Luz touched her pocket absently.

Jimmer ripped her hand away. "You want more? Go get more — chew yourself into oblivion!"

"No —"

"Go on — I mean it! Bon voyage!"

"I don't want it."

"And when you go, don't come back. Not for Ig and not for anyone. Kill yourself quick instead of slow, and save us all the hurt."

"I don't want it," Luz told him and told herself.

But she did want it, wanted it badly, wanted it even more in the following days, when she was not to go back to Ig. She was not helpful, according to Jimmer, or rather she would be tremendously helpful if she would just stay the fuck away. Her waking hours yawned before her without Ig to suck them up, and without the root, each day was a greenhouse for worry. But she did not seek out more. She read Sacajawea's birth of Little Pomp and John Muir's campaign for Yosemite until her eyes gave in to headache, until tremors began in her bowels and shuddered outward from there. Soon, her only project was making it outside to evacuate in a timely manner and back in again. Each of the four stairs rising into the Blue Bird took on its own personality, presented its unique challenges — the staggering height of the first, the tricky wedge of the third. She vomited everything she had in her and otherwise emptied herself, first in privacy and then, when she could not make it to privacy, out in the open. People gawked, but Luz did not notice them. In this way word spread that Luz was sick. One day Dallas came, and another Ray, each bringing water and news of Ig's progress. The second time Ray came he stayed, insisting on placing a bucket beside Luz and tending to her.

Cramps turned her inside out and, forgetting, she asked where all the pain was coming from. "You've been chewing a tranquilizer," Ray said. "You're going through withdrawal."

Eventually, Luz spoke only to moan apologies. "I was supposed to be better than her people, but I'm not," she said. "Not . . . not . . . not." Her wet head in Ray's lap was his forgiveness.

When Jimmer came, Ray asked after Ig.

"Sleeping," Jimmer said. "Dallas is with her. You're welcome to go see for yourself. The little one would like that."

"I'm needed here," Ray said, an unconvincing line from a badly written play. The truth was that anything that came out of Luz was easier than Ig's pleading eyes, pinched between the featureless venom-fat pustules of her face, asking, *Why are you*

440

hurting me?

Jimmer allowed Ray his dishonesty. Intervention was a young man's game, and he'd already exhausted himself with Luz, the wretch. "How's she doing?"

"She comes in and out," Ray said. He touched her dank brow. "She keeps forgetting where she is. She's always shivering."

Jimmer felt Luz's wrist, then put his head near hers and listened. He placed a bundle of sticks in a shell, lit it, and wafted the smoke toward Luz, who was no longer with them but off in an arctic tube where a sourceless echo said, *You are supposed to be here,* and, *What does that mean, babygirl, to set a bunch of uranium free?*

At dusk, Jimmer returned, empty-handed. Luz was caught in some demonic REM cycle — catatonic as a corpse, then suddenly her yellow-edged eyes open but unseeing, still watching whatever scenes played out in her mind. Each time she awoke Ray gave her water and she took it, briefly, before collapsing again. Ray told Jimmer this. And also that if he lost Luz he'd lose everything.

"If she makes it through the night she'll come out," Jimmer said.

"You're sure?" asked Ray.

"Let's get her through the night." There was something Jimmer was not saying, but

Ray could not bring himself to demand it.

And so the two of them sat quietly for some time. Jimmer grew angry at the approaching mountains and all the sorrow they brought, while Ray found himself inclined to pray. He was rusty at it, his prayers not his own but borrowed from the boys in the desert, recycled entreaties once offered to him, god of chemical reprieve. They went, *Just let everything be okay, could you? I'm hurting here. Isn't there something you can do for me? There's got to be something you can do for me. I can't sleep. I can't eat — I've got fear like you get the shits. It comes for me in the night, a black thing. It curls around my head. Mine are little winged demons, a cloud of them. I see them everywhere. Don't you have some way to make them leave? I only want my old self back. I can't remember what it was like not to hurt.*

Suddenly, light invaded the rear of the bus, a riot of dust tumbling in. Ray stayed where he was, Luz's head heavy in his lap. He would not stop touching her, not now and not ever.

Though Ray did not look up, he knew Levi's easy walk, the splay of his thick hands, his hard gourd of a torso. Levi approached Ray where he sat with Luz. Ray kept his gaze down, on Levi's right foot, where his two smallest toes should have been, where a knob of jaundiced skin twitched instead. The dowser spoke to Jimmer only. "This is not a good idea."

Jimmer said nothing.

"Stop this, Jimmer. It's fucking nonsense."

Just then, Luz woke with one of her desperate gasps. Ray held her, whispered her all kinds of prayers. To the others he said, "She's nearly through the worst of it, I think."

The dowser said, "What the hell do you know about it?"

"I've been here with her."

"So I've heard. She could die. Did you know that?"

Ray looked up to Jimmer. "Is that true?"

"I don't know," Jimmer admitted.

Levi squatted down beside Ray. "It's true," he said tenderly. He took some root from his pouch. "She needs this."

Luz, only half there, would surely take anything anyone gave her.

"No," said Ray. "You can't do that."

"I have to," said Levi. "You'll kill her."

Ray said, "Jimmer, tell him he can't do this. She's come too far for this."

"He might be right," Jimmer said. "No one has ever stopped cold."

"No," said Ray, hunching over his girl. He

said this many times.

Levi put a large, soft hand on Ray's shoulder. "Her death will be on you. I'm not sure you're grasping that."

Ray shrugged his hand off. "On me? How do you figure that, friend? You're the one force-feeding her that shit."

Again, Jimmer said, "No one has ever stopped."

Then, from the dusty halo churning at the rear of the bus, someone said, "I stopped."

"Dal," Jimmer said.

It was Dallas, Ig in her arms, a lumpy puppet.

"When?" Levi demanded.

"After," she said, an aquifer of understanding between them.

Levi opened his mouth. But then, as if absorbing the blast wave of these two syllables, he lost his balance, tumbled out of his squat beside Ray and onto his rump on the floor of the bus. Somehow, he was still all coiled potential there. He might have sprung up in rage and embarrassment, might have shaken Dallas, might have hit her, hit Ig, might have shrieked in her face all his injured rage until the sound itself forced her out, and Ig too. They waited.

Finally, Levi said quietly, "You didn't tell me."

"I didn't know I had to," said Dallas.

Then, Luz spoke. She was asking for Ig. She sat up and reached for the girl. Dallas paused, but laid Ig in her mother's lap. Luz took Ig — swollen Ig and poisoned Ig and ruined Ig — and held her.

Levi kneeled beside them. "Luz, you need to take this nib. You're sick. You could die. Just chew a little."

Ray whispered, "Don't, Luz."

Luz did not look at either of them. She kissed Ig, then muttered something into the baby's lumpy dome. The baby began to cry, a cry crimped by her injuries. Dallas went to take her again but Luz looked up, pleading for more time.

Levi raised the purplish strip of root. "Just a little bit, my girl, just to get you through."

Luz spoke again, louder. "Leave us alone."

Levi said, "Luz, you —"

"Please. Everyone. Leave us alone."

No one moved until Dallas said, "Let's go."

They went.

Hanging high above the colony, the crests of the dunes were wind-smudged, but the air outside the bus was funeral-still. Levi turned to Dallas. "You've always been willful."

"Fuck off," said Dallas before she left. "I love you, but you have got to fuck off."

Jimmer glanced at Levi, then told Ray, "Keep her hydrated. And bring that little one back to me when you can." He went after Dallas.

Ray expected Levi to leave, too — hoped he would. But Levi stayed, watching Dallas and Jimmer until they disappeared, Jimmer's hand on Dallas's back.

Levi rubbed his bare head. "Are they . . . *together*?" Apparently he expected an answer.

"Jimmer and Dal?" said Ray. "I don't know, man. I'm out of the loop."

Levi sighed, looked up at the dune sea, then gathered up his robe and began to piss. He was ample all the way down, Ray noticed.

"The women in my life are turning on me," Levi said. "Everything I do, I do for them. I think about them day and night. Everything I've done has been to make them comfortable. I worry for them. I take care of them. Every single thing I do is for them and they don't even see me anymore." He gave his penis a mournful shake, dropped his robe, and looked at Ray. "I can't even trust Dallas anymore. I've lost her. She's another person. The things I've

446

done, to keep them comfortable . . ." He exhaled again and looked past Ray, to the looming toothy range. "Things are changing all around me. 'Force-feeding.' Did Luz say that?"

"I —"

"I know she didn't say that. I've never forced anyone to do anything in my life."

"How about your little harem here?"

"Harem?"

Ray touched the notch of scar at his brow. "That's why you did this to me out there. Because I'm not useful to you."

Levi shook this off. "The dune curates. Some are called here —"

"Cut the bullshit, man. I'm a threat to you."

Levi pinched one broad brow between his fingers, then the other, as though trying to wring the irritation from them. "Do you have any idea what it would take to threaten me? That's not rhetorical. I sincerely want to know. Because I've never felt threatened or otherwise afraid of anyone in my entire life and I am curious about that sensation."

"You attacked me because I wasn't useful to you. Because you weren't interested in fucking me."

"No." Levi smiled, a sick crescent in the leaving light. "That we did for fun."

Levi turned and raised his arms to the colony around him. "The whole natural world is arrayed against you, Ray. I can hear it. There is a certain order of things here — everywhere, really. You'll fit in somewhere, but not here. Surely you've felt that."

Ray had.

"Luz belongs here," Levi said. "Dallas and Jimmer belong here. Estrella, too."

An involuntary spasm of disgust crossed Ray's face — a gift for the dowser. Levi accepted it. "Yes, I know about *Estrella*. I know everything."

Ray turned to reenter the Blue Bird. "Don't call her that."

"You know," said Levi, "I could find those people — Estrella's people." Whimsy and titillation picked up speed inside him, as if this were a spontaneous road trip he was planning. "I could find them in a day! Why don't I bring them here and we can see what they think of you?"

"Bring them here?" Ray scoffed. "Go ahead! Call on them. Make a day of it. Let me give you their address. Oh, damn, I don't have it on me. But you know what? I think they're in the phone book."

Levi's amusement was almost perceptible, a living breathing thing. "Funny," he said.

"I know where I am. Do you know where you are?"

Luz found the rootless world hot and lacking, scooped out, herself a bored husk blowing through. In her beige sobriety she clung to the idea of Ig, whose reported recuperation was the only gift life had left her. They were hardly alone together, for the sake of both their healing, so she tried to get by on conjuring the child's oddness and affection. But when Dallas or Jimmer brought Ig for a visit, the child was staggeringly hurtful, enjoying nothing more than dropping something, having Luz pick it up, and then dropping it again. Worse, the baby was in a Ray phase these days, putting her sourness on the shelf only when he was near.

With her newly clear head, Luz was free to feel acutely this injury and all the others she'd postponed with the root. She felt all the time. There seemed no intermission to her new stirrings — the guilt and shame and self-loathing were physical, concrete

450

burdens, and heavy. Boredom flopped on her chest. Regret sagged in her gut. The daisy chain of Ig's scars was a yoke she dragged from her neck. On her own and too awake, Luz recalled the corridor of her withdrawal, the arctic tube, the passageway in which she'd been trapped for such a long time. She'd come upon objects there: the scarf with its rusty stain, the bonfire circle of mostly women, mostly young, mostly pretty. She had come upon some artifacts and not come upon others. No rainbow chuckwallas or blue chupacabras in the corridor, and all the trees were wither-rooted and dead. Evidence in the corridor, breadcrumbs of reason: Jimmer the healer, Cody the grower, Nico the mechanic and the muscle.

Objects and artifacts and evidence and epiphanies: No one's name was their name. Everyone here was running from something.

She managed to gain weight, thanks to Cody, who came in to make sure she always had something to eat. Luz watched him warily on these deliveries. She'd thought him an errand boy at best, but saw now that Cody was smarter than he pretended to be. One day, remembering a ruby-red orb hovering like a chandelier in her withdrawal corridor, she said, "Can I ask you something?"

Cody said, "Will it stop you always eyeballing me?"

"It might."

"So ask.",

"Where did that grapefruit come from?"

"What?"

"When I first came here, I had a grapefruit."

"You didn't have no grapefruit."

"I did. Dallas brought it to me. We ate it with Ig."

"You might have imagined it. I still dream of dairy."

"You don't grow grapefruits in the vans, Cody."

He silently conceded.

"You don't have citrus trees."

"No, ma'am."

"So where did it come from?"

He rubbed his tight mouth. "That's one of those questions you're better off not asking."

"I need to know," she said.

Cody looked at her, somber and a little angry. "Levi wanted you to have it. He really cares about you, you know."

"Where did he get it?"

The kid said nothing.

"What's he doing out there, Cody?"

That secret intelligence flashed in his eyes. "That's another one of them questions," he said.

And that was how the last of her whole lush and infinite miracle world dissolved, finally, leaving behind only its brutal scaffolding: sun of suns, drought of droughts, no rain, no rivers, an impossible pile of sand approaching an unforgiving range. Barren and bereft and lifeless, just like the pamphlets said. Leave or die. No more complicated than that. No other dimension, no buried menagerie and no trick of the eye or ear or heart could make it otherwise.

When Ray visited later that day, he visited a dingy solar-powered school bus in a madman's colony, an outpost in the cruel tradition of outposts, peopled by prostitutes and loners and rejects and criminals and liars, their sheriff a con and a thief and surely worse.

Luz felt this disillusionment severely, with no root to blur its edges.

She stroked Ray's temples. "Do you miss your heartcolors?"

"More like I thought you would. I was afraid you'd be disappointed. I don't have any desert visions after all."

"Me neither," Luz admitted. "I wanted to,

but I don't."

She took Ray's hand as though it were an egg. "You were right," she said, "about Levi. About the primer. There aren't any new animals out there. No spontaneous rivers or wandering trees. Probably no warheads pointed at us, no Operation Glassjaw. I wanted there to be — I wanted to be important. I wanted all day, every day, especially with you gone. Especially for Ig. But there isn't. There just isn't."

Ray looked at her in their old way, the trembling swell that meant all the ways and reasons he loved her were at that instant rising in him. They kissed: horse and wagon and a new wondrous not knowing which was which, another swell, a swan dive, a splash of warmth from her flush cheeks to her throat and to the filling pools of her eyes. She pulled him to her, guided him into her, present, untentative, nothing abstract about it. Luz kept her eyes open, whispered, "It's you, is it you?" Ray said, "It is," more certain than he had been in a long time. Neither came, nor pretended to. They simply uncoupled after a time and lay together, wet with each other's sweat.

Luz said, "Stay here, next to me." He did, though he was somewhere else, too. "What is it, Ray?"

"Nothing. I can't say. Nothing."

"You can. It's us. Only us."

Ray put his hand in her hair. He kissed her forehead and saw that she was right.

"I just . . . I don't know how to say this. I just have this feeling like she knows . . ."

"Who knows?"

"We shouldn't have done it, Luz. We shouldn't have taken her." In his mind, beneath the shame of his approaching confession and the relief it promised, he marveled at all the ways he was still capable of letting Luz down. But he went on. He said, "I'm afraid of her, I think. Of Ig. There's something . . . odd about her."

He imagined her disappointment would be an audible thing, barely, like the sound of pigeons flying low through an open empty promenade, the hiss of sea foam dying at high tide, the scrapes of Sal's carving tools against ancient soapstone, the rasp of salty bleached sand beneath a board strapped to a healer's feet. He closed his eyes and waited for Luz to give up on him. This newly awakened Luz, her severe eyes always threatening to cry, could retreat into herself whenever she wanted.

But she did not retreat. "I know," she said. "I've seen it. We'll go. It will be better when we go. We'll get her someplace stable."

Ray nodded. "Someplace with walls and water."

"Water walls."

"Waterfalls."

"Rainbows in the mist."

"Misty mornings."

"Misty mountains."

"Mountain streams."

"Marshes."

"Creeks and eddies."

"Rivers and inlets."

"Lagoons."

"New moons."

"No sand."

"No sand."

"Estuaries."

"Where, Ray?"

"What about Wisconsin?"

"Yes. Yes, Wisconsin."

"You have to tell him."

The ripple took the colony to a road, and that road led them to a ghostly horseshoe of crumbling whitewashed adobe. At the center of the square stood three dead salt cedars, their trunks and low-hanging limbs papered in playbills bleached to blank, except the buried layers, which read NOW PLAYING AT MARLA BENOIT'S AMARGOSA OPERA HOUSE.

The lock on the entrance had been popped off. In the lightless lobby of the theater Luz opened a door marked MADEMOISELLES, thinking that to use a toilet might be nice, before she got on with this unpleasantness. But it seemed a bag of dry cement had exploded inside the ladies' room. Shards of mirror rivered the floor. The far wall yawned where a sink had been. The toilet lay on its side, cracked in half. Similar scene in the men's room, so she went back outside to squat.

In the theater itself it was very dark, and she had to stand for some time before her sun-clenched eyes accepted the rows of red velvet seats crusted with dust, veins of wires overhead reaching for a long-gone chandelier and Levi sitting on the apron of the bare stage. The curtain crumpled behind him, fallen its final fall. A toothless organ waited in the wing at stage left. Luz did not feel afraid, as she'd thought she might.

Levi said, "I remember this place. I saw a documentary about it in school. Marla Benoit moved here from Paris, married a miner. They were on their way to Goldfield and got a flat tire here. He got a job in the talc mines. She convinced the Borax Works to build her an opera house. People came to see her, later, but for a long time she danced alone every night. She painted herself an audience so she'd always sell out."

He nodded to the close, filthy walls. It was true, an audience had been painted there and remained beneath the grime, crowded into boxes and balconies, aficionados in their finery, pearly opera glasses resting on the breasts of the ladies, some teeth still relatively bright. A bishop, captured in mid-whisper, leaning in to another clergyman who would never hear the secret opinion of his holiness, his snide disapproval or breathless admiration. A madame with a starched ruff and a cat on her lap, both cat and mistress ever alert to the production at hand, the cat's tail ever curled in contentment. In the rear balcony sat a king and queen, eternal patrons, never to age or philander or remove their pale hands from the arms of their chairs. A swarthy gentleman in emerald bloomers, leading a lace-shrouded señora by the hand. Running late perhaps, as they always were, but now forever stranded in the entryway without any usher to soothe their embarrassment. ("Forgive our Luz," her agent said into her earpiece, "she was on island time.") The Spanish couple's late arrival surely disturbed two milk-skinned women, their paper fans paused. Behind them a man with a sly thin mustache, a playbill in his hand, eternally considering whether to adjust the gold chain of one maid's necklace, never to determine whether she would be scandalized by the flirtation or welcome it. A juggler from the Orient, pins aloft, his bare chest gleaming with effort. A lone lord in a cobalt vest, his hand to his beard, ignoring the elderly noblewomen murmuring at his elbow. His eyes closed, he listens — only listens — to the sighs of the stage below, made of pine hauled from Illinois by twenty-mule team, to the creaks of the chairs upholstered in devoré velvet sailed from New York to San Francisco around the finger of Patagonia, then sewed by Marla Benoit, by lamplight, she herself listening for the return of her whiskey-sick husband or word of a mine collapse, never uncertain which she might prefer. Eyes closed, the listening lord hears the tinny kiss of the prima ballerina assoluta's needle to its primitive thimble, both procured by trade from a Shoshone weaving woman. He hears Marla Benoit load mesquite into the woodstove in winter, the antelope-leather soles of her pointe shoes whispering across the stage in rehearsal, her ravenous moaning from beneath the petite president of the Borax Works. Then, he hears nothing for a very long time, save for a family of kangaroo rats nesting in the walls, Mojav looters disemboweling the building of its copper pipes and chandelier, an overheated Bureau of Conservation survey team and then, finally, the boyhood memories of a cuckolded dowser.

"She was mad, probably," said Levi. "The documentary had one recording of her performance and in it she played a doll — a jewelry box ballerina, and I thought she was one come to life. Freaky makeup and these jerky movements. It scared the hell out of me. I wonder what happened to her."

How sad he was, all of a sudden, how hunched and timid, how he leaned on his own idea of himself. The theatergoers all saw it, through their pearl-embellished binoculars or with their own unaided eyes. The gossiping priest and the decorous king and queen, the busty ladies and their randy suitor, the tardy couple from far away, even the Oriental juggler saw it, distracted as he was — even the listening lord with his eyes closed. How could Luz have missed it?

"I need to tell you something," she said. Luz approached the apron and sat beside a coffee can footlight. "It's Ray and me. I wanted you to know that. It's not that I don't care about you . . ."

"I get it," said Levi, his hand waving languid in the musty air. "You love me but you love him more. It's all so damn adult."

"Yes," she allowed. "I do care about you, deeply —"

A beaky scrape came from the rear of the theater as its doors were pried wide open. Some colony scavengers wandered in, seeking shade. Luz watched them and they her. She would have liked Ray to be there with her, but he was unwelcome just about everywhere now.

"You care about me," Levi prompted.

461

"Deeply."

Luz dropped her voice. "Yes. And there's — there's something else." More people filed into the unlit theater. Luz looked to Levi to dismiss them, but he waved them down the aisle. Dallas and Cass were among them. Nico, too. "Have a seat," Levi said. "Welcome to dress rehearsals at the Lovelorn Theater. Luz was just practicing her heartbreaker monologue. You were right," he told her. "You're not very good at this. Very wooden, if I may offer a note."

Luz looked at her lap. "Should we talk later?" she whispered.

"Why? We have no secrets here. Come," he called to the people in the back. "Plenty of room up front. Up," he said to Luz. He popped up, some mystic vim animating him all of a sudden. "Stand up! You're collapsing your diaphragm. Up, up!"

Luz stood. There were more people in the audience than she thought.

Levi waited until their velvet-covered chairs stopped creaking. "Now, again, with the whole body. Take it from, 'There's something else.' "

"There's something else," Luz said, a reflex. "I — I can't go through with it. The plan. I can't make her into a symbol. I thought I could — I wanted to be able to

— but I can't."

"She can't!" he called to the back wall.

"I have to think about what's best for Ig," she whispered.

"What's that? You must *project.*"

"Levi," she said, reaching for him.

"Never turn your back to the audience," he said, pointing her shoulders forward. "Very basic."

Luz hesitated.

"Go on," he said. "The show must go on."

She said nothing.

Levi said, "This affects all of them. They have a right to hear you say it. Just as I do."

"I have to think about what's best for Ig," she said.

"What's best for her." He smiled. "The plan *is* what's best for her." The others nodded. "What's best for us is best for her."

"It's just — all the exposure, Levi. It scares me."

Levi took her face and held it. "Of course it does, Luz. Everything worth doing is done in the shadow of death."

Someone moaned in assent.

"But I'll be right beside you," he said, squeezing. " 'Do not fear, for I am with you.' 'I will uphold you with my righteous right hand.' "

Luz had heard these lines before. " 'What

463

time I am afraid, I will trust in thee.' "

He flung her free. "Exactly! Think about what brought you here, about all that was sacrificed so you would come to *this* place at *this* moment!"

Luz did. She saw Ray's flat feet carrying him down the road, his prophet eyes watering above the cobalt scarf, the bloated bighorn floating in that golden pool of poison. She saw her mother submerged beneath gray waves at Point Dume, her pretty dress aswirl in the current. Perhaps it had all been arranged with a purpose in mind. Perhaps the prairie dog had marched through the starlet's front door intending to be their chaperone and spirit guide. She wanted to believe in these things still. To believe in cause and purpose.

"Levi," Luz said, "she's my daughter." She had never called Ig this, and hoped it did not sound so false as it felt.

"*Your* daughter?" Levi wheeled away, bewildered. "She belongs to all of us."

The crowd agreed.

"She is a child of the dune sea!"

Luz stood still while the crowd erupted. This seemed somehow her stage direction. "I'm sorry," she said quietly. "I won't allow it."

The two were silent for a moment, then

Levi stepped downstage. "Here is where I ask what happened to you. When did you become so possessive? Were you always this way? Was I blind to it? Have I led us down a wayward path?"

No, said the crowd. *No.*

"You used to be so . . ." He sighed. "Open."

"No I didn't," she said. "I never was."

She wanted him to be right, even still. She wanted to be the person he once mistook her for: open and purposeful all at once. But she was meager, shut. That was, after all this supposed transformation, all this movement and light, her rotten way.

"Levi, even if we did it, it wouldn't work." The crowd mumbled its disagreement. "It won't," Luz said to them. "The range will be on us any day now. You all know that. No video will stop that. No campaign. No one will care about me — a Mojav — a kidnapper. It won't stop anything." She turned back to Levi. "You found me and Ig. You know that no one else was coming for us. No one cares about Baby Dunn."

"Did I ever tell you how we found you?" he said.

"Yes," she said, "the bighorn."

"You were all but dead. Dehydrated, hyperthermic, full-blown sunstroke. Completely unresponsive. But Ig? Ig was wide awake. Conscious. Alert. Calm. She was taking everything in. Watching you go. She was at home there, witnessing."

Luz shook her head.

"You see?" he asked his audience. "You see how clarity can melt into suspicion? Without mindfulness? Without vigilance? You used to be among us, Luz. You were once with us, of us." He was using her name but no longer addressing her. "But something has contaminated you. Some vexation, some poisonous, nihilistic seed. I've seen all this, in the sweat lodge and beyond. So clearly. The range, your withdrawal into the self, allowing harm to befall our Ig. They're all connected."

The crowd sat rapt.

"My loves, there are contaminants among us. We have allowed negativity to propagate, a toxic yeast rising in our midst, and we have done nothing. I count myself among the complacent. But no more! The time has come to purge ourselves of these toxicities, cleanse our community of doubt, hesitation, misgiving, skepticism. Reinvigorate our cause from within and without!"

Yes! many said.

"We all want to know, 'What next?' First let us purify our intent. Reinvigorate our purpose. Each of us must rid our spirits of their innermost burdens and transgressions. We must expel the poison from our singular body. Do this and the path will be made plain. Do this and we will endure. We will thrive. Forever and ever. We will meet this range and meet our fate there!"

Luz tried to flee, but there were only walls at the wings. She turned around and tried to find an opening in the curtain behind her. Feeling their eyes on her, hearing their snickers and jeers, she clawed at the velvet. She could not find the opening. Finally she turned, faced them, stepped off the apron and pushed herself up the aisle and out the open door.

Patient had always wondered what it felt like — says all men wonder. Considers occasional homicidal impulses "fundamental component of masculine socialization." Says his companion [alias "Nico"] had done it — in the war — and Nico knew patient had not — says "I knew what he thought of me." Predominant motivation for initial attack was curiosity, he says — specifically regarding the physical sensation — "new sensory data interested me." Ask what kind of data: "in this case crushing a skull, I suppose." Patient didn't know potential victim at time — saw "only a Mojav" — "an empty bladder I had no interest in filling." Attributes outburst partly to environment — notes that "the desert at night has no restraints." Patient admits wanting to kill there — thought he in fact had, for a time. Ask what he remembers from attack itself: "the give of the spade" — borrowed from another community member — says his immediate thought

468

was "must remember to return this to him." Patient describes lack of profound metamorphosis — disappointed by this, initially — but says soon realized that disappointment in itself was surprising — asks when was the last time I had been truly surprised by my life. Patient also recalls hand tingling — says he was relieved — "one less thing I had to worry about." Ask what else he worried about: other group members — "they wanted all I had." Patient says person in his position must never underestimate anyone — says other men "thought they could do what I did." Ask what: patient ignores — says he was "holding them off" but efforts had a "cost" — says everything does. Ask what cost: patient ignores. Ask if he means former lover, "Dallas" — was she motivation for arson incident, later? Patient denies this — says he didn't do it for her — not initial attack and not arson incident. Admits he told Dallas fire was part of larger plan — but plan did not occur to him until *after* fire — when she inquired about his motives. Says dune sea "offered the solution" at that time — patient "only had to listen." Ask why "solution" resonated with him: it would "solve everything" and "give [Dallas] something the old man couldn't" — admits to arson but maintains he had no larger plan — "I was hurting" — says women at camp were "losing their goddamn minds." Ask if he means Dallas or "Luz": both — "also Ray." Says "everything I hated most in the world was in there" — "all my troubles inside, copulating" — patient says he hated bus itself — the vehicle — from before, when he and Dallas had resided there — "before I was called away." Ask what called him away — stillborn? Patient denies — says he understood Dallas's need for space — compares to Luz's termination of affair — considers Luz cruel, selfish — "piecemeal and secretive" — "vindictive back and forth." Says she "took more" from him. Ask what she took, his plan, the child "Ig"? Patient says question is too literal. Says we've been over this — expresses frustration — says he was lost — "completely alone" — "rejected by two women I loved deeply" — forced to watch them with other men — "my own people" — says he began to fear for his status in community — describes other men in group as "power-thirsty" — was around this time he began to fear dune sea. Ask what he feared: expressed frustration — "I've told you all this" — wondered if dune had "betrayed" him — says others said it had. Ask if this motivated arson, subsequent violence? Patient denies — reiterates he had no plan at time of arson — "except taking a two-by-four from the bonfire and holding it beneath the snout of the bus until the fire took in the chassis" — says he had had visions of "the monster box of the bus wrapped in fire" — "a burp of flame when [the fire] found a sludge of fuel in the bottom of the old gas tank." Patient says he is tired of repeating himself — says he has always been open with me — says he is "not one of those men who pretends he never learned to express his inner world [. . .] because he's too lazy to deal with his shit" — "I do the work" — says he is "not a cowboy" — says he is sensitive now "and was sensitive then." Asks why I find bus incident significant — why do I keep coming back to it? — says he knows what I am trying to do — insists arson "had nothing to do with" subsequent incidents — "Nothing to do with what happened to them, later" — says he has been honest with me — says it is my turn to be honest with him — "Why do you keep asking after plans and patterns?" — wants to know why am I convinced acts were premeditated. Ask patient what he thinks: expresses frustration — "classic psycho-bullshit smoke and mirrors" — "the emperor wears no clothes!" Eventually, patient asks if I really want to know what he thinks — says first "they told you to watch out for me" — "I'm brilliant" — "a manipulator." Then says I have a deeper motivation — says arson was "a crime of passion" — says I need him "incapable of the intensity and nakedness that phrase suggests." Patient says I am afraid he feels more than I do. Ask like what: "more sensations" — "more deeply" — "more often." Says I am starting to realize that I am "the one who is incapable of a crime of passion" — says I have never felt true passion — speculates that I "have doubted the very concept of passion" until meeting him — says I am beginning to realize that there are "subterranean emotional spheres" to which I will "never tunnel" — patient says I have "lived grayly" — "rounding out the fat belly of the bell curve" — says I am starting to realize — "truly grasp" — that "in the not too distant future [my] heart will stop its plugging" — it will be "dead inside [me]" and I "have not once used it." Repeatedly denies premeditation — says he had "no plan but pain" — says he "just wanted them to burn."

After Levi's performance at Marla Benoit's opera house, Dallas and Jimmer took Ig. Dallas's words, "We'll take her." A workaday phrase embedded in consolation and friendship, extended beneath the dead salt cedars, where Dallas found Luz trying not to cry. "This will pass, Luz. Levi's riled now. He's hurting. He gets this way. But it's all coming from a place of love. Believe me. You three will work through this. This will pass. He just needs sleep. You too. We'll watch Ig for the night. So you can get some rest. We'll take her."

A phrase drained of meaning until filled again. Still just a thing people say when Luz and Ray fell asleep that night, curled into each other like the two lake fossils they'd found on a walk in another life up a mountain called Lookout. To consider otherwise would have been to admit their complete and profound aloneness.

The lovers woke with acridity in their lungs, the air replaced with hot black smoke. Ray reached for Luz, assuming her asleep from her stillness, roused her, and together they made their way to the front door. The rubber aisle was melted, scalding their forearms as they crawled. Ray heard but did not feel the sizzle of his palms when he grasped the lever to open the door. It would not give. Struggling for breath, Ray managed to kick the door open. He and Luz tumbled into the cool arms of the desert dawn, coughing.

The whole colony was there, it seemed, and together they watched the Blue Bird go phoenix, aglow in sunset colors, red-orange and throbbing. Inside, Sacajawea, John Muir, Lewis and Clark, William Mulholland, John Wesley Powell. The starlet's scarf and Ray's father's Leatherman. Ig's bed and tub and play place. The primer.

Not until well after they escaped the bus would it occur to Ray that Luz had not been asleep, inside. Not until the adrenaline left him limp would he think to wonder why she had not reached for him. Not until they poured water down their scorched throats would he wonder why she had not reached at all, nor panicked, nor screamed. Not until after the ash flakes snowed down on them, not until after the explosion that made glass of the sand beneath, the fire flickering on the walls of the opera house, its windows like knowing open eyes. Not until after they had watched the burning bus charred to a carcass would he recall seeing her open eyes, small flames in them. Only then would Ray recall the unmoving body of his love, resigned to die.

Dallas

Transfixing, the fire. Extraordinary. Even the little one felt it.

The Girls

We watched.

Jimmer

We were more together there than we had been in some time.

Dallas

Which is what made us see so clearly.

Cody

When you think of it, the trouble started with them, with Luz and then her man.

The Girls

They were poison.

476

Jimmer

It's true that certain combinations of individuals can be literally toxic, on a chemical level.

The Girls

We tried to love them, but they were poison.

Dallas

Except the little one.

The Girls

We made choices — whatever else they were, they were choices.

Jimmer

In a context of such unity, one feels deviation as an agony.

Dallas

We could sense this man turning on us.

Cody

Ray wanted to hurt Levi, who was us.

Jimmer

You could sense malice rising in him.

Dallas

He screamed, but he had no voice.

Cody

We found out later his vocal cords were singed.

Jimmer

A soundless scream portends death, almost always.

The Girls

He went for Levi's throat.

Jimmer

He was after us, too, for we all felt and breathed and lived as one.

The Girls

A beautiful feeling, harmony. It had to be protected.

Dallas

Nico stepped in.

Cody

Straight dropped him.

The Girls

The rest of us came like gnats to a wet eye.

Ray welcomed the beating. The way he saw it he had all kinds of evil shit inside him and perhaps the blows might knead it out. For example: he hated Ig. He hated the time she'd had with Luz, the things she'd allowed to happen, the days she spent freely tottering about while he was entombed in a talc mine. He hated how open she was with her wants, her bare manipulations, how even her dishonesty was honest. He hated her cruelty, hated how grand it made him feel when she cast Luz aside in favor of him. He hated her for being so fond of him and for, yes, ruining his life. He hated her because it was easier than hating the bereft dust and the dropless clouds, the sun, the night, the Earth and its thin envelope of ruined air. He took the blows in silence. Their hands were his own, trembling as he struggled to give the men their inoculations. The laughing man on the TV, the dowser, Luz in everyone else's arms. Sal and Sal's figurines and Sal's slut mother. His own mother and her cleaning supplies. The wet bits of cork floating in her vintage California chardonnay. Luz. Luz. Luz. Every single thing she did. His quiet hate was light and there was nothing in his life that could not absorb it and reflect it back to him at the same time, nothing that would not beget more, like the joke or legend of which he recalled only the punch line: turtles all the way down. Except Ig. To hate Ig was to stop the spiral of his rage. Her innocence was the boundary, the vessel, for to hate her was to hate himself, to allow all the blackness inside him to pool around him, to skip his lifetime's worth of middlemen, to concentrate on her strange skin, her amphibian eyes, her haunting moans, repulse himself with them and punish himself this way.

The beating helped, too. He watched globules of his own blood bead black on the sand.

Luz was unable to stop it. Eventually, the crowd dispersed of its own accord, as if each participant's savagery had all at once run its course. They drifted away.

Luz sat beside Ray, but did not touch his wounds. What could she have done for him that he could not do for himself? She sat;

he lay. Wisconsin a mirage, burned off. They both grieved it in silence.

At some point, Levi summoned them.

"I'm sorry about all that," Levi said to Ray, the pulp of him. Jimmer was with him in his dome, and Nico, too. Jimmer offered some salve. Ray, his throat singed, gestured his decline.

"Where's Ig?" Luz asked.

"Yes, Ig," said Levi. "I'm glad you asked."

"Where is she?" Luz asked.

"Dal has her," Jimmer said softly.

"What have you noticed about Ig?" Levi asked. "What do you see when you see her?"

Luz said nothing.

"I know you know she's different, Luz. Atypical, an anomaly. Do you know why?"

"Let me see her, please."

"I know why." He went on. "I believe Ig is touched. Her moaning is of the same frequency as the dune's song."

Jimmer nodded his assent. "She hears this place powerfully. More so than any of us."

Luz said, "Levi, we've been through this."

"We're going through it again," Levi said. "But we're taking a different trail this time. The direct route."

"What are you talking about?" though she knew. How long had she known? It was hard to say.

"We'll be taking Ig now."

"What?"

Jimmer said, "She needs to be here."

Luz told them this was fucking madness. She said certainly they were insane. "Give her to you? You're delusional." No one seemed to hear her.

"We can take care of her. Keep her well," said Jimmer.

"Who is 'we'?"

"All of us. Everyone."

"Not me," said Luz. "Not Ray."

Ray was looking to his lap.

Levi said, "Ray is a contagion."

A spasm went through the men, but Jimmer neutralized it. "Please, gentlemen."

"I apologize," Levi said to Ray. "This has nothing to do with you. With either of you, really."

He was right, Luz knew. She was obsolete. She saw it in Ray's eyes, in Jimmer's twitching hand, heard it in Levi's level voice. Luz went into her corridor again. Ray was at one end and Ig was at the other. The algebra of the situation was balancing itself in her mind. Dallas was a better mother than she'd ever be — that was true, even before Levi said, "If you leave Ig, I will let you go. More than that. I'll give you a vehicle, food, water. I'll show you the way out. You'll go on with your life like you were meant to. Like you planned. The two of you."

There was not much else to say. Or there was plenty to say, but Ray's vocal cords had been burned to useless, and anything Luz could say felt futile, another handful of hot sand in the mouth. These decisions had been made before this discussion — before the prairie dog crossed their threshold. So though there was much to say, they said none of it.

"You can see her again, before you go," Jimmer offered.

Luz said, quietly, "I wouldn't survive that."

The next day there were rumors of rain. Atypically dark clouds a promise in the west, a crackling anticipation lost on Luz. She had gone into herself, Ray could see, though she made some efforts to feign okayness, even saluted the black glass smear where the Blue Bird had been and said, "Good-bye, house."

Ray was tired. Wisconsin throbbed dimly in the east, and he resolved to put one foot in front of the other, even though they were driving. Levi had honored his word, outfitted one of his better lorries with walls of water kegs and tarps and food. He'd made a map, all alluvial fans and gullies, the way out in the washes. After Nico delivered all this, Luz looked at the well-equipped lorry as though it injured her. "He really wants us gone," she said.

Ray found a pen. On the back of his hand he wrote, *Don't you?*

"Don't I what?"

Want us gone?

"I do. That's the problem."

On his forearm: *We're not her people.*

"No."

Never were.

"No."

On his palm he wrote,

You're okay.

"Yes."

~~*You're*~~ *okay.*

We're

"I know."

~~*You're*~~ *okay.*

~~*We're*~~

She'll be

"I know."

But these were just words she was saying.

They were ready to go. Some people woke from their siestas and emerged to watch them leave. No one spoke. Luz and Ray dawdled a little, though they were not sure why until Dallas appeared, Ig in her arms.

The girl's big head swiveled around a little, taking everything in. Her freckles, the divots in her head, all the injuries visited upon her in so short a time. Luz quietly took Ray's hand.

She wanted Ig to reach for her, to plead for her, to fling herself from Dallas's arms and wail. She wanted this and *more, more, more. Mama, I've got so much want in me.* But Ig was silent, luminous as a candle, still and indifferent.

Dallas said, "Say 'bye-bye,' Ig."

Ig did not.

Luz clasped Ray's hand tighter, for fear she would reach up and touch the baby's soft skin, her colorless hair — it would be her undoing.

Luz did not reach for Ig, but Ig did reach for Luz. One spindly arm outstretched between them, her grub fingers curling and uncurling. Luz watched it. Ray watched her watch it. *Take it,* he said in his mind, this prayer all his own. Luz stood, unmoving, as if hypnotized by the pale hand, its frank and tender need, and then she leaned back, away, forever out of reach.

"Her name is Estrella," she told Dallas. "After my mother."

Dallas nodded, then turned. As they went, Ig moaned and clucked a little, to Dallas.

Luz and Ray watched them until Ig's pale halo dissolved into the blinding glory of the dune.

Those sounds stayed with them as they fled, though Ray — all fear and blessed anticipation — would hear nothing beneath the fearsome whine of the lorry. But Luz kept on hearing those Ig sounds, her seer's song. She tried to hear the ways it harmonized with the dune, though what she heard was the engine working, dead scrub crunching, dry sand yielding when they dived into the wash. She tried and tried and soon all she heard was her trying, Ig crying — no, that was her. Her breath shuddered, heart thundered, and so she did not hear the actual thunder at their back, nor the sky opening up. She did not smell the rain coming.

What she felt, beyond the painful range of Ig, was the astonishing relief of quitting. Taking her rightful position in that long line of runners and flakes. Those were her people salting mines, jumping claims, forging bond certificates, fudging the rail route, sending dudes searching for lost gollers. Following the plow and yellowing the news. Antsy pioneers, con artists and sooners, dowsers and gurus, Pentecosts and Scientologists. Muscle heads, pill-poppers, pep talkers, drama queens and commuters. Fluffers, carpetbaggers, migrant pickers disappeared, entrepreneurs in never-were garages, all those servers. She was all of them, at last. Malibu Barbie and Manzanar. San Simeon and San Quentin. Neverland Ranch and Alcatraz. She was Boyle Heights, Fruitvale, La Habra. Koreatown, Cambodia Town, Filipinotown, Japantown, Little Tokyo, Little Seoul, Little Manila, Little Saigon, Little Taipei, Little Moscow, Little Kabul, Little Arabia, Little Persia, Little Armenia, Little Pakistan, Little India, Little Italy, Little Ethiopia, Venice Beach. Drained lakes, sulfur seas, yucca forests dried to paper, redwoods blighted and departed, sequoias and pinyon pines tinder for a never-satisfied wildfire. These were her people. Speculators and opportunists, carnival barkers and realtors, imagineers, cowards and dreamers and girls. Mojavs. Eyes peeled for the flash of ore, the flash of camera, the wet flesh of fruit. Gold, fame, citrus. Every erotic currency harvested green or yellow or the profound underground black of oil gone red-brown when slid between two fingers. Clear — whatever color you want it to be. The color of diamonds kissed by light. Bathe in it, fling it into the air, carpet the desert in Bermuda and Buffalo and Kentucky blue. Blast it into the night sky, burble it at every porte cochere and waiting room atrium, adorn it with koi, trout, dolphins, killer whales. Freeze it with freezing machines and glide down atop it in the sunshine. Hold it icy against your injuries. Cut it with sugar, with liquor, with pesticide, blast for gold or gas with it, grow creatures with it. Ride it, spray it into the street, swim in it, soak in it, drink it in, piss it away.

The flood came upon them like an animal, like a vengeful live thing, earth-colored and savagely fast. Ray took it for a sandalanche at first, as the wriggling fingers surrounded the lorry. Its true properties came to them both at the same time. They looked at each other.

"It's water, Ray. Is it water?"

Ray attempted to pronounce "Everything okay," but his withered cords did not permit it. The flood lifted the lorry. The truck was afloat, no longer their own, and silty dun water around their ankles proved it.

Luz leaned over the edge of the lorry and baptized her hand. "Beautiful."

Ray braked and steered, but these efforts were as useless as his voice. He remembered some rescue training, some advice for preserving one's aliveness. Against great pain he tried to say *Stay.*

But Luz's hand was on the handle. Ray reached for it as she swung the door open. She said, coolly and with a hard grace, "I have to go, baby."

Ray lunged for her. But she was out of the lorry, stepping to her waist in the opaque rage of water. It pushed her and she lurched, nearly fell, but her face was serene. Ray scrambled to pull her in, but she would not allow it.

She would not allow it. Ray's phrase years later, in Wisconsin, the Carolinas. In Greencastle, Indiana, where the soybeans no longer grew.

"I'm okay," Luz shouted back over the miraculous roar of water, all those prayers answered late. "I'd be okay," she revised, smiling before she slipped forever under, "if I could just get my feet under me."

489

ACKNOWLEDGMENTS

This novel is indebted to too many books, films, artists, and writers to list, but the following deserve specific acknowledgment: *The Control of Nature* by John McPhee, *Beyond the Hundredth Meridian* by Wallace Stegner, *Cadillac Desert* by Marc Reisner, *The Worst Hard Time* by Timothy Egan, *The American Religion* by Harold Bloom, *Under the Banner of Heaven* by Jon Krakauer, *Demon Camp* by Jennifer Percy, *The Art of Dowsing* by Richard Webster, *Into Eternity* directed by Michael Madsen, and *Picture Me* directed by Ole Schell and Sara Ziff.

Billy Dunn's sermon on sulfur is based on that by Pastor Deacon Fred of Landover Baptist Church, entitled "Friends in Christ, Do You Have Demons in Your Colon?" Ray's poetic influences are K. A. Hays & Will Schutt. Jimmer's homeopathic remedies are informed by pamphlets on the topic published by the Aurand Press of Lancaster, Pennsylvania. Luz's rooty epiphanies about nature imagery are inspired by the artwork of Anna Kell.

Finally, my sincere gratitude for the expertise of Ben Marsh, Chris Helvey and Henry Brean, and for generous support from the Creative Writing Program at Princeton University and the John Simon Guggenheim Memorial Foundation.

ABOUT THE AUTHOR

Claire Vaye Watkins is the author of *Battleborn* and a National Book Foundation "5 Under 35" fiction writer, as well as the recipient of the Story Prize, the American Academy of Arts and Letters's Rosenthal Family Foundation Award, and a Guggenheim Fellowship, among many other honors. Her stories and essays have appeared in *Granta, One Story, The Paris Review, Ploughshares, Glimmer Train, Best of the West 2011, Best of the Southwest 2013,* and elsewhere. An assistant professor at the University of Michigan, Watkins has also taught at Bucknell and Princeton, and she and her husband, the writer Derek Palacio, are codirectors of the Mojave School, a creative writing workshop for teenagers in rural Nevada.